P9-CRH-128

Praise for four authors who turn up the heat...

Lora Leigh

"Insanely scorching and truly outstanding."
—*Romance Junkies*

"Guaranteed to heat up the cold winter nights."
—*Fresh Fiction*

Angela Knight

"If you like . . . pages that sizzle in your hand, you're going to love Angela Knight."
—*New York Times* bestselling author J. R. Ward

"The future belongs to Knight!"
—Emma Holly

Anya Bast

"A grand escape into a paranormal world brimming with sensual delight."
—*Wild on Books*

"Bast's writing is . . . exquisite in its richness, and sinfully hot."
—Ilona Andrews

Allyson James

"Will keep you enthralled until the very last word!"
—*USA Today* bestselling author Cheyenne McCray

"Deliciously erotic."
—*Romance Reviews Today*

Hot for the Holidays

Lora Leigh

Angela Knight

Anya Bast

Allyson James

JOVE BOOKS, NEW YORK

THE BERKLEY PUBLISHING GROUP
Published by the Penguin Group
Penguin Group (USA) Inc.
375 Hudson Street, New York, New York 10014, USA
Penguin Group (Canada), 90 Eglinton Avenue East, Suite 700, Toronto, Ontario M4P 2Y3, Canada
(a division of Pearson Penguin Canada Inc.)
Penguin Books Ltd., 80 Strand, London WC2R 0RL, England
Penguin Group Ireland, 25 St. Stephen's Green, Dublin 2, Ireland (a division of Penguin Books Ltd.)
Penguin Group (Australia), 250 Camberwell Road, Camberwell, Victoria 3124, Australia
(a division of Pearson Australia Group Pty. Ltd.)
Penguin Books India Pvt. Ltd., 11 Community Centre, Panchsheel Park, New Delhi—110 017, India
Penguin Group (NZ), 67 Apollo Drive, Rosedale, North Shore 0632, New Zealand
(a division of Pearson New Zealand Ltd.)
Penguin Books (South Africa) (Pty.) Ltd., 24 Sturdee Avenue, Rosebank, Johannesburg 2196, South Africa

Penguin Books Ltd., Registered Offices: 80 Strand, London WC2R 0RL, England

This is a work of fiction. Names, characters, places, and incidents either are the product of the authors' imaginations or are used fictitiously, and any resemblance to actual persons, living or dead, business establishments, events, or locales is entirely coincidental. The publisher does not have any control over and does not assume any responsibility for author or third-party websites or their content.

HOT FOR THE HOLIDAYS

A Jove Book / published by arrangement with Lora Leigh Inc. and the authors

PRINTING HISTORY
Jove mass-market edition / October 2009

Collection copyright © 2009 by Penguin Group (USA) Inc.
"Vampire's Ball" by Angela Knight copyright © 2009 by Julie Woodcock.
"A Little Night Magic" by Allyson James copyright © 2009 by Jennifer Ashley.
"Sweet Enchantment" by Anya Bast copyright © 2009 by Anya Bast.
"A Christmas Kiss" by Lora Leigh copyright © 2009 by Lora Leigh.
Cover photographs by Shutterstock.
Cover design by George Long.
Text design by Laura K. Corless.

ISBN: 978-0-515-14700-1

JOVE®
Jove Books are published by The Berkley Publishing Group,
a division of Penguin Group (USA) Inc.,
375 Hudson Street, New York, New York 10014.
JOVE® is a registered trademark of Penguin Group (USA) Inc.
The "J" design is a trademark of Penguin Group (USA) Inc.

PRINTED IN THE UNITED STATES OF AMERICA

10 9 8 7 6 5 4 3 2 1

CONTENTS

Vampire's Ball

Angela Knight

ONE

*C*hristmas had come to Walsh Drive. Every house on the block was draped in swags of icicle lights that shone through the dancing swirl of snow. Firs, cedars, and pines stood framed in frosted windows, trimmed in glittering ornaments and twinkling lights. A plastic Santa waved from a neighbor's yard, his recorded "Ho ho ho!" booming through the night, his painted face glowing.

God, she hated Christmas.

Kat Danilo pulled into her dark driveway, aching in every muscle. She'd taught three classes at the club today—two Healthy Groovin' and one Kickbox to Fitness—and she was in desperate need of a long, hot soak and a cup of chamomile tea.

After she made sure her mother was okay. Mary Danilo never did well this close to Christmas.

One more week. All they had to do was get through one more week, and they'd be okay. There'd be dark days, yes, but at least there wouldn't be Santas and Christmas trees everywhere you looked, triggering memories better left buried.

Kat's stomach balled into its accustomed knot when she

got out of her little red Ford Focus. Snow crunched loudly underfoot as she approached the front door. Her hand shook in the act of unlocking the dead bolt, making the keys jingle. "Mom?" She swallowed and licked dry lips, tried for a sunny tone. "Mom, I'm home."

"In here, baby." Her mother's voice sounded bright, excited.

Kat slumped in relief. It was going to be a good night. She blew out a breath and entered the foyer.

The stranger rose as Kat walked into the living room. Shining blond hair curled around the woman's shoulders, contrasting with a deep cobalt cable-knit sweater that accented the sapphire blue of her eyes. Dark jeans made the most of her impressive height and long legs. An athletic woman, Kat judged, fit and comfortable in her own skin.

Mary stood too, a head shorter than the blonde, a certain jittery excitement in her tired eyes. "Kat, this is Grace du Lac. She's your stepmother."

Kat froze. "I . . . don't understand."

Mary gave her a smile that was a trifle too bright, a bit too wide. "She's your father's wife."

Kat rocked back on her heels and eyed Grace warily. The family dynamics here were potentially touchy, to say the least. As far as Kat knew, her father had been a drunken one-night stand shortly after Mary's truly ugly divorce. Either the condom had broken, or too many rum and Cokes had blunted her mother's sense of self-preservation. Either way, Kat had come along nine months later.

"Lance met Mary long before our marriage," Grace explained. There was not even a flicker of jealousy on her elegant features. She looked no older than Kat herself; apparently John Lance had a taste for cradle robbing.

"Oh." Kat slid her hands into her jacket pockets, struggling to figure out why the woman was here. "Has something happened to . . . my father?" It felt strange to say the words. "My father" was a phrase she'd rarely spoken.

"Oh, no. He's just on a mission. I was deputized to explain things."

Mission? "What things, exactly?" Kat took a step closer, studying Grace with a suspicion she didn't bother to hide. "I'm sorry, but I don't understand any of this. My mother tried to contact John after she realized she was pregnant, but he'd vanished off the face of the earth. We never heard a single word from him all the time I was growing up. Now you pop up twenty-six years later. Why now? What do you want?"

"Sometimes I could kick my husband's ass." Grace shook her head in disgust. "The knights have always had a cavalier attitude toward their children."

"Knights? I thought his last name was Lance."

"Actually, it's Lancelot du Lac, Knight of the Round Table."

Kat laughed, amused by the sarcastic image. The chuckle died as she gazed into Grace's utterly serious eyes. Good God, the woman meant it. *Is she some kind of nut?*

The blonde studied Kat for a long moment before her blue gaze hardened in resolution. "Time to quit stalling and get it over with." She reached out and gently laid a hand against Kat's cheek. Her palm felt seductively kind. Soothing.

Frowning, Kat started to pull back, only to discover she couldn't move. She opened her mouth to demand what the woman was doing.

Which was when knowledge slammed into her brain in a hurricane of images, emotions, information that battered her senses until the room spun. She didn't even feel herself hit the floor.

Kat lay flat on her back, staring at the ceiling. Her aching head swam—which was no surprise, since her world had violently realigned in the last five minutes. She felt as if someone had picked up her brain and shaken it like a snow globe.

"Kat!" Mary thumped to her knees beside her, eyes wide with panic. "Kat, are you all right?"

"Fine," she mumbled, an automatic lie instilled by years of soothing her mother's fears. "'M fine, Mom."

A surprisingly strong hand closed over her forearm, pulled her easily into a sitting position. "You sure about that?" Grace knelt at her side, a frown of concern drawing her blond brows down. "I gave you the whole package. It's a lot to deal with."

Kat stared at her. "You're a witch." It wasn't possible, yet she knew it was true. The knowledge felt utterly solid, as if it were something she'd always known, observed, believed. *Objects fall down instead of up. Grace du Lac is a witch with fantastic magical powers.*

"Yes." Grace's gaze didn't even falter at the admission.

"My father is one of the Knights of the Round Table. And he's a vampire." She took a deep breath. "And the reason you're here is because I could become a witch too."

Grace nodded. "We could use someone like you right now. But that's not my decision." She rose, pulling Kat to her feet with an easy strength that was far from human. "Ridge is going to have to make that call."

Two Days Later

He'd fought Nazi soldiers, communist spies, and demon-infected terrorists. Dealing with Kat Danilo should be a piece of cake. Yet somehow, Ridge Champion had an ugly feeling his newest mission wasn't going to be that easy.

Ridge pulled his Porsche 911 into the driveway of 344 Walsh Drive and switched off its rumbling engine. Ice-crusted snow crackled under his Armani loafers as he stepped out of the car. Striding up the curving brick walkway, he eyed the three-story Victorian. Snow was rare in Charlotte, North Carolina, yet icicles hung from the gray-trimmed eaves. The house's wooden siding was as white as the landscape, and more snow dusted its steeply pitched black roof. A very pretty house, solidly middle-class.

He stepped onto the porch and thumbed the doorbell,

sending a cheery four-note chime ringing through the interior.

The gleaming black door swung open a moment later, revealing a woman who had to be Kat's mother. The skimpy dossier he'd read said Mary Danilo was fifty-five, but she looked considerably older, her face gaunt, hollows under the blue eyes, lines of pain cutting grooves around her mouth. The beige slacks and sweater were too big for her thin body. Her smile looked forced as she opened the door wide and stepped back. "Come in, come in out of the cold." She extended a hand as he stepped inside. "I'm Mary Danilo, Kat's mother."

"Ridge Champion." Her fingers felt thin, fragile, and cold in his careful handshake. He wished he could do something about her obvious anxiety.

"May I take your coat?" She gestured toward the mass of heavy black wool that draped his shoulders.

"No, I'm fine." They needed to get moving.

Mary nodded, and turned to lead the way through the tiled foyer and into the living room. "Kat'll be down in a second. Last-minute primping. Not that she's vain, but she likes to look nice, and . . ." As if losing track of where the sentence was going, Mary trailed off. "Grace said . . ." She broke off again and studied him anxiously. Finally she took a deep breath, as if gathering her courage. "Grace said you're a vampire."

He met her gaze steadily. "Yes, ma'am."

"I didn't want to believe her. It sounds crazy. There's no such thing. But . . . I couldn't *not* believe."

"No," Ridge said. "She wouldn't let you do anything else."

"Oh." She twisted her hands together, staring up at him.

"Your daughter will be safe with me," Ridge told her gently. "Most of what you've heard about vampires is myth. Crosses don't bother us, we don't drain people's blood, and we're not undead. We certainly don't sleep in coffins. We're the good guys. And I would never hurt an innocent."

"Grace told me that. But Kat's my only child."

"I know, ma'am. She'll be safe with me."

The searching doubt didn't fade from her eyes, though finally she nodded. "Thank you."

Unfortunately, there wasn't a hell of a lot more he could say to convince her. Unlike Grace du Lac, Ridge wasn't a Maja, able to induce belief with a spell.

"Mom?" The voice came from somewhere upstairs, sounding far too sexy for a woman who still lived with her mother at the age of twenty-six. "Zip me up, please?"

"Coming." Mary shot him a harried, apologetic smile and left the room. Her footsteps sounded on a stairway somewhere out of sight.

Ridge tucked his hands in his overcoat pockets and studied his surroundings. The walls were painted a soft, elegant cream, the couch and chairs were covered in pale gold slipcovers, and a potted palm occupied a woven basket in the corner. There wasn't so much as a Santa figurine to be seen.

And why was that? He frowned slightly.

Idly, Ridge wandered over to the golden marble fireplace, where an eight-by-ten photo occupied the center of a white wooden mantel. From the center of a sterling silver frame the teenaged girl smiled in the kind of stiffly posed shot taken for senior yearbooks. A pretty blonde who looked vaguely like Mary Danilo, she wore a heart-shaped locket around her neck engraved with initials Ridge couldn't quite make out. Candles stood to either side of the frame as though it were a shrine.

He frowned. Was this Kat?

"Mom, are you sure you're going to be okay?" The woman's voice carried clearly to his vampire hearing, surprisingly throaty, flavored with the South, smooth and rich as Kentucky bourbon.

Ridge shifted, uncomfortable at his involuntary eavesdropping.

"I'm fine, Kat." The answer sounded too tense to be entirely honest.

"I can cancel."

"No! No, this is too important."

"Are you sure? I can tell him to forget it."

"No. I need to know. If you can find out . . . I'd like to know. Maybe . . . I think it would help. Maybe."

"This'll work, Mom. I know it will. You saw what Grace could do."

"But you've got to stay safe. Promise me you won't endanger yourself. I couldn't stand it if . . ."

"Nothing's going to happen to me, Mom. I can take care of myself."

Yeah, well, that's what I'm here to find out, Ridge thought grimly.

High heels clicked on the stairs, followed by the softer pad of rubber soles. Ridge turned to greet his date.

And caught his breath.

Kat Danilo paused in the hall doorway, a long, slim candle of a woman. Cream silk skimmed down a lithe and graceful body, draped seductively over hips, trailed into a short train. The gown was strapless, its cleavage framing round, sun-kissed breasts. An artful slit permitted glimpses of a gently muscled calf and one spiked gold heel.

Kat advanced to meet him, extending a hand, her smile bright and easy. In contrast to the formality of her gown, her hair was a short, spiky blond 'do that framed delicately angular features with saucy wisps.

"Ridge, this is my daughter, Katherine Danilo," Mary said with evident pride. "Kat, Ridge Champion."

Some bone-deep instinct had him bowing over those slender fingers. Unlike her mother's, her hand felt warm and surprisingly strong. Her eyes crinkled at the corners as she smiled, a clear and crystalline blue. He thought he saw a hint of indigo in their depths.

She wore the same gold heart locket as the girl in the picture, but her features were stronger, her gaze years wiser. So who was that in the photo? A sister?

That dossier he'd read was beginning to seem even thinner than he'd thought. Which made him wonder what had been kept from him, and why. The Majae's Council often played inscrutable games, even with the vampires of Avalon.

"Hello, Ridge." The girl's lips looked full and tempting, slicked with bronze gloss. He wanted to taste them. That Kentucky bourbon voice sounded like an invitation to sin.

"It's my pleasure, Kat." Or it would be, if he wasn't careful. How the hell was he supposed to maintain his objectivity with a woman who made his every cell thrum with need?

Unfortunately, he had no choice. There was too much at stake here—starting with Kat Danilo's life.

TWO

The vampire drove a black Porsche. And what's more, he looked like the kind of vampire who'd drive a black Porsche.

Kat eyed Ridge Champion in the dashboard lights as he drove with speed and skill. Hair that looked as darkly silky as Russian sable, thick brows slashing over cat-green eyes. A profile that could have been chiseled by Michelangelo. Lips a little sulky, a strong cleft chin, nose a Greco-Roman sweep. And, God help her, dimples that flashed when he smiled. What the hell kind of grown man had dimples? If he hadn't been a vampire, she'd have figured he was gay.

Gay? Kat winced. Apparently, being really nervous brought out the catty bitch in her.

Her mouth tasted as if she'd eaten a bag of cotton balls. Animated cotton balls, currently tumbling around in her lurching stomach. She tried to work up enough spit to swallow.

He whipped the Porsche between a pair of stone columns. Kat blinked at the houses that rolled past. Middle-class suburbia, nice but decidedly down-market from the Porsche. "You live here?"

"Not exactly."

He pulled into the driveway of a bland brick split-level. Garage doors opened and then closed again behind the car's sleek taillights as he braked to a silken stop. Kat started to reach for the door handle. . . .

The universe twisted itself inside out, taking her stomach along for the ride. A hot white starburst exploded in front of her eyes, blinding her. Kat clung to the door, blinking furiously, as the world settled into some kind of weird new configuration. Her stomach settled with it. "What the hell was that?"

The vampire looked at her and smiled. "Magic."

"Yeah, I kind of figured that from the psychic sucker punch." Kat gazed out the windshield and her jaw dropped in astonishment.

They were now outside, surrounded by expensive cars in a rainbow of colors. Porches, BMWs, Cadillacs, Rolls-Royces. The only thing that kept the lot from looking like valet parking at the Academy Awards was three beaters: a rusting VW bug, a panel van that appeared to date from 1972, and an ancient Model T in serious need of a paint job.

Light exploded in the corner of her eye. She jerked around to look out the passenger window. A 1957 cherry red Thunderbird had appeared in the parking space next to them. The well-dressed driver got out and went around to open the door for his date.

Kat was still gaping when Ridge opened her own door and extended a hand to help her out. Cautious of her skirt's silken train, she took his hand. It felt broad and warm under hers as he tugged her from her seat and threaded her fingers into the crook of his arm.

"Where are we?" Tilting her head back, Kat gazed upward. She couldn't recall a sky quite so beautiful, so incredibly black, or strewn with so many glittering stars.

Ridge followed her dazzled stare, and a slight smile curved his absurdly beautiful mouth. "This is the Mageverse."

"The what?" She searched the magical memories she'd acquired from Grace. Unfortunately, her knowledge apparently had some very large holes.

"The Mageverse. It's a parallel universe where magic is a natural force, like gravity or magnetism back home." He started down the row of cars, guiding her along. "This is where we live, where we draw on the magic that we use on Earth."

His biceps felt round and firm under the warm wool of his coat sleeve. She looked up into his elegant profile, frowning. "But how did we get here?"

Ridge lifted one broad shoulder in a half shrug. "That house we stopped at. There's a spell gate on the floor of the garage. When a car drives into it equipped with the trigger spell, it transports the car to the Mageverse."

"Oh." She tilted her head, eyeing him curiously. Her fingers stole unconsciously to her locket, absently rasped it back and forth over its chain. "I thought you did it."

"Me?" He shot her a surprised look. "Vampires can't do magic. Well, not that kind of magic. I can turn myself into a wolf or heal some really ugly gunshot wounds, but nothing outside my own body. You need a Maja for that."

"Why? I mean, if you could turn yourself into an animal—which sounds pretty damn major to me—why not other kinds of magic?"

"Why does gravity pull down instead of push up? That's just the way it works."

They joined a stream of richly clad people leaving the parking lot. Kat hunched inside her overcoat and studied the crowd as they walked. About half wore tuxedos or gowns in some shade of white, from eggshell to cream. The remaining women were dressed in a rainbow of vivid colors in silk and velvet, the men in black tuxes. Come to think of it, Grace had provided her with the white gown she wore. Some kind of color coding?

They clipped around a stand of trees with the rest of the well-heeled herd. The sight that greeted them stopped Kat in her tracks.

The five-story castle looked as if it had been transported directly from medieval England, complete with moat and thick stone walls. She could almost see Merlin standing on the ramparts, magic pouring from his hands.

Ridge gave her arm a little tug to get her moving again. As they walked across the wooden drawbridge, Kat looked over the edge at the moat below. A reflection of the full moon danced on the water's mirrored surface.

They passed under a portcullis into a courtyard decorated with rosebushes and topiary. Statues of medieval knights and ladies gleamed in the moonlight like graceful ghosts. A keep towered in the center of it all, soaring against the black sky, spotlights illuminating its massive cream stone walls. Heart hammering with nervous excitement, Kat let the vampire lead her through the keep's towering oak doors.

They gave up their coats to a lovely young woman manning a coat check in the foyer, then wandered into the huge ballroom beyond.

The first thing Kat saw when they entered was a Christmas tree that had to be fifty feet tall, a massive, noble fir draped in thousands of white lights. The ornaments—a glittering collection of balls in white, silver, and gold—were easily the size of Kat's head. It was so damned impressive, she barely noticed the usual stab of Christmas agony.

Dancers swirled around the huge tree, to the strains of some hidden orchestra. Kat was instantly grateful for the magical knowledge of waltzing Grace had given her at the same time as the dress.

"Would you like something to drink?" Ridge asked over the buzz of voices and laughter.

Kat licked dry lips. "Yes, please." Something with alcohol, if she was really lucky. She needed to numb her fluttering nervousness.

So damned much rested on this.

Ridge led her across the gleaming white and black checkerboard expanse of the marble floor to the other side of the room. Three huge tables stood lining the long wall, spread with a dazzling selection of appetizers. A towering ice sculpture stood on the central table, depicting a woman's arm thrust upward, holding a sword that shone with condensation.

"The Lady in the Lake," Ridge said. "Didn't happen like that, but Arthur loves that story."

"You know King Arthur?" Kat's voice spiraled upward into an embarrassing squeak.

"Yep." He nodded. "In fact, there he is."

The man who stepped into the center of the room didn't look like an immortal vampire knight. He was dressed in a tux, for one thing, though he wore his curling dark hair in a shoulder-length style, and a short, neatly trimmed beard framed his square jaw. Though not tall, he was as muscular as Ridge, and an air of power lingered around him like cologne. He lifted a hand, and the music stopped. "May I have your attention, please?"

Dancers stepped away from each other and turned to listen. The ones in white studied Arthur with the same staggered, wide-eyed fascination Kat felt. The rest listened with evident respect.

"As you've probably heard," Arthur said, "we're recruiting."

This drew a dry chuckle from a few people, though others looked grim.

"Those of you in white are Latents—the mortal descendants of the knights and ladies of the Round Table. And like all Latents, you have inherited the genetic potential to become immortal. Vampires, in the case of the men, while the women could transform into Majae."

"Please don't call us witches," a dark-haired woman in a red velvet gown called. "We don't like it."

"And believe me, you don't want to piss Morgana Le Fay off." Arthur smiled as the group chuckled. "Morgana and her fellow Majae worked a spell to find all the Latents who could survive the transition without going mad." He paused, his expression going grim. "Obviously, we didn't invite the Latents who'd be driven insane by the process."

"Nobody wants to deal with a case of Mageverse Fever," Ridge murmured in Kat's ear. "We're usually forced to kill the poor bastards—hopefully *before* they start piling up victims."

"But just because you can safely become one of us, that doesn't mean you should." The smile dropped away from Arthur's face. Suddenly there was something very old and very tired in his eyes. "Despite what you may think, we're not really immortal. We may not age, but we can be killed. And recently, a great many very brave Magekind died in some very ugly ways."

He began to pace around the silent circle of the crowd, pausing here and there to stare into someone's eyes. No one spoke, or shifted, or coughed. It almost seemed no one dared breathe.

"Your respective escorts have the task of deciding if you should become one of us. It's their responsibility to determine if you have the intelligence and courage to join us in our fight. It's not a decision to be made lightly. Any mistakes you make may cost not only your lives, but the lives of the rest of us as well. And worse, you could kill the innocents who depend on us for protection."

Arthur paused again, this time directly in front of Kat. She caught her breath as her heart began to pound in furious lunges. Those dark eyes bored into hers. She had the feeling he saw the deep hidden core of rage, the craving for revenge that roiled inside her.

And the fear, carefully hidden and barely acknowledged.

At last he turned away. "Fifteen hundred years ago," Arthur continued in a quiet tone that still carried to every corner of the room, "Merlin tested me and the members of my court to determine if we were up to the task of protecting mankind from its own suicidal impulses. Those of us who passed his tests drank from his magical grail and became immortal. Now it's our turn to determine if you are up to the task. We need you, but only if you are willing to pay the price."

The former king lifted his voice until it rang around the room. "If you are not willing to risk death, to fight and die with us, please leave now. We will honor you for your honesty and sacrifice, for it's no easy thing to refuse the promise of power. But if you stay, know the risks. Rest assured, your Magekind sponsor does. He or she will not make the decision lightly."

Arthur paused, sweeping his gaze over the crowd. His mouth twitched in a slight smile. "Now that I've killed the mood, have a nice evening."

On cue, the music rose again. People drew together, heads tilting as conversation began to buzz.

"You still want that punch?" Ridge asked.

"Is it alcoholic?"

He grinned. "I think so."

"God, yes."

Laughing softly, he started toward the punch bowl. Kat licked her dry lips, and frowned at the sudden sensation that someone was staring at her.

She turned to meet the stare of a tall, brawny blond man with such sharply chiseled features, he could have posed for an Armani ad. His eyes were pale and gray as winter ice, and just as cold. "I couldn't help but notice your necklace." In contrast to his gaze, his smile was as charming and warm as a sunny day. "It's lovely. Where did you get it?"

Kat's fingers closed over the engraved heart. "It was my sister's."

His smile widened. "Really?"

She went still, going on the alert. "She died."

"Did she?" Sympathy, rich as cream, filled his eyes. "I'm so sorry."

"Trey?" An older dark-haired man appeared at his elbow. "I've got someone I'd like you to meet, son."

"Sorry to bring up painful memories," the blond said, and turned away with his father.

Kat frowned after him, tense. It wasn't the first time she'd met a man who made her instincts howl. But here, among people who were, by definition, the good guys? She snorted in disgust at herself.

She was getting as paranoid as her mother.

THREE

$\mathcal{A}$ delicate crystal cup appeared before Kat's eyes, held in a strong brown hand. "You making friends with the werewolves too?"

"Werewolves?" Startled, she looked up at Ridge. "I thought you were all either vampires or witches."

"Majae," he corrected, and took a sip of his own cup. The contents were a delicate pink. Apparently he wasn't restricted to blood. "They don't like the 'w' word, remember?"

"Majae. And vamps are called Magi." Kat sipped, and smiled at the spicy-sweet bite of alcohol blended with fruit. "Grace gave me the lecture. She didn't say anything about werewolves, though."

"We didn't know about them until recently." He rested a warm hand on the small of her back, and she walked along with him. "Seems Merlin didn't entirely trust us, so he created a race of Direwolves to make sure we didn't step over the line. They're immune to magic, so in a fight they'd probably kick our collective asses."

"So why'd Arthur invite them?"

Ridge shrugged. "Why not? They're our allies now, and it's Christmas. Arthur invited all kinds of people to the party." He nodded at a small glowing figure that darted past through the air, looking rather like a giant firefly. "Fairies, dragons, a shape-shifting unicorn or two."

"Y'all have interesting friends." Absently, Kat put her drained cup on a passing tray. As the tray retreated, she did a double take. No waiter carried it. It just glided along through the air, apparently surfing on a wave of sparks. "I am definitely not in Kansas anymore."

"Want to dance, Dorothy?" Ridge gave her a rakish smile and held out a hand.

"Why not?" She rested her palm on his and let the vampire lead her into the ballroom.

The Latent waltzed very well, following his lead with an athletic ease and grace. Her train had some kind of wristband she'd hooked one hand through, and she held her arm out to the side so the skirt swirled around them like water. The slit flashed glimpses of long leg that heated his libido to a smoky simmer.

He found his gaze lingering on her sultry mouth under its coat of bronze gloss. Her scent was intoxicating—female flesh, some exotic floral perfume, Latent potential singing a siren song in her blood. The combination made his fangs ache.

It was far too easy to imagine how she'd taste.

He'd never Turned a Latent—doing that kind of thing without permission could get you an order of execution. Mageverse Fever was nothing to screw around with.

But he'd heard there was no experience quite like having a woman Change as you spilled yourself into her. Merlin's Gift igniting in her cells, activated by contact with a vampire's magic. . . .

Yeah. They said it was something.

Assuming you could ignore the cost she could end up paying for all that power.

Janice, screaming as she burned in the demon's fire . . .

Ridge smelled her blazing hair as her shrieks of agony deafened him. The magical flames seared him as he tried to beat them out with his bare hands. . . .

Too late. Too goddamn late.

His feet faltered, and he lost the rhythm of the dance.

"Hey, you okay?"

Janice was gone. The eyes that looked up at him were Kat's, blue and smoky and concerned.

"Fine," Ridge said curtly. "I need some air." He released her and strode toward the French doors that led out into the moonlit garden.

It was warmer out there than it had any business being this time of year. Apparently one of the Majae had cast a spell to ensure it was just cool enough to be pleasant on a dancer's heated skin. Ridge drew in a calming breath and walked across the stone-paved patio.

Kat trailed him, frowning in concern. "You sure you're all right?"

He turned to look down into her lovely moonlit face. "Why do you want to do this? Become a Maja?"

She gave him a smile that looked a little too tight as she caught up her locket in long fingers and began to rasp it along its gold chain. "Well, immortality sounds pretty cool."

Impatiently, he waved off the statement. "Somehow I doubt you're stupid enough to really believe that."

Her blond brows flew upward, and she drew back, visibly offended. "I'm not stupid at all."

"Good. Because Arthur wasn't kidding when he said you need to be damned sure you want to do this. It can get you killed in some really ugly ways."

Her gaze went chilly. "Not being immortal is no guarantee you'll die in bed, Ridge. And I like the idea of being able to defend myself."

There was a bitter note to that Southern Comfort drawl. "Is there a particular reason you need to be able to defend yourself?"

She turned away and moved to the stone balustrade. "The world is full of predators."

"True." He followed her to study her expressionless profile. "And we tend to encounter a lot of them in this job. Mostly because we go out and look for them. If you stay human, you'd have a reasonable chance of avoiding all those killers."

"Only if you're lucky. Not everybody's lucky." Her fingers found her necklace again.

"Who do you know that was that unlucky?" Realization dawned. "The girl in the picture on your mantel? The one who owned that necklace?" He reached for the locket.

Kat lifted one delicate shoulder in a half shrug, pulling away before he could touch her. Her fingers tightened protectively around the locket.

Ridge brushed his fingertips along the line of her jaw. Her skin felt warm, silken. She automatically looked up at him. The pain in her eyes deflated his own useless anger at past failures. "I'm sorry," he said softly. "I just don't want to see you hurt."

Her mouth twisted into a bitter line. "It's a little late for that." But as she studied his expression in the moonlight, the tension in her face slowly melted into sympathy. "You're grieving too."

He looked off over the gently rolling lawn. Its clusters of moonlit trees glowed with the soft magic of the Mageverse. "A friend of mine died in the Dragon War. She . . . burned. One of the demons threw a fireball and hit her. She was standing six feet away, but there was nothing I could do. I didn't have the magic to put it out. And neither did she." Ghostly shrieks rose in his ears again.

"A lover?" There was no pity in those lovely eyes, only understanding. Yes, Kat had her own memories that sliced the mind like broken glass.

"We hadn't been together like that in decades. But she was the one who made me a vampire. You never forget the one who Changes you, whether there's real love there or not. Watching her die . . ."

"Hurt." Kat said it as if she knew how utterly inadequate the word was to express such howling agony.

"Yes."

She rose on her tiptoes, caught the back of his neck, and drew his head down until she could reach his mouth. It was a surprisingly tender kiss, less an act of passion than an offer of comfort.

Her lips felt exquisitely soft as they brushed over his, a delicate seduction. She started to draw back.

Ridge caught her nape, felt the cool silk of her short hair against his fingers, impossibly soft. Opening his lips, he deepened the kiss, drinking in her taste, savoring the sweet comfort she offered.

Kat responded with a tiny moan, a whimper of breath against his mouth. She leaned into him, the silk of her gown warm from her body, her breasts lush and full against his chest. Her long legs moved restlessly, brushing his thighs.

Her scent filled his head, some delicate perfume tinged with jasmine. And beneath that, the heady musk of female arousal. He hardened in a hot, sweet rush, his balls going tight.

Vampire hearing picked up the rush of her pulse, the sea tide of her blood. His fangs slid from their housing in his jaw. He bent his head, nuzzling, and she tilted her chin, giving him access to the big, pulsing vein. . . .

What the hell am I doing? The thought blew through the smoky heat of his arousal, chill as a sudden draft. Ridge blinked.

Oh, hell, he was losing it. If he didn't stop this, he'd be balls-deep in her and coming before he knew what hit him.

And that was a really bad idea. Tempting, yes—Merlin's Cup, he was tempted—but there was no way he could maintain his objectivity if he banged the girl.

No, not banged, a voice whispered from the back of his brain. Nothing with this woman would be as simple as a bang. Kat Danilo wasn't the kind of woman a man used for meaningless physical release. She might draw you in with that pretty body, but she'd snare you tight with her intelligence, with her questing mind and dry wit. Not to mention the subtler temptations of shared grief.

That might be the most dangerous snare of all.

There was far too much Grace had kept from him when she'd asked him to sponsor Lance's daughter.

Stepping away from Kat took a surprising amount of effort. She looked up at him, those beautiful eyes a little dazed, a bit disappointed. His fangs twinged in frustration.

"I think we'd better go back inside," Ridge managed hoarsely, "and dance."

They drove through the moonlit night, the Porsche's headlights spearing the darkness. In the green glow from the dash, Ridge shot Kat a look of concern. She'd danced and joked throughout the evening, teasing him subtly with a brush of fingertips here, a ripple of laughter there. She knew just how much he wanted her now, and she'd seemed determined to test his control.

But as the evening wore on, Ridge had sensed a growing tension in her. Now as they drove into her housing development, the tension hit a vibrating peak that irritated him like the rasp of sandpaper over bare skin. *Does she think I'm going to lunge for her throat?*

Yet, as they wheeled into the driveway, Kat's attention seemed focused on the house rather than him. She was out of the car before he had time to turn off the engine.

Ridge's brows shot up as he watched her clip up the brick walkway as fast as her tight skirt would allow, fumbling her keys out of her overcoat pocket as she went. He opened the car door and strode after her.

"Mom?" she called as she wrestled the door open.

"Baby?" Her mother's voice floated from somewhere upstairs.

Kat's shoulders slumped in relief. "I'm home!"

She turned and gave Ridge a smile as he walked up behind her. "I had a lovely evening."

"That's good." Ridge studied her with narrow eyes. "What were you so afraid of?" He could smell the fading scent of her fear, hear her heartbeat slowing its desperate thump. "I was starting to wonder if you thought I was going to jump you."

Kat looked honestly startled. "Oh, no. Nothing like that." Her laughter sounded a bit forced. "I just . . . worry about my mom. I guess I'm a little paranoid."

"You want me to check the house?"

"No. No, that's fine. We're fine."

Ridge tucked his hands in his overcoat pockets and studied her thoughtfully. "All right. If you're sure."

"I'm sure." That smile was definitely forced.

"Look, we need to meet tomorrow night. I'd like a better idea of how you'd handle yourself in a fight."

Her blond brows lifted. "Ridge, I'm a fitness instructor."

"I'm aware of that." The dossier had mentioned that much at least. "But being fit doesn't mean you know what to do when someone's trying to hurt you."

He got the distinct impression she was grinding her teeth, but she restricted herself to a nod. "You're the boss."

"Yes. I am. I'll pick you up at seven."

FOUR

$\mathcal{R}$idge's house was a three-story Mediterranean villa in golden stucco, its windows arched, its low roof red ceramic tile. Impressive though it was, it looked modest next to towering Mageverse neighbors that included a Germanic castle and a sprawling Gilded Age mansion.

"Who builds these houses?" Kat asked, eyeing the crenellated walls towering over the trees next door.

Ridge shrugged. "Majae, usually. It takes a lot of magic to build a house like this. Generally you barter services, though a Maja may give you a house as a gesture of gratitude."

She grinned, swinging the athletic bag she carried in one hand. "And what did you do to win a witch's gratitude?"

"Saved her from a Death Cult assassin." His smile was sly and very male. "She was very, very grateful."

"I'll bet."

He led her inside, past plaster walls, wrought iron fixtures, and timber-trussed ceilings. Their feet padded over gleaming tile floors in warm shades of rose, gold, and cream. The combined effect was both intensely masculine and very beautiful.

Yep, that had been one grateful witch, all right.

At last Kat followed Ridge into a cavern of a room with a towering ceiling supported by heavy dark timbers. Padded mats covered the floor, sinking underfoot with every step.

"We'll work out here," Ridge told her, and gestured at an arched hallway. "You'll find a bathroom down that corridor where you can change."

The bath in question was nothing short of sybaritic, Kat discovered, all smooth cream marble with pale gold accents. You could practically swim laps in the tub, while the shower was an elegant freestanding affair with multiple showerheads protruding from the rounded glass walls.

It was all enough to give a girl ideas, especially after last night's toe-curling kiss.

The memory of Ridge's mouth had left her shifting restlessly in the sheets all night. He'd felt so tall and deliciously strong against her, yet he'd touched her with exquisite care, as if she was something fragile and valuable. The simple brush of those lips had been enough to leave her aching.

When her tongue touched the tip of one fang, Kat had felt a strange erotic jolt, a delicious blend of fear and desire. Ridge was so utterly unlike any other lover she'd ever had. Next to his elegant restraint, every other man seemed a fumbling boy in retrospect, overeager and graceless.

Kat might have thought Ridge a little too cool, in fact, had she not sensed the patient predator beneath his gentleman's mask.

Vampire.

Grace had told her the genetic spell that was the Gift could only be triggered by making love to one of the Magekind. Which meant Kat would have to brave that dark and alien masculinity. Feel those fangs break her skin, that thick cock pump into her sex.

Dry-mouthed, Kat began to undress. Her nipples stood stiff and aching as she took off her bra. She shivered in anticipation and bent to dig hastily in her workout bag for her clothes.

*W*hile Kat changed, Ridge retreated to his own room two floors above to don a pair of loose cotton pants. Barefoot, he padded back downstairs a few minutes later.

To stop in his tracks and stare.

Kat was bent double in the center of the room, one hand wrapped around her left ankle as she stretched, chest flat against her thigh. Her legs were amazingly long and deliciously bare, displayed by a pair of thin cotton shorts. When she straightened, he saw she wore a cropped tank that revealed a tight, lean belly. Her breasts rode her chest in round little handfuls that made him want to peel that thin tank off for a better look.

As he watched with hungry interest, she bounced on her bare toes, eyeing him. "What now?"

Somehow he resisted the impulse to suck in his stomach. He knew his body was hard and strong from years of swinging a sword in practice bouts against his fellow Magekind.

But immortal, ageless vampire or not, he was still a guy.

Ignoring his ego, Ridge stepped closer and gave her a come-ahead gesture with his fingers. "Show me what you can do. Hit me."

He'd trained his share of Majae over the years, and he knew what to expect. An awkward swat he'd barely feel, delivered with a complete lack of speed or skill. And no strength whatsoever.

Smoky blue eyes narrowed as she stepped up to him. That was all the warning she got.

Kat came up off the floor, her fist blurring at his chin with the full weight of her body behind it, clean and hard as a heavyweight's jab. If he'd been human, she'd have bloodied his nose. As it was, he barely ducked in time to avoid the punch. The breeze of her fist fanned his hair.

Her eyes narrowed, delicate lip curling up in a feral snarl, as anger crackled like a lightning strike in those cool blue eyes. Kat didn't like missing.

She came after him then, throwing first a left, then a right, snapping both punches with speed and skill and no hesitation at all. When he automatically avoided both, she whirled into a spinning kick he was forced to knock aside with a thrust of his forearm.

She didn't even stop for breath. Every blow was harder, faster, punch flowing into punch flowing into kick. She picked her targets like a pro, aiming for ribs, head, knees, ankles at seeming random.

Just to see what she'd do, he finally started throwing punches of his own, human-slow at first. She blocked them with all the strength and speed her Latent genetics gave her.

"You've done a hell of a lot more than teach kickboxing," he commented, jerking aside to avoid a kick that would have knocked a human cold. He caught her ankle and flipped her like a poker chip.

Kat hit the ground on her back and rolled to her feet, as cleanly and easily as if she'd practiced it a thousand times. She probably had. "Black belt." She was breathing a little faster now, but the anger was gone from her gaze. She'd obviously realized she couldn't afford the luxury of rage against someone like him.

Ridge snaked a fist past her guard and popped her on the nose. He pulled it, but it still rocked her head back.

She retreated, smooth and graceful as a dancer. Her guard never dropped. He watched anger flicker in her eyes, then melt away into intense concentration. He could almost taste the determination that gave her blue gaze a cool, metallic glint.

His own eyes narrowed in response. *Let's see what you can really do, Kat Danilo. Let's see just how far you'll go.*

Kat went after the vampire with everything she had, every skill she'd built over fifteen years of martial arts training. That was saying something. As a Latent, she was faster and stronger than most women and a good percentage of men. She'd brought down brawny male fighters twice her weight.

Yet trying to hit the vampire was like punching water. He flowed aside from every punch, every kick. Then he'd flick out a casual hand, shoot right past her guard, and slap her just hard enough to sting. She never even saw the blows coming.

He was beginning to piss her off. That was bad. Getting angry was the first step to losing. *Stay cool, Kat. Stay in control.*

She couldn't afford to lose. She had to prove she was worthy of the Gift.

Breathing hard, sweat rolling down her thighs, her arms, Kat took a step back and began to circle. Ridge moved with her, all warrior's grace. At least he was sweating, hard muscle gone slick and gleaming under the lights. Those loose pants of his had slid down, riding low over his hips, revealing a teasing glimpse of dark hair snaking down his belly.

His green eyes burned at her, intense, hot. Hungry. His sensual mouth curled in a smile she suddenly wanted to bite.

I've never seen any man more beautiful.

The thought streaked past her guard like one of his taunting little slaps. She caught her breath.

He lifted his fists, raising his guard. Muscle flexed and rolled. His biceps bunched, tight and round. There was an intriguing little pucker high on his shoulder that looked like the scar from a gunshot wound. A second scar, this one long and slashing, ran down one side of his abdomen and disappeared into his waistband. She wanted to trace it with her fingers.

Focus, dammit.

What the hell was wrong with her? She never got distracted during a bout. Though to be fair, none of her opponents fought half-naked.

Or looked like Ridge Champion. Sweat-slicked, strong, so deliciously male.

Focus, Kat!

To force her mind back to business, she spun into a roundhouse kick. He ducked under her slashing leg, kicked out a foot, snagged her ankle, and dumped her on her ass.

Ridge pounced before she could roll away, one hand capturing her wrists, legs twining around hers, his big body crushing her into the mat.

Kat snapped into action, trying the half-dozen tricks she knew to get out of this kind of hold. None of them worked. He even jerked his head out of range of her attempted head-butt. And smiled.

Think, dammit. He's too freaking strong. You're going to have to out-think him.

"All right," Kat gasped, forcing her muscles to relax, watching him under half-closed lids. "You win."

"Do I?" That sensual mouth twitched. "There's a promising admission." He relaxed fractionally, strong legs loosening their grip on her thighs. His lids drooped to a lazy half-mast, and he lowered his head.

Kat went still under the kiss. It was slow, lazy, a thorough exploration of her mouth, as exquisitely tempting as the one the night before.

No, even more so. Sweat and effort gave his body a sultry heat that eroded her sense of discipline. She could feel him going hard against her belly, the long width as intriguing as his soft, sinful lips.

Kat opened for him with a moan. Her head spun, and she let herself yield. His free hand slid up to cup her breast, sending teasing heat spiraling despite the thick fabric of her athletic bra.

She squirmed, letting her legs fall apart. He nudged her chin up to give her throat a teasing nibble, then lifted his weight to allow her to spread her legs around his. She braced a palm against his muscular ribs. . . .

And gained precisely the leverage she needed.

With a twist of her legs and a heaving thrust of her arms, Kat threw him off and bounced to her feet, falling into a combat crouch. "Let's try that again," she growled through gritted teeth.

And Ridge, lying flat on his back, began to laugh.

Frustrated, she raked her sweaty hair out of her eyes and glared at him. "What's so damned funny?"

"Grace did explain how you actually become a Maja, I trust?"

"Yeah, we have to have . . ." She trailed off. "Oh."

"Yeah." He gestured at the erection still tenting his pants. "Oh."

She blinked at him, trying to decide whether to feel triumphant or moronic. "You mean I passed your test."

He chuckled, folding his arms behind his head as he gazed up at her. "Honey, you knocked it out of the park."

"I thought I had to beat you." Kat frowned in confusion.

He snorted. "Not very damned likely. I'm an eighty-year-old vampire with sixty years of combat experience, and I once deadlifted a Cadillac off a pedestrian. You're good, but you ain't *that* good."

Realization struck. "I never had a prayer."

"You did better than I expected." He grimaced. "Then again, I didn't expect you to be able to throw a punch without detailed instructions and a map. Most new Majae can't."

Puzzled, Kat dropped to her knees on the mat. "So what the hell was the point?"

Ridge knelt in front of her like the sensei he could have been. "I wanted to know if you could think on your feet. If you'd panic when faced with overwhelming odds. Whether you could take a punch without running home to Mommy."

She raised a brow. "And?"

"And you don't panic. When you got pissed off, you controlled it instead of making stupid mistakes. Pain doesn't stop you. And you kept fighting long after anybody with any sense would have thrown in the towel. What's more, you just played me for a sucker, which is both embarrassing and seriously impressive."

Her heart was thundering a heavy metal beat in her ears. "So you'll make me a Maja?"

The humor faded from his eyes, leaving his expression grim. "Yeah. We need people like you. I just hope you don't end up regretting it." He rose to his feet. "Come on. I don't know about you, but I could use a bath."

Kat blinked, imagining Ridge naked and covered in bubbles. *Oh, this is going to be good.*

FIVE

She'd been right, Kat decided. You could swim laps in Ridge's tub.

He was down on one knee, testing the water temperature and adding some mysterious oil that formed aromatic clouds of bubbles. His back looked deliciously broad, muscle flexing and working as he moved, and she contemplated it in happy anticipation.

When the tub was filled and fragrant, he stood and turned toward her. He stood tall and impossibly handsome in the golden light of the candles that rested on every flat surface. They'd all burst simultaneously into flame when he and Kat walked into the room.

Ridge claimed the candles were magic, but she suspected they'd been ignited by the sheer lust in the air. You could almost see it, sparking and swirling around them like amorous fireflies.

He moved toward her, his eyes heavy-lidded with need. A long, distinct shape strained against the soft cotton of his pants. She wanted to tug down his waistband for a shameless ogle.

Ridge tipped her chin up for his kiss. If he felt the same

impatience she did, he hid it well, taking his time with the slow mating of mouths, teasing, stroking, lip-to-lip, tongue dancing around tongue. Kat sighed, relaxing into his solid strength. His hands came to rest, one cupping her butt, the other on the dip of her waist.

The kiss spun on, lazy and drugging. The taste of him intoxicated—a hint of salt, a trace of mint, and over it all, that dazzling masculinity.

Deep inside her, something woke, responded with a hot leap of need. Something furious and demanding that had never risen for another man.

The Gift?

The thought shot a little shiver of mingled excitement and fear through her. Grace had given her a rough idea what to expect, but how was it going to feel? Magic igniting in her every cell, changing her, making her immortal. Something other than human. . . .

"Shhh," Ridge breathed against her mouth. He drew back enough to smile into her eyes. "There's nothing to be afraid of."

Ha. Showed how much he knew. That, or she was a coward, because she could think of any number of things to fear.

Mostly failure.

But then he caught the hem of her top, peeled it smoothly off, and tossed it aside with an offhand little flip. Her bra followed a moment later.

She swallowed, looking up at him uncertainly as he gazed down at her breasts in the warm candlelight. Did he think them too small? Too big?

You never knew with guys.

"Lovely," Ridge sighed, and she relaxed at the honest delight in his eyes. He lifted one hand, gently brushing his palm over one erect nipple before slowly cupping her in warm, gentle fingers.

Kat let her head fall back at the feather-soft pleasure as he stroked her. His fingers traced delicate patterns over the full curves, brushing the tight peak, thumb sliding back and forth.

"Sweet." She sighed. "It feels so sweet."

One corner of his mouth kicked up. "Yes. It does."

He dropped to one knee and caught the waistband of her shorts and panties in both hands. Tugged slowly downward. Leaned forward to press a kiss to her belly, right below her navel. She giggled at the ticklish sensation.

"God," Ridge murmured, still drawing the shorts down, "you've got the longest legs."

She smiled shyly and stepped out of the bottoms, bracing one hand on his broad shoulder.

He knelt there, gazing up at her, admiring. His green eyes looked almost black, shadowed by the fall of his hair over his forehead.

Then he leaned forward, and his mouth found her.

Kat gasped, startled, as his tongue slipped across her clit. The hot, wet pleasure hit her like a silken lash, fiery yet impossibly sweet.

He spread her lips for better access, and licked lazily. First tiny flicks, then exquisite little circles. He reached between her legs. The sensation of one finger slipping deep tore a gasp from her lips. She threaded her hands into the cool silk of his hair and held on for dear life.

He drew back just as she was about to spill over.

"Ridge!" she protested, as he rose to his feet with that pacing panther grace. "Has anybody ever mentioned you've got a sadistic streak?"

He smiled, very male, just shy of smug. "A time or two." And he pulled down the waistband of his cotton pants. His cock sprang free.

She forgot her irritation in anticipation. His erection looked delicious, a thick, rosy length that jutted from his muscular belly.

He ignored her shameless, hungry gape and calmly drew his pants down his brawny thighs, stepped out of them, and straightened.

And let her stare.

God, he was beautiful. Kat was no stranger to physical power—there were plenty of muscular men at the gym—

but there was a sculpted elegance to Ridge's body you didn't get from pumping iron. His was a warrior's build, long and lean, with a swordsman's grace and agility.

A big hand closed over hers, shocking her out of her lust-induced trance. Smiling indulgently, Ridge guided her over the side of the tub and down into the delightfully warm water.

Kat sighed in pleasure as she sank onto the low bench just beneath the foamy surface. Little wavelets sloshed as he joined her, drawing her back into his arms.

Picking up a bar of fragrant soap, he began to run it over her skin, lazily stroking. Kat let her eyelids slide closed, the better to concentrate on all the wonderful sensations.

Bubbles caressed her arms, her breasts, as gentle currents swirled around her body, seductively warm. The cake of soap felt slick, cool, as he stroked it over her nipples, around her arms, down her torso to her legs.

She let her head fall back against his shoulder. "I feel like melting chocolate. Like there's not a bone in my entire body."

"Mmm," he purred. "That's okay. I'm hard enough for both of us."

Kat chuckled without opening her eyes. "You're a bad, bad man, Ridge Champion."

"And getting worse every minute." The cake of soap slid wickedly between her legs. He turned it on edge, used its slick, rounded surface to maddening effect. Kat caught her breath in delight as it slid over her clit, teasing until she squirmed.

"Like that?" he rumbled in her ear, his voice deep, almost thrumming.

"Mmm." She couldn't seem to manage anything more coherent.

"How about this?" Fingers replaced the soap, slick and skilled. Circled, danced, strummed. She panted, rolling her hips in tiny, needy jerks as he tormented her gently.

His mouth found the side of her neck, nibbled until she turned her head to find his lips blindly. They kissed, his hands skimming her with soapy fingers. He stroked nipples, followed the curve of breasts, traced belly button and hip bone. Found erogenous zones she didn't even know she had, and played over them until she quivered in response.

No lover had ever made her body leap like this. Lost in the hot honey rise of passion, she reached back and hooked an arm around his neck, arching into his hands, gasping.

No, she'd never had a man like this.

*E*very fluid movement of her long, lush body was an act of seduction. She twisted and rolled, stroking herself against him like a cat, purring and lazy with pleasure. Her nipples jutted, hard and pink and sweet as candy atop breasts that filled his hands with satin warmth. Foam rolled down her body, hissing and popping in gentle accompaniment to the lapping of warm water around them.

Ridge was hard as marble against her ass, and his fangs ached with the need to taste her. Her heartbeat pumped a demanding beat in his ears. He knew he must have wanted a woman this much in his decades as a vampire.

But damned if he could remember when.

Need beat in his blood, pulsed in the root of his fangs and the thick jut of his cock. He felt like distilled lust, a pure and blazing psychic heat. He wasn't sure how much longer he could keep from claiming her.

Sliding a finger deep into creamy flesh, Ridge moaned. God, she felt so tight, yet so impossibly slick and ready. The thought of how she'd feel clasping him made him shudder.

Kat rolled her head against his shoulder, arching her neck in invitation. He bent his head to kiss her there again . . .

And felt the big vein pulsing against his lips in thumping temptation. His eyes slid closed, and he pressed the tips of his fangs against that vein.

"Yes." She gasped. Her Southern Comfort voice sounded even more throaty, and her gaze met his, fey and witchy with need. "Do it. Take me."

He somehow wrestled enough self-control to ask, "You sure?"

"Yes!"

The hunger demanded he fall on her like a wolf, but he fought it back and kissed her there slow, teasing.

Then he bit. Her flesh gave under the sharp slice of his fangs, blood filling his mouth. She arched with a shocked little cry. He started feeding pleasure back to her in long pulses, keeping time with every swallow of her blood.

She felt the first bright, scarlet sting of his teeth as a sudden shock. But delight flooded in behind the flash of pain—a dark, intense pleasure that was somehow all feral male, as if he magically shared what he felt.

All the while, those big hands stroked, one tugging slippery nipples, the other seeking between her thighs. Sliding parted fingers back and forth around her clit until long curls of delight spiraled up her spine like red ribbons.

The orgasm took her by surprise, a dazzling explosion that made sparks flash in front of her eyes. She cried out.

He growled at the sound. Lifted his head.

Before she quite knew what was happening, he rolled with her, sweeping her under his body, bracing her backside on the seat rimming the tub. Then he was between her thighs and inside her in one long, breathtaking lunge. Kat yowled again at the sheer overwhelming wonder of the sensation.

It felt like he filled her to the throat, deliciously ruthless, surrounding her in slick male muscle, hot and wet and very, very ready. With a rumbling growl, he began to thrust.

Kat hooked her heels over his ass and ground back at him, giving as good as she got, mindless with the clawing rise of need. Wanting more. On the razored verge of something she couldn't identify. Something she had to have, if only . . .

Thrust. Thrust. Thrust. More. Only a little bit more, and she'd . . .

He roared, a deep bellow of passion, stiffening against her, pulsing deep.

At first she thought it was another orgasm. Hot white, blinding, a delicious, searing pleasure that had her convulsing against him.

And then the pleasure bled away, and she could see again. It seemed she was somewhere else, a room she recognized.

And she saw—

R idge threw back his head and roared again as his orgasm pulsed in liquid fire. The pounding intensity of it made him shudder and gasp.

Until at last he collapsed, wrapping himself around Kat in exhausted, desperate gratitude.

A thought penetrated his dazed lassitude. *We're going to have to do this again. Takes three, maybe four times to activate the Gift. Thank Merlin.*

It came to him that the edge of the tub was probably digging into her butt, so he rolled over with her, draping her across his body. "Damn, Kat," he said, half-laughing as he lifted his head to look down into her face. "You've kicked my . . ."

He broke off. Her eyes were wide, unfocused, her expression blank. He jerked upright in alarm, but she only lolled limply in his arms. "Kat! Kat, what's . . . ?"

"Mom," she whimpered. Not exactly the word a man wanted to hear from his new lover. Then she blinked and snapped into focus, her eyes widening in terror. One small hand clamped onto his shoulder, nails digging deep. "Ridge! Ridge, there's something wrong with my mother!"

SIX

*K*at scrambled out of the bath, naked, wet, bubbles streaming down her luscious backside. Ridge would have been entranced by the view, had it not been for the panic in her eyes. He levered himself out of the tub and handed her a towel as she looked around in panicked helplessness. "What did you see?"

Kat took the towel automatically. "Just a flash of her face. She looked asleep. But I felt a sense of terror, like there's something horribly wrong." Fear and doubt warred on her face in heartbreaking combination. "Maybe I just imagined it."

"You saw this just as you came?" He strode toward the bathroom door, drying his shoulders with the towel he'd snatched off its rack.

"Yes." She padded after him, her clothes bundled in her hands. "Does that make a difference?"

"Yeah. You haven't come into your Gift yet—we haven't made love often enough—but many Latents get visions the first time. If you saw it, it either has happened or is about to."

Kat's face paled, and she swayed. Seeing her stagger

from the corner of one eye, Ridge turned and caught her elbow.

"My mother's suicidal." Her eyes looked huge, and she pulled away from him to begin dragging on her clothes, though foam still clung to her wet skin. She hadn't taken the time to use that towel. "Mama's battled clinical depression for years, but it's worse in the Christmas season. She's attempted suicide twice, but I always got to her in time."

Ridge cursed, a rolling string of gutter Latin he'd picked up from Arthur.

Kat met his gaze and swallowed, obviously fighting to control her panic. "We've got to get back now, Ridge."

He nodded sharply and headed for the wrought iron staircase. "There's no time to fool with the car. I'll get Grace."

$\mathcal{R}$idge found the cell phone where he'd left it, upstairs on his dresser. It was not, of course, a real cell phone—such a thing wouldn't work in the Mageverse—but when Ridge spoke the word "Grace" into it, the magical device nonetheless chirped obligingly.

He was acutely aware that Kat watched him anxiously, damp but dressed.

"This had better be good," a male voice growled.

"Your daughter thinks your old lover just attempted suicide. That good enough for you?"

Lance's reply was a single pungent curse. "Grace?" he said. "We need to get over to Ridge's now." There was a gratifying urgency in that "now."

The air rippled into a gate just as Ridge pulled a shirt over his head. Grace and Lancelot stepped through.

"Where's your mother?" Grace demanded of Kat, the gate still rippling the air behind them.

"In her bedroom, I think. She looked asleep, but I have the feeling there's something wrong. Really wrong." Kat took a deep breath and balled her hands into fists, obviously working to get her fear under control. "Fatally wrong."

Without another word, Grace turned, gesturing. The gate rippled again, now revealing a bed with a woman lying in a fetal ball under an embroidered quilt.

"Mom!" Kat lunged through the gate, and Ridge followed, Grace and Lance at his heels. Ridge was barely aware of the ripple of magic surging over his skin as he dove through the dimensional door.

*K*at's stomach rolled itself into a quivering, ice-filled ball as she plunged into her mother's bedroom. Mary appeared deeply asleep, and Kat found herself hoping she'd just scared the hell out of everyone for nothing.

But when she grabbed her mother's shoulder and shook her with a loud "Mom!" the still form did not respond.

"She's alive," Grace said grimly. "Barely." The Maja reached past Kat, putting one slim palm in the center of her mother's chest.

Ridge's warm hands closed gently around Kat's shoulders and drew her away from the bed. "Give Grace room to work, babe."

As Kat watched anxiously, Grace's fingers began to glow. Sparks spilled from her flesh, dancing over Mary's body, cutting spirals around the woman's still arms and legs, circling her head in a halo of light.

Kat caught her breath. Grace's magic had made her believe in witches, but actually seeing the otherworldly light show at work around her own mother was something else again. *This is real. All of it. Vampire knights, witches, Merlin, all of it. Real.* "Is she going to be all right?"

Grace grunted, but made no answer, an expression of deep concentration on her face.

"I think we'd better go downstairs and wait," said the dark-haired stranger who'd accompanied Grace. "It's not a good idea to distract her when she's doing work this delicate."

Kat looked up at him. This man must be Grace's husband. Which made him . . .

Her knees went weak.

Ridge caught her forearm and steadied her. "You going to be okay?" His steady green gaze was dark with compassion.

Kat took a deep breath and blew it out, managed a quick nod. As Ridge guided her toward the door, her gaze fell on a small pill bottle beside the bed. She scooped it up and was not surprised to find it empty. A glance at the label confirmed her suspicions.

Sleeping pills.

"Dammit, Mom." Anger stiffened her back. Kat pulled away from Ridge's supporting hand and stalked out to clatter down the stairs. "God forbid she leave another bloody corpse for me to find. This is the third fucking time she's pulled this stunt."

Kat didn't look back to see if the men were following her as she made for the kitchen. They'd need coffee to get through this. At least, she would; she had no idea what stressed vamps drank.

Besides, there was something soothing and familiar about the ritual of making coffee. At least it gave her something to do with her hands.

"I gather this has happened before," Lancelot said as she put the pot on to brew.

Kat glanced over at him. He was almost ridiculously handsome, with dark, thick brows arching over eyes the color of warm sherry. His hair was thick and curly, his cheekbones broad, his nose narrow over a wide, curving mouth. It was obvious why her mother had fallen into bed with him twenty-six years ago.

It was impossible to think of him as her father. For God's sake, the man looked only a few years older than she was. Thirty or so, tops, though she knew he had to be sixteen hundred years old, at least.

Yet as she studied him, Kat realized there was something vaguely familiar about the shape of his face. *Damn, he looks like me.* She saw a softer, feminine version of those angular features every time she looked in a mirror.

The shape of his eyes and chin, the curve of his mouth. Yet because he appeared to be only a few years older than she was, strangers would probably mistake him for her older brother.

"Kat," Ridge prompted her softly, "do you know why your mother would do something like this?"

She went to the china hutch for the sterling silver coffee set her mother used for guests, then added three cups and saucers and carried the heavy tray back to the central island where the coffeepot hissed. "I had a sister."

"I remember," Lancelot said unexpectedly. "Mary mentioned her. She was a little girl at the time. Seven or so. She was spending the weekend with Mary's ex-husband." A deep frown line formed between his thick brows. "The divorce had just been finalized."

Which was why Mary was out getting drunk. "Karen had a stormy childhood. Spent a lot of time shuttling back and forth between her father's house and Mom's. Me . . ." Kat managed not to let her gaze slide toward Lancelot. *I had no father.* "I stayed with Mom all the time, which became kind of an issue. Karen accused Mom of favoring me, but Mom said it wasn't true. Said I was just younger, needed her more." She shrugged. "It got really bad when Karen hit eighteen. Typical teenage stuff. Beer, boys. Lots and lots of really bad attitude."

But Kat had worshipped her beautiful big sister anyway. Cheerleader and boy magnet, Karen had been as blond and popular as a living Barbie doll. Ten-year-old Kat had probably annoyed the daylights out of her, constantly tagging at her heels. "There was this boy. She said his name was Jimmy Chosen, and that he was a college senior. Mom tried to get him to come to the house, but he kept making excuses, ducking her invitations. That really set off all her mommy alarms."

"I'd imagine so," Lancelot said.

"Then, that Christmas Eve, Mom found a package of condoms in a pocket when she went to wash Karen's coat.

It all hit the fan. Lots of screaming, lots of crying. Mom threatened to throw Karen out if she kept dating Jimmy."

"Probably not the best way to handle the situation," Ridge observed, moving over beside her.

"No, which is just one of the reasons Momma periodically tries to eat entire bottles of Seconal." Kat gave him a slightly bitter smile. He brushed a comforting hand across the small of her back. Feeling oddly soothed, she continued, "I heard Karen get up before dawn Christmas morning and attempt to sneak out of the house. I got up and begged her not to go—I was afraid Mom really would throw her out. Karen threatened to kick my ass if I ratted on her. Swore she'd be back in an hour, long before Mom woke up. So I went back to bed." She stared down at her own reflection in the shining surface of the coffeepot without really seeing it. "I wish to God I'd been the little snitch Karen always swore I was. If I had been . . . "

She broke off to transfer the coffee into the silver pot, then picked up the loaded tray and led the way into the living room. "By the time two hours had passed, I knew Karen was in serious danger of getting caught."

Sitting down on the couch, Kat began to fill the delicate cups. Ridge sat down next to her as Lancelot took one of the armchairs. "We lived in one of those lakeside developments then, very upscale. I knew Karen liked to meet her boyfriends out beside the lake, where there was a shady stretch of grass. So I went to get her."

She glanced up. Lance was watching her, his gaze brooding. "The day before, I'd seen a dog dead on the highway. Been hit by multiple cars, I guess. Probably a truck or two. Its body was all ripped up, red ropes of . . . Well." Her voice sounded distant to her own ears. "Karen lay on the grass in her favorite picnic spot. And I thought when I saw her that she looked just like that dog. I wouldn't have known who she was if it wasn't for her long, pretty blond hair. I recognized the hair."

"Sweet Jesu." A muscle flexed in Lancelot's handsome

jaw, and his eyes looked . . . haunted. As if he was remembering something just as unpleasant.

Ridge caught Kat's cold hands in his own big, warm ones, stilling her mechanical efforts with the coffee. "I'm sorry."

"I know." She managed a tight smile for the compassion in his eyes. "I ran back home, screaming. Mom didn't believe me at first, thought I had to be wrong. But then we walked to the lake . . . " Kat broke off for a long moment. "We spent Christmas day talking to cops."

"And you were ten years old." Lancelot rubbed both hands over his face. "Merlin's balls, girl, I'm sorry."

Now that she'd started telling the story, Kat felt unable to stop. "Some of the cops thought it must have been some kind of animal. Maybe a bear. Something big, with claws, though nobody could say how a bear had gotten to the middle of Lakeside Village without being seen."

Next to her, Ridge stiffened and shot Lance a significant glance.

"Mom and I knew they were wrong. It had to be Jimmy Chosen, especially since it turned out there was no Jimmy Chosen anywhere in town. Not enrolled at the college, not anywhere. And he was never caught." She stirred her coffee slowly. "Ever since then, we've tried to deal. I started taking martial arts, became something of a jock in school. Ran track, played basketball, the whole bit. Momma tried to hold it together for my sake, struggled with periodic bouts of depression."

"But it got worse." Ridge rested a hand on her knee, a silent offer of support.

Kat nodded. "When I left home at twenty-one, determined to become a cop, Mom attempted suicide the first time. She was convinced I was going to end up like Karen. So I gave up the cop idea and moved back home. Got a job at the fitness center I worked out at. Spent the rest of my time trying to make sure Mom kept taking her meds."

"And then Grace showed up." Lancelot picked up one of the coffee cups and started adding cream and sugar, his movements as mechanical as her own.

"I had hoped that by gaining the Gift—by becoming a witch—I could find Karen's killer and finally get some justice. Lay Mom's ghosts to rest." Kat's fingers stole to the heart locket.

Ridge nodded at it. "That's hers, isn't it? Karen's?"

"She was wearing it when . . . I hoped I could use it to home in on him. The killer. But Mom—she's never liked me getting out of her sight, particularly not with a man. I thought she'd know I was safe with you, especially after Grace worked her magic. But apparently her old demons got the better of her."

A long silence trailed by, broken only by the hum of the refrigerator.

"She's stable."

Kat looked up. Grace smiled at her from the door to the living room. She looked drained, pale. "I've saved her life, repaired the worst of the damage to her body. But her brain . . . She's very, very ill." The woman dropped into the chair next to her husband. "She's been suffering for years. It's going to take a lot of neurochemical work, plus some very delicate repairs of all that burned-in psychic trauma. All beyond my skill. I've made arrangements to gate her to the Healing Clinic."

"Good." Lancelot gave Kat a reassuring smile. "They'll be able to help your mother there."

Kat frowned. "Healing Clinic?"

"The Magekind can heal most physical injuries, but sometimes we—or our mortal relatives—need outside help," Grace explained. "There's very little the clinic's healers can't do something about."

"Good," Kat said grimly. "My mother needs all the help she can get."

SEVEN

When the four trooped back upstairs, they found Mary still deeply asleep, though Grace assured Kat it was no longer the unhealthy coma they'd found her in.

Grace conjured another gate, and Lancelot carried Mary through it, directly into the room his wife had arranged at the clinic.

It was reassuringly pleasant, Kat decided, glancing around as she helped tuck her mother into bed. The furniture was homey rather than the kind of stark, utilitarian setup one would find in a regular clinic. The blond wood of the bed, nightstand, and dresser was engraved with twining vines and flowers, and the thick quilt appeared handmade.

Her attention fell uneasily on a pretty ceramic pitcher and matching mug on the bedside table. Both were painted with elegant pink roses. "You may want to take those out of here," Kat told the woman Grace had identified as the healer on duty. "The mood she's in now, she might try to break one and use the shards on herself."

The healer, a slender redhead, gave her a steady, sympathetic look. "You couldn't break either of those with a sledgehammer. Don't worry, dear. We'll take good care of your mother."

"When will she wake up?"

"We'll keep her asleep until Petra, the spiritual healer, arrives in the morning. They'll begin work then. We'll call you when she's recovered."

Kat frowned. "Shouldn't I be there when she wakes? Mom won't know where she is."

"She won't be afraid, Kat. Petra is very good with this kind of case."

"She is," Lancelot put in. "Petra helped my daughter-in-law Caroline deal with the aftereffects of the Dragon War." He grimaced. "Post-traumatic stress from the final battle has kept all our healers busy."

"Yeah," Ridge agreed. "I've been meaning to see Petra myself."

Well, that was a pretty solid recommendation. "So when will I be able to see my mother?"

The healer shrugged. "I can't say for sure, since I'm not a psyche specialist. But given her condition, I'd say at least a week."

"By then, Petra will have her healthier than she's been since Karen died," Grace told Kat kindly. "She'll feel as if she's been reborn."

Kat stared in astonishment. "In one week?" God, what if they'd been able to get this kind of help fifteen years ago? How much pain could have been avoided? For that matter, what about all the other mentally ill people on Earth? What about all the sick and dying, the starving, the victims of war and genocide? "Well, aren't we fortunate," she said, then winced at the bitterness in her own voice. She sounded like an ungrateful bitch. "I'm sorry. Thank you so much for everything you're doing for my mother. I'm very grateful, and I know she will be."

The healer waved the thanks away. "Think nothing of it, dear." She studied Kat a moment, her gaze penetrating. "When was the last time you ate? You look a little pale."

"Ah." Kat frowned, trying to remember. "I had dinner around five P.M."

"It's almost three in the morning now. You should get something."

"I'll take care of her." Ridge rested a strong hand on her shoulder. She gave him yet another tired smile. Seemed she'd been doing that a lot tonight, probably because he'd been beside her for every step of this ordeal.

Something to think about, there.

"Sounds good." The healer touched Kat on the shoulder. "Try to get some rest. You've had a rough night."

She nodded mutely and followed the others out of the room as the healer bustled off to check on another patient.

Together, Kat, Ridge, Grace, and Lancelot walked down the hall to a reception area. Comfortable armchairs clustered around a crackling fireplace trimmed with pine boughs and Christmas lights.

Lance opened the gleaming front door, and the four exited to descend a set of stone steps to the cobblestone street beyond.

The sky was still dark, but streetlamps shed pools of warm, bright light. The air felt cold and sharp against Kat's face, and snowflakes danced and fluttered through the shafts of light.

"I am sorry," Lancelot said roughly, turning to face Kat, shoulders drawing back under her gaze. "I wish I had known your mother had gotten pregnant."

"But you did find us eventually." Kat eyed him, tucking her hands into the pockets of her jeans. "So it wasn't impossible, if you'd bothered to check. Which might have been the logical thing to do, considering you hadn't worn a condom."

"We don't," Lancelot said, the words clipped. "The Gift is genetic. Unmarried knights"—he slanted a glance at his wife—"are expected to father children whenever possible. Sexually transmitted diseases aren't a problem for us, so . . ."

She stiffened, stared. "You got my mother pregnant on *purpose*?"

"I didn't know whether she was fertile, or if she'd made arrangements of her own." He sighed. "I know that sounds callous."

"It is callous—Dad." Kat rocked forward on her toes and glared up into his eyes. "Regardless of all the other shit that happened, you gave her another mouth to feed and did absolutely nothing to help support me."

Lancelot met her furious gaze without flinching, though a flush spread across his high cheekbones. "Yes, I got her pregnant. And no, I made no effort to find out if she needed help. I can't change that, but I would if I could. And I will do everything in my power to make it right."

Yeah, right, Kat thought bitterly.

Lancelot pulled a thick gold signet ring off his finger. "I asked Grace to prepare this for you. If you need me, say my name, and it will bring me to you. At any time." A muscle flexed in his jaw. "And yes, I know it would have been nice to have it fifteen years ago."

In her anger, Kat wanted to snarl something dramatic and throw the ring in his face. But judging by the icy dignity in his eyes, he was expecting just that, so she gave him a slight, cold nod instead and accepted it. "Thank you."

He gave her a courtier's bow that looked automatic and completely natural, then reached for his wife's hand. "We'll see you later, Kat. Ridge."

The four exchanged nods—Grace's was a little cool— then turned and went their separate ways.

Silence spun out between Ridge and Kat, filled only by the click of their heels on the cobblestones. "I don't understand how she can just ignore what he does." Her voice sounded clipped to her own ears, smoky with anger and frustration.

"Grace?" Ridge slanted her a look.

"Yeah. I mean, the man is a legendary seducer. He and Arthur's wife . . ."

"Legends often exaggerate. It really wasn't that simple. Besides, Grace and Lance are Truebonded. Neither of them could cheat now even if they wanted to."

"Truebonded?" She glanced over at him, curious.

"A deep magical union Magekind couples create. True-bonded partners can sense each other's emotions, even thoughts. They can use the bond to reinforce one another's powers magically. It's the most profound kind of marriage two people can share."

She frowned deeply, considering the idea. "Doesn't sound like you'd have a lot of privacy."

"I'm told you learn how and when to give each other space."

Looking up into his handsome face, Kat found herself wondering what it would be like to share that kind of relationship with Ridge.

It sounded . . . intriguing.

Kat leaned against the gleaming stone countertop in Ridge's kitchen, sipped her wine, and watched him chop salad vegetables with impressive skill.

For a man who didn't eat, he certainly seemed to know his way around a kitchen. The mouthwatering smell of cooking meat curled up from the oven, where a steak was currently on the broil.

"There's something you need to know," Ridge began as he tossed the salad. "It may make the situation with Lance a little more understandable. And besides, nobody needs to become a Maja without knowing this stuff."

She studied him over the rim of her wineglass. The Riesling was delicately fruity and sweet. "And that would be?"

"Only about one in a hundred of our children can become Magekind without going insane," Ridge told her bluntly. "And it's not an insanity that we can treat. That's why the Magi are under orders not to use protection when they have sex. We need every Latent we can get in order to have any chance of finding one who can survive the Gift."

Kat's eyes widened. "But that means—"

"We have to watch the vast majority of our children

die of old age. Lance told me once that he'd lost fifty-two children and grandchildren that way, before he decided he could no longer stand to have any contact with his mortal offspring."

"Fifty-two?" If the loss of one child had almost driven her mother insane, how had Lance tolerated watching child after child die?

"Then there's the problem of raising mortal children in the Mageverse, among immortals who do magic without even thinking about it." He turned toward the stove, opened the oven door, and reached in with a pair of tongs to turn the steak. "The results are often not particularly positive for the child."

"How?" Kat frowned, chilled.

"Well, take Sir Bors's son." Closing the oven door again, Ridge turned to lean against the counter, muscles shifting as he crossed his arms. "He was so furious when he was denied the chance to become immortal that he became a follower of a magical demon. He attempted to sacrifice Arthur in an act of death magic that would have destroyed us all. Luckily, Arthur and his knights got to him first."

"My God." Kat rubbed her hands over her face. "So you're saying if I become a Maja, I won't be able to risk children."

Ridge shrugged. "You can have them. You may not want to raise them. Many Majae put their children up for adoption on Mortal Earth. That way the child has a chance of a reasonably happy life, without ever knowing about the one-in-a-hundred chance of winning the genetic lottery."

"And that's the real reason Lancelot made no attempt to contact my mother."

"Yeah, that would be it."

After Kat ate, she and Ridge retreated to his bedroom. "Sun'll be coming up in an hour," he told her. "I'll go into the Daysleep then."

Kat nodded. Grace had told her vampires had to sleep during the day as their bodies recharged. They needed the magical energies of the Mageverse every bit as much as blood.

Ridge stepped closer and drew her into his arms. "But I've found over the years," he purred, "you can do a lot in an hour."

EIGHT

A shaft of rose light woke Kat. She opened her eyes to the sight of a glowing stained-glass window, apparently designed to render the sunlight safe to vampire skin.

She blinked sleepily, enjoying the play of color through the muscular unicorn the window depicted. Roses wreathed its thick blue neck as it pranced through a sunlit wood to greet a blond lady in a long medieval gown in dark blue and gold. Ivy twined up the great animal's spiral horn. The woman looked as besotted with the unicorn as he did with her no-doubt virginal self.

Kat sympathized. She felt pretty besotted herself.

Turning on her side, she gazed down into Ridge's sleeping face, painted in glowing color in the window's light. He appeared younger asleep, his handsome features relaxed, almost boyish. A curl of dark hair brushed his forehead. His shoulders looked very broad and tanned against the soft linen sheets.

He'd made such slow, sweet love to her the night before. When they'd come, she'd seen magic burst around them like a fireworks display, though thankfully there had been no horrific visions.

Today they would make love for the third time. Chances were she'd come into her full Gift then. Ridge had said sometimes it took more than three times, though never less.

Kat almost found herself hoping it would be more, because afterward, Ridge would have no reason to stay.

Would he?

Settling onto her elbow, she frowned uneasily at the thought. Was she allowing herself to get too involved? As supportive as he'd been, she was nothing more than an assignment to him. A pleasant assignment, maybe, but still, just another mission, like all his others over six decades as a vampire of Avalon.

But Kat knew she would not forget him. Ever. She'd never had a lover like him, and it wasn't just the biting—which was a hell of a lot more fun than she ever would have thought. Nor was it simply his lovemaking, spectacular and life-changing though it was.

It was the look on his face when he'd seen her fear for her mother, the compassion in his eyes when she'd told him about her sister's death. And the way he'd held her before the sun came up, his arms warm and strong. As if she were something precious.

As if she were more than an assignment.

Ridge stirred, green eyes slowly opening. The sun must have set.

He smiled the moment he saw her, a lazy, sated curve of the lips, and stretched, his beautiful torso arching as he extended brawny arms. He caught her waist and tumbled her down across his chest. "That was a serious look you were wearing when I opened my eyes."

"Thinking."

"You know, if it's about your sister, you don't have to go through with this." His gaze turned serious. "I'm sure Lance and Grace would be happy to help me track that bastard down and take care of him. You'd have your closure."

Kat studied him. "But I thought you guys needed the reinforcements."

"Yeah, but as I told you last night, there's a price to pay, and it's pretty steep. You can still back out."

She hesitated. "No, actually, I can't. I need to do this, Ridge. That monster murdered my sister, destroyed my childhood, and drove my mother crazy. I want to get the bastard myself. I have to."

Then a new thought struck. Kat tilted her head, considering it. "And too, there's the way Grace saved my mother. If I had that kind of ability, I could keep people from suffering the way I did. I could stop bastards like my sister's killer before they had the chance to ruin so many lives. That's worth a little sacrifice."

Ridge nodded slowly. "Yeah, I've always thought so. I've never regretted becoming Magekind because we do so much good. But it's not a choice to make casually."

"I'm not making it casually." Kat bent down and kissed him slowly, thoroughly, before lifting her head again. "But I am making it."

Ridge smiled. One big hand lifted to trace the line of her cheekbone. "Have I told you how beautiful you are?"

Kat blinked at the change of subject. "Umm."

"Guess not." He caught her by the back of the head and drew her down. "You are"—he breathed against her mouth—"incredibly beautiful. Those big, smoky eyes, those soft lips . . ." He kissed her, taking his time, a slow seduction of tongue and teeth and lip, teasing, yet so gentle her breath caught. His fingers traced the line of her jaw, the rounded curve of her chin, and came to rest on her pulse, pounding hard in her throat.

Kat moaned, shivering a little at the sweet pleasures he spun with his lips, his tongue, his long fingers, the motions so delicate, yet producing such intense sensations.

"You're good," she panted. "Damn, you're so good."

He smiled as he nibbled his way down toward her breasts. "You're so inspiring."

When his mouth found her nipple, the pure, intense delight drew her spine into a bow. He rumbled in response to her hot reaction and settled down to lick, tongue swirling, teeth gently raking. She bit her lip and let her eyes drift closed.

God, it really did feel incredible. Each sensation seemed more intense than it ever had before, as if her every cell had become sensitized to his touch.

He gave one nipple a delicate nibble, using just enough tooth, just enough pressure. Swirls of candied heat made her writhe. Unable to help herself, she twined her legs around his waist and rocked her hips slowly against his. She felt his cock jutting ferociously hard against her soft belly. Seduced, Kat reached between them and wrapped her fingers around the shaft. Warm satin over steel. She moaned in anticipation.

Ridge growled something, a hot male rumble of encouragement. Kat continued to explore. The head of the big organ felt like velvet, soft and a little nubby. A slick tear of arousal met her fingertips, and she smeared it over the hot tip. He sucked in a breath.

And rolled with her, tumbling her onto her back. He rose, spread her legs with his big hands, started to lower his head. "Sixty-nine," Kat managed to gasp.

The sound he made was so raw and ripe with anticipation, she shuddered. Ridge rearranged himself, head down along her body, giving her access to the hard jut of his shaft. She wrapped one hand around it, angled it downward, and sucked the round, warm head into her mouth. Salty, musky, a little astringent, but so deliciously, utterly male.

Best of all, it was Ridge—Ridge who had comforted her, who had offered the solid support of his strength through the nightmare of her mother's latest meltdown. Ridge, with his powerful body and kind eyes.

Kat opened her mouth wide and raised her head, sucking him in, taking him so deep, her throat muscles clenched in discomfort. She didn't care. Closing her lips tight around the smooth satin shaft, she suckled in long, rippling pulls, intent on giving him pleasure.

He made a strangled sound of agonized delight. Kat grinned a little smugly around him.

And then male fingers spread her delicate lower lips, and his tongue found sensitive flesh. She almost jolted into orbit herself.

His tongue circled her clit, tracing tiny, delicate patterns. His dark hair tickled the inside of her thighs as he worked, an extra flourish of delight.

With a purring hum of pleasure, Kat suckled, one hand cuddling the soft furry pouch of his balls, the other sliding up and down his shaft. Losing herself in the sweet eroticism of his cock, his mouth, his tongue.

Losing herself in him.

Ridge looked up along her body, watching the play of smooth muscle in her belly, the flex of those strong thighs as she writhed under his touch. He gave her a slow lick, dancing his tongue around her clit as he slid a finger inside her. She was hot, deliciously wet, snugly tight. His cock twitched in hungry anticipation. She rewarded it with another mind-blowing suckle and swirl that made the muscles in his legs jerk and his toes twitch.

He shuttered his eyes and watched the magic dance. Sparks of it eddied around them to his vampire vision as her body readied itself for the Gift. Ridge could almost taste it, foaming like champagne on his tongue.

His beautiful, magic Kat. So damn young, yet with such ancient eyes. The same pain and tragedy that had broken her mother had made her strong, tempered her like a sword blade in a forge.

I'm in love with her.

The thought sliced through his mental guard, ringing with truth. He caught his breath, half in fear, half in sheer, dazzled delight. The smell of her filled his senses, her taste flooded his mouth. He felt intoxicated. Kat-drunk.

And Ridge knew in that moment that he had to find a

way to keep her. Letting her get away was just not an option, any more than he could live without oxygen.

His lips peeled back from his teeth, and he jolted back onto his heels. His cock protested losing the delightful contact with her mouth, but he ignored it, grabbed her by the hips, and pulled her around until their bodies were aligned.

"Ridge!" She laughed, catching his wrists as he spread her legs wide.

He caught his cock in hand, aimed for her rosy, glistening opening, and thrust his way home.

"Ridge!" Her beautiful eyes widened, but not in pain. "Oh, God!"

Half-crazed from a need that was far more than a craving for release, he began to thrust in long, sawing drives of his cock, plunging in and out. She felt so incredibly slick and tight as she gripped him, the friction glorious. He wasn't sure he could hold on, but he was damned well going to try.

Teeth gritted against the pleasure, Ridge bucked against her. And with every thrust, magic gathered around them in a hot dance of light.

Head spinning at the sheer feral sensation of his cock plunging inside her, Kat clung to Ridge's sweating shoulders. She felt a savage pressure building, coiling tighter and tighter inside her belly, until she had to writhe. Her legs coiled around his hips, tightening instinctively, dragging her hips harder against his, seeking that last bit of sweet friction.

Something flashed at the edges of her vision. Automatically, Kat's eyes shifted to track the glow. The small golden orb promptly exploded like a silent skyrocket, spilling sparks over her skin. She gasped at the hot pinpricks of pleasure.

Ridge kept thrusting. He felt huge, a thick, tunneling possession that pulled and twisted at her inner flesh, filling her utterly. More fireballs appeared, popping like bubbles, spilling bright sparks over them both.

Kat yowled as his cock drove deep and magic showered her skin.

He nuzzled her throat. She automatically tilted her chin, knowing what he wanted. Giving him access.

Ridge bit deep, his fangs sinking into her flesh even as he drove to his full length in her sex. He stiffened, coming as he drank.

And the world detonated.

The magic burst from Ridge, a searing explosion that triggered an answering burst in Kat. Fire blazed up from deep inside her every cell, a silent whirling detonation. Clinging helplessly to his broad shoulders, she watched the room disappear into dazzle, as if a small sun had suddenly exploded right in the center of her chest. Heat seared her, as intense and furious as the pleasure of her orgasm.

Magic shot between them like a fountain, spearing through Ridge's chest and out her back, then arching around to pierce Kat again. Growing brighter with every circuit until it formed a blazing loop of energy.

Suddenly she could feel what he felt—every pulse of his cock, the tight creamy grip of her own sex, the rake of her nails down his back. Something seemed to click between them, locking down, linking them mind to mind, heart to heart.

Kat screamed, a long, singing note of pleasure and pain as the magic built and built and built. She barely heard Ridge's answering howl.

The birth of Kat's power thundered in Ridge's ears like the roar of tornado-force winds. He could only wrap both arms around her and hold on for dear life. Her blood filled his mouth as her sex milked his cock, and he writhed.

Never in his life had he felt anything like this.

Then it all just . . . stopped. The eye-searing energy disappeared, leaving him clinging blindly to her lithe, sweat-slick body. Kat fell limp under him, her strong legs releasing their desperate hold, her fingers relaxing their grip on his shoulders. His skin stung, and he suspected she'd dug her nails deep.

"My God." She gasped. They were both panting. "What the hell was that?"

Ridge gently disengaged his fangs from her throat and licked the blood away. "That," he said, his voice hoarse, "was magic. You're a Maja now, Kat Danilo."

NINE

*K*at lay dazzled and panting. With a last, sated groan, Ridge collapsed beside her. She could feel his pleasure echoing in her own body like a deep thrum in her cells. *Incredible.* She wasn't sure if it was his thought or her own. *Never felt anything like that.*

Magic swirled around her like dust motes in a shaft of sunlight, a dancing glitter. Half-hypnotized by the swirling patterns, she watched the tiny flashes dance around her head. Every time she inhaled, she breathed them in.

Experimentally, Kat puffed out a breath. Magic rolled from her mouth in a glowing plume, reminding her of chilly childhood mornings when she'd watch her breath mist.

"You look stoned." Ridge rolled onto one elbow, watching her with an indulgent expression.

"I feel stoned. Sort of . . . floating." Kat frowned suddenly. "Is it real? The magic, I mean?"

"Oh, yeah. I don't see it often, but sometimes when it's particularly dense, vampires can perceive it. And I'm told Majae see it all the time. After a while, you quit noticing it as much."

He looked different, she realized. Vivid, sharply solid.

More real somehow. When she looked away, she could feel his presence like a low hum.

As if he was a concentration of pure magic.

A weaker hum came from a closed door across the room. "There's something magic in the closet."

"Wouldn't be surprised." He yawned hugely.

Curious, Kat rolled out of bed and swung the door open. A pile of metal objects lay heaped on the floor. Kneeling, she picked up a helmet, scorched and dented. There was a cuirass too, along with greaves, gauntlets, and other assorted bits of armor. All of it was blackened, as if it had been through a fire, and most of the pieces showed dents and smears of old blood.

"I should have cleaned and repaired it, but I didn't have the heart. Some bad memories there." Ridge said from behind her.

"You were hurt." She could feel the magical echo of old wounds, a reverberation of pain in her own flesh.

"Not as bad as some." His voice was grim. "I lived."

The flow of magic in the dented helm seemed to be disrupted. Acting on pure instinct, she fed her own power into it, straightening and reinforcing the flow. Light swirled around the helm, and the dents disappeared, leaving it gleaming as if brand-new again.

"Cool!" Kat looked around at Ridge, surprised. "It wants to be whole. I wonder if I could fix it all . . . " Extending her hands over the pile of battered armor, she concentrated, sending a wave of magic swirling over it.

When she dropped her hands again, it was all repaired and shining. "Damn. That was . . . surprisingly easy." Kat cocked her head, considering the pile, mentally tracing the smooth flow of magic. "All I had to do was straighten the kinks in the energy patterns, and everything popped right back out."

"Can you make armor of your own?" He knelt beside her and lifted a long sword out of the pile, then handed it to her. "Creating the stuff's a bit harder."

"You mean copy it? Maybe scaled to fit me?" She

weighed the big blade in her hands. It was well-balanced, but definitely made for a vampire's strength. Too heavy for her by far. Transferring the weapon to her left hand, she bit her lip and concentrated. Magic swirled into her right hand, formed a column of light, solidified.

The new blade was shorter, lighter. She handed Ridge the original, then extended the copy, weighing it in her hands. The balance was a little off. She dissolved it and tried again. Better, but still off. Tried again until she was satisfied.

"What do you think?" She handed the sword to Ridge.

He took it, held it at full extension, then gave it a slow swing, careful in the limited space. "Good work." Handing it back, he eyed her. "You know how to use that?"

Kat nodded. "My sensei taught me a little kendo, and I fenced competitively in college. I'm not a knight, but I know which end of the blade goes in the target."

Next she tackled the armor, dragging magic in and pouring it out, following the patterns of force in Ridge's armor. It was, she thought, a bit like singing a song someone else had written. Her first try at a full suit was a bit misshapen, but she kept working, destroying the suit and recreating it until she was satisfied.

Finally Kat stepped up to the full-length mirror and considered her gleaming reflection. Her head ached from the effort of all that ferocious concentration, but at least the thing looked right. The armored plates followed the contours of her body, and the joints matched her own, with no gaps to allow a weapon to penetrate. She twisted back and forth to test the armor's flexibility. And smiled in satisfaction. It was light as construction paper, but strong as the steel it appeared to be.

So she'd passed the first test she'd set herself. "Okay, now let's try the hard part." She reached down the gorget of her armor and drew out the silver locket she'd been wearing for days now. Concentrated.

"Uhh, Kat . . . " Ridge said uneasily.

She ignored him, all her focus on pouring magic into the

locket and listening to the returning echo of energy. First came a familiar scent she hadn't smelled in so many years, she'd almost forgotten it.

Kat found herself smiling. "Cherry lip gloss and my mother's Nicole perfume. My sister always filched Mom's perfume when she went out."

Then another odor cut through the familiar smell. Like the smell of dog fur, only ranker, tinged with the copper taint of blood and the nauseating reek of death. Kat sent more magic pouring into the necklace. "Show me. Let me see him!"

At first nothing happened. She gritted her teeth and concentrated harder on the killer's feral reek.

"Are you sure you should try to do this now?" Ridge's green eyes narrowed in worry.

"No, but I have to do it anyway." Her heart raced with a sense of urgency. "I've got this really bad feeling." As if something horrible was going to happen if she didn't act *now*.

The scent vanished. "Shit! I've lost it."

"Don't try to force the magic." Ridge dropped a hand on her armored shoulder, encouraging her to meet his eyes. "It's like fighting. If you overthink it, you get in your own way."

That made sense, thanks to all those years of martial arts training. She forced rigid muscles to loosen, then sent her magic rolling into the locket again.

A woman shrieked. Kat jumped, eyes snapping wide. "That's *real*. That's happening now!"

Somewhere, Karen's killer was closing in on another victim.

Ridge bent to jerk his jeans off the floor. "We've got to get to her." He stepped into the pants, jerked them up his legs, zipped, grabbed his sword. "Open a dimension gate."

"How the hell . . . Oh." She remembered the swirling iris of magic Grace had created, the rippling sensation as she'd stepped through. Gathering her magic, Kat sent it pouring into the air.

It began as a single glowing point that rapidly expanded into a swirling opening that showed a view of moonlit trees.

Another scream rang out, raw with pure panic.

"Bloody hell," Ridge snarled, and leaped through the gate. Kat shot after him, praying the dimensional door wouldn't dissolve with them halfway through.

Leaves crunched underfoot as they landed, and she puffed out a relieved breath. Still dressed in her conjured armor, Kat lifted the sword she held. Ridge had grabbed his own blade before he jumped, but he wore only the jeans. She bit her lip and concentrated, but his armor did not appear. "Nothing's happening!"

"We're on mortal Earth," he hissed back, scanning the night with narrow eyes. "Magic doesn't work as easily here. Try again."

Kat sought her magic again. After a moment she found it: a thin, burning thread glowing inside her mind, instead of surrounding her as it did in the Mageverse.

No wonder magic was harder to use here.

Reaching deep, Kat concentrated ferociously on the armor she'd repaired. Called it.

And watched in satisfaction as it swirled into being around Ridge, covering him in magical steel.

He didn't even look down to watch it appear, instead tilting his head back, inhaling deeply as if seeking a scent. "This way." He set off, moving swiftly and silently through the woods.

Another scream rang out, and he broke into a run, bounding through the night with a vampire's blurring speed. Kat conjured a light and raced after him in its bobbing glow.

Ridge grabbed her, dragging her to a halt just before she charged headlong into a clearing. He held a finger to his lips and pointed silently.

"Won't do you any good to scream, bitch." A big man stalked a slender blonde, who backed away from him in evident terror. Kat had the ugly feeling he was familiar somehow, as if she'd seen him before. A chilling thought, considering his next words. "I'm going to rip out your heart and eat it."

"Why?" the blonde cried. "You said you loved me!"

"And you bought it!" He laughed. "Stupid little cunt. None of you bitches are anything to me but gullible meat."

Kat's lips peeled back from her teeth in a silent snarl of rage. Meat? Her sister? This poor girl? *Meat?*

A scream tore from her throat, a shriek of distilled fury. She jerked out of Ridge's hold, swinging her sword up as she charged into the clearing. *I'm gonna hack that bastard's head off his shoulders.*

"Kat!" Ridge snapped. "Wait!"

She ignored him, wanting only to kill, to make the bastard pay for years of fear, anguish, and guilt, of missed childhood Christmases and birthdays experienced as grief instead of joy. Make him pay for her mother's suffering. Make him feel all the pain he'd caused.

The man whirled in surprise as she exploded out of the dark. "What the fuck?"

"It's your turn to die, you son of a bitch!"

She got a glimpse of blond hair, of a big, muscular body, of cold eyes widening with a trace of astonished fear.

And then she was on him, her blade swinging in a long, flat arc. By rights, it should have hacked his head from his shoulders.

He ducked. Moving far faster than a human had any business moving, in a fluid explosion of speed.

And he laughed at her. "I always wanted to kill a Maja."

What? How did he know about . . . ?

A gleaming blur tore past her. "Why don't you try a vampire instead, you bastard? Or don't you like fighting somebody that can kick your ass?"

Ridge didn't hesitate when the killer ducked his first whirling blow. He just kept hacking, swinging his sword in great arcs that twisted effortlessly into flashing thrusts. "Kat, dammit, get the girl out!"

Ridge was right—the victim was the priority. Kat threw

a look over her shoulder. The blonde just stood there, white-faced and wide-eyed, as if paralyzed by sheer fear. Kat bolted over to grab the girl's hand and jerk her back toward the woods. "Come on!"

"No!" the killer bellowed. "She's mine! My prey!" Magic burst from the center of his chest in a bright blue explosion. His glowing outline grew. And grew. And grew.

When it vanished, a huge figure towered there, looking like something out of a horror movie. Easily the height of a grizzly bear, the thing was lean, with a long wolf head and cold blue eyes. His fur was the same blond as his human hair, thickening to a mane on his head and bushing around his naked genitals. Where the hell had his clothes gone?

"Kat, get that girl out *now*!" Ridge bellowed again.

Kat whirled to drag the girl away even as she realized the monster was the blond man they'd seen at the party, the one who'd been so interested in her locket. She'd felt his evil then, but she'd ignored her instincts.

Ridge had told her the man and his father were werewolves, but she hadn't imagined anything like this towering monster. No wonder the cops had believed Karen had been attacked by some kind of animal.

She had been.

"Come *on*!" Kat hauled furiously on the blonde's arm, dragging her out of the clearing by main strength.

"What . . . what are they?" The girl stumbled, staring over her shoulder as the vampire charged the towering werewolf, sword flashing in great arcs. "What are *you*?" Like Karen, she couldn't have been more than eighteen. She even looked like Kat's sister—same long blond hair and big blue eyes in a heart-shaped face.

"Don't worry about it!" A gate. They needed a gate. She reached for the magic . . .

And Ridge shouted in pain.

Kat jerked around. Blood rolled down the vampire's armored side from a huge gash that ripped across his cuirass.

In the flashing instant it took her to register her lover's

injury, the werewolf was on Kat and the girl, snarling mouth gaped wide to reveal teeth the length of her fingers, clawed hands reaching. Kat shoved the girl clear and swung her sword at the monster's torso.

He threw himself back, avoiding her stroke, then lunged again. She hacked at the clawed hand swinging at her face.

Fast. God, he was fast. He darted right past her guard with that enormous reach. Even as she threw herself back, she felt claws rake her torso, heard the shriek of metal tearing like paper. It didn't hurt. *I'm not going to get out of this alive.* The thought cut through the furious blur of action. There was no fear in it, just cold reason. Just her brain's calculation of the odds.

Fuck it. If I die, I die. But I'm taking this bastard with me.

Kat flew into full extension, the kind of fencer's lunge she'd used in college, thrusting her blade toward the monster's chest. And it bit deep.

He roared in pain and fury. She didn't see the blow coming until it hit her with the force of an armored Humvee. Pain detonated in her shoulder, a bright and sickening blast, and she went flying. Hit the ground hard, light bursting in her head as she struck. Blinking, Kat stared blankly at the moonlit trees overhead. She'd never been hit that hard in her life.

Get the fuck up, Kat!

Somehow she rolled to her feet, staggering, shaking her head, sick and aching.

Ridge had faced off with the monster again, despite the scarlet flow that slicked the right side of his armor.

The girl was crawling on the leafy ground, trying to get away from them all, blood running down her face. Impossible to tell if it was her own.

We need reinforcements. The thought slashed through Kat's consciousness a breath before she remembered the ring her father had given her.

"Lancelot du Lac!" she bellowed. "Dammit, I need you!"

And nothing happened.

TEN

"*L*ancelot!" Kat bellowed again. Nothing.

So much for his magic ring. *"Say my name, and it will bring me to you,"* my ass. The bastard had never been there for her before. Why should he ride to the rescue, just because she happened to be fighting nine feet of psychotic fur?

Shaking off the growing dizziness—she suspected a concussion—Kat lifted her sword and prepared to charge.

"What?" her father snapped from behind her. Then: "Holy God! How did you piss off a Direwolf?"

The relief she felt was so great, she wanted to kiss his handsome, irritated face. "That's the bastard that killed my sister."

Lancelot swore.

Ridge ducked a vicious clawed strike, came up, thrust, missed when the werewolf twisted aside like a matador. Kat raced toward them, swinging her own sword up. Damned if she'd let that monster kill Ridge too.

Before she could reach her target, a streak of black fur shot past her with a snarl like a chain saw. She jerked back—*another one?*—and almost swung her sword at the great black wolf. Then she realized it was slashing at the Direwolf's huge muscled haunches with fanged jaws.

Lancelot had vanished. Where'd he . . . ? Holy hell, *he'd become the wolf*. Ridge had said shape-shifting was a vampire ability.

At least the blond girl was making good use of the distraction the vampires had provided. On her feet again, she staggered from the clearing, throwing panicked glances back over her shoulder as she ran. Her would-be killer howled in frustration, but couldn't get past Ridge and Lancelot to follow.

Where the hell was Grace? Kat had hoped the other woman would come with her husband, but apparently not. Too bad, because they could have used a Maja who knew what the hell she was doing.

Well, Kat had a sword and a couple of vampires. That would have to be enough.

She focused on the towering monster. Ridge and wolf Lance were circling him, one distracting him while the other darted in to slash with sword or teeth. Kat slid into the space between them, looking for an opening for her own assault.

Now—while he was focused on Ridge. Kat lunged, swinging her sword.

He wheeled, quicker than any cat. One huge hand snapped around her armored neck and jerked her right off her feet. His other hand wrapped around her helmeted head, started to pull . . . *Oh, Jesus, he's going to rip my head right off my shoulders!* She yowled in terror and swung her sword, but he was too close, and the blade's guard glanced harmlessly off his shoulder.

The werewolf howled in agony, his clawed hand losing its grip. Kat fell like a rock, hitting the ground in a teeth-rattling heap of armor and blade.

Over her head, Lancelot the wolf had buried his fanged jaws in the werewolf's groin. The monster swung one enormous paw, catching the vampire across the skull. Lance's furry body went flying, slamming with vicious force into a tree. The wolf bounced off the trunk, hit the ground, rolled.

And did not get up.

"Lancelot!" Kat's heart seemed to freeze in her chest.

Ridge assessed the situation with all the skill his sixty years of combat experience gave him.

We're screwed.

Kat had taken a raking stroke down her torso, Ridge was wounded, and Lance was unconscious. At least they had all done damage to the . . .

Magic flared and pulsed around the Direwolf, blinding and blue. When the glare died, the creature had become a golden-furred wolf the size of a pony. It gathered itself to dive on Kat, who still lay stunned at its feet.

Ridge stepped in, swinging his sword like a baseball bat. The wolf fled, snapping. Before Ridge could catch it, magic swirled around the big beast again, and the Direwolf was back, injuries fully healed by his magical transformation.

Yeah. We're screwed.

He could heal his own wounds by transforming—so could Lance, when he regained consciousness—but there was always a moment of disorientation to the process. It wasn't much, but the Direwolf wouldn't need much of an opening to lay one of them open with those claws.

The son of a bitch was not only nine feet tall, with the strength to match, he was incredibly fast. It was no surprise they were having so much trouble defeating him: Direwolves had been created by Merlin himself to kill rogue Magekind. Too bad the alien wizard hadn't realized the problem they'd face if a *Direwolf* went rogue.

If they could get a call to the Mageverse, they could bring in reinforcements. Unfortunately, Kat was having trouble with her magic. Which was no surprise; Ridge knew more about using magic than she did.

Kat was up at last and running toward Lancelot, apparently intent on helping her father. The werewolf lunged after her, jaws snapping. Ridge cursed and raced in the creature's wake. The monster whirled on him, a long arm lashing out. Metal shrieked as those huge claws ripped a hunk out of his helm. Blood flew. He ignored it, swung his sword. Cursed under his breath as the Direwolf ducked with that incredible speed and agility. Ridge continued his attack, forcing the monster away from Kat, who whirled away from Lancelot and moved to help him.

They had one chance—and it wasn't much of one. If he and Kat could Truebond, they could reinforce each other's power and experience.

Normally it would take hours of work and magic to form the intense psychic link of a Truebond. Luckily, Ridge and Kat were already partially linked from triggering her Gift earlier that evening. If he could deepen that link . . .

He found the thin connection already fading in the back of his mind and threw his consciousness along it. *Kat . . .*

Ridge? Astonishment rang in her mental voice. *How . . . ?*

We've got to Truebond. Combining our abilities is the only chance we've got to beat this bastard and survive.

But I don't know how!

I do. He hoped.

He'd better.

Open to me. Ridge's voice whispered the words in her mind, a seductive mental purr. *Reach out to me. Use your magic.* His gaze met hers, intense, demanding. He didn't seem aware of the towering furred figure stalking him.

If this doesn't work, we're both dead. So I'd better make it work. Concentrating hard, Kat caught at that mental cord to his consciousness, simultaneously drawing on the magic in her own core.

Bind us, he breathed, staring deep into her eyes. *Braid us.*

Behind him, the Direwolf's cold blue eyes narrowed, seeing Ridge's distraction.

Ridge . . .

Don't worry about him. Concentrate on me.

Kat saw what he wanted her to do; the image was so plain in his mind. She caught her breath as she realized in a flash the risks and implications. The connection would be so strong, the death of one would kill the other.

So we just won't die, he said, even as he pivoted like a dancer, swinging his sword in a hard arc that drove the werewolf back.

Kat grabbed the magic, forced it into the thread, raw energy pouring faster and faster, binding them tighter. Mind to mind, heart to heart, will to will, as frozen seconds ticked past. The werewolf's lips drew back from those dagger-blade fangs as he circled them, waiting for his chance.

In slow motion, Kat watched the monster's clawed hand draw back. Ridge lunged at him, deliberately focusing the creature's attention even as his bond with Kat grew stronger. His magic flowed into her as hers flooded him, a burning circuit of power that brightened with every passing second.

Her muscles grew stronger, responding to his strength. Her skin felt hot, swollen. Kat lifted the sword and waited for her opening, even as her heart howled at the risk.

Ridge swung his sword, deliberately leaving himself wide open. The Direwolf lunged just as it had before, clawed hand catching the vampire's chest, ripping through armor and flesh and muscle. Ridge bellowed in pain, keeping the creature's attention. The towering beast's lips drew back from his teeth, and he prepared to rip out his foe's throat.

Kat stepped up behind the werewolf, leaped upward with all the vampire strength Ridge had loaned her through the Truebond. Her sword swung in a blinding arc of steel and magic, slicing into the werewolf's thick neck. She felt the crunch of bone against her blade, and then the great head spun from the beast's shoulders. It hit the ground, eyes wide with astonishment in the instant before they glazed into death. The massive body slowly crumpled, collapsing in a pile of fur and claws beside its severed head.

Kat didn't stop to gloat. Ridge toppled, his body convulsing from the fatal wound he'd deliberately invited from the monster's claws. She hit the ground beside him and planted a hand in the center of his bloody armor. Light flared around her palm as she gave him back the magic he'd loaned her. In a flash of light and power, he transformed into a wolf.

And scrambled to all four feet, his horrific injuries instantly healed.

Kat wanted to throw her arms around him, but there wasn't time. Lancelot needed her. She wheeled . . .

Just as a gate whirled into glowing being halfway across the clearing. Grace leaped through it, racing for her fallen husband with fear vivid on her pale face. "Lance!"

The moment her hand touched the wolf's furry head, he shifted in an explosion of light. Lancelot raised his now-human head wearily and gave his wife a tired smile. "Took you long enough."

ELEVEN

*I*t turned out Grace and Lancelot had been working a
terrorist bombing at an Iraqi school when they'd gotten Kat's call. Grace had stayed behind to help dig injured
children from the wreckage while Lance had gone to help
Kat.

"Scared the shit out of me when I felt him lose consciousness through the Truebond," Grace told them once
Ridge had returned to human form. "I was afraid I wouldn't
get to him in time, but there was this little boy who was
dying." She shrugged. "I had to heal the child first, and that
took time."

"As well you should have," Lance told her, rising to his
feet and offering his wife a hand up. "I can take care of
myself."

Grace rolled her eyes. "Yeah. Right."

Kat frowned. "Speaking of magic, we need to find that
girl the Direwolf tried to kill. He'd caught her with his
claws at least once, and she's going to need healing."

"And that's just the physical damage," Ridge said, his
face grim. "The psychological stuff is going to be even
rougher."

Grace nodded. "Better let me take care of that. I've had a lot more experience in dealing with that kind of psychic injury."

"What are you going to do?" Kat asked, curious.

The Maja raked a lock of long hair back from her face with scratched and bloody fingers. Apparently she had her own injuries from digging through all that Iraqi rubble. "Blunt the kid's memories. And it needs to be done now, before they burn in and she winds up with post-traumatic stress." She caught her husband's arm and gave it a tug. "Come on. Use that vampire nose of yours and find her for me."

Lance cast a grim glance toward the werewolf's body. "Then we're gonna have to contact the bastard's father and tell him what happened. He's not going to like hearing he raised a serial killer."

Grace winced and sighed. "No. We'd better take Arthur and Morgana along. We'll need all the firepower we can get, if we're going to have to break news like that." She twined her fingers with her husband's, and the couple started to turn away.

"Lance . . ." Kat said.

The big knight looked back at her. "Yeah?"

"Thank you for riding to the rescue."

He shrugged. "Hey, you're my daughter."

She gave him the first genuine smile she'd had for him. "Yeah, that I am."

*K*at listened to the fire crackle as it shed a golden glow over Ridge's gloriously naked body. He lay sprawled on the huge fur throw she'd conjured in front of the fireplace, his skin contrasting with the dark, shimmering mink.

Selecting a strawberry from the silver tray at her elbow, she took a tart, juicy bite, then another sip from her champagne glass. "I could get used to this magic thing."

Ridge's long fingers curled around his own glass, lids

dipping lazily over brilliant green eyes. "It does have its appeal." He wasn't talking about the champagne, either. She could feel the sexual heat humming through him as he admired the full curve of her breasts and the line of her long legs.

Kat smiled at him and chose another strawberry. Took a slow, taunting bite. His rumble of male hunger made her grin.

For the first time in her life, she felt beautiful. Struck by the thought, Kat considered it. She'd always known she was reasonably attractive—she'd been hit on often enough, though she'd never really felt comfortable with male admiration. Maybe because she'd never really trusted any of those men.

She trusted Ridge. Would have trusted him even without the Truebond.

He smiled at her, sensuous and lazy. *I trust you too, babe.*

"Good, because you're stuck with me." She hesitated, a new and vulnerable thought flashing through her mind. *Does he mind? We're connected now. We couldn't break the Truebond if we wanted to.*

Of course, Ridge read that flash of insecurity. "I wouldn't have it any other way." His green eyes met hers in the firelight, serious and intent. "Kat, I love you." And he meant it. She could feel the love in his mind, a pure, warm glow.

She smiled in delight, basking in that lovely sensation. "And I love you, Ridge Champion." He sat up, put his glass aside, and reached for her. Kat fell into his arms with a soft moan, quickly muffled by his kiss.

Ridge tasted of champagne and his own distinct male heat. His tongue entered her mouth, a slow, tempting slide, rich with seduction. His body pressed against hers, all hard, hair-roughened muscle. She let her fingers drift over him, exploring the warm ridges of definition, the shape of his back, his broad shoulders, his strong throat. He purred in pleasure against her fingertips, a delightful male rumble. And began to explore her in turn, finding curves and hollows, tracing the contours of a jutting nipple until she quivered at the arousing, velvet sensations.

Each sensation had a lovely, shimmering echo as he experienced what she did, returning the pleasure in a sweet feedback loop. Making love to Ridge had always been amazing, but the Truebond gave passion an entirely new dimension. For one thing, she could feel what felt best to him, could zero in on precisely the right pressure, the right combination of nail and fingertip and tongue and tooth to drive the delight even higher.

Somehow that rising passion quickly turned into a sensual contest there on the thick fur throw, as each sought to drive the other crazy.

Ridge won by simply lifting her onto her knees, spreading her legs, and pinning her astride his face with a hand on each of her thighs. All her helpless squirming did her no good at all against his vampire strength.

"No fair!" Kat gasped, and moaned as he dragged his tongue the length of her sex.

His only answer was a wicked little chuckle as he settled down to lick swirling circles around her clit.

God, the sensations were mind-blowing. Ridge's mouth felt so hot, so perfect, as he used his tongue in tiny, delicate little flicks. Even as she gasped, he reached up her body to find one nipple. His fingers strummed and plucked the furled bud, creating jolt after sweet burning jolt of delight, like a series of delicious electric shocks.

But Kat wasn't so easily overwhelmed. She twisted with the agility of a natural athlete, reached back, and found his cock. Big as it was, it made an easy target. A smile of satisfaction curling her mouth, she began stroking her fingers along the hard, sensitive shaft, tracing the long, snaking veins, the plump head and fat, furry balls.

He growled at her from between her thighs. She had no trouble translating the sound, even without the Truebond. *Keep that up, and this will be over too soon.*

Then you'll just have to exert a little self-control, won't you?

He punished her with a particularly long, evil stroke of his tongue that ripped a gasp of pleasure from her mouth. Writhing, she returned the favor with a stroke of her fingers from the base of his cock to its head, smearing the silken drop of pre-cum over the sensitive curve.

The sensations were so intense, their mutual arousal was so hot, neither of them could hold out long. Soon Ridge tumbled her onto her back, rose over her like a hot-eyed wave, and spread her wide.

Kat gasped as he positioned his thick organ at her opening and drove home in one hard lunge. The sensation of being so utterly filled blended with his sensation of filling her. The mental reverberation seemed to make their very bones vibrate. They yowled in chorus.

Ridge started thrusting. Kat rolled her hips to meet him, grinding hard, desperate for every bit of friction, hungry for the hot release of climax.

Even as he powered into her, thrust rolling into thrust, Ridge tipped up her chin. Knowing what he wanted, she gave him her throat.

The sweet, piercing pain of his bite edged the hot pleasure of entry and retreat. Kat screamed out, overwhelmed by the complex brew of sensations. Ridge bellowed in reply, shooting into climax at her heels, in a whirling, dizzy detonation.

Afterward, they collapsed together in a limp, boneless pile, breathing hard in happy exhaustion. "I don't think I can move," Kat moaned.

"You don't need to move," Ridge murmured, sounding thoroughly sated. "We'll just lay right here and pant."

Kat smiled, watching sparks of magic swirl dizzily around them, as if dancing on the air currents they'd stirred up. She followed one particular bit of glittering green with her eyes. Something about it reminded her of something she hadn't thought about in years. "I've got this memory. I must have been really young."

Ridge turned his head to look at her, surprised at the remembered image in her thoughts. "A Christmas tree? I didn't think you had any good memories of Christmas trees."

"This was . . . before. I must have been eight or so, because all I remember thinking about is how beautiful it was. A green Christmas tree light shining on the surface of a ball. One of those old-fashioned ones, cut out in a faceted mirrored shape in the middle. I thought it was the prettiest thing I'd ever seen."

Acting on sheer impulse, she spread her hands and concentrated. Magic flew from her palms, spinning into the empty corner beside the fireplace. The corner that needed something.

The swirling magic formed a column of green light, flashing and glittering. When the blaze of energy disappeared, a live fir stood in the corner, decorated with colorful balls, striped candy canes, and long strings of silver tinsel. Magic flickered and swirled around the tree's limbs in bright reds, greens, yellows, and blues. Christmas colors.

At the very top of the tree stood a blond angel dressed in white robes, with feathered wings spreading from her slender shoulders. Her delicate face looked just like Karen's.

Looking up at the angel's serene and lovely features, Kat felt her eyes sting. She'd always felt pain at the sight of a Christmas tree, but there was a sweetness to the ache now, a weary satisfaction. "I got him for you," she told the angel.

"Yeah, you did." Ridge's fingers threaded with hers as he looked up at the tree. "It's beautiful."

For a long moment, they lay silent, watching the light flicker off tinsel and fragile, gleaming balls. "I spoke to that healer at Mom's clinic," Kat told him at last. "Petra said I can go see Mom tomorrow. She's . . . healed." Kat smiled up at the angel. "Just in time for Christmas."

"That's wonderful." Ridge sat up and reached for his discarded jeans, dug around in a pocket. "Personally, I've been thinking about how I want to celebrate New Year's."

The box he produced was small, covered in dark blue velvet. When he flipped its top open, the ring's central ruby glittered in the light of the Christmas tree, surrounded by a circle of smaller emeralds. The Truebond told her he'd asked Grace to create the ring for him while Kat had been busy with the healer.

"Will you marry me?" His lips curled up even as he asked the question, his green eyes glowing with the love he felt.

She went into his arms with a low laugh of delight. "God, yes!"

Christmas was never going to be the same.

A Little
Night Magic

Allyson James

PROLOGUE

I am Coyote. I run on the wind; I invade your dreams. I know your darkest secrets, your most depraved desires. I know what it is you crave deep in the night.

The gods call me Trickster. They laugh at me but they fear and distrust me.

They are right to fear. I have no boundaries, no restrictions. I do as I please, screw whom I please, bestow bounty or terrible misfortune, as I choose.

I am Coyote. I am Chaos.

Enjoy your dreams.

ONE

"I'm here to stay," Jamison Kee said.

Naomi stared over rows of red and white poinsettias at Jamison, who'd walked back into her life as suddenly as he'd walked out of it. He had his hands stuffed into the pockets of his jeans jacket, dark eyes quiet, easy as you please.

She'd woken not half an hour ago to the sound of hammering on her roof. *Wrong time of year for a woodpecker.* Her deaf daughter, Julie, bouncing up and down excitedly, had nearly dragged Naomi out of bed and out of the room, too excited to stop and sign.

Throwing a coat over her sleeping shirt and exercise shorts, Naomi had picked up a baseball bat and marched outside.

She'd looked up to see Jamison Kee on her porch roof, hammer in hand, like he belonged there. Julie pointed up at him and yelled in joy.

"What happened to your roof?" Jamison had asked, holding a nail to another shingle. "It's a fucking mess."

Naomi had stood there with mouth open, unable to speak, unable to think. She'd turned and slammed back into the house.

Jamison had still been on the roof when she emerged again, dressed. Julie had climbed up the ladder to take Jamison coffee. Both ex-lover and daughter looked over the edge of the porch roof at her as she'd stalked to the greenhouse to check on the poinsettias she'd promised to take to the Ghost Train celebration.

Damn him for still looking so good. Black hair, brown eyes, honed body, at home in jeans and jacket and cowboy boots. A Navajo shaman with a gorgeous ass.

She heard the door to the greenhouse open behind her and knew it was him. Naomi walked around the table, happier with it between her and Jamison and her emotions.

"What are all those for?" he asked, his voice as dark and rich as she remembered. He'd lulled her with his voice the first night she'd met him, and if she wasn't careful, he'd lull her with it now.

"The Ghost Train." She leaned over to pluck off a dead leaf.

"You don't believe in the Ghost Train."

"Neither do you," she shot back. "But it brings in my biggest week of business for the year. No way am I going to argue that it doesn't exist."

Jamison didn't answer. The Ghost Train legend—that a ghostly steam train glided into Magellan on the empty railroad bed every Christmas Eve—was bullshit as far as Naomi was concerned. Plenty of people believed it, though, including the loads of tourists who came every year to the festivities. Jamison also knew it was bogus, but he kept his mouth shut. People liked to believe in things.

Jamison's silence continued. He could do that, stand in place and simply *be*, for hours on end if he wanted to. She'd liked that about him—liked that he'd brought equilibrium back to her life. Peace.

Which he'd shattered by disappearing one fine morning. Naomi had awakened to her daughter standing sorrowfully by her bed and signing, *Jamison's gone.*

"What do you want, Jamison?"

"To tell you why I went to Mexico, and why I came back."

Naomi finally glanced up at him. Mistake. He was even better looking than she remembered, his body harder and stronger, his face bearing a new grimness.

She viciously squirted water on an ailing poinsettia. "Don't bother. I know what you're going to say—that you needed 'time,' but then you changed your mind and decided you wanted to see me again. Well, guess what? I don't want to hear it." She made her voice firm but couldn't bring herself to look at him again. "I got over you, Jamison. I don't want you back, and I don't give a shit where you were or what you were doing. So clear your stuff out of your studio and go."

"I checked the studio this morning. I was surprised you didn't throw everything out. Or burn it down."

Naomi slammed the water bottle back to the table. "I couldn't risk that some half-finished sculpture might be worth a frigging fortune, and that wouldn't be fair to your family. It's not their fault you went walkabout. They say you do this all the time. I can't believe how *sick* I got of people asking me if you were off working on a new sculpture."

"I'm sorry about that," Jamison said. "I really am."

"So, what, after two years without hearing anything from you I should just say, 'Golly gee, glad you're back, let's kiss and make up'? Forget it."

She swung away but felt Jamison move behind her, his warmth on her back.

"I'm not leaving again, Naomi," he said softly. "That's what I came to explain. I'm here to stay. For always."

Naomi tried to make herself pull away, maybe put the table between them again. Instead she turned and let herself look into his dark eyes, to see again the man she'd fallen in love with.

She'd met Jamison through one of her cousins in the vast Hansen clan, Heather, who owned Magellan's New Age store called Paradox. Heather had invited Jamison, a noted Navajo storyteller, to come down from Chinle to talk to her study group about Native American myth. Naomi had gone and taken Julie, thinking it would be good to teach her about Navajo culture, since they lived so close to the Navajo Nation.

She'd expected an old man with a lined face and white hair. Instead, Heather had brought out a broad-shouldered, muscular man of about thirty-five, easy in his own skin, with sin-dark eyes and a mesmerizing voice.

Jamison had asked to be introduced to Naomi after his talk, because he'd watched Naomi sign his entire lecture to Julie. He'd smiled at Naomi, the sensuality of him making her breath catch. Jamison had invited Naomi and Julie to grab coffee with him, so Julie could ask him questions, he said, before he made his long drive back to Chinle.

Then next thing Naomi knew, Jamison was spending the night in her bed and making pancakes for breakfast the next morning. He never did go back to Chinle.

Jamison had made Naomi fall in love again, had taught her to feel again against her better judgment. He'd made love like an angel, his body sealed to hers, his mouth taking away all pain. Deep in the night he whispered that he loved her, that they were soul mates, together forever.

Soul mates, my ass.

Damn all magic-seeking, shamanistic men with gorgeous bodies and long cocks. Jamison had laughed at Naomi for being an Unbeliever—a person who lived in Magellan and didn't buy the crap about it being at a confluence of vortexes or a center of mystical energy—then went on drawing circles and chanting and whatever it was he did in the art studio he'd built himself in her back yard. And she'd loved him like crazy.

Their first wild night together flashed through Naomi's mind as Jamison slid his fingers behind her neck. She remembered every touch, every kiss, the feel of him invading her body, and her ready surrender.

He smelled of sweat and denim, winter sunshine and wind. As always, she sensed something wild in him, like an animal or lightning, she was never sure which.

Her skin prickled where his fingertips brushed her. He leaned closer, lips nearly touching hers.

He was waiting for her to kiss him, to make the first move. Once she did, once she acknowledged his touch, his kiss would turn hard, possessive. Jamison always did that, making her feel like she was in control, then taking that control away in an instant.

As Naomi willed herself not to respond, Jamison began brushing soft kisses to the corners of her mouth. His lips were smooth, his breath warm.

Warmth tingled through her body and pooled between her legs. She burned for him. She wanted him to lay her back on the pile of potting soil next to them and screw her right there, anything to ease the ache.

Naomi slid her hands down his back, over the hard leather of his belt to his slim butt cupped by tight jeans. She loved his backside, remembering it taut and bronze-colored against her white sheets.

"Let's go inside," he said against her mouth.

Naomi dragged in a sharp breath, and cold poured over her. "No."

"Naomi . . ."

"No." She almost cried as she pushed Jamison away. "You always do this to me. You kiss me until I want you so much, I'll do anything you say. I won't do it this time. I'm busy. I have a business to run and plants to get to the depot."

"Let me help you."

"No, thanks."

"It's a big job. You need me."

She slammed her arms over her chest. "I needed you so many times in the last two years. Where were you then? Oh, I forgot, somewhere in Mexico."

"Do you think this is easy for me? To love you so much it rips me to pieces to know I hurt you?"

"Don't flatter yourself. I did fine without you."

"Why? Did you start seeing someone else?"

She wanted to laugh. "In Magellan? Who? I'm related

to half the town, and I've known the other half far too long. Besides, I don't *need* a man in my life."

Jamison relaxed. "Good. That makes things easier."

"Easier for who?"

"Easier for me. I don't have to worry about anyone else getting hurt." He finally stepped away from her, his big body tense and tight. "I told you, I'm staying, Naomi. In Magellan, in the house. With you."

"Oh, really? Well, what if I don't want you to?"

"That doesn't matter. I'll sleep on the sofa if you don't want me in your bed. I'm not leaving you and Julie alone, because they'll be coming."

His eyes held a darkness she'd never seen. "Who will?"

"People I pissed off in Mexico."

"What kind of people? Shit, Jamison, don't tell me you got involved with drug runners."

A hard smile flitted across his face. "There are more dangers out there than drug runners, believe me. I'm one of those dangers. I'm staying here to protect you. For now. For always."

From the look in his eyes, he wasn't joking, he wasn't exaggerating. She felt a qualm of fear. *Julie.*

"Give me your keys," he said, holding out his hand. "I'll bring the truck around."

"I left them in the ignition. Paco Medina is putting on a new tire for me."

"Don't leave them there again. Lock your truck and keep the keys with you. Or better still, with me. Get Julie, and I'll meet you at the truck."

Jamison turned around, hands in his jacket pockets, and strode out of the greenhouse. Naomi's palms sweated, her heart pounded, and her lips were raw from his kiss.

There was a part of Jamison that she'd never understood, never reached. Jamison had known so much, had seen so much. He'd grown up in poverty, which had been conquered only by his entire family's hard work and Jamison's sought-after sculptures. Naomi might be an Unbeliever, but she realized Jamison knew things she couldn't even begin to comprehend. Something had happened in Mexico that frightened even him. Whatever scared Jamison had to be damned dangerous.

She wished with all her strength that she could hold on to that fear and not be distracted by how nice his ass looked as he walked away from her.

*J*amison let Naomi drive to the depot, not trusting himself behind a wheel yet. The Ghost Train was a popular holiday tradition, and everyone in town seemed to be at the old depot to help decorate. Jamison was greeted left and right by people happy to see him again, asking him how he was, where he'd been. Jamison hadn't realized he'd made so many friends during his short sojourn here, but Naomi didn't seem surprised.

Jamison was as friendly and polite as possible, but insisted that he, Naomi, and Julie return home right away. He wanted this over with; he'd looked forward to this moment since he'd finally broken out of his cage and started the thousand mile journey home.

The Changers had been fools to try to force him to bind to one of their own. He'd already been half-bound to Naomi, but if he didn't complete the bond quickly, she'd be in grave danger.

When they walked into the house, Naomi slammed her purse on the kitchen counter. "Julie, go tell Mrs. Medina I told you to help her. I need to talk to Jamison."

Julie's smile grew sly. "Are you going to kiss?"

Jamison felt his own smile grow, but Naomi shot him an irritated look. "No, we're going to talk."

Julie shrugged, grinned once more, and ran out of the house, toward the open door of Hansen's Garden Center, which backed onto Naomi's property. The Medina family, who ran the nursery with Naomi, adored Julie and would take care of her.

Naomi faced Jamison in silence. Gods, she was beautiful. The wind had pulled Naomi's brown hair into fantastic tangles, and her cheeks were pink with cold and anger. The cold poked her nipples into tight buds as well, obvious even through her sweatshirt. He itched to grasp her breasts again, feel the velvet areolas, the hard little points.

Naomi started talking, and Jamison struggled to focus on her words. The animal in him wanted to take over, and focusing was difficult.

"All right," she said. "If you insist on explaining. Why *did* you disappear for twenty-four months, then charge back in like you expected me to be waiting? How long will you be gone for next time?"

"I told you, I'm staying. For good."

"Why?"

"To protect you from my enemies."

"What enemies? Jamison, if you don't tell me what's going on, I'll explode."

Not an hour ago, she'd been too angry to want his explanation, but he knew Naomi couldn't stand *not* to know. She probably thought he'd taken off to some Native American enclave where he'd spent days in a peyote haze and seduced every female who came along. The peyote part had been true, though not by his choice.

Jamison shucked his jacket and laid it on a stool at her breakfast bar. "It would be easier to show you." He held out his hand. "Come upstairs with me?"

She folded her arms across her chest, pushing her enticing breasts higher. "Something in Julie's room you want to see?"

He let a smile touch his mouth. "This isn't about sex. I promise." *At least, not yet.*

Naomi's eyes went flint-hard. Jamison loved her eyes. They were the color of turquoise, a beautiful blue green that defied description. He'd never liked blue eyes until he'd seen hers.

She walked past him, her arms still folded, and started up the stairs.

Naomi's house was an old Craftsman bungalow, built in

the 1920s and renovated several times through the years. The result was a modernized but solid, cozy house, with a large living room and kitchen below and two bedrooms and a bath upstairs. Julie's room was on the right at the top of the staircase, Naomi's on the left. Naomi marched into her own sunny bedroom and waited for Jamison, winter sunshine picking out golden highlights in her hair.

Jamison's wariness prickled as he walked inside. There were too many windows. Naomi's room had views northeast, northwest, and southeast, the bedroom running the entire length of the house. It wasn't the axis Jamison would have picked on which to orient a bedroom, but people in Magellan built their houses according to street planning, not alignment with the four winds.

Jamison quietly pulled the blinds down on the thick-paned windows while Naomi watched him in silence. He turned around and toed off his boots at the same time he pulled off his sweatshirt.

He didn't miss how Naomi's gaze went to his chest, to his own nipples, which were dark and tight. He liked that she didn't look away as he undid his turquoise belt buckle and slid off his jeans.

Her face went pink as she gazed at his ordinary cotton briefs. He was hard behind them—how the hell could he help it? Jamison tugged off his socks then, without modesty, pulled off the briefs.

The way her gaze swiveled to his needy arousal was gratifying. She'd always liked to look at him, lord knew why. She'd wet her lips like she was eager to savor every inch of him.

Two years without Naomi had been way too damn long. He loved every molecule of the woman. *Why do I love her?* he'd once asked his grandfather, who was a much better shaman than Jamison could ever hope to be. Was it some kind of trickster magic? Jamison had spent his entire life on the Navajo reservation, scoffing at white people and white ways. Then a woman with blue green eyes had smiled at him, and he'd fallen like boulders in an avalanche.

He'd fallen so hard he'd moved into her house in the middle of a white man's town. In the middle of a community who believed that the ghost of a steam train chugged through their little town every Christmas. The gods had to be laughing their asses off at him. Except Jamison hadn't felt humiliated. He'd been happy.

Jamison crossed his hands over his chest and closed his eyes. He drew on the stillness he'd learned deep in drug-induced dreams, looking for the center of calm that nothing could breach.

He found the beast right where he'd left it. The beast had terrified Jamison the first time, and he'd been convinced he'd been put under a spell or cursed by a sorcerer. The Changers in Mexico had explained everything to him. Whatever else they'd done, they'd at least let him understand.

Jamison's mouth always changed first. His flat human teeth enlarged and elongated, becoming sharp canines, top and bottom. His face pushed forward, his jaw and tongue re-forming to fit the new mouth. The strangest feeling was the whiskers poking out sharp and hard from the sides of his face.

The mouth took the longest, then the rest of his head followed rapidly. Ears pricked, his hearing sharpened, and his eyes became round and wide. His spine narrowed and lengthened, and claws erupted on his now huge feline feet. He fell to all fours, feeling a long tail twitching behind him.

He wanted to roar but stifled it; there was enough of his own consciousness left to realize what would happen if someone heard a wildcat snarl in Naomi's bedroom. He lifted his gaze to Naomi, his world now black-and-white, the edges rounded and slightly concave. She stared back at him, her red-lipped mouth open, her blue green eyes wide.

His beautiful, brave lady didn't scream or faint. She simply gaped at him for a moment then said, "Jamison, what the *fuck*?"

TWO

This couldn't be happening. Naomi stared at the mountain lion that gazed back at her from the middle of her bedroom rug. A mountain lion. In her bedroom.

Jamison Kee had turned from a magnificently nude man into a mountain lion.

He looked back at her with the large dark eyes of a hunting cat, his lips parted to show huge, sharp teeth. She'd never seen a mountain lion this close before—never seen one at all, in fact, except in a zoo or through a pair of strong binoculars. She noted every detail—the light tawny color of his pelt; the black around his muzzle and the tip of his tail; the round, pricked ears; the heavy muscles of his shoulders and chest.

He looked bigger than she thought mountain lions were—his head would reach her chest if she were brave enough to go to him. And his eyes held intelligence. Jamison's intelligence.

"Jamison," she whispered.

The mountain lion growled softly. Then its face began to flatten as it rose on its hind legs. The transformation she'd witnessed happened in reverse, and in a few seconds, Jamison stood on his flat feet, naked in front of her.

They stared at each other in dead silence for a full minute. Then, as though to make sure she got the point, Jamison morphed back into the mountain lion.

"Jamison, why are you doing this to me?"

The mountain lion padded toward her. Naomi stood frozen, unable to run, unsure she wanted to run.

She was right, his head came up to her chest. He butted against her like a tabby cat, rumbling in his throat as he stroked his forehead across her breasts.

Naomi didn't like how her body flushed with heat, how her nipples tightened. She tentatively pushed him away, and he turned his head into her hand, rubbing his whiskers against it.

She started to laugh. "That tickles."

The mountain lion reared up and placed his paws gently on her shoulders. The look in his eyes was almost amused as he swiped a rough tongue across her cheek.

"Jamison."

The cat morphed back into Jamison. Now she had his tall, naked body against her clothed body. He leaned down and licked her neck, his hot breath sending fire through every nerve. He gently bit where he'd licked.

"Please tell me that was a trick," she said. "You're playing a trick on me."

"No, love. It's what I am."

Naomi ran her hand through his warm hair, which had come out of the braid when he'd changed. He lifted his head and looked at her, his dark eyes holding the edge of danger she'd sensed before.

"I can smell you," he whispered. "So ripe and hot. You're scared, but you want to fuck me."

She nodded, her breath quick. Her blood was so hot she feared it would boil in her veins. She could smell him as well: aroused male, sweat, and dust.

Jamison pressed his thumbs to the corners of her mouth, opening her to take his deep kiss. He scraped his tongue through her mouth, his teeth catching on her lips.

The kiss in the greenhouse had been tame and tentative. This one contained wild animal strength. He snaked his fingers through her hair, pulling her head back, moving to bite her throat. She arched against him, the small pain of his bite arousing her like crazy.

She felt his penis pressing her abdomen as though Jamison wanted to crawl inside her clothes with her. He shuddered, mouth closing over her neck, sucking.

Naomi's breasts hurt where they rubbed his chest, tips swollen and hot as fire. She pried at her shirt, trying to free herself, and Jamison yanked the shirt off over her head. He made short work of her bra, unsnapping it and tossing it aside, before his hand went to her pants.

Naomi helped him unbutton and unzip, shoving her pants down and then her panties. No slow seduction this time—Jamison could spin out lovemaking for hours, but that careful, sinfully lazy man had disappeared.

He growled, a real, rumbling wildcat growl as his hands went to her naked buttocks. The space between her legs was wet, hot, needy. He rubbed his tip there but didn't enter.

"I'll try to go slow," he said. "I don't know if I can."

"I don't care." She touched his face. "I need you."

Jamison lifted her, and she eagerly locked her legs around him. He took two steps to the bed, holding her firmly, and then he lowered her to the mattress.

That was the only thing he did gently. He grabbed her ankles and spread her legs, and then climbed on top of her.

She'd craved his warm weight for two years, had fought to forget what it felt like. But as he kissed her, she knew she hadn't forgotten one fraction of him. She knew every touch, every pressure of him, the smell of his sweat, the heat of his body.

His eyes had changed. His look was fierce, possessive, where years before it had been only loving and tender.

"You're mine," he said with another animal growl.

She was too far gone to hear him. "Do me, Jamison. Please. I need you to."

He smiled a triumphant smile. The lion shone out of his

eyes as he collapsed onto her and entered her with one fast, tight thrust.

*J*amison threw back his head as he slid inside her. *Back where I belong.* Images of what he'd been through flashed in his mind then fled, resolving in the beautiful face of Naomi.

Please. I need you to. Her words rang in the room, mixing with his own—*You're mine.*

He drove into her, his cock aching as her walls closed around him for the first time in two years. He felt nothing except her sweet clench on him. She was hot and slick, and he slid in and out, hard and fast, no barriers between them.

Naomi arched, her mouth twisted in pleasure. He squeezed one of her nipples between thumb and fingers, liking how she cried out at the pressure.

Two years. Two damn, long, empty years without Naomi. He hated the people who'd caged him, who'd taken his freedom in exchange for knowledge. They hadn't wanted him to return to Naomi, to take refuge in her.

The bed creaked and banged against the floor. Naomi lifted her legs and wound them around his buttocks, her heels digging into his back. She rocked her hips, taking him deep, deeper, and he groaned with the joy of it.

Damn, it had never been like this before. They'd had great sex in the past, but now he wanted to pound into her, harder, harder, until she screamed. She was responding, her sheath so wet, her hips moving with his rhythm.

He wanted to come inside her, and then flip her over and pull her hips back against his and do it again. He wanted to do what he'd never done with her, press his finger to her anal star and ready her to take him that way.

He kissed her again, their lips swollen, Naomi nipping at him. His body dripped with sweat. It was hot in here, so hot, and she felt so fucking good. Fire spread from where they joined, and flared through every nerve ending until his entire body burned.

"I'm going to come," he whispered.

She locked her hands around his shoulders, encouraging him with her hips and legs. "Yes. Please, please. I need it."

He thrust into her five more times, groaning like a maniac with each one. His balls were so tight, his skin stretched until he couldn't stand it.

Then the surge came, and he was pumping his seed high and hot into her. He snaked his hand between them, massaging her. She screamed and bucked, coming at the same time he did.

He wanted to stay inside her, but they were both so wet that he slid right out as soon as his cock slackened the slightest bit. Jamison landed next to her, his legs tangled in hers, both of them breathing hard.

He drew his hand across his forehead, finding his hair soaked with sweat. Naomi lay limply, her swollen breasts rising and falling. He stroked them, feeling her heart beating swiftly beneath her skin.

"Damn." Jamison panted. He let his head flop to the pillow, his breath too ragged for speech.

Naomi nodded tiredly. "I know."

Jamison wrapped his arms around her and spooned her back against him. "I missed you so much."

"I missed you every minute," she said. "Every second of every minute for two years."

Pain twisted his heart even as his erection tightened, wanting more. "They wouldn't let me come back to you. I tried so hard." Even now, they hunted him. They hadn't let him go—he'd escaped, and he knew the Alpha wouldn't let him live for that transgression. "But I'm here to stay. I'm never leaving again. I promise."

Naomi said nothing. He couldn't tell whether she believed him or not.

Jamison stroked her hair. She had thick hair, silken and

beautiful. She didn't like to wear it long; she cut it when it reached past her neck.

"I want you again," he said.

He expected her to say she wanted to sleep instead, but to his delight, she turned over and smiled at him. It was a wicked smile, one that made every blood vessel inside him heat.

"Please," she said in a seductive voice.

"Damn, I missed you."

He pulled her to her hands and knees and entered her. The lovemaking was faster this time, but just as intense.

Not long later, they fell again, landing together on the bed. Jamison had just enough strength to pull a quilt over their bodies before he fell into a black, untroubled sleep.

*N*aomi was stirring tomato sauce on the stove not long later, when she felt Jamison's arms come around her from behind. She closed her eyes briefly, enjoying the sensation of him.

Julie, perched on a stool at the breakfast bar, grinned at them both. Her hands started to move. "Mom and Jamison, sitting in a tree. K-I-S-S-I-N-G."

"Where did you learn that?" Jamison asked her.

"My teacher," Julie answered.

Naomi said, "She says that if Julie mainstreams in high school, she'll need to know all the silly things hearing kids learn growing up."

Julie was homeschooled because schools for the deaf were expensive and heartbreakingly far away. A teacher from Santa Fe, specializing in deaf children, came out to Magellan three days a week to teach Julie. In a few years, when Julie was ready to attend junior high, she'd be going to Tucson to stay with Naomi's parents and attend the deaf day school there. Naomi wanted Julie to have the best education possible, but at the same time, she didn't look forward to the day Julie would pack her things and leave.

Jamison kissed Naomi's neck. He'd showered, and now smelled of shampoo and soap. He rummaged in the refrigerator to pull out soft drinks for himself and Julie. Jamison never touched alcohol; he said it clouded both his artistic and shamanistic abilities.

Caffeine must not, because he guzzled coffee, tea, and soft drinks by the gallon. Naomi suspected that another reason Jamison didn't drink was because his father had been an alcoholic, and he'd died in a single-car accident on a lonely road in the middle of the Navajo reservation.

Jamison sat down with Julie and became the Jamison Naomi had known before. He told Julie stories and made her laugh while Naomi finished cooking. He helped clean up the dishes afterward, and then he and Julie settled in for some serious TV watching, Christmas special after Christmas special.

Naomi sat a little apart from them. Jamison's lovemaking upstairs had been incredible, nothing short of explosive. Jamison had always been good, but that. *God.* Her whole body throbbed just thinking about it.

The intensity had been more than about going two years without sex. Jamison had turned into a live, dangerous animal right in front of her, slapping down her Unbeliever skepticism. Then he'd made love to her with animal wildness, showing her he'd changed more than just in shape.

Jamison put Julie to bed himself, and then he came downstairs and checked that the doors and windows were secure. He took Naomi by the hand. "Come with me. I need to show you something."

"You mean there's more?" she asked. "I don't know if I can take more."

"You need to understand." Jamison pressed a brief kiss to her lips, one that told her his fires hadn't been dampened at all.

She locked her fingers around his, and he led her outside, heading for the art studio that waited silently in the corner of the yard, away from the now-empty parking lot of Hansen's Garden Center. Back here, in the private world Jamison had carved for himself, all was quiet and serene.

He unlocked the padlock on the door of the studio and ushered Naomi into his sanctuary.

THREE

Jamison loved his art studio. He'd constructed it like he would a hogan, but the roof was copper sheeting with a huge skylight to let in the sunshine as he worked. The door faced due east, and he'd scattered corn to bless the studio before he'd moved in his sculpting tools.

In the middle of the room a table held the chisels with which he created the sculptures that for some reason people paid big money for. He sculpted what moved him, from stones nature put in his way—an abstract hawk, the stillness of a wolf watching his prey. He breathed a prayer and a bit of magic into every piece.

He also sculpted things from scrap iron, or custom designed decorative wrought iron for extra money. His iron-working tools stood against the north wall with an acetylene torch that he'd refilled when he cleaned up this morning and scraps of twisted iron he'd been working on before he'd gone.

Jamison led Naomi inside and jerked the cover from the sculpture he'd been working on the night he'd left. The head of a mountain lion peered out of orange red stone, its shoulders ending in a jagged line of reddish rock. Naomi reached out and touched it with one slender finger, her eyes filled with wonder.

Jamison had found the nearly smooth red sandstone in a wash near the Pink Cliffs and hauled it the twenty-five miles back here. He'd let the stone rest for a few months before he'd taken out his tools and carved what he saw inside it.

"I don't understand," Naomi said.

Jamison put his hand on the sculpture, the porous stone cool and rough. "I was working on this that night. It was freezing out here, but I couldn't stop. The sculpture was coming—like magic. And then . . . " He trailed off.

He couldn't explain the terror, the feeling that he'd been choking, dying. Watching his hands and arms change before his eyes, suddenly finding himself on all fours thinking and seeing like a wildcat.

Naomi's blue green eyes were wide. "You were sculpting a mountain lion, and then you changed into one?"

Jamison caressed the stone. "It scared the shit out of me. I thought I'd gone insane. When I changed back, with my clothes all ripped, I was afraid a skinwalker had cursed me. Then I changed to the lion again, and again. I couldn't stop it, couldn't control it."

"Why didn't you call for me?"

"And tell you what? That I kept turning into a mountain lion?" He shook his head. "I was so scared I'd hurt you, hurt Julie."

"So you just left?"

"I didn't trust myself to come back into the house and say good-bye. I had to go."

"You told your family," she said, hurt. "They knew you'd gone to Mexico, but they wouldn't tell me anything more."

"I called my grandfather on the way out of town. I told him to get word to you, but he decided you shouldn't be told everything. He wanted to prevent you from coming after me, he said, which would have been too dangerous. He was right."

"So he knew where you were the whole time?" Naomi's voice rang with anger and outrage.

"He knew I'd gone to Mexico, but not exactly where. Even I didn't know exactly where I was going."

"He should have told me. I know he doesn't approve of me. He says I bewitched you, which I always thought was funny, since I'm a notorious Unbeliever."

"He isn't wrong." Jamison crossed to her, but he didn't reach for her. If he touched her, he'd want to keep on touching her, to drag her upstairs and have sex with her again. Maybe have sex with her right here. He needed her every second.

"You did something to me, Naomi. You made this Diné boy leave the land of his people so he could lie in your bed. And I don't regret one second of that choice."

"Just tell me what happened in Mexico."

Jamison walked away from her, around the other side of the half-finished statue. The mating frenzy still hadn't left him, and if he was going to talk, he needed to be as far from her as he could be. "I went to Mexico to find people like me, other Changers. I needed to know what was happening to me."

"How did you even know where to look for them?"

"Coyote told me."

Her brows shot up. "Coyote, the drifter?"

The man who called himself Coyote was a Native American, from what tribe Naomi had never discovered, who liked to hang around the streets of Magellan. He didn't seem to be homeless, but no one knew where he lived or where he went when he disappeared. He was a big man with black hair, youngish and amiable, always joking with the locals and entertaining the tourists.

Coyote always greeted Julie with a big smile and would crouch down on his heels to speak sign language with her. Naomi had once asked him where he'd learned to sign, and he'd shrugged broad shoulders and said, "Around." The townspeople regarded him as mysterious, sometimes annoying, but harmless.

"Don't tell me Coyote is—what did you call it?—a Changer too?" Naomi said.

"No, he's Coyote."

"Huh? I'm lost."

"He's Coyote the god," Jamison said gently.

Naomi the Unbeliever gave him a skeptical look. "How could he be? He hangs out with bikers at the the Crossroads Bar."

Jamison stifled a laugh. As though gods were above fraternizing with bikers.

"Coyote does whatever he wants, and he has fun at the Crossroads." Jamison sobered. "I was standing in here, sweating and terrified, and all of a sudden he was at the door. He knew what had happened. He told me that other Changers could help me and told me how to find them. He drove me down to Nogales and across the border himself, in a ratty pickup. Then he disappeared. Literally. Truck and all."

Naomi ran her fingers along the sculpted head of the lion. "How did you get the rest of the way?"

"Walked. Hitched. I found the other Changers in the mountain ranges in Durango—pretty much in-the-middle-of-nowhere Mexico. I thought some parts of the Navajo Nation were remote, but they're roaring civilization compared to this place. The Changers were there, all right."

"And they took you in?"

"They beat me up, stripped me naked, stole everything I had, and locked me in a cage."

Naomi looked at him in shock. "Oh, God, Jamison. Why?"

"To teach me obedience. I threatened the Alpha."

"Why did you threaten the Alpha? What's an Alpha?"

He gave her a wry smile. "I didn't, not intentionally. But when I showed up out of the blue, the pack leader took it as an attack by a dominant."

"Mountain lions have packs?" Her voice shook. "I thought they were solitary."

"Natural mountain lions are, but not Changers. They

have a hierarchy, like wolves or African lions, and my scent and my approach wasn't submissive enough for them." Jamison folded his arms across his chest, uncomfortable with the memory. "It was partly my fault. They kept telling me to yield to their power, but the Alpha pissed me off so much I wouldn't. The Changers feared I wanted to take over their little pack, even though I told them I didn't give a damn and didn't even want to stay. They've become inbred and paranoid, though I can't really blame them. There's no place in the world for them."

Naomi studied him, worried. "Is there a place in the world for you?"

"I think so." Jamison started to pace the tiny space, restless. "The Changers hid themselves away down there. They'd fled from many parts of the world to survive together. But they spoke of others out there who manage to live among normal human beings. I plan to be one of those."

"But what if you have no choice?" She rubbed her arms. "You already seem different."

"Different?" He'd tried so hard to remain solidly himself. "Different how?"

"The Jamison I knew would never pace. And he wouldn't *not* talk for an hour when he saw someone he knew. You rushed us out of the depot in twenty minutes. And the sex today was . . . "

He stopped. "Was what?"

"Phenomenal. You've always been the best lover, but . . . wow."

Jamison couldn't help grinning, remembering the amazing joy when he'd shot his seed inside her. "It was powerful. Maybe two years of abstinence fed it?"

"Were you abstinent?"

She looked straight at him, but he saw the pain in her eyes. She wanted to believe he'd been true to her, but feared his answer.

"The Changers had weird rules about sex." Jamison made himself stop pacing and lean against a table, pretending to relax. "Every sexual encounter you had, and who you had it with, meant something. The leader could screw whoever he wanted, in whatever form he wanted to. The next cat down could screw anyone she wanted, but had to submit to the Alpha. And so on. They tried to put me at the bottom, at the mercy of everyone, but no way was I letting myself be used like a sex slave. They said I could participate in the group orgies if I stayed chained up, but I declined."

Naomi smiled suddenly, like the sun lighting up the sky. "I know you, Jamison. You didn't just decline."

"No, I pretty much told them what I thought about their sexual perversions, in vivid terms. Navajos are a modest people."

"Modest, my ass. This afternoon you stripped in my bedroom, ripped off my clothes, and jumped my bones."

Jamison warmed, thinking of the glorious feel of her clenched around him. "I pulled down the shades first." He came to her. "Besides, it was you. I've never been able to resist you."

Her gaze moved to his lips, and his pulse started to throb. "You haven't finished your story," she said.

"It's almost done. Another way I fought their sexual advances was to tell them I already had a mate. This puzzled them, because according to the Alpha, Changers should only take Changer mates. Even Changers who mainstream don't marry."

"A mate." Naomi's voice went quiet.

"That's what they call it." Jamison cupped her cheek. "It sounds more intimate than girlfriend, but less intimate than lover."

"Did you mean me?"

He laughed softly. "Of course I meant you. My lover with the turquoise eyes." He pressed a kiss to the corner of her mouth.

"Why were they so cruel to you?"

Jamison brushed a strand of hair back from her forehead. "They did teach me things, like how to control the

Change, and how to calm the beast inside me so I didn't
savage everything in sight. I learned how to be contained,
controlled. It took a long time. They were right to keep
me caged at first. I tried to rip out the throats of everyone
I saw."

She slid her arms around his waist. "I can't believe
that."

"I'd never felt like that in my life. I was a killer, and I
wanted to kill. Me, the storyteller who reads to children."
Jamison remembered his fear and self-loathing, his cer-
tainty he couldn't trust himself with anyone he loved. "But
the Changers taught me how to focus the killing instinct to
what was necessary—hunting game or moving up in the
pack. Not that they were about to let me move up. They
taught me, but the Alpha didn't trust me."

"You got away from them, though."

Jamison nodded. "Once I got used to the Change and
made it clear I wasn't going to challenge the Alpha, they
let me have more freedom. Not much, but more. The Alpha
had some idea of using me as a guard for the pack, but he
couldn't trust me enough. So he decided that, to enforce
my loyalty to him, I should mate with one of his females."

The worry returned to Naomi's eyes. She was trying to
listen and be understanding, but he preferred her flash of
jealousy to total indifference.

"Was she pretty?" Naomi asked, trying to sound casual.

Jamison wanted to laugh. "She'd lived in the remote
desert most of her life, and I don't think she'd combed her
hair in five years. She was a beautiful mountain lion, but as
a woman . . . let's just say she let herself go."

Naomi didn't look amused. "Are you telling me this because you think it's what I want to hear?"

"Because it's the truth, love. I didn't want to take her as
mate, either as a cat or as a human. I wanted to get out of
there, get home, and find you." He lost his smile. "But they
didn't want me to go."

"Then how did you get here?"

"I escaped." Jamison closed his eyes, remembering the

pain of the spelled chains. He'd drawn on his own limited shaman magic to counteract the spells, but it had been brute strength that finally broke them.

"It took me a long time, but I finally escaped their compound. And they chased me. They're still hunting me."

Naomi touched his face. "Is that why you said your enemies were looking for you?"

"Yes." Jamison kissed the line of her hair. Her scent was intoxicating. "I had to come back here to protect you. The Alpha knew I was only partially bonded to you—he could smell it. I heard him tell his seconds that he had to get rid of you before he could fully bond me to the female."

"Get rid of me." Naomi's beautiful eyes filled with alarm. "I bet he didn't mean persuade me to break up with you."

"The Alpha has lived apart from civilization so long he knows only one method of dealing with something in his way." Jamison felt grim. "Kill it."

FOUR

$\mathscr{N}$aomi went still. She gazed into Jamison's dark eyes, windows to the man she'd thought she knew.

"Kill it," she repeated.

Jamison touched his lips to her hair again. "The Alpha is a vicious bastard," he said softly. "As soon as I understood what he planned, I doubled my efforts to escape, to get back to you. I won't let anything happen to you, Naomi, I promise."

Naomi thought about the way Jamison had not let her do anything alone since he'd arrived. Every step of the way he'd been right beside her and Julie.

"Julie," Naomi said, watery fear washing through her. Julie was sleeping alone in the house.

"They're not here yet," Jamison said as though reading her thoughts. "I can smell them, and they haven't found me or Magellan. They'll figure it out sooner or later, but it gives me a little time to complete the bond with you."

She frowned up at him. "What do you mean, complete the bond? Won't that make them more determined to kill me?"

"Once I am completely bonded to my mate, they can't touch you. There's powerful magic in the bond. It's not just a civil agreement, like marriage. No Changer will dare touch another's mate on pain of death. Changers bond only once, and after that, never again. There is no divorce, no remarriage. If you bond with me it will be forever. For both of us."

"*If* I bond with you?" she repeated. "You're giving me a choice?"

He was standing toe-to-toe with her, his arms like strong wings on her back. "If you don't want to complete the bond with me, I'll go, draw them away from you."

"But if you leave, is that any guarantee they won't find me and try to eliminate me anyway?"

His mouth turned down. "No, it's no guarantee. I'm sorry, Naomi. If I'd known all this three years ago, I never would have moved in with you. I'd never even have asked you to have coffee with me."

"That would have been a shame," Naomi said softly.

"But you'd be safe now. You wouldn't have to know any of this."

"I wouldn't have known happiness, either. Or what it was like to truly fall in love."

Jamison said nothing, but his eyes filled with anguish. "I think when I met you, the Changer in me started to bond to you at once."

Naomi had felt it too, she realized now. When Jamison had come home with her the night she'd met him, and they'd made love in the white moonlight, she'd known that she'd waited all her life for this man. A man with midnight-dark eyes and a warm, liquid voice.

Having him quietly move in and start helping her at the garden center had seemed so natural. They'd started driving up to Chinle every other weekend to visit his mom and sister and his vast extended family. They were warm, calm people, like Jamison, and they'd instantly absorbed her into their ranks. She'd feared that they would be angry at Jamison for pairing himself with a white woman, but their attitude seemed to be that if Jamison liked her, she must be all right.

Only Jamison's grandfather hadn't been enchanted with Naomi. He spoke little to her, sometimes pretending she wasn't in the same room with him. Jamison had told her not to worry about it, but Naomi hated that the most respected member of Jamison's family didn't like her. She felt like she'd failed Jamison in some way, though Jamison hadn't understood that when she'd told him. "Grandfather has always been difficult," Jamison had said.

Naomi smiled a little. "So great sex is not enough to complete the bond?"

Jamison grinned back. "There's a ritual Changers have to follow to bond to their mates. I've heard of a shaman up in the White Mountains, an Apache, who can do it. If you're willing, we'll go see him tomorrow."

"Tomorrow's Christmas Eve. I have to take Julie to the Ghost Train."

"We'll be back long before the celebration starts."

"Why not a Navajo shaman? Aren't there several in your family, not to mention your grandfather?"

"This Apache is a Changer, one of the ones who managed to sync with the rest of the world."

Naomi frowned. "If he's a Changer, why didn't Coyote send you to him instead of driving you to Mexico to be locked in a cage for two years?"

Jamison blew out his breath. "You know, I don't know." He smiled, his warm, to-die-for smile. "Come with me tomorrow, and we'll find out. That is, if you're willing."

Naomi clenched her jaw. "Don't worry. I don't think I want to let you out of my sight again."

Jamison leaned down and kissed her. "I'll make sure you don't regret it, love. I promise you."

Jamison told Naomi that Julie should be taken somewhere safe for the day, because it would be too dangerous for her to accompany them. Naomi, her heart squeezing, agreed. Julie didn't want to be left behind, but on the other hand, she viewed staying with Naomi's old high school friend, Nicole, in Flagstaff and playing with her kids as a fun vacation. Nicole would bring Julie back to Magellan tonight for the Ghost Train, and hopefully by then this bonding thing would protect Julie too.

It was midmorning by the time Naomi drove with Jamison out of Flag and along the 87 up into the mountains. An hour later, Naomi turned onto the winding highway that rolled across the top of the Mogollon Rim and into the White Mountains.

It had been cold in Magellan and snowy in Flagstaff, but up here, winter had settled in hard. Glittering drifts piled on either side of the plowed highways, and the tall ponderosa pines were mantled in snow.

Naomi loved the beauty of it, though part of her looked forward to spending a balmy Christmas day under the palm trees with her folks in Tucson. She wondered briefly what her parents would say when she brought Jamison with her and told them he was back in her life. She glanced at Jamison, who lounged comfortably beside her, sunglasses shielding his eyes from the glare of sun on snow. Her parents would be delighted. Jamison charmed everyone.

They stopped in the Apache community of Hon Dah for hot coffee, and Jamison asked a convenience store clerk if he knew a shaman called Alex Clay.

Naomi wasn't really surprised when the Apache man grinned and said, "Hey, Jamison. How've you been?"

He and Jamison talked about mutual acquaintances and family members for a moment, then the man continued.

"Yeah, I know old Alex. He lives down by Whiteriver. I'm not sure exactly where. He's a crazy old man, though." The clerk mimed lifting a bottle and drinking.

"Thanks." Jamison paid for the coffees and held a steaming cup to Naomi. "If anyone else asks about him, you never saw me."

The man flashed a sunny smile. "Sure. I don't gossip."

"Like hell he doesn't," Jamison said under his breath as they climbed back into Naomi's truck. "But he doesn't like strangers and won't tell them anything."

"Where to now?" Naomi asked as she put the truck in gear.

"We go to Whiteriver and ask around."

She gave him a dark look. "So this Alex Clay doesn't have an address?"

"You've lived in a town too long, love. Someone will know where he lives and give us directions."

It had already taken hours to drive along snaking highways through snow and traffic, and there was the Ghost Train celebration to get back for. "He doesn't have a cell phone or anything?" Naomi asked, exasperated. "Some way we can call him and ask where he lives?"

"Probably not. If he's anything like my grandfather, he'll think cell phones were invented by evil spirits to enslave humanity."

"Yeah?" She subsided. "He might be right about that."

Jamison studied her a moment, his sunglasses still. "Grandfather likes you, Naomi. He's just not comfortable with non-Indians."

"It's all right."

Jamison slid his hand to her thigh, his touch warm. "He'll come around."

"Really, it's all right." As long as Jamison was beside her, she thought, making her feel loved and wanted, she could put up with the silent disapproval of his grandfather.

Whiteriver was a small community, but it was busy today with last-minute Christmas shoppers as well as hunters and skiers up from the desert cities. Jamison talked to several people, who, for an interesting change, had never met him. At last Jamison jumped back into the truck with a smile on his face and kissed her.

"Go that way," he said, pointing down a side street.

Naomi followed Jamison's directions. Soon they were out of town, following a tiny ribbon of road through snowy paradise. Naomi drove carefully, keeping an eye out for stray elk, other cars, or citified hunters who might mistake a red Ford pickup for a deer.

After half an hour, the pavement ended and they followed

a washboard road through the woods. The road had been plowed, which meant people lived back here, but Naomi winced as her tires ground through frozen potholes.

Finally Jamison pointed to a tiny house in the shadow of the trees. Smoke rolled from its chimney. "Here, I think."

Naomi parked in front of the house, but Jamison put his hand on her arm when she started to open the truck's door. "Wait a few minutes. Let him get used to the idea that we're here."

Naomi was impatient to get on with it, but she recognized that she had to do this Jamison's way.

"One thing I don't understand," Naomi said as they waited. "If the Alpha of these Changers thought you were such a threat, why didn't he try to kill you right away when you came along? Why keep you alive and try to make you part of the pack?"

Jamison smiled a chill smile. "Because the Alpha is a snob. Apparently, I'm a purebred Changer. One of the Alpha's missions in life is to keep the Changers' blood from being diluted. That's why he wanted to mate me to one of his—to breed more purebloods."

"Ick. Like you're a racehorse."

"That's how I saw it. It drove him crazy when I told him that the woman I claimed as mate wasn't a Changer at all."

Naomi shuddered. "That's why he wants to keep you from being with me? How bizarre."

"He's fanatical about genetics and inheritance for some reason. What I've learned is that Changers in the Americas were originally shamans from a tribe that has long since vanished—divided into and absorbed by other tribes. The shamans became so attuned to the animals they watched and prayed to that they learned their essences, their spirits, and could eventually take their shapes."

"You mean like skinwalkers?"

Jamison sketched a symbol in the air that he'd told her was a sign against evil. "Not like skinwalkers. A skinwalker wraps himself in the hide of a freshly killed animal and then morphs into its shape. Skinwalkers are evil and dangerous. These shamans understood the spirits of the animals, they could become an animal. It was the animal gods' gift to them. In my case, the mountain lion."

"Can Changers be other animals? Not just mountain lions?"

"Depending on the original shaman they descended from, yes, though it's usually a predator. Wolves, coyotes, hawks."

"If you are a pureblood," Naomi said, "that would mean your father was a Changer. Or your mother. Right?"

"Both my families have the genetic strain, the researchers in the pack told me. But apparently the ability to change doesn't manifest in every generation. If anyone else in my family can change, they've never admitted it."

"The researchers?" Naomi picked up on the word.

Jamison went silent a moment. "They had a lab. They had money. Everything was state-of-the-art."

Naomi reached over and plucked off his sunglasses. Behind them his eyes were filled with memories of pain. "They hurt you," she whispered.

"They had to make sure I was worthy to be allowed to live. They took a lot of *samples*."

She didn't like the way he said samples. "You only need a strand of hair to check DNA."

"They checked so many things. My stamina, my strength, my endurance."

"They tortured you, you mean." Anger surged through her, wild and furious. "Those Changers had better not come up here after you, because they'll have to deal with me."

Jamison smiled a little, but he said, "Don't even think about fighting them, Naomi. They're dangerous and well trained."

His tone made her subside, but Naomi wanted to scream in frustration. They'd hurt him and caged him while she'd been living obliviously in Magellan, angry at Jamison for deserting her.

If she'd known what was going on, she could have found

some way to rescue him—how, she had no idea. But she was related to half of Hopi County and must know someone who could have helped her. Putting her connections together with Jamison's huge family, she could have raised a formidable army.

Jamison put his arm around her shoulders. "I got away, and I'm back. Thinking of you, needing to get back here to you, kept me alive, kept me from giving up hope."

Naomi's throat ached. "And here I was pissed at you for not calling me."

Jamison pulled her close and buried his face in her neck. "But I'm glad you were here not knowing. It kept you safe."

His warmth was much better than the heater running full blast. She turned her head and met his mouth with hers. She loved having him here, with his satin-smooth lips on hers.

"Let's do this bond thing," she whispered. "I don't want to lose you again."

Jamison caressed her face, his hand sliding into her coat to cup her breast. "The bond means I protect you, and no one else touches you."

"Good."

Jamison started to kiss her again, then glanced out the front window. The door of the house stood open. "Ah, it looks like Mr. Clay is ready for us."

"Good," Naomi repeated and snapped off the engine.

FIVE

*J*amison realized before they'd spent ten minutes inside
Alex Clay's tiny and rather smelly house why Coyote
hadn't sent him here to learn about being a Changer. The
man was insane.

The thin, elderly Apache shuffled around his one-room
house, gathering up bits of trash and piling them on a worn
blanket in the center of the room. He muttered to himself,
paused to extensively scratch an armpit, then plopped
cross-legged onto the blanket and closed his eyes.

Jamison gestured for Naomi to sit facing the old man,
and Jamison sat next to her, letting his thigh touch hers.

Alex kept his eyes closed as he rummaged through a
leather pouch. He brought out stones—turquoise, onyx,
and a white stone Jamison couldn't identify.

He began muttering to himself again, but Jamison
couldn't understand what he said. Alex wasn't speaking
any Native American language Jamison recognized, and he
knew many.

Naomi looked sideways at him, and Jamison shrugged,
though his heart constricted with uncertainty. He wanted—
needed—this bond with Naomi, and he grew impatient.

Impatience was something new to Jamison. He'd been raised to be calm and accepting, not acting until nature or the gods showed him the right path. Since his first Change, he'd been more volatile, less willing to wait for someone else to tell him what to do.

Had he ever been patient? he wondered. Or just stubborn? Had he only wanted to show off to others that he could sit in meditation longer than they could? To show that he didn't need to rush around looking for happiness? That he could sit like a lump and wait for grass to grow on him better than anyone else? Idiot.

Naomi had never waited for life to show her what to do. She faced her problems full-on and did what she had to do. She'd left her husband in Phoenix when he made it clear he blamed Naomi for Julie's deafness. She'd returned to her people, took over her parents' business when they retired, and made something of her life. When Jamison had disappeared, she hadn't folded up and stopped. She'd gotten mad and kept on living.

Naomi embraced life, the good and bad of it. She was an Unbeliever, yet she indulged her neighbors' obsession with the Ghost Train and took in Jamison's Changer ability with good grace.

Jamison put his hand on hers. He liked the feel of her skin, always warm, on his. She laced her fingers through his and gave him a little smile, which made his blood sing.

Jamison had been raised not to interrupt his elders, but he sensed that this man could go on rocking and mouthing nonsense for days if he wasn't stopped.

"Sir," he said in a low voice. "Mr. Clay."

Alex Clay didn't look up or stop chanting. But after another minute or two, he wound down to silence. He rose, took a bundle of herbs from a basket in the corner, and tossed it into his wood-burning stove. A sweet but acrid smell permeated the room.

"I think that's a controlled substance," Naomi hissed. Jamison gave her the barest nod.

The old man sat in front of them again. He took

Jamison's hand in his then Naomi's. He closed his eyes and began chanting in a low drone as the room filled with heady smoke.

Alex put their hands together and started piling the stones on top of them. The turquoise and onyx felt warm, the white stones strangely cool. Naomi's eyelids drooped from the smoke, and Jamison wished the man would open a window or something.

Alex suddenly opened his eyes. They were wide and black, full of more intelligence than his rambling muttering had led Jamison to believe. He put his hand on their joined hands and squeezed. Naomi winced, and Jamison felt the pain of stones pressing into his skin.

Just as suddenly the old man let go and raked the stones back to the blanket.

"One hundred dollars," he said clearly. "Cash."

Naomi raised her brows. Jamison bit the inside of his mouth, pulled out his wallet, and counted five twenties into the man's outstretched hand.

Jamison helped Naomi to her feet while Alex recounted the money and stuffed it inside the pouch with the stones.

As they made to leave, Jamison turned back.

"I don't mean to question you," he said. "But you are a Changer, aren't you?"

The old man chuckled. He didn't move, but suddenly his body shrank and his clothes collapsed inward. Naomi gasped.

An elderly hawk emerged from the clothes, shaking its feathers. It glared at them with yellow eyes, put one wing over its head, and went to sleep.

"So that's it?" Naomi asked as she started the truck. "Now we're bonded?"

"No." Jamison sighed, frustration and disappointment warring within him. "I think that was the biggest load of bullshit I've ever gone through. He's not a real shaman."

"But you gave him a hundred dollars."

"He needs food and fuel for the winter. I bet he shafts a lot of people, and they go along with it because they feel sorry for him."

"He really is a Changer, though. He didn't fake that."

Jamison shook his head, glum. "But there was no bonding. You're still vulnerable."

"Then so are you."

Jamison tried to contain the anger boiling through him. "Let's get back to Magellan. The weather's changing."

Naomi peered at the sky, which had moved from blue to gray while they'd been inside, clouds lowering. Storms could gather fast in the mountains. Jamison remembered a summer day he'd been hiking on Humphreys Peak, one of the sacred mountains of the Navajo near Flagstaff. One small cloud had been hovering over the summit when he started, but within an hour, he was dodging lightning strikes and a deluge of hail.

Naomi said nothing as she inched the truck back toward the main road. As they snaked northward through the reservation, flakes of snow began to dust the windshield.

"What do we do now?" Naomi asked. "Who else can perform the bonding thing?"

Naomi faced the road like she faced everything, chin up, with bring-it-on sass. A defeat was only a minor setback to her.

"I don't know anyone else," Jamison said. "Except the Alpha who held me captive, and I don't plan to ask him."

"What about this Coyote? He knew where the Changers were in Mexico, maybe he knows where some others are around here."

"He's not exactly trustworthy."

"He's nice to Julie. And it's worth a shot."

She had a point. "I'll try to track him down," Jamison conceded. "I'll check out the Crossroads Bar and see if anyone knows where he's staying. If he shows up at the Ghost Train tonight, I'll try to corner him there."

"Or I will. I'd like to know why he shunted you off to Mexico and didn't tell me. If he's some powerful god, he could have at least called."

Jamison chuckled. Coyote the mighty trickster god would meet his match in Naomi.

"Damn, the snow is picking up," she said.

The black strip of road they'd reached was deserted, and snow fell thick and fast. They had miles to go before they met the northbound highway, and then they'd have to crest a summit before twisting back down to the plateau.

Naomi set her jaw, slowed the truck, and drove carefully and intently. Five miles later, wind slapped them halfway across the road, and the windshield was covered with white.

"Shit." Naomi pumped her breaks. The truck obediently slowed, listing sharply to the right as the wheels went into the shoulder. They stopped, the truck rocking, and the whiteout blizzard struck full force.

Naomi sat still, hands locked around the wheel, eyes wide. Jamison unbuckled his seat belt, slid across the cab to her, and put his arms around her.

"We'll be all right." He turned her face to his, smoothing her cheek with his thumb. "There's no other traffic, and when the storm lets up, they'll send out the plows."

"Julie . . ."

"Is snug and safe with your friend in Flagstaff. We'll just have to think of a way to keep ourselves warm." He licked her ear.

She relaxed enough to smile. "I missed you, Jamison."

"I missed you too, love." Her hair smelled so good. It always had. He nibbled her earlobe, liking the little noise of pleasure she made.

Naomi turned her head and kissed him. He melted into her, feeling her hot mouth, her questing tongue. He remembered falling asleep inside her last night, her warmth filling his empty spaces.

"You're mine," he murmured. His entire body flushed with heat. "Mine."

She kept kissing him, her lips so soft. He imagined her lips sliding around his heavy erection, and his body throbbed.

"I'm going to do another sculpture and sell it," he said. "Then use the money to buy you the biggest diamond ring you ever saw."

She stilled. "Diamond?"

"It's the custom of your people for a man to give a diamond ring when he asks a woman to marry him, isn't it?"

Naomi's turquoise eyes went wide. "Are you asking me to marry you?"

"I plan to, when the time is right."

"Jamison . . ."

He kissed her again, finished with words. He let his fingers move to the button of her jeans, then her zipper. She jumped. "What are you doing?"

He grinned. "Celebrating that you're going to let me ask you to marry me. Besides, who's going to see us in a blizzard?" He kissed her again, then he tugged at her open jeans. "Pull these down."

Naomi gave him an amazed look, then she quickly slid the jeans and her panties down over her butt. Jamison moved his hand between her legs, feeling her liquid heat.

"The seat is cold." Her eyes widened, then she dissolved into laughter.

Jamison reached behind the seat, where she'd stowed a neatly folded blanket along with her emergency supplies. She was always so practical.

Naomi half rose, and he slid the blanket under her. "Better?"

"Better."

"Good." Jamison leaned down into her lap and moved his tongue into her slick heat.

$\mathcal{R}$esponsible Naomi never dreamed she'd let a man go down on her in the front cab of her truck on a major highway. Of course, snow was piling up on the windows, blotting out the world. She should worry about how much gas and battery life her truck had, but right now those concerns seemed irrelevant.

Jamison had a magic tongue. He licked and kissed her, using fingers to spread her. She let her head drop back.

"Jamison."

"Mmm hmm?" he asked, his mouth busy.

"I'm glad you came back."

"Mmm. So am I."

His hot tongue contrasted sharply with the cool air in the cab. She needed his mouth and what it did.

His tongue moved across her labia, parting the lips, then tickled her swollen berry. He suckled her, pulling the nub into his mouth, the tiny pain of his teeth arousing as hell.

She looked down at his satin black hair and strong back, marveling that this man wanted her. Three years ago, when he'd said in his lecture, "Navajo legend says that this world is the fourth level of worlds we've ascended to," his smooth voice had made her wet. She'd never thought listening to a creation myth would make her want to take a man to bed.

This incredible man everyone liked wanted her, and he showed her now by jabbing his tongue straight into her cream. She moaned out loud, her fingers furrowing his hair.

He went on driving her crazy, his neck muscles working as he drank her. Her hips moved frantically, her juices pouring out of her and over his tongue.

"Jamison," she screamed.

"That's my girl," he whispered into her skin.

He kept his mouth on her, moving with her frenzy until she suddenly broke. She had no idea what she shouted or what she did, but she was squeezing with her thighs, raking her fingers across his back.

Finally he raised his head, his smile stretched wide. "Don't kill me, love. I want to do more later."

Naomi collapsed against the seat, panting. "Sorry."

"I was teasing." Jamison licked his lips as he sat up, his eyes hot and full of sin. "I like it a little rough."

Naomi dragged in long breaths, fire still raging in her core. Before she could reason out what she was doing, she unbuckled and unzipped Jamison's jeans and lowered her head to his lap.

"Naomi . . ."

"Payback," Naomi said and swirled her tongue around his stiff cock. "Sit there and take it."

Jamison made a raw noise, fist closing on her hair. He tasted so good, better than she remembered. She wanted to suck him into her mouth and keep on sucking, to let him know how much she missed him. He rocked his hips like he wanted to fuck her mouth, and she opened wide for him.

"Damn, I missed you," he said.

Naomi was slightly surprised at herself, but the new wildness in him touched a wildness in her. And what the hell? If they were going to freeze to death out here, they might as well go out having fun.

Naomi suckled and licked his cock until he groaned and shot a sweet stream into her mouth. She sat up again, triumphant, and reached for the tissues she kept in the glove compartment.

Then she noticed the silence. "Oh my God, it stopped snowing."

The blizzard had slowed, and a snowless wind had blown chunks of white from the front window.

Naomi wiped her mouth and jerked her jeans up with shaking fingers. "We'd better stop this."

Jamison's smile was wicked. He drew her against him, kissing her neck, under her hair, his breath hot. "Why, so we don't embarrass the highway workers?"

"I was thinking we'd be the ones embarrassed, sitting here with our pants down."

Jamison licked her ear, and she felt the ridge of his already hard erection against her thigh. "Hope they get here soon," he rasped. "I want to do more in a more comfortable setting."

"Maybe you should take a look at how stuck we are. The cold might do us good."

"I don't think anything will cool me down from being with you."

"Even so."

Jamison laughed and kissed her again, then he zipped

up his jeans, pulled on gloves, and opened the door. Freezing air rushed into the cab, cut off abruptly as he slammed the door again.

Storms up here could diminish just as quickly as they blew in. Jamison brushed the remains of the snow from the windshield and Naomi could see the road, or at least a thick blanket of white with reflective markers sticking up through it. Even with her four-wheel drive, the road would be impassible for a while, the snow too soft and slick. They'd have to wait for a plow.

Jamison walked around the truck, the wind whipping his hair. He retied part of a tarp that had come loose in her pickup bed, brushing snow from the top of it.

Towering pine trees grew thickly on either side of the road, and Naomi saw something moving under them. An elk maybe? Or a deer?

It came closer, a large animal lumbering on four legs. Elks were big and could be dangerous if they charged.

Jamison turned around and stilled. It was a bear. Two bears, one shadowing the other.

Black bears roamed these mountains, but Naomi would have thought this deep into winter they'd be hibernating. These bears didn't look lean and hungry, and were nowhere near sleepy.

They stopped, snouts swiveling to point straight at Jamison. They sniffed the air, then with enraged growls, they charged.

SIX

*N*aomi screamed. As Jamison leapt back into the cab, Naomi instinctively slammed the truck into drive and stomped on the accelerator. The pickup lurched forward a few inches, then the tires spun, digging them deeper into snow and mud.

"Stop!" Jamison said in a commanding voice. He was yanking off his coat, shoving the boots from his feet.

"Making noise might scare them away."

"Those aren't bears," Jamison said grimly as he hauled off his shirt and kicked out of his jeans. "They're Changers."

Naked now, he grabbed Naomi by the back of her neck and gave her a rough kiss. "Stay in here."

He slammed open the door, changing into a snarling mountain lion as he jumped from the cab. The bears charged. Naomi cried out as Jamison met them head-on, teeth and claws clashing.

Holy shit. She couldn't just sit here and watch them tear Jamison apart. Maybe she could scare them, distract them. She punched the horn, letting it sound in loud bursts. One bear jerked its head up, then as the other bear tackled Jamison, the first bear rushed the truck.

The cab rocked as the bear slammed into it. It was a Changer, Jamison said. That meant the bear could morph into a human who could open doors and drag her out into the snow.

She slammed the locks shut and flipped open her cell phone, punching 9-1-1 and praying she had reception. "Hey," she shouted at the person who answered. "We're stuck in the snow, and bears are attacking."

The calm-voiced woman on the other end asked her where she was and promised help was on the way. She advised Naomi to stay inside the truck with the doors locked.

"You think?" Naomi screamed as the bear slammed its paws into the driver-side window. Glass shattered and cold air poured in.

The bear suddenly howled and went down when a huge, tawny-colored beast jumped on it. A wolf? Naomi wondered as the two animals rolled away. Could this get any worse?

A moment later she wished she hadn't thought that. Another mountain lion bounded out of the woods, this one nearly twice Jamison's size. He was snarling, foam flecking his red mouth. The bear with Jamison backed off, and the two mountain lions met with a crash and a wildcat scream.

The bear hovered outside the fight, breath steaming in the air. He was watching like a referee, his head moving back and forth as the two combatants wrestled and struggled.

"Jamison," Naomi sobbed.

The broken window darkened, and Naomi whipped her head around to see the man who called himself Coyote standing next to her, stark naked and breathing hard. Gone was the man who wandered Magellan's streets and teased tourists, who smiled at Julie and signed to her. His eyes were yellow and glittering, his lips pulled back from pointed canines.

"Get out," Coyote said to Naomi. He yanked open the

door and unlocked her seat belt himself, pulling her out by the arm. The bear that had been attacked lay still, groaning, the snow stained red around it.

"If you stay in there, they'll crush the truck," Coyote said.

"If I'm out here, they'll crush me."

Coyote ripped the tarp from her truck bed and pulled out a shotgun, one she hadn't put there.

He thrust the gun into her shaking arms. "You know how to use this?"

Naomi nodded, hands automatically moving to hold the gun in a safe position.

"Good. Defend yourself. Shoot to kill, because they'll kill you if you don't."

He turned away, not seeming to notice the cold and snow, even though he was bare-ass naked. He threw back his head and let out a ferocious howl. Then he started running at the second bear, morphing into a beast as he went.

He was bigger than a wolf, huge and muscled, but his face was pointed and foxlike. A coyote's face.

The second bear roared, turning to meet the threat, and both went down in a tangle of limbs. Jamison was still fighting the other mountain lion, the two cats springing apart to circle each other before slamming together again.

Naomi charged around the truck, the shotgun cradled in her arms. She cocked it and sighted, but she couldn't shoot for fear of hitting Jamison.

Wind suddenly howled down the highway, stirring up the drifts. The sky darkened with impossible speed and snow started to fly. The driving flakes stung Naomi's cheeks, and white clouded her vision. The red truck was ten paces away from her, but in a matter of seconds, she could barely see it.

The bear that Coyote had already wounded struggled to its feet behind her. Naomi swung around and aimed at it, but it morphed into a human and stumbled toward the truck. He leaned heavily against the hood, blood streaming from his shoulder.

Naomi moved toward him, still aiming the gun. "I called nine-one-one," she yelled. "You just stay right there."

The man gazed at her like he hadn't heard. He had black hair and eyes so dark she saw them through the whirling snow. "There's sorcery in this," he said with a harsh accent. "Are you doing sorcery?"

"The only sorcery I have is right here." Naomi sighted down the barrel to make her point.

"If you are not, then . . . " The man's eyes widened in horror and he stared past Naomi at the fight between Jamison and the other mountain lion. "He's doing it. He's a sorcerer. Shoot him! Shoot him, now!"

Did he mean Jamison? Or the second cat? Naomi swung around and looked over the gun at the mountain lions. But they were locked together, Jamison's ears flat against his head.

A few feet from them, Coyote morphed into a man, lifted the bear he fought, and threw it to the ground.

The man next to Naomi emitted a moan of distress and started for the fallen bear. To Naomi's astonishment, the bear on the ground morphed into a woman with tangled dark hair. She lay still, her arm bent at an unnatural angle.

Unperturbed, Coyote walked back to Naomi as the man fell to his knees beside the woman. Coyote was a huge man, easily six and a half feet tall with bulging muscles filling out his body. He had the dark skin of a Native American, long black hair, and black dark eyes. His face had a flat look, as if his nose had once been broken, maybe in a biker bar?

Coyote put his hands on his hips, watching the mountain lions fight. Jamison was going to lose. Naomi's heart thumped as the larger cat drew claws along Jamison's side and bright red streaks erupted on Jamison's fur.

"Do something!" she screamed at Coyote.

"He's the Alpha," Coyote grunted, gesturing at the cats. "If I interfere, Jamison automatically loses."

"The Alpha? You mean the Changer who locked Jamison in a cage and treated him like a lab rat?"

Coyote didn't answer. Naomi's blood ran hot. She uncocked the gun and moved toward the fighting pair, treading carefully in the snow. Maybe Coyote's assistance would negate the testosterone contest, but would that happen if Jamison's own mate helped him?

Naomi dug her boots into the snowy ground. She cocked the gun, and as soon as the Alpha flung Jamison underneath him, she shoved the barrel of the gun into the creature's neck.

"Let him go," she shouted.

The mountain lion screamed. With lightning speed, he yanked his head around and leapt at Naomi.

Naomi shot. The boom of the gun deafened her, and several things happened at once.

Coyote dragged Naomi out from under the Alpha's flailing claws at the same time Jamison flung the Alpha to the ground. Blood spattered across the snow, but the Alpha rolled away, still alive.

Naomi's shot had ripped into his side, but he'd been moving fast, and she hadn't killed him. Jamison morphed back into his human form with a grunt of pain, his skin scored and bleeding.

The Alpha stood upright, his wildcat body changing to that of a tall man. But his shape shimmered and changed again, unfolding into something even taller. He was huge, his hair tangled and coarse, his eyes red. An overpowering stench rolled off him.

"A skinwalker," the man who'd been a bear rasped. "He's a fucking skinwalker."

"Son of a bitch," Jamison panted.

The Alpha clutched his side, blood pouring from it. He snarled, then turned and loped off under the trees. Coyote started after him, but after the Alpha had run five paces, the man vanished. The snow whirled where he'd been, then the storm stopped. The wind died away, and clouds parted to let the sun through.

Jamison collapsed. Naomi dropped the shotgun and caught him in her arms, kneeling with him in the snow. He was bleeding from many wounds, but his eyes were clear and alert.

"I'm all right," he rasped. "A lot of scratches and bites, but nothing too deep."

"You're a good fighter, Jamison," Coyote said above Naomi. "No wonder he was afraid of you."

Naomi turned toward Coyote then immediately whipped away when she saw the man's very long, flaccid cock hanging right next to her.

"He's a skinwalker," the male bear Changer snarled. He limped toward them, supporting the woman, who was pale but upright. "All this time. We will tell the pack, choose a new leader."

The woman looked at Jamison with narrowed eyes. "Do you wish to challenge for Alpha?" She spoke with an accent that told Naomi English wasn't her first language.

Jamison shook his head. "I'm staying here." He glared up at Coyote. "Why did you send me to be trained by a skinwalker?"

"I didn't know. I never met the man until today." Coyote gazed off into the woods where the Alpha had disappeared. "He must be a damn good skinwalker if he fooled you all for so long."

"He will not be allowed to return to us," the man vowed. "We will retreat, and I will care for my mate. We have no quarrel with you, Jamison."

Jamison sat up, brushing the snow off his body. Like Coyote and the other two, he didn't seem to notice the cold. "Then why did you attack me?"

"On the orders of our Alpha," the man said. He spat into the snow. "But we take no orders from skinwalkers."

Without another word, the man and woman turned and walked together into the woods, each supporting the other.

"Will they be all right?" Naomi asked.

Coyote grunted. "They're Changers. They'll heal quickly, and the skinwalker will be more interested in coming after Jamison."

Naomi looked at him in fear. "But I wounded him. I drove him off."

"Temporarily," Jamison said. "We'd better go."

He started to climb to his feet, and Coyote and Naomi grasped his arms to help him. Coyote didn't have a scratch on him, though the hair on his chest was damp with sweat.

Jamison walked to the truck without limping, leaving large footprints in the snow. He opened the passenger door and reached for his clothes.

Coyote pulled jeans and a flannel shirt from under the tarp in the truck bed and started dressing without hurry.

"Were you riding back there this whole time?" Naomi demanded.

"Yep."

Naomi's face went hot. She'd let herself scream without restraint when Jamison went down on her, and then she'd happily sucked Jamison off, thinking they were cut off and alone. From the grin on Coyote's face, he'd heard everything.

"I figured you'd need me," he said, his yellow eyes dancing with amusement. "You mind giving me a lift back to town?"

"Do I have a choice?" Naomi glared at him. "And wipe that disgusting look off your face or I'll charge you for the gas."

SEVEN

*H*e would be coming. Jamison knew that as they drove out of the mountains, following the flashing yellow light of the plow. By the time they reached lower elevations, the snow had gone, and bare desert greeted them under blue sky.

Coyote rode in the truck's cab with them, squishing Jamison between himself and Naomi. Jamison didn't mind sitting right next to Naomi, where he could rest his hand on her thigh. She was scared and angry, and he wanted her so much he could barely sit still.

She'd leapt to his defense, damning the rules of Changer combat to protect her mate. The bonding ceremony the Apache had done might have been bogus, but Naomi possessed the courage of a true mate. He'd find a way to bind her to him in the Changer way. He had to.

They arrived in Magellan as the sun set, the tattered clouds to the south streaked brilliant red. The Ghost Train celebration would begin in a few hours. All businesses in Magellan closed for it, including Hansen's Garden Center, so the parking lot was deserted when they reached the house.

Coyote went straight to the refrigerator and started rummaging around until he came out with a can of beer.

"You're staying?" Jamison asked him.

"You need me to."

"I know." Jamison stripped off his shirt as he went into the downstairs bathroom. Naomi followed.

Her worried look turned to one of surprise when she saw that Jamison's torso had almost healed. The long scratches on his skin already had closed and scarred over. Jamison dabbed off the remaining blood with a washcloth.

"Why do you and Coyote think the skinwalker will come back?" Naomi asked him. "We defeated him, didn't we?"

"Not quite. He wasn't fighting to kill. He was fighting to see what I could do. What I *would* do." Jamison dried himself and twined his loose hair into a braid. "And now we know his secret. He'll have to return and kill us."

"Why? If he disappeared, how would we know how to find him? Who would we tell?"

"The Alpha, or whoever he is, is crazed about honor. You and I and Coyote made him lose face as well as control over the pack." Jamison nodded grimly. "He'll recover, and then he'll come."

Naomi slid her arms around him, and Jamison pulled her warm body close. "I never realized what you went through," she said softly. "Thinking of what they did to you makes me so angry."

Jamison buried his face in her neck, kissed her skin. He knew he'd never have survived without the memory of her. He'd think of how good she smelled when she first woke up, warm and sweet, her sex juices scenting her from whatever arousing dream she'd been having. Making love to her in the morning had been the best thing in the world.

The idea that, after he'd left, some other man might have made love to her as the sun rose, had also kept Jamison alive in the cage and determined to get back to her. To fight for her, if necessary. Two years hadn't made much difference in the savage possessiveness that spiked in Jamison every time he saw her.

"I kept going because I wanted to come back to you," he said. "Whether you were waiting for me or not, I wanted to see you again."

Coyote darkened the doorway, and Naomi broke the embrace. Jamison didn't want to let her go, needing the feel of her body against his.

"Ready for the Ghost Train?" Coyote asked. "Sounds like fun."

Naomi bit her lip. "Maybe we shouldn't go. Julie shouldn't, anyway. Nicole needs to keep her in Flag."

"Nah." Coyote shook his head. "Julie's been looking forward to it all year, and she's invited me special. Don't disappoint her." He gave them his pointed-toothed grin. "Me, I wouldn't miss it for the world."

*N*aomi still had misgivings, but the thought of being somewhere bright and cheerful surrounded by friends appealed to her.

"Skinwalkers hate light and fire," Jamison said on the way over. "And crowds. We'll be safer there than at home right now."

Magellan's railway depot was typical of those built in the Southwest during the great railroad boom of the end of the nineteenth century. Crafted from wood and stucco, the depot was one long, narrow room, with a station office in the back. It had been built in 1890 to service tracks that connected the main line in Winslow to the mountain and mining towns to the south. In the 1930s, the service up to the mountains had been discontinued and the depot closed. Over the years the railroad company had removed the rails and ties from the railroad bed, but the raised bed was still there, empty and unused.

Then an enterprising town planner claimed he'd found a story of a "ghost train," which rumbled through Magellan each Christmas. He'd started a celebration on Christmas Eve to greet the ghosts as they rode past. The depot was restored, the event planned, word sent out. It worked. The

Ghost Train celebration had become a Magellan tradition, and people came from all over the Southwest to see it.

By the time Naomi, Jamison, and Coyote arrived at the depot, it was lit from top to bottom, and a huge Christmas tree glittered in one corner. Candles flickered inside luminarias on the depot porch and the low walls surrounding the platform. The poinsettias Naomi had provided were holding up well, lending brilliant color inside and out.

If skinwalkers didn't like light and fire, they wouldn't like this place. Naomi nervously watched the dark desert beyond the depot, but nothing more frightening came out of it than a few rough-looking bikers, riding up to join in the celebration.

Julie, unhurt and unworried, ran inside with Naomi's friend Nicole and hugged Jamison. Maude McGuire was already there with her husband, Magellan's chief of police. Maude walked around with a large cookie jar, taking donations for the historical society. She greeted Naomi with a wave and a smile, but the smile didn't reach her eyes. Her daughter Amy had been missing for a year now, with no word whether she was dead or alive.

"I might know someone who can help them," Jamison said into Naomi's ear. She jumped, still nervous.

"Help who? The McGuires?"

"I know a woman, a half-Navajo from Many Farms, who investigates mysterious happenings. If I talk to her, she might be able to look into their daughter's disappearance. If nothing else has helped, it's worth a shot."

"Do you know everyone on the Navajo Nation?" Naomi asked. "In the entire Southwest?"

Jamison allowed a smile to touch his eyes. "Janet Begay went to school with my youngest sister. Janet moved off to Flagstaff, and I haven't seen her since, but I can track her down. And it's my mother who knows everyone in the Southwest. She just tells me all the gossip."

Beside her, Julie squealed. Naomi swung around, heart pounding, but Julie was waving madly to Coyote. He smiled at Julie, a friendly look that softened his face, and he lifted Julie up on his shoulders.

Naomi glanced around the bright depot, which seemed warm and safe. But after the celebration the town would grow dark again, lying vulnerable to attack.

"Julie can't come home with us tonight," she said.

"No," Jamison agreed.

"Will she be safe if she goes back with Nicole?"

"Safer than she will be at home. But I want you to stay in Magellan with me."

Naomi looked at Julie laughing at Coyote, her hands moving in quick signs. "Because you think the skinwalker will come after me if I'm separated from you?"

"I wouldn't be able to keep you safe. And if you're with Julie, he'll take her too."

"Damn it."

"I'm so sorry, Naomi."

His eyes were dark and grim, and Naomi touched his shoulder. "I'll help you defeat it. I'm scared as hell, but I'm not letting it hurt my mate."

Jamison gave her one of his warm, sinful smiles. At the same time someone cried, "The Ghost Train is coming!"

Everyone hurried out onto the platform. Jamison and Naomi followed more slowly, and Coyote came behind them, Julie holding his hand.

The night was clear, the mountain storms having stayed in the mountains. Stars filled the horizon in an opaque sheet of white. It was so beautiful, but Naomi had learned how much evil the empty desert held.

Naomi's cousin Heather shushed everyone. "Can you feel it?" she said. "The heat of the steam? Can you hear the wheels on the track?"

"Yes," someone else whispered. "The Ghost Train has returned to Magellan."

Coyote stared at the empty track bed and then back at Jamison. "They're crazy," he murmured. "There's nothing there."

Jamison shrugged. Julie signed silently to Coyote, *We know, but everyone likes it.*

Coyote threw back his head and laughed, which earned him glares. After a few minutes of people murmuring about the Ghost Train's presence, Heather sighed. "It's moving on now. Shall we send it on its way?"

As one, everyone on the platform waved as though they were seeing off old friends. "Good night! Merry Christmas! See you next year!"

"Time to go," Coyote said. His laughter was gone.

Jamison explained to Julie that she'd be going back to Flagstaff, but they'd come for her tomorrow to open presents and make the journey to Tucson to her grandparents' house. He spoke with confidence that by tomorrow, everything would be all right.

Julie wasn't stupid. She looked anxiously at Naomi, then signed to Coyote that she expected him to take good care of her mother and Jamison.

"I will," Coyote said. He leaned down and kissed Julie's hair. "I'll keep them safe, sweetie. Promise."

Jamison put his arms around Naomi as Julie got into Nicole's SUV. "She'll be fine with them. And if anything happens to us, your folks will take care of her."

Naomi's heart beat faster. She knew her family would help Julie more than Julie's own father would, but the thought of leaving the little girl alone made her crazed.

She turned in Jamison's arms. "Let's get this bastard."

Jamison smiled and kissed her. "That's my girl."

*W*hen they reached the house, Coyote in tow, Jamison flipped on all the lights, inside and out. The flood of light made him feel better, but he knew it wouldn't last. Coyote seated himself next to the Christmas tree in the living room, snapped the shotgun open, and started to clean it.

Naomi decided to make sandwiches while they waited, and while she was occupied, Jamison went out to his studio.

He unlocked it, turned on the lights, and looked around. The wrought iron project he'd started two years ago still hung on the wall, his equipment ready for use.

Jamison wrapped the unfinished stone mountain lion in heavy cloths and carried it out. He didn't lock the studio this time, and he set the padlock on the ground inside the door. When he reached the house, Naomi was still making sandwiches. Coyote had put aside the shotgun and turned on the television.

Jamison took the sculpture upstairs to Julie's room and placed it on a shelf in her closet. He smiled at the clutter of little-girl things in her bedroom: magazine pictures of current male stars, posters of unicorns and ballet dancers, and stuffed animals all over the bed. Books spilled off shelves and lay in piles on the floor, from the latest young adult novel to classics like the Narnia series to the Navajo storybooks Jamison had given her. In Julie's silent life, books were her connection with the world.

Naomi set a plate with a sandwich on the breakfast bar, and Jamison leaned on the counter to eat it. He wasn't hungry, too keyed up, but he knew he shouldn't drain his strength.

He caught Naomi as she turned away. He skimmed his hands up her back and kissed her lips, unable to keep from touching her.

"So we just wait for him to attack?" she asked in a quiet voice.

"It's better this way. We have a base here, and it will be safer than going out to hunt him. He'll come tonight."

He kissed her. She melted into him, her fear and adrenaline flowing up to him. He wanted nothing more than to take her upstairs, bury himself in her, draw strength from her for the coming fight.

From the way Naomi kissed him back, she wanted it too. She pressed her thumbs to the corners of his mouth, put her tongue inside. Her hips rose to his, rubbing his hardness, which itched for her.

"Nice," Coyote said. "Want to fuck while we wait?"

Jamison eased away from Naomi in regret. "It might not be a good idea."

"I meant with me," Coyote said.

Naomi gave him a withering glance. "Don't you wish."

"I do wish. That's why I asked."

"Keep your paws off my mate," Jamison said, torn between amusement and possessiveness. *Trickster gods.*

"I meant with both of you."

"No," Jamison and Naomi said at the same time, and Jamison laughed.

Coyote shrugged his massive shoulders and turned away. "TV it is, then. You have HBO?"

EIGHT

The skinwalker struck just after one.

Naomi lay against Jamison on the sofa, her warm head on his shoulder, while he and Coyote watched an old horror movie. Coyote had laughed all the way through the movie, pointing out flaws in the plot, claiming no werewolf would act like that. And anyway, there was no such thing as werewolves, he said; only Changers who could take wolf form.

Jamison didn't notice the movie, listening for every noise outside.

He knew the skinwalker had arrived when the house suddenly went black. The television noise ceased abruptly and the pinprick lights on the Christmas tree died. Jamison picked up a flashlight from the coffee table and pressed it into Naomi's hands. He heard Coyote reach for and lift the now-loaded shotgun.

Something scraped on the boards of the porch. The doorknob rattled then there was more scraping, then silence. Jamison saw Naomi's eyes glitter in what little moonlight penetrated the windows, saw the glisten of the shotgun's barrel, held steady by Coyote.

They heard a quiet splinter of glass in the back door's window, then the latch clicked and the hinges creaked. A huge creature stood in the open doorway, blocking the light outside.

His stench was overpowering. Jamison's sense of smell had developed sharply since his Changer ability had manifested, and the odor made him want to vomit.

Beside him, Naomi clicked on the flashlight and shone it full on the creature. He must have been eight feet tall, his skin crusted with blood from his earlier wound. His eyes were huge and red, teeth jagged. He was a far cry from the clean-shaven, controlled Alpha Jamison knew. Skinwalkers could take the shapes of their victims, so he must have killed the real Alpha a long time ago and stepped into his life.

The skinwalker roared and charged into the kitchen. Coyote brought the shotgun up and fired.

The gun's roar blotted out all other sound. The creature moved fast, spinning away from the shot, and Jamison couldn't tell if he'd been hit. A second later the skinwalker was back on his feet and crashing toward them.

Jamison shoved Naomi at Coyote. "Get her out of here!"

Naomi screamed as Coyote grabbed her and hauled her to the front door. Jamison began ripping off his clothes, willing the change to come.

Changing without stilling his mind could be painful and made him nauseous, but he had no choice. His limbs jerked as they became the strong legs of a mountain lion, his face aching as the shift took him.

The skinwalker lunged, trying to get past Jamison to Naomi. Jamison knew the strategy: Kill the mate, weaken the Changer.

Jamison leapt, twisting to plant all four paws into the giant creature's chest. The skinwalker's foul stench nearly overwhelmed him, but he held his breath and raked his claws across the being's flesh.

The skinwalker wrapped two huge arms around Jamison and threw him across the kitchen. Jamison regained his feet, running back at the skinwalker as soon as his claws touched the floor.

His full-on attack gave Coyote time to get Naomi out the front door. The skinwalker threw Jamison aside again and charged after them.

The lights of Naomi's pickup sliced across on the skinwalker's body, and he threw up one hand to block the glare. The truck roared at him. Coyote hunched over the wheel, Naomi next to him with the shotgun.

The skinwalker leapt into the house again, shoving Jamison in front of him. The truck's tires squealed as it turned at the last minute.

"Jamison!" Naomi shouted, then Coyote gunned the truck into the street, carrying Naomi to safety.

"Just you and me now," Jamison said.

Skinwalkers could move fast. Legend said they could keep up with speeding trucks, even fly, and Jamison's heart beat wildly in fear that the creature would simply turn and chase Naomi. But the skinwalker stalked Jamison, flicking into the human form of the Alpha Changer Jamison had known for two years.

"I never trusted you," the Alpha hissed.

Jamison morphed back into his own human form. "Looks like you had good reason. Why pretend to be a Changer? Why fool everyone for so long?"

"Changers have a pack. Skinwalkers are alone."

Was it that simple? Jamison wondered. The skinwalker was lonely?

"And as an Alpha Changer you could control others," Jamison said. "Don't bullshit me."

"You were always resistant to the rules. Why? Did you know what I was?"

"The others are sheep," Jamison said in contempt. "They're too scared to exist in the world alongside human beings, they were happy you provided a place they could hide. I didn't want to hide."

"You love your human mate. Pathetic. Changers are stronger when they mate with Changers."

"You inbred the pack down there so much you weakened them. You liked that, so they'd be subordinate to you, and you could continue your charade."

"They could be an army."

"An army afraid to leave their caves? I was surprised to see Matto and Lira up here, but I guess you convinced them I was dangerous to the pack."

"You are dangerous. To me. You die now."

Jamison was morphing back into his cat form before the skinwalker finished his sentence. The skinwalker snarled and lunged at him, the Alpha's form gone now, but instead of fighting, Jamison turned and raced out the back door.

The skinwalker laughed. It came after him, faster than thought. Jamison slammed open the studio and plunged into the darkness inside.

Tables of Jamison's equipment crashed to the floor as the skinwalker charged in behind him. Jamison felt the skinwalker's hands around his neck, yanking him off the floor. The skinwalker began to squeeze while Jamison scratched and fought.

With the last of his strength, Jamison raked him with his back claws, then twisted away, morphing to human as he landed.

The pain of the sudden change sent him to his knees. The skinwalker grabbed him in the dark, and Jamison kicked him away frantically.

He knew by heart where everything in his studio lay. That way, when he worked in a creative frenzy, he could reach out and pick up the exact tool he needed without having to search for it.

He knew how far he had to reach to close his hands around his acetylene torch and lighter. He cranked the torch on full blast right into the skinwalker's face.

The skinwalker screamed. The blue white light of the torch lit the room in a blinding flash. Jamison screwed up his eyes, but kept the torch on the skinwalker.

The skinwalker caught fire. He flailed, screaming, straight into Jamison. He knocked the canister from

Jamison's hands with amazing strength, and the torch exploded into flame on the floor.

The wooden sides of the studio caught quickly, fire licking the dry wood. The copper and glass roof groaned—it wouldn't burn, but if the walls went, the hot metal would crush everything beneath it.

Jamison crawled toward the door, choking on smoke. Behind him, the skinwalker stayed upright, roaring and burning. The creature lunged at Jamison, catching him in his fiery hands. Jamison struggled, but the smoke was suffocating him, flame scoring his flesh.

The studio walls collapsed slowly around them. Jamison morphed back into the mountain lion, fire singeing his fur. The heat was unbearable, his once peaceful studio an inferno.

With a tearing sound, the roof came down. Jamison kicked away from the skinwalker and flattened himself against the stone floor, his body raging with pain. Pieces of glass and wrought iron flew past him like hail.

A section of roof bowed in front of him, scattering the remains of a wall. Jamison leapt for the flame-filled tunnel it created, letting his mountain lion instincts take over. The cat squeezed through the tiny opening, scrambling for the cold desert night.

But the opening was too small, and his cat's body became wedged in the rubble. He was burning, dying, smoke filling his lungs. At least the skinwalker wouldn't make it out, he thought in some satisfaction. And he'd saved the mountain lion sculpture for Naomi.

He dragged in one more breath, feeling his oxygen-starved limbs tingle, his heart trying to beat. His vision went dark.

Hands on his shoulders hurt like hell, and he regained enough strength to snarl. Then his body was being dragged out into the cold, and he heard Naomi swearing and crying.

Coyote started hitting him. Not hitting, he realized as his senses came back, slapping the fire out of his fur. Jamison forced himself to roll over in the cold gravel, then he lay panting, sucking the crisp desert air into his lungs.

The remains of his studio roared with flame. He opened his eyes to see Naomi stretched beside him, weeping. He touched his cat's tongue to her forehead. *Be well, my mate.*

Somewhere beyond this hell he heard the faint wail of sirens as Magellan's fire crew raced toward Naomi's house. With the last of his strength, Jamison morphed back to his human form and lay still.

NINE

"Don't you ever do that to me again." Naomi buried her face in Jamison's chest on her bed, loving the sound of his heartbeat beneath her ear. "Don't you dare decide to send me away and then rush into danger."

She'd thought she'd die when she'd seen the flames erupting from behind her house. She'd made Coyote turn the damn truck around and go back. Thank God she'd spotted Jamison half sticking out from the burning rubble of the studio. She'd raced to him without thought, reaching into the flames to pull him out.

The paramedics had given him oxygen when they'd arrived, but by that time Jamison's burns had decreased dramatically, his Changer body having healed him. The paramedics gave him a once-over then sent him home.

The studio lay in a charred, smoking ruin. The firemen didn't mention finding a corpse inside, and Naomi wondered what had happened to the skinwalker.

In bed in her bedroom, Jamison brushed Naomi's hair from her face and kissed her. "If Coyote hadn't taken you away, the skinwalker would have killed you. He was trying to weaken me by killing my mate. And he'd have been right. Without you, I'd have wanted to die."

"So you let him corner you in your studio?" Naomi said angrily. "Good plan."

"I knew if I could lure him to the studio, I'd have the means to kill him. They don't like fire, remember?" Jamison grinned. "Who says art isn't useful?"

"But you might have died too. You had no way of knowing whether you could get out."

Jamison kissed the corner of her mouth. "If I hadn't killed him, he'd have come after you. I'd do anything to keep that from happening."

Naomi rose on her elbows. "Don't die for me, Jamison. I need you alive."

"You got along all right the two years I was gone."

"No, I didn't." She pulled back the sheets and slid on top of him, thighs straddling his. "I told you I did, but it was bullshit. A part of me was missing, like there was a hole in my life. I need you, and not because you're handy repairing my roof or making pretty sculptures."

Jamison's grin was wicked. "Is it because you need a man between your legs? Please say yes."

"Only partly." Her blood warmed, but she wasn't finished yelling at him yet. "I need to see you every day. I need to hear your beautiful voice. I love how you love Julie and how you made her believe in you. I love *you*, not just how you make love. Although you're good in that department too." She moved her hips, feeling the hard ridge of his erection. He was so solid under her, so male.

"Good," Jamison said in his dark voice. "Because you're a beautiful woman, you're sitting naked on top of me, and your breasts are tight and right where I can touch them." He traced a swollen bud with his thumb.

"So now it's time for seduction?" she asked.

"I hope so." His hand drifted up her back, protective, supportive. "You're going to marry me, aren't you? Even if the Changer bond didn't work, we can bind in the human way."

Naomi's heart squeezed both in joy and regret. Two days before, she'd never heard of the Changer bond, but now she wished they'd have been able to complete it. It meant so much to Jamison.

"I'll marry you," she said. *Now, tomorrow, whenever you want.*

Jamison pulled her down to hold her tight. "Thank you. I'll try to make it a hell of a lot better than your first marriage."

Naomi laughed. "You won't have to work hard for that."

"But I am going to work at it. Because you've done so much for me." He stroked her hair. "I love that you take what life throws at you and face it head-on. I love that you took in a stuck-up Navajo storyteller and made him your love slave."

"You aren't stuck up." She marveled at how he could think that. "You have time for everyone."

"Because you taught me. I thought I was so smart, coming down here to teach white people what life was all about. You and Julie blew away my prejudices with one cup of coffee." His grin widened. "I noticed you didn't argue about the love-slave part."

"I don't mind having a love slave. What are you going to do about it?"

"I'm going to cup your breasts in my hands." He did so, thumbs stroking her areolas. "Then I'm going to lift you a little bit." He slid his hand under her thighs, coaxing her to rise. "Then I'm going to enter you. And I don't feel like being gentle."

In spite of his words, his touch was tenderness itself as he lowered her onto him.

His next thrust was not so calm. Jamison tightened his grip on her hips and pulled her onto him, stabbing deep into her.

"I love it," she whispered, her head dropping back. "Jamison, I don't care that the bonding ceremony didn't work. I love you."

"Love you too," Jamison said, then his rumbling voice drifted into groans, and he made love to her as though he'd never let her go.

*O*utside, something stirred under the remains of the smoldering copper roof. A blackened hand pushed away a sheet of hot roofing, and a monster crawled out. He was a burned husk, hair gone, eyes blind, but he moved with determination. *Kill.*

He sensed something sitting in wait for him, a white presence, though he couldn't see it. He stopped.

Coyote, in his animal form, put one paw onto the remains of the skinwalker and pulled back in distaste.

"Why don't you just die?" he growled.

"I am a skinwalker," the thing rasped. "More powerful than any Changer. I will kill you."

"Bad luck for you," Coyote said. "I'm not a Changer."

He blew his breath onto the skinwalker. The half-dead beast screamed once, then shuddered, mewled, and dissolved into dust.

"Done," Coyote said in a deep voice.

He looked up at the house. Even though the windows were closed, Coyote's superior hearing picked up the excited sounds of sex. He licked his lips. He could climb up there and watch them. That might be fun.

He laughed, imagining the look on Naomi's face if he did.

Coyote threw back his head and gave the starlit sky one determined howl. Then he turned and loped through the deserted parking lot of Hansen's, heading down the road toward the Crossroads Bar.

*T*he depot was deserted and dark when Naomi parked the truck in front of it just before dawn. The celebration was long over, the lights extinguished, the depot locked.

Coyote's message had told them to meet him there.

He'd left the scrawled note on top of the quilt under which Jamison and Naomi had slept. Which meant he'd crept in there while they'd been naked and entwined. The shit.

Naomi and Jamison climbed to the deserted platform behind the depot. It was freezing, and their breath hung heavily in the starlit air.

The night held no terror for Naomi now. The skinwalker was dead, and Jamison was alive, and they would marry after the Christmas celebrations. Coyote helping her save Jamison was the best Christmas gift anyone could have given her.

That didn't mean it wasn't damn cold out there. "He'd better show up soon," Naomi muttered. "And I still don't understand why he sent you down to those awful people in Mexico."

Jamison slid his arm around her. "I think he did because there was no one closer to teach me. Whatever else the Changer pack did, they taught me how to control my ability and use it well. If I hadn't learned that, I probably would have gone insane, like Alex Clay. I never could have returned to you."

"Maybe," Naomi said grudgingly. "But Coyote should have checked on you."

"He's a god. He doesn't follow our rules."

"I'm just glad he was here to help you now." She shivered, thinking of what might have been. Jamison tightened his hold on her, leaning her back against him.

They waited in silence. The railroad bed stretched to the horizon, a straight man-made line running across a land creased with winding arroyos.

An icy wind whispered across Naomi's cheek. She turned to look north, in the direction of the wind, and squinted at something flickering out in the desert.

Footsteps sounded behind them on the platform. "Hey," Coyote said. He wore his usual jeans and leather coat and carried a small duffel bag over his shoulder.

"Hey yourself," Naomi answered. "Why are we here?"

Coyote grinned. "To see the real Ghost Train."

"What are you up to?" Jamison asked him, but Coyote held up his hand.

"They're coming. Look."

The chill wind touched Naomi's cheek again, and the flickering she'd seen grew brighter. A small cloud of dust drifted silently over the desert.

When the dust cleared, she saw figures moving along the railroad bed, walking single file on the raised earth. The figures were those of men and women, ghostly and nearly transparent. They were Native American, dressed in Navajo wool or in leather and skins. Silver glittered here and there along with the flash of turquoise.

"I feel this," Jamison said softly. "This is real."

"Who are they?" Naomi asked.

Coyote's voice was slow and quiet. "Magellan is a crossroads. The way is thinner here between this world and the ones below it. On this night, the land remembers the crossing of so many from life to what lies beyond."

Naomi's eyes widened. "So the Ghost Train is a train of *people*?"

"It's no coincidence that you refer to the place the highway ends and the bar there as the Crossroads. The railroad was built on top of an ancient trail. It's no coincidence that the service closed down either."

"I thought it was because it was too expensive to run," Naomi said.

Coyote chuckled. "Naomi the Unbeliever."

"She believes now," Jamison said. "She believes in what's real."

Coyote's grin vanished. "Look at the land around us. It looks flat, dry, empty. But you have lived here all your life—you know that there are hundreds of arroyos and canyons and washes that crease the land, their banks so sharp you don't see them until you're right on top of them."

"Yes," Naomi said impatiently. "I know that."

"They are cracks in the earth. Things can fall into them. And things can come out of them."

So Jamison's stories had told her. "Things," Naomi repeated. "Like the skinwalker?"

"Worse than any skinwalker you will ever see. I know this. I came from the cracks in the earth." He looked at them staring at him, but he didn't laugh. "The time is coming when you will have to believe, Unbeliever. We will need you both."

"We who?" Naomi asked, mystified.

Coyote watched the ghostly figures parading silently past without answering, then he shouldered his duffel bag.

"Time for me to go. I've got places to visit, people to save, villains to annoy." He winked at Naomi. "You two stay out of trouble. I can't always be saving your asses."

Jamison tightened his arms around Naomi. "I'll take care of her."

"And she'll take care of you." Coyote laughed. "Have to go now."

He leaned over and kissed a startled Naomi full on the mouth. Then he hoisted his bag, jumped from the platform, ran up to the top of the railroad bed, and fell into step with the walking figures. Coyote was real, substantial and colorful against his pale companions.

He headed south with them, the line now stretching as far as they could see. A cold wind rippled the dried desert grasses, then the entire column of figures wavered and vanished. Coyote vanished with them.

The two on the platform stood in silence, staring at the empty desert.

Jamison blew out his breath. "I've seen a lot, but I've never seen anything like that."

"Was it real?" Naomi asked, her voice hushed.

"It was real," a new voice grated beside them.

Naomi swung around. An elderly Navajo man, bundled in a fleece-lined jacket, was standing next to them, watching the place where Coyote had vanished.

"Grandfather," Jamison said. "What are you doing here?"

"I came to pay my respects to the Ghost Train."

Naomi noticed he spoke English, not Navajo. She wondered at the courtesy, the first he'd ever shown her.

Grandfather Kee looked at Jamison with warm, dark eyes. "You are strong, Jamison. Coyote did well for you."

"Are you a Changer?" Naomi asked. "Jamison told me it ran in families."

The old man shook his head. "I am a descendant of the original Changer tribe, yes, but I do not have the talent. I did not know Jamison did, either, until Jamison told me Coyote was taking him away." Tears gathered in his eyes. "But I knew that where Coyote sent you would strengthen you, prepare you. And he was right. You made it home, you defeated a skinwalker. You are very strong, and he knew it. He feared you."

"How do you know all this?" Naomi asked him.

"Coyote told me." Grandfather Kee smiled a little. "Coyote told me many things. About how you tried to bond like a Changer."

Jamison nodded, and Naomi again felt the sadness of their failure. "We tried. It didn't work."

To Naomi's amazement, Grandfather Kee burst out laughing. She'd never heard him laugh before.

"Jamison, you are such a fool," he said. "You think a ceremony with turquoise and smoke is what it takes to make a bond. Did you not tell me that when you took coffee with this woman the first time you knew she was meant for you?"

"Yes," Jamison said slowly.

"When you were born, your grandmother prophesied that you would find happiness only outside your own kind. You were so angry about that, remember? And didn't you tell me after you met Naomi that your grandmother had been right?"

"Yes to everything, Grandfather."

"You are already bonded to her, Jamison. You are bonded by spirit and by soul. By love. I knew it when you first brought Naomi home."

"I thought you didn't approve of me," Naomi said.

"Not true, child. I saw how much in love you both were, and how much Jamison loved your daughter. It reminded me of what your grandmother and I had together, what I had lost. While I am happy for you, it also makes me sad." His dark eyes filled. "I am only half a man without her."

Jamison's eyes grew moist. "Grandfather." He enfolded the man in a heartfelt hug.

Grandfather Kee pulled Naomi down to give her a kiss on the cheek. He took her hand and Jamison's and pressed them together.

"You are one," he said. "The bond between you is true. I am shaman. I can see."

Naomi's hopeful gaze met Jamison's, and Jamison realized that his grandfather was right. The instant connection he'd felt with Naomi had been his destiny fulfilling itself. And hers. During his absence she'd remained true to him, even while telling herself she shouldn't. She hadn't sought comfort elsewhere or even gotten rid of his things.

Julie had known, and his grandfather had known. Even Coyote had known.

"Why didn't the Alpha know?" Naomi asked. "You said that he thought we hadn't completed the bond."

"He wasn't a true Changer," Grandfather Kee said. "He just wanted to be one."

"I guess I need to catch up too," Jamison said.

Naomi laughed in her beautiful, unself-conscious way. Her smile was wicked. "I can think of many things we can catch up on."

Jamison's grandfather regarded her with twinkling dark eyes. "After your Christmas day in Tucson, you will come to see us and bring young Julie. We all miss her."

"We'll be there," Jamison said. He embraced his grandfather again, his eyes wet. "Thank you."

Grandfather Kee squeezed Jamison's shoulders, gave him a dignified nod, then turned and walked away, fading like the ghosts into the lingering darkness.

Jamison took Naomi's hand, led her to her warm, familiar truck, and drove her home.

*   *   *

Later as Naomi snuggled down on Jamison's bare shoulder, she murmured, "We have so many homes now. This one, my folks' place in Tucson, and your family in Chinle. Kind of nice for an only child."

"Julie's an only child," Jamison said in a speculative voice.

Naomi laughed and kissed the tip of his nose. "If we keep this up, she won't be for long."

Jamison's eyes warmed, his kiss when he pulled her down to him both loving and heat-stirring. "Then as the years go by, we'll have even more homes to go to on Christmas."

"Fine with me." Naomi opened her arms as he slid on top of her. "My Changer mate. I wouldn't have it any other way."

Allyson James writes nationally bestselling, award-winning romances, mysteries, and mainstream fiction under several pseudonyms. She lives in the desert Southwest with her husband and cats and spends most of her time in the world of her stories. A list of Allyson's current books and upcoming releases can be found on her website, www.allysonjames.com, or contact Allyson via e-mail at allysonjames@cox.net. And keep an eye out for *Stormwalker* by Allyson James, coming in Spring 2010!

Sweet
Enchantment

Anya Bast

ONE

*B*ella had vowed to never bind her life to this man's. Now here she was, about to do it. Worse, she'd made the decision only two seconds after learning of his predicament.

Ronan still didn't know she'd entered his cell. He knelt before her, his arms extended to either side, his wrists wrapped in heavy charmed iron chain, and his gaze fastened on the cracked cement floor of the cell.

How low the great mage of the Seelie Court had sunk. The only charmed iron chain in the whole of the Seelie Rose Tower resided within the walls of Her Majesty's Prison, and he was wrapped in every inch of it. His dark hair hung over his face, and his biceps and muscular bare back flexed as he moved uncomfortably against his bonds.

Bella liked the fact that the mage, Ronan Achaius Quinn, was in such a subservient position to her. He wasn't a man who was subservient to anyone unless forced by charmed iron to be so.

For a moment she allowed her gaze to trace over him. She'd never seen a more beautifully made man in her life. Not before the day she'd clapped eyes on him and not af-

terward. The sight of him made a woman want the iron silk
of his body rubbing up against hers, made carnal thoughts
crowd the most prudish of female minds.

His long black hair shadowed his square jaw, the sensual
pout of his mouth, and the icy blue eyes that were known
for being able to draw the truth from the worst of liars. He
wore only a pair of loose black trousers, leaving his feet
and upper half bare. Ronan always wore black, even here
in prison. His sculpted, powerful body moved a little as
he tried to find the comfort his captors were so set on not
giving him. He was strong not only in body and mind, but
in magick too. However, the charmed iron neutralized the
abilities he possessed. It was his sorcerer's skills that normally kept him very high in the Summer Queen's graces.

Not so tonight.

The Seelie wanted to kill him and she could hardly blame
them. However, she couldn't allow it. She couldn't let Ronan
come to harm, no matter what lay between them or what
he'd done to land himself here. It didn't matter that once he'd
shredded her heart. It didn't matter that she'd vowed never to
offer any part of herself to him ever again. She'd been a fool
to think she could ever keep a promise like that.

❧ "I can smell your perfume, Bella," Ronan said in a broken, gravelly voice, without looking up. "I've never forgotten your scent. I know it's you."

She shivered at his words and then shook it off. It was
silly to think it was romantic. He was a mage, after all,
even when stripped of his magick by charmed iron. He had
a nose for different scents because of his work. His power
was innate, allowing him to twist leaf, flower, and herb into
powerful spells.

Not only was he a mage, he was only just on the barest
side of Seelie. Ronan possessed Unseelie blood, enough
to allow him to cast dark spells. The Summer Queen, the
Seelie Royal, allowed him to remain in the Rose Tower
because of the strength of his magick and, undoubtedly,
his physical beauty. And perhaps there was a part of her
that enjoyed thumbing her nose at the Shadow King, the

Unseelie Royal, by denying him one of his strongest court members.

Ronan was one of the few members of the Seelie Court who possessed Unseelie blood, but he wasn't the only one who had it.

She cleared her throat. "Ronan, it's been a long time."

"The last time we spoke in more than just passing, it wasn't a happy occasion."

A slight tremor shook her body. No, it hadn't been a happy occasion at all. Ronan had broken her heart into so many pieces it had taken decades to put back together. Maybe it still wasn't healed.

"Yes, and look at you now." Her voice held the bitter edge of memory.

She walked around his body, her expensive gold and white heels clicking on the gritty cell floor and the trailing edge of her pure white stole brushing through dirt. She'd been at a Seelie Court ball sharing conversation with her dearest friend, Aislinn, when she'd received the news of Ronan's arrest. It was cold outside—almost Yule. The Seelie often held balls, but they were especially frequent during this time of the year. Despite all that lay between them, not the foulest Unseelie goblin could have stopped her from racing to the prison.

She came to a halt in front of him.

Pulling against his chains, biceps flexing, he finally looked up at her. His hair slipped over his forehead, and he gave his head a sharp shake to move it to the side. The man was handsome enough to break any woman's heart, and he'd broken more than just hers, Bella was certain. He was much older than she was—though they appeared the same age. That was the way it worked with nearly immortal *Tuatha Dé Danann*. Once they reached the age of thirty, their aging slowed to a crawl. However that didn't hold for experience. At nearly a century her senior, he had far more life experience than she did, and that meant he'd broken far more hearts. He had kept his affairs quiet since their breakup, however. She had to give him that much. At least she hadn't had to endure watching other women on his arm.

His gaze roved over her body—clad in a filmy white and gold gown. She knew what he saw. The dress was low-cut, delving deeply at her cleavage, and it was tight, appearing to be painted onto her waist and hips and dipping down to the small of her back. He looked at her like he wasn't in chains, like she didn't hold his fate in her hands. He looked at her like he had a right. It piqued her that he thought he could stare at her like that. It did other things too. Things it shouldn't.

"It's been a long time, Bella." He paused, swallowed. "You're still the most beautiful woman ever to walk the streets of Piefferburg." His voice was rich and deep, full of the sincerity she'd fallen for once.

Her cheeks heated. Anger welled, and she forced herself not to pull the stole around her body.

She slipped a hand to her hip. "What were you thinking, taking a job from the Phaendir? Are you insane? You had to know that if you were caught the Summer Queen would want to kill you."

He slanted her the cocky grin she knew so well. "Insane? Well, you know me, Bella. What do you think?"

She turned her face away and bit her lower lip. "They plan to take your head for this. Your status as the Summer Queen's pet mage won't protect you. *No one* allies with the Phaendir and escapes the consequences."

"I've lived almost two hundred years, Bella. It won't be a tragedy for the world to give me up, or for me to give the world up."

"Sweet Danu, Ronan! "Do you have some kind of death wish? Is that why you did this?"

He only bowed his head in response, arms pulling at his bonds.

She paced away from him, toward the cell door, folding her arms over her chest and wrapping her stole more closely around her against the chill. The cold permeating her bones had less to do with the damp prison than with what she was about to do. She halted and closed her eyes, gathering her courage.

How could she just rip her heart out of her chest and lay it on a slab to be sacrificed—again—this way? But the alternative . . . She couldn't bear to think about it.

"Ronan," she started, turning toward him. "I've told the Summer Queen I'm taking you as my husband and she agreed to it." She paused. "We're getting married, you and I. It will protect you. It's the only thing that will save you from the Wild Hunt."

The Wild Hunt went out every night and gathered the souls of those fae who'd died. After the Summer Queen took Ronan's head, the Hunt would be coming for him.

Ronan raised his head, but said nothing. For the first time in the thirty years she'd known him, apparently her words had struck him speechless. Finally, "Bella—"

"I can't watch them kill you, no matter how stupid you are." She lifted her chin. "I will marry you, but it will be in name only. You'll get no . . . privileges from me. No money, because I'll want you to sign a prenuptial agreement. You'll have to live with me, of course, but my apartment is large and there's only Lolly, my housekeeper, and I there now. We'll be able to stay somewhat separated." She pressed her lips together. "You'll get to keep your life. It's a good deal."

"So the great Bella Rhiannon Caliste Mac Lyr of a pure *Tuatha Dé Danann* bloodline has finally selected a suitor and he's a prisoner slated for death. A man who pulled a job for the Phaendir, no less. Marked forever for scorn in the Rose Tower. A thief with Unseelie blood. The Seelie are laughing at you right now. Back at the ball you rushed from, they're snickering behind their gloved hands and into snifters of cognac at this whole situation."

All true, but it didn't matter. "You're not a suitor." Her voice came out in a harsh snap. "Once you were, maybe, thirty years ago. Briefly. Right now you're just an old friend whose ass needs saving." She turned away from him. "I can't tell you how much I'm sacrificing to do this."

Emotionally. Psychologically. "Aren't you even going to say thank you?"

"I'm going to say no."

"No?" She whirled. "What? You can't say no. You—"

He gave his head a shake and looked up at her. His normally icy blue pupils were wide and dark, his hands clenched. "I want you, Bella, but when we come together, we do it my way. On my terms. I'll make you mine, not the other way around."

Danu, the arrogance. Nothing about him had changed. "The only thing you'll ever lay claim to is the worms that will nibble your flesh when your headless body is buried."

She whirled and went for the door, then halted, laying her hand against the cool steel frame and closing her eyes for a moment. It figured this was happening at Yuletide, the time of greatest darkness throughout the year. Even as stupid and stubborn as he was, she wouldn't let him die. She'd go to the Summer Queen and figure out a way to force him to marry her.

She'd save his life today and he could hate her for it tomorrow.

Ronan bowed his head and made fists, working the blood through his arms and trying to ignore the slight sting of the iron. It was an effective torture for the fae. Normally charmed iron not only nulled a fae's magick, it made him sick. Eventually, if the iron was left on the skin for too long, it would kill. However as a mage who was particularly susceptible to the metal, he'd worked for years on developing a resistance to it. He murmured under his breath and blue green magick sparked in his palms. His magick wasn't as strong as when he didn't have charmed iron touching his skin, but it was strong enough.

Bloody hell, could it be? Did Bella still have a flicker of feeling for him? He thought he'd killed that off along with everything else good in his life a long time ago. For the first time in decades, hope flared to life inside him.

Maybe he had something to live for after all.

He needed to find out for certain. That meant there was no way he was going to rot in here any longer. Not with Bella out there still caring for him.

And, *bloody hell*, she'd looked so good. His hands curled involuntarily remembering how satiny smooth her skin looked. He couldn't wait to run his fingers over it, his tongue. That dress she'd been wearing was like sin woven into fabric the way it showcased her full, delectable breasts and how it tapered down her long, slender, kissable back. He wanted to plunge his hands into her thick fall of dark hair, wanted her legs around his waist while he fucked her until she couldn't see straight. He wanted to put his claim on her, make her his in every way he could. It had been a long time since he'd been with a woman.

None but Bella would do.

Bella was his. He'd given her up once, but he'd learned his lesson. No way was he ever doing it again.

Ronan began to plot his escape.

TWO

$\mathcal{B}$ ella crossed the stone floor of her living room, feeling the chill of the night even through her slippers. Not even the thickly woven rugs her people were so famous for could keep out the cold. Wrapping her silk bathrobe more firmly around her, she sank onto a settee in front of the well-insulated floor-to-ceiling sheet of glass that served as her apartment's outside wall. She had a wonderful view of Piefferburg from the third-to-top floor of the Seelie Court residence. Only the Summer Queen above her had a better view, and perhaps Aislinn Christiana Guinevere Finvarra, her even more highly placed friend.

The building was organized by social rank. Bella's blood was very pure, her parentage nearly pristine Seelie *Tuatha Dé Danann*—no Unseelie, trooping fae, or wilding blood at all. As far as was public knowledge, anyway. Bella had suspected for a long time that she carried Unseelie in her gene pool. But as far as the Summer Court was concerned, she was descended from the original *Tuatha Dé Danann* bloodlines of Ireland. They themselves had been immigrants from Scandinavia, and before that . . . Well, no one knew for certain, but there was much speculation about their origin.

When she'd gone to the Summer Queen to demand Ronan's hand even though he'd told her no, she'd expected the queen to agree because of Bella's high placement at court. The Summer Queen had denied her petition, however, wanting to see blood flow. Not even her rank and Ronan's previously high status would sway the Seelie Royal. The queen wanted Ronan's head and now she had every reason to take it.

Ronan would die in the morning. The Wild Hunt would collect his soul the next night. Bella had to resign herself to the reality of the situation.

Her stomach leaden, she glanced down at the large square that separated the Seelie and Unseelie Courts. The Seelie Court was called the Rose Tower because it was constructed of rose quartz. The Unseelie Court was referred to as the Black Tower because—never to be outdone—it was made from black quartz. The delivery of large quantities of each had been allowed by human society and the Phaendir, and magick had been employed to make them useable as construction material.

Below her she could barely make out two figures—brownies, she thought—cavorting and playing in the softly falling snow. The whole city was awash in Yule parties at this time of the season. Elderberry wine, the traditionally favored drink of the fae, flowed fast and furiously. Mortals even risked passage beyond the city limits to partake of the festivities, though not all would make it back. That was the rule of Piefferburg, a prison sometimes called Purgatory, borrowing from human Christian tradition, by those who lived here. No fae could leave the city, but humans could enter, so long as they understood they became prey to anything that lived here once they passed the boundaries.

They still came. The fools.

The Phaendir, a powerful guild of druids, had created and still controlled the borders of Piefferburg with warding. They called it a "resettlement area."

If one wanted to be philosophical about it, the fate of the fae was poetic punishment for the horrible fae race wars of the early 1600s that had decimated their population and left them easy prey to their common enemy, the Phaendir. The wars had forced the fae from the underground, and the humans had panicked in the face of the truth—the fae were real.

On top of the wars, a mysterious sickness called Watt Syndrome had also befallen them. Some thought the illness had been created by the Phaendir. However it had come about, the result was the same—it had further weakened them.

That's when the Phaendir had allied with the humans to imprison them in an area of what had then been the New World, founded by a human named Jules Piefferburg.

These days the sects of fae who'd warred in the 1600s had reached an uneasy peace. Trapped together in Piefferburg, they were united against the Phaendir because that old human saying was true—the enemy of my enemy is my friend. Most fae felt a surprising lack of animosity toward humans who'd been so frightened of the fae and so manipulated by the Phaendir.

But not *all* of the fae felt that way.

These days the humans weren't just frightened of the fae, they were also highly fascinated by them. They passed the borders of Piefferburg knowing they took their lives in their hands, yet unable to resist the draw. It had always been that way, since the dawn of human evolution. Humans were like moths drawn to the seductive and magickal faery flame. It was one of the reasons the fae had chosen to go underground so many thousands of years ago.

The Summer Queen had even allowed a human film crew to stay in residence at the Seelie Court. They produced a television show for the mortals called *Faemous*, which followed the social frolicking of the Rose Tower. Apparently it was the most popular program on human television. Humans were so enthralled with them that they would sit on a couch and watch fae lives played out rather than live their own lives. It was ridiculous, in Bella's opinion.

Never to be outdone, the Shadow King, who ruled the

Unseelie Court, had allowed a film crew in too, but they'd quickly become someone's appetizers, or so Bella had heard.

She gazed across the great square to the hulking black quartz high-rise of the Unseelie Court, a place forever locked in a cold war with the shining Rose Tower. The Summer Queen only allowed in those with the untainted blood of the Seelie *Tuatha Dé Danann*, and even they were subject to a strict hierarchy. Although the occasional Unseelie nobles, if they possessed certain qualities, were permitted residence.

The Shadow King of the Unseelie Court took all kinds, any monster with fae blood, any creature bred between two immortals. The only prerequisite for being a member of the Black Tower was a willingness to spill blood, either into your mouth or onto the floor, it didn't matter.

Ronan would be welcome. So, maybe, would she, since she wielded the dark arts. But the thought of living in such violence and chaos, among such monsters, made her shudder.

As she watched the soft white flakes of snow fall into the velvety darkness, movement caught her eye across the square. Lifting off into the black was the Lord of the Wild Hunt and his entourage. That mysterious figure and his Host made her blood ice more than Jack Frost's Yuletide decoration of her windows. No one knew the man's identity. All anyone knew was that he was a member of the Unseelie Court, and that he and his Host sometimes meted out brutal punishment to those fae who broke the law. They also reaped the souls of the Fae after they died and escorted them to the afterlife. Every night they collected them.

They'd be coming for Ronan soon.

She turned her face away from the sight of the Lord of the Hunt's Host rising into the dark, snowy skies on massive stallion hooves and the soft padded feet of netherworld hounds. To distract herself from her thoughts, she grabbed the remote and flipped the TV on across the room. *Faemous* exploded onto the screen. She should have known; her housekeeper loved the twenty-four-hour-a-day coverage of the court as much as the humans.

As she went to turn it off, Ronan's face filled the huge dimension of the screen. Bella paused.

In other news, Ronan Achaius Quinn, once celebrated Seelie Court mage, is scheduled for a morning beheading after working for the Phaendir without the Summer Queen's leave. It's unknown what sort of job he performed for the Phaendir, but it was enough to incur Her Majesty's wrath.

A photo of herself popped onto the screen and Bella rolled her eyes.

One must wonder how Bella Rhiannon Caliste Mac Lyr is feeling tonight. After a scorching romance all thought long extinguished some thirty years ago, today she attempted to save the mage's life by marrying him. As we know, she has resisted all suitors and has done so for the last three decades, ever since they parted ways. Apparently our suspicions about her still holding a torch for Ronan were correct. The announcer's voice lowered a bit, and you could practically hear the arch of the human male's brow. *Word is, he said no. We wonder—*

Bella flipped the TV off. She threw the remote to the settee and looked around her spacious, luxurious . . . empty apartment. There had been a moment or two when she'd been looking forward to sharing this space with someone . . . with Ronan. The announcer on *Faemous* had been right—she'd never stopped carrying a torch for him. For decades she'd tried very hard to hide that from the rest of the court, but now it would be apparent to all and she would be a laughingstock.

She didn't regret it. She'd done all she could to save his mangy hide. His death would not weigh on her conscience.

It would only weigh on her heart.

Making a noise of disgust that echoed through her living room and into her darkened kitchen, and made her feel even lonelier than she had a moment ago, she turned and walked into her bedroom. This place was huge, yet she felt strangled most of the time. The Seelie Court was the most luxurious place in Piefferburg, yet to Bella it felt like a morgue. Stifling, too close. She longed just once to go beyond the bounds of the court and see the rest of Pief-ferburg, like the *Ceantar Láir*, fae suburbs as they were called, where the trooping fae that weren't a part of the courts or the wild places lived. Or even the Boundary Lands, where vine and tree grew within and intertwined with the shambles of old buildings, and where the wild and solitary fae had made their homes.

She also dreamt of seeing the human world. Like many fae, she wondered what it would be like to be free. Rumor had it Ronan had seen it. Ronan had been everywhere, seen everything. He was allowed so much more freedom as a partial-blood Seelie mage than she was as a pureblood Seelie *Tuatha Dé*.

The irony was that she wasn't pureblood Seelie at all.

It was a secret she'd only ever shared with her best friend, Aislinn. Bella could twist curses with her thoughts. She'd first noticed it around the time she'd turned seven, the same time a fae's magick normally began to awaken.

Her mother and father had lived in the Rose Tower's courtyard, next to a great Seelie lady who didn't like children. The neighbor's pride and joy had been an elaborate flower garden in her yard which she kept nourished with her magick even through the dead of winter. One day Aislinn accidently left her favorite doll at the edge of the garden and the lady had incinerated it on the spot, making Bella's best friend cry. Bella had been so angry that she'd stood in her parents' yard and stared hard at her neighbor's labor, those roses, lilies, and orchids she kept so perfectly tended, and had wished them to wilt and die.

By the morning Bella's will had been done. All that was left of the woman's beautiful garden was rows of drooping gray flower heads and scorched grass.

That was Unseelie magick, dark magick. Bella had begun to wonder about her bloodline. Began to suspect. And then she'd noticed some of her other stray dark thoughts begin to manifest: her wish that her mother's piano would be destroyed so she wouldn't have to take lessons anymore; her hope that the water main in the school would break so they would have a free day.

And then she'd known for certain she was strong Unseelie.

She'd wondered if her mother had had an affair with one of the Unseelie court males, but the Rose and Black Towers had almost no interaction at all. In addition, her mother's blood hardly ran hot, and she was not at all inclined to passion or impulsiveness. No, it was more likely that her father was really her father, but that somewhere down her genetic line someone had strayed to Unseelie and by some trick of fate the blood had shown up so gloriously bright in her.

Unwilling to worry them, Bella had never confronted her parents about her dark art. If she was discovered with Unseelie blood, the Summer Queen would banish her entire family from the Rose Tower and, as their money was dependent on the court, they'd be left destitute. She'd simply learned to lock down her thoughts with an iron will, not allowing herself to do any damage to anyone, making sure she didn't inadvertently back any negative thoughts with magick.

Luckily her ability to manipulate physical flame had also developed and she could present that soft, benign magickal face to the world. She could blow out candles from across the room and make the fire in her hearth grow brighter or dimmer—that's all that power was strong enough for. But strength of magick wasn't a prized asset in the Rose Tower. Here it was all about your bloodline . . . and your fashion sense.

It was better for people to think her a weak *Tuatha Dé Danann* with pure blood than the powerful Unseelie she suspected she was.

Bella had confided her secret in Aislinn because Aislinn also possessed Unseelie blood. It had forged a bond between them and they became closer than sisters. Perhaps some subconscious link had drawn them to be friends in childhood; Bella didn't know. She was just grateful they had each other to lean on.

Maybe Ronan suspected the blight on her bloodline. Maybe that was why he'd rejected her . . . twice.

"Stubborn man," she muttered and slammed her bedroom door shut.

*L*ying awake in her bed, Bella heard a slight sound a moment before a huge hand closed over her mouth. Terror jolted through her veins and she kicked and struggled until Ronan's face came into view.

"Don't scream."

She shook her head and he released her. Bella scrambled back away from him a little. "You scared a year off my life, Ronan! How did you get out? Why are you here?"

"I'm here because you're here, Bell."

Bell. Once she'd loved it when he'd called her that.

"Bel*la*."

"I came because I had to talk to you."

"Talk to me? You broke out of prison just to talk to me?" She blinked. Was she still dreaming? Nope, wide awake. "You're slated for death in the morning."

He grinned. "Did you really think I was going to stick around for that?"

"I never thought you had a choice."

He was not wearing a shirt. The realization slammed into her fast and hard. Not only was Ronan in her bedroom in the middle of the night, he was shirtless. A bare-chested Ronan was her worst weakness. She refused to let her gaze slide down past his broad shoulders to that muscular, golden silk-over-steel expanse. If she looked at his chest, she'd want to glide her hands over it, and she couldn't afford such brainless impulses right now.

"Seems I did."

"You turned down my offer of marriage. Did you prefer death to being with me?"

"You're being dramatic."

"Am I?" She made a frustrated sound and looked away from him. "Look, I don't want to bicker with you right now.

I was sleeping. What gives you the right to break in here and harass me?" She waved her hand. "Just go off and try to escape. Good luck with that, by the way. I predict you'll be back in charmed iron by morning."

"You weren't sleeping."

"How do you know?" She hadn't been, of course. How could she sleep knowing the morning would bring his head rolling across the throne room floor?

"I remember the way you breathe when you sleep, Bella."

Her chest tightened and all rational thought left her for a moment. They'd never had sex, but they *had* slept together once. Just once. He'd held her from twilight until dawn. It was one of the times in her life when she'd felt perfectly content, so she recalled it vividly. "That was decades ago and it was only one time. There's no way you could remember that."

A slight smile twisted his full mouth and his light blue eyes glittered in the half light. "Yes, it was decades ago, but I memorized how you breathe that night. I replay it in my dreams."

She went motionless, caught breathless with her gaze locked on his. She had no idea what to say to that, and definitely didn't know how to feel. The moonlight streamed in through the window, bleaching the color from his face and painting it in shades of silver. His eyes were serious, focused—intent on her in a way that made her shiver. As if he'd decided she was his. After the rejection. After all these years.

Suddenly she knew how to feel—*angry.*

"I have to go soon. Before I leave, I have things I need to say to you."

"You have nothing to say that I want to hear." Her breath hissed from between her clenched teeth. "Where are you going?"

"I can't tell you."

She threw her hands up. "How did you get out of the prison?"

He flashed a cocky smile. "Did you really think they could keep me?"

"Yes, actually. They had you mired in charmed iron up to your neck." She studied him. "If you could escape, why didn't you do it earlier?"

"I didn't have a reason until you came to see me, Bella. You still care about me. There's still a seed of emotion in you for me. I thought I'd crushed it a long time ago, but it's still there." He held out a hand to her.

What? Her mind whirled with all the implications of his words.

She looked toward the door, needing a way out. There might be a bit of truth to what he said, but it wasn't something she wanted to face right now. He'd hurt her so badly. The last thing she needed was to show him her soft underbelly again and allow him to snap out another bloody chunk.

"You presume too much," she said in her best icy voice.

He dropped his hand.

A hard pounding on her front door made her jump. The Summer Queen's Imperial Guard, most likely. She leapt from the bed and grabbed his hand, pulling him toward her walk-in closet.

He resisted a little. "Where are you leading me?"

"I have a secret room behind my shoe rack."

"Why do you have a secret room?"

She glanced at him. "Do you think I would serve in a place as treacherous as the Summer Queen's court without a safe place to go?"

She flipped on the light and pulled a knob on the wall containing her dozens of pairs of designer shoes. A panel slid open and she pushed him through.

He hesitated, looking back at her. "How do I know you won't turn me over to them?"

"You don't." She gave him a final shove and closed the panel back in place.

THREE

$\mathcal{F}$lipping the closet light back off and going into her bedroom, she grabbed her bathrobe off the end of the bed. By now Lolly, her house hobgoblin, should've answered the door.

"Can I help you?" Bella asked, squinting against the light in the foyer and tying her silk wrap more firmly around her. Lolly, a knobby, wrinkled hobgoblin of about five feet tall, stood near the two guards. A more loyal housekeeper was never to be found, and right now Lolly looked upset that the keepers of fae law were shadowing their doorstep. The guards were both dressed in head-to-toe rose and gold metal and wearing heavy black boots and helms. Shining swords hung at their sides. The fae had never really gotten on board with firearms.

The Imperial Guard was primarily made up of lower-blood sons and daughters of the *Tuatha Dé*. All were fiercely loyal to their queen. They had unmatched speed and strength and were well suited for their position.

"We're very sorry to disturb you, my lady. We are looking for an escaped prisoner," said the one on the left.

She crossed her arms over her chest. "Ronan Achaius Quinn, no doubt."

"Yes, Miss Mac Lyr."

Bella smiled at Lolly, who stood as if ready to defend her mistress's home with her life. "Thank you for answering the door. You can go back to bed, dear."

Lolly nodded once, glared at the guard, and melted back down the darkened hallway.

Bella turned her attention back to the men. "As you are already aware, since all of Piefferburg and the free world is also aware, I asked Ronan Quinn to marry me to save him from the Wild Hunt and he refused. He chose *death* over marriage to me. Why do you think he would come here?"

"By order of the Summer Queen, we're checking everywhere."

She stepped to the side and used a supercilious tone of voice. "All right, then, search my apartment if you feel the need, but it's a waste of your time and mine. I'd prefer to be sleeping."

"Apologies, my lady."

She waved her hand dismissively and they moved past her. Sinking down on the edge of her couch, she watched as they searched her place. The soft recessed lighting of the room glowed on their rose and gold armor as they respectfully moved pieces of furniture and checked possible hiding places. She held her breath as they investigated her walk-in closet, but they found nothing.

"Thank you for your attention to this matter. You serve Her Majesty well," Bella said, escorting them to the door. "I hope you find the bastard. Since he refused me, I'd just as soon see his head roll."

"Causing his head to roll is our objective, my lady. Have a restful night," one of them replied as they left.

Once the door closed, Bella leaned her hand against the wall and slumped a little, releasing the breath she'd been holding.

The sound of shuffling slippers met her ears. "Is everything all right, my lady?"

Bella straightened and smiled at her housekeeper. "It's fine, Lolly. I just don't like having the Imperial Guard looking for a fugitive in my home, especially when it's the man who has made me the laughingstock of the court . . . twice."

Lolly nodded her wizened brown head. "It's been an eventful day, to say the least. Would you like me to make you some peppermint tea?"

"That's kind of you, but I'm exhausted. I think I'll just retire for the night and hope no one else pounds on our door. You should get some sleep too."

Lolly bowed her head and turned. "As you wish, my lady."

After the light in the hallway had flipped off and Lolly's bedroom door was once again closed, Bella hurried in and released Ronan from the hidey-hole. "They're gone," she said, and then gasped as he pressed her backward, crowding her against the closet wall behind her. Magick snapped around his head like a blue halo, maybe triggered by . . . what? His emotions? Could his emotions be that strong where she was concerned? It seemed unlikely.

"Ronan, what are you doing?" Her voice came out a touch too breathy for her own peace of mind.

He said nothing in response; he only stared down at her with his eyes heavily lidded. Shadows concealed half his face, but she could still tell his expression was serious, and there were sexual intentions in his eyes that made her stomach tighten and anticipation pool a little farther south. Ronan didn't touch her, didn't even kiss her. He only dipped his head so she could feel the heat of his mouth near hers, scent the mint on his breath. He remained so close to her skin that heat radiated from his body and warmed her.

Her hands made fists at her sides as she fought her reaction to him tooth and nail. No way was she going to make this easy for him, not after what he'd done to her. No way was she just going to give in to him now. She was no longer the young, naïve woman she'd been the first time they'd been together. She was no longer dazzled by his good looks and power.

Although the touch of him apparently dazzled her body.

She moved a little, hyperaware of all the changes his proximity was eliciting in her. This was not good. This was not something she wanted, but the only way to get it to stop was to get away from him.

"Back away from me." Her voice sounded surprisingly even. It was a Yuletide miracle that she could sound so calm right now.

"No." He pressed in closer and she lost her breath for a moment. His mouth came down so close to hers that she could feel the words he spoke. "I need you."

Something she'd been holding in, all penned up and tightly lidded, bubbled up from her depths, bringing with it a swell of emotion. It burst over her like a berry in her mouth, sweet and luscious, making her melt against him for a moment and close her eyes. It would be so easy to give in, to forget and just allow this. There was still a part of her that wanted him so much, more than anything.

"It was never that I didn't care about you," Ronan whispered. "Bella, don't you know that?"

"How could I know that?" Her eyes popped open and she pushed him backward, which had all of the effect of trying to move a boulder, but he stepped back anyway. "Get out, Ronan. I've tried to save your butt twice now and I'm done. Get out, and good luck." She started to force her way past him, but he caught her by the elbow.

"You still care about me."

She closed her eyes again. "Ronan . . . "

"I'm leaving now, but I'm coming back for you. You're mine, Bella. You always were and you still are."

She wrenched her arm from his grasp and turned from him. "You've got no right to call me *yours*. You threw me away years ago, you bastard."

"I made a mistake. I've regretted it for years. I thought at the time it was the right thing for you."

Bella stopped short, but didn't turn around.

"I was wrong. I have wanted to turn back the clock for decades now, make the other choice. I didn't know until tonight that you still carried any residual feeling for me."

He paused. "But you do, don't you? Otherwise you never would've offered marriage to save me."

She said nothing for several moments, her hands clenched tightly at her sides and her mind in a whirl of surprise and confusion. Her words had left her completely. She didn't know what to say anyway. How dare he tell her these things after he'd rejected her all those years ago and left her alone!

"I'm going to the Boundary Lands. There's something there I need to retrieve, something I didn't think mattered until you came to me at the prison. Now this object means everything. It will save my neck and make it possible for us to be together."

The Boundary Lands. A little thrill went through her at the prospect.

She turned and studied him, her brow knitting. Memories of the years following his rejection of her welled up. A muscle in her jaw worked. "This object you need to get from the Boundary Lands, it's what you stole for the Phaendir, isn't it?"

"Yes."

"What is it?"

"I can't tell you, for your own safety. I'm going to retrieve this object, and when I come back, you're mine, Bella."

"I'm not yours. I'll never be yours. You made sure of that three decades ago."

He smiled, but it didn't reach his eyes. He didn't believe her. Why should he? She barely believed herself. This man held a power over her that she could not deny. "As you wish."

"I'll see you safely out of the building and into the square. I'll wish you luck and then we're saying good-bye. *Forever.*"

His eyes clouded black for a moment. "I'll take what I can get from you, but this doesn't mean it's the end. Now that I know you have a seed of emotion for me, I intend to make it grow."

She stared at him, unable to believe the words he'd just

uttered or the ferocity behind them. Not in the last thirty years could she have imagined she'd be hearing them from him. "It's too late."

"It's never too late. I want you and I won't give up until you're mine."

"You didn't want me before. What makes you think I want you now?"

That made him blink. *Good*. His level of confidence where she was concerned disarmed and annoyed her. Her head was still spinning from the last twenty-four hours.

She turned and stalked into her bedroom, where she dressed in a pair of jeans, a warm gray sweater, and a pair of black boots.

He was lucky she had a whole stack of Yule gifts in her closet at the moment, waiting to be wrapped. Some of them were clothing items for men. After she found him a black sweater, a coat, and a pair of boots, she grabbed her own coat and they made their way out of the building.

Her shoes crunched the snow on the cobblestones as they kept to the shadows along the edges of the square. The Imperial Guard marched at the far end of the open expanse, a sight that made Bella far colder than the winter air biting through her heavy burgundy coat.

Above their heads, the Wild Hunt returned to the Unseelie Court, their pockets stuffed full of fresh souls, perhaps. The air above Bella and Ronan stirred, and the soft sounds of wings and the baying of the hounds broke the snow-laden quiet.

But Ronan's soul wasn't in that mysterious dark man's possession. At least, not yet.

A block away, two revelers laughed and drunkenly slapped each other on the back, on their way home from a Yuletide fete, no doubt. All the evergreens around the edges of the square gave off a gentle glow of festivity, dressed with lights and ornaments. Even the much abused and hated statue of Jules Piefferburg, founder and architect of the fae prison, was dressed in Yuletide finery. He even had a sprig of holly tucked behind one charmed iron ear.

Normally they dressed the statue as a woman or adorned it in rotten fruits and vegetables. If it hadn't been made of charmed iron, much worse would have been done.

"There, you're in the square. Good luck, Ronan. I sincerely wish you well. May you successfully evade the guard and return with the object, victorious." She turned back toward her building.

A hand clamped down over her wrist. "Don't put me too far from your mind, Bella. I'm coming back for you."

She turned back to him with wide eyes, her surprised breath huffing out white in the cold air. "Let go of me. All I have to do is scream and the guards will come running."

Magick tingled against her skin. A bolt of blue darted across his pupils, like lightning. "You wouldn't. I know you wouldn't."

"Don't make assumptions when your life is at stake."

A rustling came from nearby. The tromp of imperial boots in the snow. Suddenly panicked for him, she pushed him backward into the shadows and then followed. The reaction was instantaneous; she needed to protect him. It proved everything he'd said, but she wasn't about to admit it.

"Ronan Achaius Quinn and Bella Rhiannon Caliste Mac Lyr, stop in the name of the Summer Queen."

"Gods damn it. They saw you," Ronan growled. In one smooth move, he had her over his shoulder and was running along the wall toward the shadows between the buildings.

The guards shouted and gave chase, boots in multitude crushing the snow and ice in pursuit. Ronan muttered a few words of Old Maejian, the ancient language of the *Tuatha Dé*, and a duplicate image of Ronan and Bella split from their bodies and headed in the opposite direction, running across the square while they—the real they—melted seamlessly into the inkiness of the space near the base of the Rose Tower.

The guards took the bait, changed directions, and followed the illusion. Magick like Ronan's came in handy.

"Let me down!"

He stopped and eased her to the snowy pavement. He'd covered their snow tracks with another illusion. He paced away from her, pushing a hand through his hair. "Bloody hell, Bella. You have to come with me now. I didn't want this. It's too dangerous."

"Yes, well, I don't want to go either." Even though a part of her did. He was going to the Boundary Lands and she very much wanted to see them.

And maybe that wasn't the only reason she wanted to go with him.

"I'll tell them I coerced you into going with me."

"The guards clearly saw me trying to protect you, Ronan."

He swore under his breath. "It doesn't matter. Once I have the object, I'll be able to bargain with the Summer Queen for anything."

She tried, and failed, to imagine what could compel the Summer Queen to forgive Ronan of all his trespasses, and Bella's too. Her voice lowered. "What did you do for the Phaendir, Ronan?"

He smiled, his teeth white against his golden skin. "I stole something *for* them and then I stole it *from* them. Something very rare and powerful."

FOUR

$\mathcal{R}$onan studied Bella as she walked under the soft glow
of the intermittent streetlights with snowflakes catching in her long dark hair and on the shoulders of her burgundy coat. She glanced at him. She'd drawn her normally lush mouth into a thin line and narrowed her eyes.

They were making their way farther into the *Ceantar Láir*, the area where most of the fae in Purgatory lived, the trooping fae—all those who didn't belong to one of the courts and weren't wildlings. The *Ceantar Láir* formed a half ring between downtown Piefferburg and the Boundary Lands, and there was a lot of water in it and many bridges. They were walking because any other sort of transport right now was too risky. Metal amplified tracking spells.

"Give it up, Bella."

"I'll never give anything up to you." She continued her march.

He missed a step at the venom in her voice and watched her walk past him. His objective was to make that a lie. Right now he lived for it. He wanted her to give everything up to him. He wanted to fuck her luscious body from twilight to morn—every way she'd allow him—with no sounds issuing from her lips but sighs, moans, entreaties for more, and his name.

The phrase *I love you* wouldn't go amiss either.

He picked up his pace to catch up. "You don't even know where you're going so fast."

"Anywhere far away from you is acceptable."

"You wound me." He fell into step beside her.

"I'd like to do more than just wound you."

"You just saved my head, Bella. I don't believe it, unless you mean something else," he finished with a suggestive lilt to his voice.

She colored a little. With skin as fair as hers, it was easy to see even in the gentle glow of the streetlights. "I'm only coming with you because I have to."

"Okay." He shrugged one broad shoulder. "Like I said, I'll take what I can get from you. Before we travel to the outreaches of Piefferburg, we need to visit a friend. I need the ingredients for a spell for magickal countermeasures."

"What kind of countermeasures?"

"I need to block their tracking spell. Even now they're figuring out where we are and coming after us. Is your magick strong enough to block a tracking spell?"

Bella hugged herself. "You know it's not."

"Then we need to make a stop first. Afterward we'll find somewhere to sleep. It's cold and we're both exhausted."

She eyed the rows of neat houses they passed. Each of them was unique to the type of fae it housed. The brownies' abodes were small and round, while the Formorian houses were large enough to shelter a family of giants. The effect was discombobulation, unevenness, chaos. So unlike the neat suburban neighborhoods of the humans, where all the houses looked alike and everyone cut the grass to exactly three inches.

Dear Gods, how Ronan loved Piefferburg. He'd been beyond the borders, thanks to the Phaendir. He'd seen the human world. All the fae wanted out of here, but he couldn't see why. There was no magick out there.

"I guess hotels are out," she muttered.

"In a normal hotel, even with countermeasures, the guard would track us so fast our heads would spin off our shoulders." He grinned. "Never fear. I know the perfect place."

She gave him a suspicious sidelong glance. "Where?"

"A love hotel."

Her steps faltered. "A *what*?" Her gorgeous brown eyes grew wide.

"You've lived a sheltered life. A love hotel is a totally anonymous establishment. You check in via an unmonitored computer system and pay cash for the room. Very popular with the affair-having set. Small, simple rooms, since usually people don't go there for the décor."

"They go there for the bed."

"They go there to fuck."

She averted her gaze, looking straight ahead. "No way."

"You're going if you don't want to freeze to death, or be captured by the Queen's Guard, or both."

"Why couldn't you have just left me alone? I could be home in bed right now."

His boots crunched the snow-covered ground. "Why didn't you leave *me* alone? You could have left me in my prison if you'd wanted and you didn't. I didn't want to put you in danger. I didn't want you on this journey, but maybe it's better you're out of your prison too."

"Prison? What are you talking about?"

"Come on, Bell, you know as well—"

"Bel*la*."

"—as I do that all the Seelie nobles are locked in a prison."

"Every fae in Piefferburg is a prisoner, Ronan."

"You know what I mean. The Seelie are expected to behave a certain way. They're indoctrinated into a restrictive culture and told half-truths and outright lies about the outside world. Being born into that court is akin to being born with shackles on for an eternity."

"Wow, Ronan. You never used to feel this way. When I

knew you, you weren't so negative about the Seelie. Is it because they recently tried to get rid of you?"

He shook his head. "My opinion of the Seelie Court has never changed. I petitioned the Summer Queen to reside in the Rose Tower because I had a good reason to do so, that's all."

"What was your reason?"

His reason had been her. He'd visited on an errand for the Shadow King all those years ago, had met Bella and fallen in love with her. He'd petitioned the Summer Queen immediately for residency. Circumstances being what they were, he'd been forced to eventually end his affair with Bella, but he'd never wanted to leave her proximity, so he'd remained in the Rose instead of returning to the Black. No matter how much it had hurt to see her so often and never be with her, he'd remained. "I stayed at the Rose Tower for you."

"Stop, Ronan. Just stop. You confuse me."

"Let me explain."

"No." She shook her head. "You have no idea how badly you broke my heart. I don't want to hear it. I just want to get through this." She crossed her arms over her chest and hugged herself. "Where is this hotel, anyway?"

"In good time. We're almost at my friend's place."

She looked down the quiet, snowy, house-lined street. Then she looked back at their footprints on the walk behind them, quickly being covered over with a frosting of snow. "Your friend lives in the *Ceantar Láir*?"

"No, not exactly." He murmured a low, magickally charged Maejian phrase, took two steps forward, and disappeared.

*B*ella stopped short and blinked. His hand reached out of nowhere and yanked her forward . . . into nowhere.

The world was hazy for a moment, then grew clear and sharp once more. They were no longer in the *Ceantar Láir*. A dark, gritty street now surrounded her. No snow, but the chill bit deeply into her bones. He'd stepped them into a pocket, moved them from the *Ceantar Láir* back to the downtown area with one murmured phrase and a dash of strong magick.

Bella understood instantly that this was a part of the downtown area where the Seelie weren't encouraged to visit. They were on the other side of Piefferburg Square, and the smooth black quartz of the Unseelie Court rose directly behind the small buildings to her right. This alley was nestled somewhere at the back of the Unseelie Court, right at its base.

"We're standing in the shadow of the Black Tower," Bella whispered, turning a wary circle on the snow-dusted cobblestones.

"Yes. We're right at the door of the Piefferburg witch."

"The Piefferburg witch is a friend, Ronan?" Her breath caught. "She's Unseelie."

He flashed his teeth. "So am I, Bella."

It was hard to keep in mind that he'd been a member of the Black Tower a lot longer than he'd been a resident of the Rose. "You have some of that blood, but you're not so . . . *so* Unseelie as the Piefferburg witch."

"I am very Unseelie *Tuatha Dé*. Almost one hundred percent, in fact. Only a drop of Seelie to muddy the pool. Do you have a problem with that, Shining One?" The voice was old, broken, gritty as the pavement Bella stood on. The woman's body matched. The Piefferburg witch stood in a narrow doorway, the light of a small room behind her glowing softly, invitingly. "Don't stare, child. It's rude." The wizened crone disappeared into the tiny building. "Come in, please."

Without hesitation, Ronan followed. Bella studied the doorway for a heartbeat, snowflakes drifting onto her cheeks and melting, then she entered.

Candlelight cast dancing shadows on the walls and revealed a table with three chairs. All along the walls were shelves filled with books, boxes, and jars. All of it was in terrible disarray. The scent of dried plants, herbs, and various other items used in the witch's special brand of magic assaulted Bella's nose.

The ancient-looking witch bowed with a swiftness and flexibility that Bella could not believe. "It's an honor to have such a high-ranking Seelie in my humble shop." The scorn in her voice said otherwise. "You are Bella Rhiannon Caliste Mac Lyr, descended without taint from the first Seelie *Tuatha Dé Danann*. I've seen you on *Faemous*, of course."

Bella didn't respond to the mockery she heard in the words.

With a wave of her hand, the crone transformed into a beautiful young blond woman wearing a shimmering green dress that hit her mid-thigh and a matching pair of kitten heels. Her makeup was flawless and beautiful; glittering bobs hung at her ears, and a matching pendant nestled in the hollow of her throat.

"Oh, my sweet Danu." One might think that living in the Rose Tower would have exposed Bella to powerful magicks, but that was not true. None of the Seelie she knew had power like this. It had all been bred out of them in an effort to keep the bloodlines true. It was ironic and a pity.

"Don't show off, Priss," said Ronan, who was examining a crystal ball on the other side of the room.

The witch pouted. "I get so few pure Seelie. Let me play."

Bella lowered her hand from her mouth and forcibly wiped the awe from her expression. "I've heard of you. You're the only witch in Purgatory."

"Incorrect." Priss the witch raised an eyebrow. "I'm the only one of my kind in all the world." She changed form again, this time to an older, pregnant woman. She wore overalls and a red kerchief wound through her auburn hair. Beautiful, maternal.

Maiden. Mother. Crone. She was all of them. A unique fae creature created from Unseelie and low-blood Seelie pairings, with unimaginable power. This was the Piefferburg witch.

Now she was back to crone. She cackled and crooked a finger at Bella. "I know what you two want and I have it." She shuffled to one of the shelves and pulled a small wooden box from it. Slanting a sly gaze at her, the witch said, "I trust you can pay?"

She had a moment of unease. Arranging for payment with the fae was fraught with double meanings, loopholes, and treachery. "What am I buying?"

Ronan answered. "Supplies to weave a cloaking spell. A way to cover our tracks and make it more difficult for the Imperial Guard to track us." He paused. "And *I'm* buying it."

"Never mind. I'm giving the ingredients to you for free, just for the pleasure of watching the will of the Summer Queen thwarted." The witch crackled again. "The circus is in town and I'll gladly pay for my seat."

Priss the witch shuffled back over to them with the box in hand. Both Bella and Ronan came close to peer inside as she pushed the carved top open on a whine of rusty hinges. Whatever was inside—Bella wasn't sure she wanted to know—smelled dry and slightly decayed.

Whatever the contents, Ronan palmed the box like it was something precious and followed Priss to another shelf, where he gathered more vials and small boxes. Then Priss led him to the back of the room, where there was a counter with a large brass bowl and mystical-looking implements that Bella couldn't name.

Priss caught Bella craning her neck to see, and she cackled. "Intrigued a bit by the dark arts, Shining One?"

Bella's spine stiffened. "I'm not afraid of it, if that's what you mean."

"A Seelie who is not afraid of the dark." The witch shook her head. "I never met one. You're lying." Summarily dismissing her, Priss turned and began fussing with the jars on her shelves in the dimly lit room.

Ronan worked at the back table while Bella peered curiously at her surroundings, wondering exactly how Priss achieved the clown car effect of such a large room existing in a space that appeared outwardly to be so tiny. Clearly her home was in an alternate pocket somewhere else within the boundaries of Piefferburg.

Leaving a scatter of dried herb on the table, Ronan approached her with the original rare wooden box in his hand. "The spell is woven. All we need to do now is set it in place." He came close enough to her so she could feel his body heat.

Ronan murmured under his breath and power swelled in the air, putting pressure in Bella's eardrums. She took a step back just as Ronan blew into the box, puffing the dry concoction into her face. Bella's body shook from the inside out, a strange sensation that made her gasp. Magick clung for a moment on her skin and in her hair before dissipating into the air. As she shook and acclimated to the spell covering her body, Ronan inhaled his own dose.

"So this will keep us safe?" Bella asked.

Ronan shrugged one shoulder. "There are countermeasures for countermeasures. I was one of the queen's mages and I know the others are all good. We can't be totally sure we're protected, but it's better than nothing."

"Better than nothing. Great."

"Thank you for your help, Priss. Can you let us out near the *Ceantar Dubh*?"

That was nowhere near the Boundary Lands. Couldn't the witchy subway system get them closer? "*Ceantar Dubh*? Why can't she let us out—" She stopped herself before she blurted out more than the witch needed to know. Bella's gaze darted to the old woman, who smiled at her. "You know, where we need to go."

"Priss's abilities in this regard are driven by the magick of the fae. The more fae in an area, the stronger her magick. Therefore, she's limited to downtown and the *Ceantar Láir*."

The witch shrugged and waved her hand. "Anything for you, Ronan. The location is set." She grinned, showing broken teeth. "As always, I thank you for your patronage."

*   *   *

"*H*ow, exactly, do you know her?" Bella asked as they stepped back into the narrow alley.

He cast a sidelong glance at her. "Jealous of an old woman?"

"First off, I'm not jealous. I'm just curious. Second, she's not always an old woman."

Ronan glanced at her and gave her a small, secretive smile. "No, that's true. Not all the time."

Bella rolled her eyes.

"I know her," Ronan said, pulling her down the alley, "because she stocks the ingredients necessary to create many of my spells. Out of all the fae in Piefferburg, with the exception of my brother, Niall, her magick is closest to my own. She's not one of my lovers."

One of his lovers. So, he had many. It pinched. Bella couldn't deny that fact. She shouldn't care, but she couldn't help that she did.

FIVE

*H*e murmured something and they stepped through another pocket, this time into a different part of the downtown area, one that Bella had been to only a handful of times, as it wasn't an upscale shopping area.

Storefronts were closed this late at night and so close to the winter solstice. Yuletide lights blinked merrily in the windows, wishing passersby a merry season filled with joy. The occasional fae could be seen walking down the cobblestone street, huddled in a coat, but this was the downtown business district and there weren't any Yuletide revelers to be seen like there were near the square.

In front of them rose a tall brick building with a red hostelry sign blinking on the front. They were at the infamous "love hotel," apparently.

"See? We're here. Knowing Priss can be very helpful." He walked into the building.

"Yes, I'm sure," Bella grumbled before following him and wondering just how many of his lovers he'd taken to this place. The thought left her stomach a little sour.

One computer stood in the small entry room, the cursor on the black screen blinking at them. Ronan went to it.

"Are you sure you trust this?" Bella asked, coming up next to him. "This place could be saturated in magick or inhabited with fae who are able to secret themselves away and spy. I mean, you said people use this place for conducting carnal affairs, right? Can you imagine all the reasons to monitor activity? Suspicious spouses? Blackmail? Pure unadulterated voyeurism?"

"The spell I cast on us will protect us from any magickal surveillance, Bella." He typed something into the computer and paid for the room with cash by feeding the bills into the appropriate slots, and a key slid out near the keyboard. "Relax. We'll get some sleep and we can continue our journey in the morning."

Her body was achy with fatigue and her muscles tight with stress. He walked to her and laid his hands on her shoulders. The heat of his touch melted through the fabric of her shirt and into her skin. She stared at the collar of his sweater, where she could see a few dark chest hairs and his smooth, warm skin over hard, rippling muscle. She couldn't stop herself from wondering what it all would feel like under her fingers, her lips. The scent of him teased her nose, a combination of his soap and aftershave—the quintessential smell that was simply him. It made her feminine muscles deep within clench with sudden desire, bringing her body to an almost abrupt sexual awareness.

Ah, Danu, just his proximity made her knees go weak. She had no defenses against this man. She hadn't had them thirty years ago and she hadn't developed any since.

"Bella, look at me."

With effort, she raised her gaze to his.

"Relax."

Fat chance of that in a *love* hotel with the one man she'd always wanted but could never have. Still, she did need to relax a little, or soon her clenched jaw would be churning out diamonds made from her teeth.

She took a deep breath and let it out slowly. "Okay, I'm relaxed." At least for a second or two.

He waved a flat plastic room key in front of her nose. "Good. Then let's get some sleep."

The room was small, barely enough space for two people to get around in. A window on the far wall revealed the lovely view of a fire escape and the brick side of the neighboring building. The bed—a king size—was the only piece of furniture. There were no dressers, no chairs, not even a lamp or a bad painting on the wall. It was clear what the room was meant for . . . and it wasn't for relaxing weekends away from home. Bella almost turned and walked the other way once she'd crossed the threshold, but Ronan caught her arm.

"There's only one bed." It was a stupid, obvious comment, but her tongue couldn't find any intelligent words at the moment.

"Don't worry, I'll take the floor."

She eyed the small space. "There's not enough floor for you to take."

"I'll manage. The rooms are small so they can pack a bunch into one building. These places make a ton of money."

"Great." She curled her lip at the garish green design of the coverlet and eyed the dark entrance to what was undoubtedly a closet-sized bathroom. "I think I prefer my apartment."

"Not all the fae are as blessed as the Seelie, Bella."

"Is the room clean, at least?"

"Spotless. It's run by the Uruisg. You know how clean-crazy they are."

The Uruisg were a breed of Scottish brownies, a slightly more nightmarish cousin to her house goblin, Lolly. Aside from being known for their cleanliness, in ancient times they'd had a tendency to harass unwary human travelers for the fun of it, back when the fae were supposed to be underground. Some of them had been unable to leave humans completely alone.

So, apparently, the Uruisg had gone from tormenting travelers to hosting them.

That was called irony.

He entered the room, pulling off his coat and his sweater with a tired groan as he went. Bella averted her eyes and lingered in the doorway. Stepping into that room was going to be like stepping into fire. She didn't want to get burned, but the flame was so very pretty.

She fidgeted and frowned. "Maybe I could get my own room."

He glanced at her and shook his head. "And if the Imperial Guard shows up? If you're in your own unlocked room, by your choice, how could I convince them I kidnapped you?"

"They *saw* me helping you, Ronan."

"I'd still try to convince them I'd coerced you."

She narrowed her eyes at him. "I thought you said we were safe with your spell on us."

He spread his hands, shirt fisted in one hand. "No one can predict the future, Bella. No one can know every possible angle. Magick is a never-ending tangle of possibilities." Ronan swept low in a courtly bow. "Please, enter, my lady. I promise I won't bite."

Maybe he wouldn't bite, but the mischievous look on his face convinced Bella he might want to nibble a bit. The problem was she wasn't completely sure she didn't want him to nibble.

She entered the room anyway.

His hands went to the top button of his pants. She looked away. "I'm going to take a shower, if you don't mind. I still have prison stink on me." At the shake of her head, he headed into the bathroom.

With a grateful sigh of relief for a few moments alone to collect her thoughts, she sank down on the bed and stared at the closed bathroom door. The water was turned on, and after a minute steam rolled from beneath the door. She wasn't going to think about Ronan naked, wet and soapy under the spray of the hot water.

So, of course, that's all she did.

Pulling off her coat, she slumped back against the pillows and recalled the first time they'd met. The Seelie Court was small in comparison with the rest of Piefferburg, but it operated through a system of social cliques. Ronan had come to the court on an errand for the Shadow King. He'd lived in the Black Tower since he'd been a child, along with his brother, who still resided there. He and Bella had met in the hallway that day and it had been like an electric shock for her. She'd been immediately smitten.

Ronan had been scheduled to be there for a week on and off, acting as a messenger for his king. At the end of that week, he'd shocked them all by applying to stay in the Rose Tower. The Shadow King was incensed. The Summer Queen allowed it because taking one of the Unseelie was a way to embarrass the Black Tower's Royal, and besides, Ronan was physically attractive and had captured the imagination of most of the women at court. It also didn't hurt that he was a powerful mage. The queen quickly employed him as one of her personal assistants.

Due to the uniqueness of the circumstances—an Unseelie coming to their side of the square, even if said individual had some Seelie blood, was highly unusual—everyone assumed he was sleeping with the queen. That he was her pet, so to speak. Even Bella had believed that to be the case at first.

But of all the women at court, Ronan seemed to have his eye set on Bella. Every time they passed each other in the corridor, his dark gaze would hold hers with such a carnal intensity that her cheeks would heat and her heart would thump. At banquets and balls he always managed to sit near her or brush against her. Bella wasn't the only one who noticed it. Aislinn had commented on Ronan's fascination with her often.

Secretly, it had thrilled her.

It had also worried her, because if the queen had taken Ronan as her lover, Her Majesty would not be pleased if he was attracted to another woman. Bella rather enjoyed her head *on* her shoulders.

So one evening Bella took matters into her own hands.

She cornered Ronan and asked him point-blank what sort of game he was playing with her life. That was when Ronan told her he wasn't sleeping with the queen . . . and then he'd kissed her.

Ronan's hadn't been the first kiss of her life, but it had been the first kiss that made her knees go weak and her toes curl. It had been the first kiss that had ever blanked her mind clean of rational thought, made her bones turn soft as warm butter. It hadn't been her last kiss from Ronan, nor had it been her last kiss, period.

Still, brushing her fingers across her mouth even now, she could recall the first touch of his lips.

They'd shared a strong romance from that day forward, though they'd never slept together. The court had buzzed about their affair and even the queen took notice. The Seelie Royal finally asked Ronan what his intentions toward Bella were and gave him her blessing if he chose to ask Bella to marry him. That's when Ronan, in front of the entire court, had declared he was finished with her.

Just like that.

In love one minute and publicly dumped the next.

Bella's heart had shattered. His rejection of her had been humiliating, but it had been her broken heart that had made her literally sick.

Even worse had been the years of having to live at court with him. She became a master at avoiding him, until she'd decided her pride couldn't allow that kind of behavior. They said hello once in a while in a corridor, made small talk when forced. She'd tried to build a wall of non-emotion between him and herself. She'd never managed it. Not quite.

Ronan emerged from the bathroom wearing only a towel around his middle. Water droplets still clung to his chest, and his dark hair was slicked back, throwing his handsome face into sharp relief.

Bella sat up against the pillows and cleared her throat. There was not even close to enough fabric covering that man. His smooth golden chest, back, and arms rippled and flexed with every movement he made. She knew it was only some primitive female mating directive that made her react to all that muscle and strength. That's what made her want to lick him all over. It had nothing whatsoever to do with the fact it was Ronan. *Nothing*. She fussed with the coverlet as Ronan moved around the edge of the bed, closer to her.

"I won't drop my towel, I swear."

Anger flared in a hot rush through her veins. She glanced at him. "It doesn't matter to me. Drop it. See if I care."

"Okay." He removed the towel and she turned her head away, but not before she got an eyeful of his narrow hips and long, wide cock.

"You're blushing, Bella. I thought you didn't care."

"Danu, Ronan." She cleared her throat again and concentrated hard on the opposite wall. It was better to change the subject and fast. Something. *Anything*. "Tell me what it's like in the Unseelie Court."

"The Unseelie Court?" He pulled on his pants and zipped them up, then worked the towel through his damp hair. "I told you my impression of the Black Tower long ago."

"Tell me again."

He shrugged. "It's dangerous, but not as bad as you've been led to believe. The Summer Queen likes to demonize the Unseelie. Although it's true it's where the dark fae live. It can be brutal and violent, but it's not the absolute evil that most of the Seelie Court believes it to be. The Seelie Royal herself is darker than many of the fae who live in the Black Tower."

Bella disagreed. The Seelie Queen's magick was dark in nature, and she had the will to spill blood—which she'd demonstrated amply over her long lifetime—but her magick could not be used directly to cause harm. She could only take life if it was in defense of herself or her court, and the darker portion of her power was never passed on to her progeny. That was the law of the Seelie and the confines of the royal station.

"But to be Unseelie one must love to spill blood, that's the saying. One must be able to kill with one's magick.

You don't enjoy spilling blood and that's why you came to Seelie."

"No, you're wrong." He shook his head. "I came to the Rose Tower for you and no other reason, Bella. If I had never met you I would still reside in the Black."

She looked away from him, her jaw locking. Right. Then why had he dumped her and broken her heart?

He dropped the towel on the bed. "My magick is dark and I can cast spells that will take someone's life. It's that capacity that makes me welcome in the Unseelie Court. I have the ability to kill with my magick; I just don't have the will." He paused and then said gently, "There are many more Seelie than you can imagine in the Summer Queen's court who have Unseelie blood."

Her gaze jerked upward and locked with his. She had the capacity to spill blood with her magick. Did he know that somehow? Did Ronan know she was Unseelie?

"*Many* Seelie carrying the DNA of the Unseelie? That's impossible. A couple, I could imagine." Herself and Aislinn, namely.

He held her gaze in a way that unsettled her. "There's more crossover than you might think. More liaisons between the Seelie and Unseelie than you can imagine. It's secret on the rose side, considered shameful, but not so much on the black."

She licked her lips and fiercely examined the fabric of the blanket covering the bed. If what Ronan said was right, they'd been fed a pack of lies about the supposed flip side of the fae coin. Even if it was possible that many more Seelie were in a predicament like hers and Aislinn's, she still wished she could shake her attraction to the dark.

Just as she wished she could shake her attraction to Ronan.

Mastering her emotions so they didn't show on her face, she commented, "Maybe one day I'll see it, the Black Tower, I mean."

"No." Ronan shook his head and pulled his shirt back over it. For a moment Bella mourned the loss of his bare chest. "It's not as bad as you think, Bella, but if I have anything to say about it, you'll never find out firsthand."

She glanced up at him. "Why? Don't you think I can handle it?"

"You can handle anything, but the Black Tower is too dangerous for someone who hasn't grown up there."

"So what's with being so protective of me?"

"You haven't figured it out yet, Bell?"

Their gazes held for a moment, until she broke away and scooted off the mattress. "I'm going to use the bathroom."

She inched around the bed and went directly into the bathroom to wash her face and shed as much clothing as she could to sleep better. When she exited, Ronan was on the floor, lying wedged on his side between the bed and the wall. She wasn't going to think for a minute about how uncomfortable he must be. He'd been the one to get himself into this situation, after all, not her.

Bella crawled onto the bed and lay down with a heavy sigh.

She wasn't going to think about what this bed was normally used for, either.

SIX

The light snicked out in the quiet air and the room sank into inkiness. Outside the window, fat snowflakes had begun to drift down again, catching and melting on the metal of the fire escape. Tomorrow night was Yule, and all the fae in Piefferburg were celebrating the coming of the longest night of the year. The day after Yule the light would begin to increase and rule the world once again.

"Why did you do it?" she asked, her voice startling in the quiet. "The job for the Phaendir? I know you won't tell me what you stole for them, but can you tell me why you did it?"

Silence.

"Ronan?"

"Sometimes you guide your life down a path where it seems like you have nothing to lose, so why not?"

"That's not really an answer." She sighed. "You're the king of non-answers and games."

He remained silent for several moments before saying, "It is an answer. You're just not listening closely enough."

Rolling to her side, she sighed again. "Ronan, you're a mystery to me. There was a time in our lives when I thought

I knew everything about you, but now you're nothing but an enigma."

"You always did like puzzles."

"Ugh. Go to sleep." Bella flopped onto her back, closed her eyes, and tried to follow her own advice, but her muscles were tight with stress.

On top of it, every couple of seconds she would hear Ronan shift on the floor, trying to get comfortable.

"Ronan, get into bed. There's no sense in you being down there when this bed could fit three people." She winced, wondering how many times the bed really had fit three people.

He crawled onto the bed. "I thought you'd never ask," he said on a groan as he lay down.

"Just remember it's an invitation to get into bed, not into *me*."

"I value my balls. I know better than to try anything with you right now."

Silence and darkness descended, intimacy closing around them like a velvet fist. His body heat radiated out and melted into her, relaxing her better than a massage. The stress leached from her body and drowsiness closed over her. Finally, she slept.

*B*ella awoke to a picture of enticement almost too strong to resist. Ronan lay on his back in just his low-slung pants, the top of his dark blue briefs visible at the waistband. His feet were bare, as was the muscled, lickable expanse of his chest. One strong arm was thrown over his face, shielding his eyes from the dawn streaming in through the uncurtained window—undoubtedly designed to get the hotel guests out of the room as quickly as possible in the morning. His other arm was thrown wide on the mattress, his hand reaching out in unconscious supplication toward her.

Bella eyed his broad hand with a mixture of alarm and contentedness.

Dear Danu, she needed counseling. Apparently this man was the worst kind of addictive drug. No matter how low her addiction brought her, a part of her still needed more. Maybe her hormones were reversed in some masochistic way, making her want only the men who were the absolute worst for her.

Her gaze skated down the smooth sweep of his chest, to the jut of his lean hip bones. Her teeth made furrows into her lower lip. It had been a long time since she'd had sex. That was obviously not a good thing, since her libido was unnaturally revved up by the sight of Ronan.

"Good morning," came Ronan's sleep-raspy voice.

Her gaze jerked to his face. She was well and fully clothed, but in that moment she felt naked in front of him. Could he tell that the sight of him excited her? Did he know that his mere presence in her bed helped her to sleep? Could he read all that on her face? "Good morning."

"Sleep okay? You've got dark smudges beneath your eyes."

"I didn't sleep enough, but I'll be all right. We should get going. I want you to get this object back, whatever it is, and clean this mess up as soon as we can so I can get back to my life." Such as it was.

"That's my plan too." He pushed up on his elbows. "Thank you for coming with me."

She finally felt able to look him in the eye again. "I only came because I had to."

He held her gaze. "Really? Is that true?"

Her impulse was to look away, but she was mesmerized by the look in his eyes. "Why did you reject me all those years ago, Ronan?"

The question had slipped out on a whisper, without her even understanding she'd asked it until it was too late. Those words had been locked up within her for so many years, it felt great to finally let them free. Even though coldness at the possibilities of Ronan's answer coated her stomach and throat. She'd imagined them all at some point over the years. *I never loved you* topped the list of her nightmares.

She barreled ahead, suddenly sorry she'd asked. "The queen was ready to allow us to marry and I really thought you"—she swallowed hard—"cared about me. Then out of the nowhere you stood up in front of the court and rejected me."

He exhaled slowly. "I was stupid, Bell. I thought I was protecting you from what our union would bring." He paused and rubbed his face with a hand, looking weary all of a sudden.

Bella blinked. That wasn't one of the answers she'd imagined. "That makes no sense. What does that mean?"

Ronan reached for her hand, but she pulled away before he could touch her. His hand closed into a fist. "You have Unseelie blood."

Her heart stopped, skipped, and then began beating rapidly. "How can you know that?" she whispered.

He shook his head. "I'm not sure how I know. It's a part of my power. I just do. Your blood sings to mine. It's one of the things that first attracted me to you, but, Bella, if they ever found out, the Summer Queen would toss you out of the Seelie Court. You don't have the novelty of powerful magick to keep yourself in her favor."

She swallowed hard. "I am aware."

He took her hands. "Imagine if we had children, you and I. Any offspring of ours would have strong, dark magick and the Seelie Court would know. I thought that if I left you, if we never created a child together, you'd be safe. Even though it would kill me to watch it, I thought you'd find yourself a Seelie nobleman and have children with only a small bit of Unseelie in them. You'd be all right."

She'd been so in love with Ronan—and so young—she'd never thought very deeply about the possibility of having children with him. Infertility was rampant among the fae, keeping their population low, but it *was* possible she and Ronan could produce offspring who had strong dark magick. And they wouldn't be able to use birth control to prevent conception because no method of birth control for the fae seemed to work. Not even condoms were effective. When a fae female conceived, it was a little like magick—it just happened, no matter if the couple had been taking every precaution.

It was dumb. She should've thought about it. After all, she remembered the disgraced Maugin family who had been banished from the Rose Tower after their child had turned up Unseelie. That family's wealth had been based on their lineage, and they'd been supported financially by the rest of the fae. Surely they'd slipped into poverty now, unless the Shadow King had taken them in. They'd lost everything. Her family would've too, if she'd been discovered as a child.

She narrowed her eyes at him. "Did you love your place at the Seelie Court more than you loved me?"

"No!" He swore low under his breath. "I don't give a damn about the Seelie Court. I'd leave it tomorrow if it weren't for you. *You* cared about your place at court, Bella. That's what I was protecting."

She stared at him in stunned silence for a several moments before whispering, "I never loved it more than I loved you, Ronan."

"I know that now, though I didn't realize it back then. I made a mistake and I paid for it. I could never move on after I let you go. I found my soul mate in you and losing you slowly destroyed me over the years. Still, better me than you, Bella. Back then I thought banishment from the Rose Tower really *would* destroy you."

"You were wrong. All I needed was you." The rest of the words she could've said left her, and all the saliva on her tongue dried up. Bella exhaled slowly and got off the bed. She needed some time to absorb what he'd told her. She'd spent years imagining he'd say something . . . well, something other than that.

Once off the bed, she whirled to face him. Seems she had words after all. "Why didn't you tell me back then why you were rejecting me? Why did you let me live all those years thinking I'd done something wrong or that you'd used me in some way?"

"I thought it was better if you hated me. I assumed that if I told you I knew you had Unseelie blood, you'd argue with me. You might have wanted to leave the Seelie Court to be with me and I couldn't allow that."

"Yes, you're right. That's exactly what I would've done."

He pushed off the bed and paced to the bathroom and back. "You're in the highest ranks of the Seelie, Bell. You've had money your whole life. You've had luxury and servants. If the Summer Queen threw you out of the Seelie Court, you'd have to give all that up. You'd live in poverty. You don't know how hard it would be—"

"Don't treat me like I'm a child, Ronan! Don't assume I'm some ignorant, lovesick woman who, in her naïveté, assumed life would be all puppies and sunshine as long as we were together. I knew back then that leaving the Seelie Court would be hard. Don't you think, knowing that I had Unseelie blood, I would have considered it?" She clenched her fists and made a frustrated sound. "All I want—*wanted*—was to be with you, Ronan. I would"— she made another sound of frustration—"*would've* given up any amount of physical luxury in order to bind my life with my soul mate's." She bored a hole into him with her gaze. "I *knew* back then you were my soul mate, Ronan. *Knew it.*"

Ronan only stood and stared at her with an unreadable expression on his face.

Bella drew a shaky breath, gathering herself, and waved a hand. "It's done now, all over with. Out of love and a desire to protect me, you made a high-handed decision that ruined my life. I get it."

"It ruined my life too, Bella. I can only say that I thought I was doing the right thing for you."

She crossed her arms over her chest. "Well, you weren't." A breath huffed out of her. "So why tell me all of this now?"

"Because now I know you always loved me as much I loved you. Because now we have a way to be together."

She stared stonily at him. "Who says it's not too late?"

"I know it's not too late. I know it because you came to me in the prison and proved that you still have feelings for me." He paused, his jaw locking. "I know it's not too late because you're mine. Then. Now. *Forever*."

She turned and walked toward the bathroom so he couldn't see the expression on her face. When she got to the doorway, her knees went doughy and she reached out to steady herself with a hand on the doorjamb. "Why didn't you ever come to me during these last thirty years? Why didn't you tell me all this sooner?"

"I thought you hated me." His voice came from right behind her, and his proximity made her shoulders tighten. "It wasn't until you came to the prison that I had any reason to believe you might still have a flicker of love left for me."

Bella closed her eyes and gritted her teeth as her world shifted a little to the left. "I don't know what to say."

"The Phaendir came to me. This object I stole for them, I never planned to let them have it. I never planned to allow the Summer Queen to have it either, but now that I know you still care for me, it gives us a chance. The Summer Queen will bargain for what I have to give her; maybe she'll even agree to protect our union, no matter how much Unseelie blood our children may have."

Gods, he wanted them to be together.

He was doing all this for her.

His hands cupped her shoulders, the heat of his body bleeding through the fabric of her sweater and into her skin. He turned her to face him, but she wouldn't look up into his eyes. "Just give me a chance, Bell, that's all I'm asking. I know I screwed up the first time. Give me a chance to show you I'm telling the truth." He tipped her chin up, forcing her to look into his face. "I never stopped loving you. It never faded and it never failed."

She blinked, her huge brown eyes coming into focus. "I can't do this. I—"

He dipped his head and stopped her words with his lips. Bella stiffened and almost pulled away, but the sensation of his mouth on hers after so many years was like a balm on an old wound—healing, nourishing. He brushed his mouth across hers as though he had all the time in the world—like he was savoring her. Then he nipped gently at her lower lip and she melted.

Ronan made a low, hungry sound in his throat and dragged her up against his bare chest, his mouth slanting over hers. He eased her lips apart and branded her tongue with his. The taste of him filled her mouth, the scent of him teased her nose, and the hard, warm press of his body against hers did things to her she could only barely recall were possible. After so many years the sexual spark was still there.

Bella grasped his upper arms, trying hard not to think about the huge bed behind them and the part of her that wasn't sure she could resist him if he pulled her toward it. She'd always been attracted to him on a primal, sexual level. Even though they'd never had sex, she knew it would be explosive between them. They shared the kind of chemistry that made it impossible for it to be any other way.

But there was so much more to love than just good sex.

She stepped back, breaking the kiss, and closed the bathroom door in his face.

SEVEN

Ronan stared at the closed door separating him from Bella. His lips felt electrified from her mouth, and his body was tight, anticipatory. His cock had gone rock hard in the very first moment of their kiss. He wanted her, had wanted her for years, craved the scent of her skin, yearned for the slide of it against his. Now he'd had a mere taste, and the need for more was nearly overwhelming. It made his hands curl involuntarily at the thought of touching her silky bare body. He forcibly caged the beast within that screamed for her.

It was an effort not to pound on the door or rip it from its hinges. He wanted to throw her down on the bed and use every sexual wile he possessed to lure her to him. If he tried hard enough, he could tempt her past her misgivings, make her forget that he'd rejected her all those years ago. If he put his mind and body into seducing her once she exited the bathroom, he could lure her into giving in to him completely . . . carnally.

But the problem was that he wanted more than just a coupling of their bodies. He wanted her heart and maybe just the slightest bit of her soul. Ronan wanted what he'd been so stupid to give up before—he wanted eternity with the one woman in the world whom he loved.

He wouldn't obtain that by letting his cock rule his head. No, he needed to be patient and regain her trust. Ronan wouldn't accept anything less than the whole of Bella.

He made a fist and almost slammed it into the wall beside the door frame as a way to vent the emotions that roiled within him. Next to the door he leaned up against the wall and rested his forehead against his forearm, trying desperately to get a handle on his lust and to calm the condition of his lower body.

It wasn't the Summer Queen's wrath or the Imperial Guard that Ronan feared might bring an end to him. It was Bella. Could he survive being this close to her and not being any closer?

The door opened, and Ronan stepped back as far as the edge of the bed would allow, clenching his hands at his sides so he wouldn't leap on her. Just the scent of her skin made him crazy. He wasn't sure how much longer he would last without a deeper taste of her. He wanted the flavor of her on his tongue. He wanted to drown in her.

She drew a long, slow breath and studied him without speaking, while Ronan's heart dropped out of his stomach at her expression. He moved his gaze downward to avoid the accusation and anger on her beautiful face and found that her body told a different story. Her spine was slightly arched, breasts thrust out a little, as if inviting him to look at them, touch them. Even her lips were parted and moist. She wet them again as she glanced at his mouth.

Bloody hell, what a dichotomy. She wanted him, but she was also frightened. No doubt terrified he'd hurt her again.

Never.

"Bella? Come here."

To his absolute amazement, she came. She walked straight into his arms. He enveloped her in his embrace, and every bit of tension he'd been holding released in a wave of silent exultation and relief. He'd waited so long for this, had imagined it so often.

It was better—much better—in reality.

For a moment, he held her close and nuzzled the top of her hair, breathing in the scent of her and letting it intoxicate him. He found a bit of bare skin and stroked it slowly, savoring the silkiness of her body and wanting more, so much more. She shuddered against him and he pulled her backward toward the bed.

With a sigh that heated his blood, she allowed it. He pushed her down onto the mattress and rolled her beneath his body, his mind and heart a riot of fantasies fulfilled. Her hair spread out around her head and she looked . . . ambushed. Ambushed and beautiful and willing. Her eyes were a bit wide and her lips parted.

Gods, he was going to have to hold himself back. All he wanted was to devour her, but he had to take this slow. What he wanted most was to give her pleasure right now, to taste her and feel her explode in orgasm against his lips and tongue. He wanted to slide deep within her and feel all her hot silk close around him, ripple and pulse as he drove them both to climax. He wanted to brand her as his and mark himself indelibly in her mind and heart.

"Ronan, I don't know about this." She stared at his mouth.

"I do. I want you, want more of you." He lowered his lips and rubbed them over her mouth slowly, making her shiver beneath him. "Give me more, Bell."

She melted against him, her fingers curling around the curve of his shoulders. He dropped his hand to the button of her jeans and undid it, then the zipper. They'd never made love before. It was difficult for fae women to conceive, but he'd been too afraid they'd manage to beat the odds and make a baby. Now Ronan wanted a baby with her more than anything, and maybe if his plan succeeded, they could work on that.

He'd work on that every single day if she'd let him.

He eased her jeans off, along with the black silk thong that made his cock hard from only a glimpse. Then she was bare and beautiful under his gaze, to his touch. He lowered his mouth to the smooth skin of her abdomen and heard her breath shudder out of her. He ran his lips down over the silky swell of her stomach, dipping his tongue into her belly button, and then went lower. She tasted better than the finest wine, and he couldn't get enough.

Placing his palms flat against her inner thighs, he opened her for his mouth. He skimmed his lips along her skin and sank his teeth lightly into the tender place where her thigh met her hip. Bella shuddered beneath him and made a sweet, low moan that heated his blood and made his cock go hard as steel.

"I can't wait to taste more of you," he murmured, blowing lightly over her beautiful sex until she squirmed beneath him. He moved up her body so he could look into her eyes. "You're gorgeous, Bella, and so aroused. You want me to do this, don't you?"

"I need you to do this." She raked her teeth against her bottom lip. "I don't care if this is a mistake," she breathed against his mouth. "I need you inside me, Ronan. I don't care if the world ends right now, that's all I want."

Ronan plunged his hands into her hair and forced her mouth to his as she pushed his jeans down past the head of his jutting cock and her fingers closed around the length. He groaned against her lips. All he wanted was to sink into her velvet softness, to lose himself inside her and become one with her.

But a sound that didn't belong had entered his awareness.

The hair on the back of Ronan's neck rose and magick in the center of his stomach twinged. He stilled and she followed suit.

"What's wrong?"

"The world ending?" he whispered. "You just might be prophetic. Get dressed, Bella."

He moved away, cursing under his breath, pulling his jeans up and reaching for his discarded sweater. Bella quickly reassembled her clothing too—a true pity.

Sounds of tromping boots and masculine shouts filtered

in from the corridor beyond their hotel room door. The Imperial Guard had found them.

"Ronan—" The rest of her sentence arrested in her throat, she looked at him with wide eyes.

He shrugged loosely. "So much for my spell. I told you there are magickal countermeasures for countermeasures."

It was also possible the witch had turned them in on purpose. The old ones loved a little chaos to ease the boredom of their lives. That's why they were hard to trust, even when you paid them well, which Ronan had a history of doing. Most of the fae weren't inherently trustworthy. Anyone who'd read Grimm knew that.

He held out a hand to Bella. "Come on. We've got to get out of here."

The guards pounded mantled fists on the door. Ronan led Bella to the window. He unlocked it and eased it up, letting in cold morning air to freeze their skin. He helped her out onto the fire escape. There was no time even to grab their coats.

He scanned the alley below them, but it was clear that was not the best way to go. "This way." He pulled her toward the sky.

"Up there? We'll be trapped on top of the building." She pulled back.

"I'm asking you to trust me, Bella. Do you?"

She took his hand.

They climbed. Behind them the door splintered open, kicked in from the boots of the guards.

They climbed faster.

The frozen metal of the railing seared his hand like fire and the *clang, clang, clang* of their shoes on the stairs sounded extra loud in the new snow of early morning. They reached the end and he helped her up onto the rooftop, just as the first shouts of the guards below them began to echo down the alley. They hadn't yet figured out that their quarry had gone up instead of down, which bought them a bit of time, but not much.

As he pulled her across the top of the narrow roof, they

passed a gargoyle hanging on the lip of the building that stared at them with a wise and bemused look on his old, pinched face.

Ronan said the words that would get them back to Priss's, but no pocket appeared, just more cold, snowy rooftop. So Priss had canceled his quick escape and had been up to no good. The next time he saw her, he'd let her know how unhappy he was. Right now he had other concerns.

The buildings in downtown Piefferburg were old, built mostly in the 1600s and 1700s and restored and renovated over the centuries. That meant they'd been built very close together, since back then there'd been no automobiles. Still, they were far enough apart that they'd have to use magick to jump rooftop to rooftop, until he ran out of juice. Once they were far enough—or he tired too much to safely get them across—they'd descend.

Muttering in Old Maejian, he wove the spell they needed to bridge the buildings and hurried across. He aimed them in the direction they needed to go—toward the Boundary Lands.

He watched her float across the last gap between the roofs. The chill had painted her cheeks rosy, made her dark eyes sparkle. A smile had overtaken her features, bright and beautiful. Despite the cold temperatures and the danger they were in, being away from the confines of the Rose Tower suited her. The pinched, severe expression she normally wore was gone.

If Ronan had his way, it would be gone forever.

He'd made a mistake thirty years ago, one that had affected them both in a negative way. He had every intention now of making it right. Fixing that wrong. He wanted Bella more than he'd ever wanted anyone in his life. She was his anchor, his hope, his love.

She was his and there was no one who could take her away from him. Not again. Not ever.

She came to a stop in front of him, her eyes still lighted and her smile still beaming. The light faltered a little as she saw the expression on his face and in his eyes. He knew how he looked. Hungry. Determined. She tried to step back, but he caught her arms and dragged her up against him, his mouth coming down against hers hot and possessively.

She didn't pull away. Making a little sound in the back of her throat, she pressed into him further. His cock noticed it. Every part of his body did. His heart really noticed it.

"Bell," he breathed out, breaking the kiss. He pressed her forehead to his chin and let out a long, slow breath. "We've wasted so much time on fear."

"Maybe too much."

He didn't like the tone of her voice, or the tremble in it.

In the distance, the commander of the Guard yelled.

"We have to get down. I don't have much power left." His magick wasn't limitless.

They left the last step of a nearby fire escape and their shoes sank into the ever-thickening layer of snow in an alley. Hearing the sounds of the Imperial Guard fanning out to search the area, he pulled her down the narrow alley and around the corner of a building, only to glimpse a force of Imperial Guards coming around the side of the same building, right for them.

They ducked back around and pressed up against the brick wall of the building behind them, both panting. The snow was coming down so heavily that it was covering their footprints. That was a stroke of luck.

"There!" Bella pointed at a vehicle some ways down the road. "If we can make it to that truck, we can hide beneath it."

With his magick almost drained to the dregs, it was their only chance.

They reached the rusty old red truck and got beneath it from the side least likely to reveal marks in the snow. He pulled her beneath him, rolling her under the warm protection of his body. Their breathing was heavy with exertion and showing white against the cold air. He hoped the queen hadn't become desperate and employed the Unseelie Court's magickical bloodhounds. If she had, they were doomed.

The boots of the Imperial Guard tromped past them in two lines and Ronan stared down into Bella's large brown eyes. They were beautiful eyes, flecked with caramel and amber. Her lips were parted and her breathing still came fast, probably more from fear than physical exertion.

As the boots stomped past them, he dropped his head and kissed her. She tasted even better when she was afraid and clinging to him. She was a strong woman and able to take care of herself, yet he liked it when she thought she needed him. He couldn't help that caveman part of himself.

After all, he needed her.

Finally the sounds of the boots disappeared into the distance and he reluctantly broke the kiss. He didn't let her go, though. This was a totally inappropriate situation for arousal, yet his body was primed for her, aching for the feel of her.

"Ronan, this isn't the time." But Ronan suspected her words lacked the rebuke she'd meant them to hold. Her facial muscles were slack and her lips rosy and swollen from his mouth. She looked warm, but he knew she had to be freezing.

He murmured one of the many spells he had memorized and wrapped magick around her body to keep the chill away. He didn't have enough power to cloak both of them, but at least she would be comfortable . . . for a while.

They needed to get to their destination and soon. Luckily they weren't far from the Boundary Lands and the place he'd hidden the object of power that the Phaendir wanted so badly. He rolled off her and helped her from beneath the truck.

Bella brushed the snow from her clothes. "Thanks for the magick, but you know it doesn't mean anything." A muscle worked in her jaw. "Neither have the kisses."

He pretended it wasn't like a stake through the heart. "That's okay, Bell. I fully expect you to push me away. Turnabout is fair play."

"Hey." Her spine snapped straight and she turned to pierce him with her gaze. "Don't act like you and me are a foregone conclusion and I'm just playing at making you pay right now."

He contemplated her for a long moment. "I would never take anything for granted with you. But even you can't deny the powerful pull between us." He paused. "Can you?"

She stared at him for a moment, her eyes going dark and her expression unreadable. Bella opened her mouth to say something, closed it, and then turned and walked away.

EIGHT

The Boundary Lands were everything Bella had imagined them to be. Covering their skeletons like hair and
flesh, trees and plants wound their way through the bones
of old structures built on the remnants of the very first set-
tlement of Piefferburg. Crumbling walls and rotting wood
combined with verdant lushness to create a place of more
beauty than Bella thought her heart could hold.

Even in the dead of winter here, fae magick kept the
plants from dying. Snow glistened on the furled heads
of roses and drifted slowly to rest on wide green leaves.
Yuletide was celebrated here by the wildling fae, and lights
nestled here and there on trees, their limbs intertwined with
red and green bulbs and sparkling ornaments.

After losing the guards, they'd walked to the edge of the
city, steering clear of every person they encountered, and
had found the boundary where all the wildling fae lived.
Letting the foliage envelop them, they'd entered, and been
unable to avoid a few of the inhabitants, but Bella felt like
here it didn't matter. This part of Piefferburg was different
from the rest, set apart like a different world, and worked
under its own set of laws. She was confident—for whatever

illogical reason—that these fae wouldn't turn them in to the Summer Queen.

He led her through a copse of birch trees, their shoes crunching over ice-laced fallen leaves. "We're almost there."

"You're not going to pull me through a pocket again, are you?"

He shook his head. "Priss is the only one capable of creating those."

He took her hand and guided her through a space between two monstrously tall birch trees. Beyond them lay a clearing with a large, aging brick structure.

Heavy lavender blooms dripped from the crumbling overhang of the building, tangled with long vines of red trumpeted flowers. She stared at the strange beauty of it—the juxtaposition of the vibrantly alive things and the dying building. By all rights the flowers shouldn't be growing, not at Yuletide, but who knew how much magick the fae caring for them possessed?

Much of the magick of the Seelie Court nobles had been bred out, choked from eons of breeding within a small population to keep the *Tuatha Dé* bloodlines true. But the magick of some of the other fae, most especially the wildling fae in the Boundary Lands, raged savage and strong.

Snow began to fall, making her gasp. She turned her face up to it, letting the flakes drift onto her face, melt, and slip down her neck. For the first time in so long, sweet Danu, she felt alive. Out here, she felt freed from the confines of the court, the queen, and her bloodline.

A warm hand pulled her up against a solid chest. Ronan's lips found hers and pressed. She opened her eyes and dissolved against him. For the first time since that fateful Yuletide ball, she just . . . allowed. Cool melted snowflakes mixed with his hot tongue as it brushed hers. He pushed her against the crumbling stone wall. Fragrant blossoms that had no business growing in the dead of winter crushed beneath their weight, releasing sweet scent to the chilly air.

"I love you, Bella," he whispered roughly against her lips in between kisses. "I never stopped."

Ronan slanted his mouth more firmly across her lips and plunged his tongue into her mouth as if to consume her. Something Bella had been holding clenched tightly in the center of her chest unraveled and released. Her muscles went loose as she threaded her fingers through the hair at the nape of his neck. Sweet pleasure suffused her, driving the chill from her bones and filling them with slow, warm honey.

He pulled her lower lip between his teeth, rasping it gently with his teeth, and her sex pulsed. Her fingers found the material of his coat and fisted. If he pushed her into this building right now and began to draw off her clothes, she would let him. She would . . .

"Hello."

She jerked in surprise at the feminine voice and pulled away from Ronan enough to look in the direction from which it came. Not far away a woman dressed in long, white, gauzy gown stood half-hidden behind the trunk of a tree.

Bella blinked. "Hello."

Ronan took a step backward. "Bella, please meet Aurora. She's a lady of the birch."

Bella had heard of them. The ladies of the birch had their roots in Czechoslovakia. They were primarily light nature-based fae, females who helped guide human females toward their dreams. There weren't many of them left. They'd largely been wiped out by the sickness. The wildings had been particularly susceptible for some reason, and owing to fae infertility they hadn't regained much strength in numbers. Only the goblins had done that.

The woman stepped toward them, a smile on her full lips. Her long reddish blond hair curled riotously past her thin shoulders, twisted through with small twigs, the leaves still attached. Oddly, it suited her. Her wide midnight blue eyes shone from a heart-shaped face, clear of any trace of makeup. She wore little to clothe her slim body, but she didn't seem cold. Her feet were bare and dirt smudged her dewy, luminous tanned skin here and there like she'd been gardening.

She was lovely. Prettier than the Summer Queen. More beautiful than any Seelie woman Bella had ever seen. And from the way she was smiling at Ronan, she knew him well.

Bella's limbs had been like warmed butter a moment ago, but now they'd gone wooden. This little twinge of jealousy was a stupid thing to feel. He'd been free to do as he wished, as she'd been free too. They'd both had lovers since their parting so many years ago. She had no claim on his romantic entanglements of the previous years.

The woman smiled and all Bella's ill feelings washed away in a moment. This person was like a part of nature herself, a wild and beautiful thing—like a refreshing rainstorm on a hot summer day or a gentle deer stepping out of the woods unexpectedly right before you. It was impossible to feel anything but joy in her presence. "I've never been with Ronan in the way you're thinking," she said warmly. "We're only friends."

Bella sucked in a breath. "Are you telepathic?"

"No. The question was in your expression."

She turned her face away.

"It's all right, Bella," Aurora said. "I understand the history you have with Ronan. I've known him for many years now, and the only woman he's ever wanted was you."

Bella looked at Ronan for confirmation of her words. He said nothing, only stared at her, his expression serious and his eyes wide and dark and very, very warm. His gaze did interesting things to her body and made her chest fill with something light. Hope?

"I still have what you gave me to keep," Aurora said, drawing them both from the way they'd fallen into each other's gaze.

He shifted to look at the birch lady. "Good. I never thought I'd come back for it."

"And yet here you are. Don't worry, it's safe."

"I thought we'd stay for a little while before heading back to the Summer Court."

"Stay as long as you'd like. You're safe here." She ducked into the structure. "Your object is this way."

Bella tried not to gawk as they followed her in. The front of the structure was crumbling brick, but that was only a fa-çade. So much in the world of the fae was not as it seemed. The ceiling was made of glass, showing the towering birch trees above that dripped with leaves, flowering vines, snow, and ice. A fire burned in a corner fireplace and comfort-able overstuffed furniture abounded in the room, all draped with cozy-looking throws. A four-poster bed dominated one corner, and a tiny kitchen occupied the opposite cor-ner. It was a small house, but it was clearly a home, very comfortable. Bella had the impression she could live here forever and be content.

"Stay here a moment," said Aurora. She exited the back of the cottage and returned with an item wrapped in cheese-cloth. She gave it to Ronan.

"Thank you for keeping it."

Aurora inclined her head and smiled. "Stay here in this cottage for as long as you'd like. We'll be watching out for you, so don't fear the guard." She looked at Bella meaning-fully. "Relax, if only for a little while. You've had a long journey and it's far from over. You both have many more miles to go before you find peace." Then she left.

Why did she think that Aurora wasn't talking about phys-ical distance, but emotional? There was a dark edge to her words that Bella didn't like. They almost felt prophetic.

"Can we trust her?"

"I would trust Aurora with my life." He paused. "I would trust her with *your* life, Bella, and that's the most precious thing in the world to me."

Ronan held her gaze, and the moment between them stretched. The look in his eyes could have kept her warm forever. Breaking the magic of it, she cleared her throat and stepped forward, toward the object. "What is it?"

He set it down on the table near the bed. "Never mind that. There's only one important thing right now." He closed the distance between them and pulled her against him, letting his hot mouth close over hers. His lips slid across her lips like silk, tasting her gently until it seemed he had to have more. Then he parted her lips and slid his tongue within.

Shivers of pleasure enveloped her. Three decades' worth of wanting welled up, and this time she didn't suppress it. *Relax.* She let it wash over her, sweeter than anything she could imagine. Surrendering to her desires, she twined her arms around his shoulders, feeling the strong bunch and flex of his muscles as he made minute movements, and made her want to run her hands—her tongue—over his warm bare skin.

He walked her back until her calves hit the edge of the bed, then dropped his hands to the button and zipper of her jeans. He worked them over her hips and down her legs, taking off her boots and socks with them and leaving her in only her thong.

NINE

She pulled his sweater up, revealing his sculpted wash-board abs. She dusted her lips across them, tasting his skin with the tip of her tongue and feeling his muscles tremble as she pushed his sweater up and over his head. The touch of her hands on him made him shiver, made him groan. It felt powerful to have that kind of an impact on a strong man like him.

She ran her palms over his chest, hardly able to believe she was here—in a place she'd never thought she'd be—with a man she'd long ago stopped hoping for. This moment had played out in her fantasies, but she'd always assumed that's what they'd stay—fantasies.

He pulled her shirt over her head and looked down at her wearing two silky bits of almost nothing, then he made a hungry sound deep in his throat and pushed her back onto the bed. For a moment he stood over her, making her shiver as his gaze swept her. He looked like he intended to devour her from head to toe.

Kicking his boots off, he followed her down onto the bed. The fabric of his jeans scraped against her bare skin as he slid between her thighs to plunge his hands into her hair and kiss her. He nipped at her lower lip and then dragged it gently through his teeth, making goose bumps erupt all over her body. Her hands strayed to the button fly of his black jeans, eager to stroke what she'd never been able to touch so many years before.

"You're mine," he growled into her ear. "I'm making love to you now and claiming you as forever mine. Do you understand that, Bella? There's no going back this time, no denying what we have between us."

Biting her lower lip, she found his gaze and nodded.

"Are you ready for—"

She stopped his words with her mouth. Breaking the kiss, she whispered, "Shut up, Ronan, and put your hands on me." To seal the deal, she cupped his cock through the fabric of his pants and stroked it. He groaned her name.

Using the pressure of his mouth, he pushed her back into the pillows while her fingers sought and freed the buttons of his jeans. There was something incredibly erotic about undressing this man and having him slowly undress her. The deliberate revealing of warm, bare flesh. The leisurely press and slide of skin against skin.

Undressing alone took her breath away.

Then they were completely naked and he was kissing her throat, nipping the tender part of her neck just under her earlobe, and Bella's rational and ordered cognition disappeared.

He rasped the edge of his teeth along her skin, raising goose bumps and making her nipples go hard, then slid his tongue along her skin, headed toward her breasts. In the back of his throat he made a low noise like the taste of her skin was intoxicating.

Stopping at one nipple and then the other, he gave both lavish attention, tracing every pucker, every hill and valley, with the tip of his tongue until she squirmed beneath him, arching her back.

He dropped down, dipping the tip of his tongue into her belly button, and then moved even lower. One strong hand planted on her inner thigh, he forced her legs to part then lowered his mouth to her sex. He teased her clit with the tip of his tongue, flicking back and forth until it grew swollen with need. Rubbing his finger around her opening, he petted her until she wanted to scream, before spearing two thick digits within and thrusting in and out. He sealed his mouth over her clit at the same time and worked it with his tongue until she writhed and bucked beneath him with the need to come.

He didn't allow it.

Building her toward an incredible, explosive climax instead, he kneed her thighs apart and braced his hands on either side of her head. The smooth head of his wide cock nudged her entrance, and all her female muscles deep within clenched in anticipation.

He stared down at her. "I haven't been with a woman since I met you, Bella. There is only you for me."

Her eyes widened and her breath caught. Then he thrust the head of his cock inside her, parting her folds and stretching her muscles. Inch by slow, mind-blowing inch, he fed her his wide, long shaft. Her head fell back into the pillows on a moan, and her spine arched as he went to the hilt inside her, filling her completely.

Tears pricked her eyes. "Ronan." His name came out broken. Grief for the years they'd lost warred with the joy of their reunion. The joy won.

Then he was thrusting in and out of her and primal lust took over.

"Look at me while you come," he commanded.

She forced her gaze to focus on his as the climax he'd withheld crashed into her with double the force. Pleasure filled every part of her body and mind as she came around his pistoning cock. Bella cried his name, tears squeezing from her eyes as sweet emotion and sexual ecstasy ruled her. As it ebbed, she held on to him, shuddering, her body eager for more.

He nipped her earlobe before dropping his head to lave over a diamond-hard nipple, nipping at it gently with the edges of his teeth. "There are so many different ways I want to take you. We have decades to make up for. Turn over."

He turned her to her stomach and slid a hand under her hips, forcing her bottom to fit against the hard jut of his cock. Parting her thighs, she dropped her head and offered herself to him completely. He ran his fingers over her sex and thrust inside, making her shudder. Then he guided the head of his cock in and drove it to the hilt in one long, hard, deep thrust that made her eyes roll back into her head.

Gliding a possessive hand from her breast, over her abdomen, and between her legs, he found her clit, engorged and sensitive, and petted it lightly as he mounted her. He slid in and out of her, slowly at first, teasingly rubbing around her swollen clit and stroking down farther to play where his cock thrust inside her, then back up through all her sensitive folds. Under his masterful touch, she was lost in a sea of pleasure and clawed the bedsheets.

He thrust faster and harder, finding her clit and rubbing it as he took her.

Pleasure built, swelled, and then exploded through her. She called his name as it crashed over her in waves, each one more intense than the last. He milked every last ounce of it from her that he could, pushing her from one stuttering climax into a second one. She heard Ronan cry her name as he came and they collapsed to the mattress in a sated tangle.

After a moment of heavy breathing, Ronan rolled to the side and dragged her along with him. The blankets and sheets were in an awful knot, and she had a twinge of regret for messing up someone else's bed, but somehow she thought that's exactly what Aurora had expected, had wanted even.

She snuggled into the curve of his body with a happy sigh. "Remember what you said on the rooftop about fear robbing us of so many years?"

He stroked her bare shoulder with his hand. "Yes." His voice rumbled out of him deep and steady. It could lull her to sleep, that voice.

"Let's not let fear steal any more time from us."

He tightened his embrace. "No, my love. No one is

stealing anything away from us now, not even the Summer Queen herself."

Bella shivered. She hoped not. That was a bridge they had yet to cross, and the queen was not the forgiving sort.

Nor was she the bargaining sort.

They stayed on the bed, letting the fire warm and illuminate the room and watching the snow gently drift down past the tree limbs above them, land on the glass ceiling, and melt. Day faded to twilight and then to darkness. Tomorrow night was Yuletide Eve. The winter solstice.

The longest night of the year.

Ronan allowed his hands to stray over her body, touching her possessively. He stroked her breasts and nipples constantly, brushed her shoulders, back, and stomach as if trying to memorize every inch of her flesh.

Often he delved between her thighs and thrust his fingers inside her over and over, let them play on her clit until she was a messy jumble of panting desire. He brought her to shuddering climax after climax until she could barely think, let alone walk.

In the middle of the night she awoke to him between her thighs, his shaft thrust within her and his hands stroking over her as though he were starving and she were sustenance he could consume through touch.

She orgasmed yet again in the dead of night with his mouth covering hers and his cock buried as deep within her as possible—joined at lips, hips, and heart.

After their shower the next morning, Ronan unwrapped the cheesecloth with Bella near him. It was a small piece, made of crystal, steel and bronze, smooth on one side and jagged on the other, making it look like a misshapen half-moon. There was part of a pattern on the front. It looked like junk, unless you were sensitive to the power it gave off. It rippled and pulsed with magick against his palm, cavorting with his own and sending little shocks up his forearm.

Bella sucked in a breath and went to touch it, but pulled her hand back at the last moment.

"Do you know what it is?"

"Oh, Danu," Bella breathed. "One of the sections of the *bosca fadbh*. It's one of three puzzle pieces that unlock part of the Book of Bindings."

He nodded. "That part of the book contains a spell that will tear down the warding around Piefferburg."

She looked up at him sharply. "This is what the Phaendir contracted you for?"

"It was being kept in a vault of a government building. I had the right skill set, magickally speaking, to break in. They contacted me, trying to appeal to my Phaendir blood, and offered me more money than I could use in three fae lifetimes. I agreed, but not because of the money. I pulled the job with the intention of never letting the Phaendir have the object."

The Phaendir were druids, strictly speaking, though both Ronan and his half brother, Niall, had a touch of druid blood as well. The Phaendir were powerful beings, powerful enough to trap and imprison all the fae of the world— as long as the fae were weakened in some way. Their magickical ability was mostly based in books and spells, in knowledge. Though over the years they had evolved a sort of magickal hive mind and that's where the power that kept up the warding around Piefferburg was stored. Still, they lacked the natural raw inner magick of the fae, lacked many of the abilities that Ronan and his *Tuatha Dé* mage brethren possessed.

It really chapped their hide too. They had hated having to come to him for help. Ronan smiled even now when he thought of it.

"Why didn't you give it to the Summer Queen? She could obtain the other pieces, and the Book of Bindings, and break the walls of Piefferburg."

He shook his head. "No, Bella. We can't get the other pieces or the book, because they are beyond the walls of Piefferburg. It's an impossible task. I wanted to ensure that the Phaendir never got their hands on this piece of the *bosca fadbh*. So I hid it here, in the lair of the most powerful fae I've ever encountered. I knew the birch lady would keep it safe. She wants peace, just as I do. Giving it to the Summer Queen will accomplish nothing. It will only assuage her ego."

Bella took the piece in her hand and stroked it with the pad of her index finger. She was still naked from the shower, and her nipples were hard from the slight chill in the air, as red and suckable as pert little berries. "It's so unassuming."

Ronan reached out and fingered a tendril of her hair. "I believe this piece is worthless in the face of having not recovered all the rest of the necessary items, but now it's my pass to freedom and to my life again. Now it's valuable. The Summer Queen will want this and will bargain with me to obtain it. She'll give me my life." He paused, holding her gaze steadily. "Will you be in that life again, Bell? This time for good?"

"What about the Unseelie blood we share? What about our potential offspring, Ronan? Aren't you still afraid we'll be exiled from the Summer Court?"

"With you at my side, I'm not afraid of anything. Are you?"

"After seeing the beauty that lies beyond the Rose Tower, how could I be?" She cupped his cheek in her hand. "I want you, Ronan. I've always wanted you, no matter the cost. I wish you could have realized that thirty years ago."

She stepped forward, closing the distance between them, and went up on her tiptoes to press her lips to his. The kiss was teasingly light and he wanted more. He caught her against him, pressing the piece of the *bosca fadbh* between them and slanting his mouth hungrily over hers. Then he lowered her to the soft mattress and kissed her lower down, taking her clit against his tongue and tasting the center of her until her cries echoed through the room and made the soft buds in the trees above the cottage explode into bloom as the magick in the air around them reacted.

He'd been in love with her since the moment he met her, and it had never abated, not in the thirty years since they'd parted ways. Now he felt flush with her, filled with the love he'd always needed from her but thought he'd never be able to accept without ruining her life, tearing her from the safety of the Seelie Court, and eventually making her resent him for it all.

He pulled her close to his body and inhaled the delicious scent of her hair. Even after all this time, he still remembered that distinctive fragrance of shampoo, perfume, and natural scent. "Ready to go back?"

Her embrace tightened a degree. "I'd rather stay here." Her voice held a note of fear in it, fear that she'd lose him again. He could feel it in her.

TEN

$\mathcal{B}$ ella didn't want to do this. Oh, dear Lady, she didn't want to face the wrath of the Summer Queen, didn't want to run the risk of Ronan disappearing from her life again.

They walked into the square, and Ronan released the glamour he'd been holding around them for the last twelve blocks. A layer of snow had fallen throughout the day and coated the square in a glimmering sheet of white and ice that reflected the silvery light of the full moon above them. Lights in the evergreens twinkled and sparkled with a Yuletide Eve merriment Bella didn't feel. Ordinarily she would be at a fete tonight, dressed to kill and drinking champagne.

Above them the clock in the center of the square struck the witching hour—winter solstice. The moment the twelfth chime ended, fireworks were launched from the top of every building, raining down sparkles and bursts of light. Booms, whizzing sounds and the joyful cries of the spectators filled the air.

Their uncertain future unfolded before them. The winter solstice was the shortest day of the year—but it also marked the point when the daylight would begin to increase. She would hold on to any bit of positive symbolism she could find.

It took only a handful of steps before the Imperial Guard marching in the square—undoubtedly on high alert—spotted them and trooped over. Harsh hands grabbed her and pulled her away as two of the men muscled Ronan to the ground and handcuffed him in iron.

"Get off me!" She shoved at the guard manhandling her, her hands finding only smooth, cold rose and gold metal.

"I abducted her," Ronan yelled. "She's been a prisoner ever since I broke out of Her Majesty's Prison. Leave her alone!"

"No." The guard released her, and she glared at the hulk who'd put bruises on her upper arms. "He's lying. I went with him of my own free will."

"Then you're under arrest too," answered the guard, turning her around and forcing the charmed iron around her wrists. She gasped at the touch of the metal against her skin and the empty way it made her feel—even her parlor-trick amount of Seelie magick was gone.

They heaved Ronan to his feet, and he gave her a look of exasperation as they hauled them off toward the reaching rose-quartz spires of the Seelie Court, past the throng that had begun to form and the camera crew of *Faemous*, who were out of breath from their run to catch some footage. Bella was sure that even now the two of them were "breaking news."

The guards pushed and prodded them up the marble staircase and down the gilded halls of the highest tower, straight to the throne room of the Summer Queen. The huge room was devoid of all but her advisors and favorites. Aislinn was there, white-faced with fear for her friend. Bella met her eyes briefly and tried to smile, but it was stiff because she was afraid too—for Ronan.

The Summer Queen, Caoilainn Elspeth Muirgheal, sat on her heavy, carved rose-quartz throne, royal buttocks cushioned by velvet. The rest of the court had adapted and changed with the times where fashion was concerned, but not the Summer Queen, who was thousands of years old. Ancient even for a *Tuatha Dé Danaan*, and of the purest blood that could be found. Her long white blond hair was coiled and pinned around her pale, oval face. Her gown seemed to be woven from starlight and gold. She was heartbreakingly beautiful. Delicate looking, but stronger than any fae with the exception of perhaps the Shadow King, her power was linked to her position as the Seelie Royal. Eyes the light blue of a husky dog's stared at them as they entered. Disapproval etched lines in her timeless face.

They came to a stop in front of her and both knelt, which was difficult to do, given the position of their hands behind their backs.

"Ronan Achaius Quinn, do you understand the severity of the charges leveled against you? Do you understand that the punishment fits the crime?" Her voice held power, strong Seelie magick, and it made all the hair on the back of Bella's neck stand on end.

"It couldn't be any worse than the punishment leveled against me before I escaped, my queen."

"Oh, Ronan, you're so young. There are fates worse than death."

The timbre of her voice made Bella shudder. It wasn't fully natural. The queen was very angry, and magick was slipping into her words.

The Summer Queen turned her frigid gaze toward Bella. "It's you I'm most surprised at. Ronan has always had a rebellious streak, but you've never caused more than a moment's stir at court. The guards tell me you say you went willingly with him. Did you help him escape the prison too?"

"No!" Ronan shouted. "Leave Bella out of this. I dragged her into this mess. It was all my fault."

"I went willingly with him," Bella raised her gaze to the queen's. "And I'd do it again."

The Summer Queen stiffened. Her spine looked rigid enough to crack. "If you care about him that much, you'll suffer his punishment alongside him."

"I have something for you, my queen," said Ronan. "Something that might sweeten your mood toward my transgression."

The queen seemed to ice over for a moment. She went perfectly still and white before speaking. "The object you stole for the Phaendir, no doubt. There's nothing you could have that would sway me in my opinion of what you have done, Ronan." She gestured to the guards. "Take them away until I've settled on a fitting fate for them both. Believe me, it will be something to impress the Unseelie."

Dark, bloody, and violent. That's the only thing that impressed the Unseelie.

The guards yanked Bella to her feet, making her gasp.

Ronan shook off the guards. "You don't want a piece of the *bosca fadbh*?"

"Halt!"

The guards immediately stopped dragging Bella and Ronan toward the side door, the one that led to the prison.

"Where is it?" The queen's voice stung Bella's skin like the lash of a frozen whip, making her wince.

"It's hidden with magick. You'll never find it on your own, but before I reveal it to you—"

"I'm the Summer Queen. What makes you think I couldn't find it?"

Bella stifled a cry. The queen's voice cut into her mind, becoming more like knife than a whip with every syllable she uttered.

"I kept it hidden from the Phaendir and I can keep it hidden from you."

His tone held a note of arrogance. Sweet Danu, they were all going to die.

Ronan continued. "I'll reveal the location of the piece, but you must agree, in front of witnesses, to several conditions."

The queen took a breath, regaining control—thank Danu—before replying. "You're not in a position to make demands, Ronan."

"Well, my queen, I have the piece." He paused. "And you don't."

For a moment Bella thought the queen might explode. Her icy, angry reserve had taken the leap to hot lava in the span of a heartbeat. "I can't do anything with your piece of the *bosca fadbh* without its mates. So you see, dear Ronan, your offer might not be as juicy as you presume."

"But if you have the piece, then the Phaendir does not. I do not need to point out that the Shadow King would also *not* have it. That should be tempting enough. And perhaps, if you don't shout *Off with his head!* I might be able to get the other pieces of the *bosca fadbh*. Perhaps even the lost Book of Bindings."

"Impossible."

"Nothing is impossible if you know the right people and pay the right price." He paused and lowered his voice. "You of all people should know that."

The queen said nothing. She only stared at him, her fingers clenching around the polished rose-quartz armrests of her throne, her perfect, beautiful face revealing no hint of what she might be thinking. The entire room seemed to hold its breath—including the guards who still loosely gripped Bella's arm.

"You're aiming far too high and assuming far too much about me, Ronan. I dislike it."

"Forgive me." He inclined his head. "I seek only to give you what the Phaendir want desperately to possess. Aren't you at least a little curious about why they want it so badly? I am."

The queen jerked her chin upward. "Before I make my decision, tell me your terms. Tell me what kind of trade you want me to make for the piece."

"I require that Bella remains unharmed and unpunished for coming with me to obtain the piece, and for her to retain her position in the Seelie Court, *no matter what*, until the natural end of her days. No matter what information may come to light about her in the future, no matter what she may do, so long as it's within the bounds of Seelie Court law."

The wording was precise and he did that for a reason. The queen was known to try and wriggle through the loopholes of a promise.

The Summer Queen eyed Bella with undisguised curiosity. "That makes me think Bella has a secret or two."

"No matter what secrets might be revealed about her, she must never be cast from the Seelie Court." Ronan's voice was steel to the Queen's ice and contained a thread of resonating magick of his own. "Not her progeny either. Or her husband. All in her family must be safe from exile."

"I take it you're not finished, since you haven't asked for your life yet."

Ronan inclined his head. "I wish to retain my life and for all charges against me to be dropped." Ronan turned and met Bella's gaze. Holding it, he finished, "And to marry Bella, if she'll have me."

The queen drummed her fingers. "You're asking for too much. *Two* lives, Ronan? No punishment for your crimes *and* a happy ending with Bella?" She shook her head. "You'll undermine my credibility, and my enemies will begin to think I'm going soft and sentimental. I can't have that." She considered them for a long moment. "I will bargain for one life. Whose is it, Ronan? Yours or Bella's?"

"No!" Bella shouted. "Don't do this, Caoilainn Elspeth Muirgheal!" Names had power, so she invoked all of the queen's. To no avail.

"Answer!" the queen demanded of Ronan.

Bella knew what Ronan would say before he said it. She had no question he would protect her life over his. Tears pricked her eyes and choked her throat. "No, Ronan, please!" The guards clamped down on Bella's arms and drew her backward. She kicked and struggled against their strength. This couldn't be happening.

Ronan met her eyes. Sorrow had turned his pupils a dark blue. "Bella's life will be spared."

"I thought as much. Now reveal the piece to me."

"Ronan! No!"

The guards' pull was something she couldn't fight, couldn't shake off. Inexorably, they dragged her backward, through the huge double doors of the throne room and into the corridor, where her cries echoed as they uncuffed her. Just as the massive doors swung shut, she glimpsed the piece of the *bosca fadbh* floating eerily in front of Ronan and a guard behind him, a silver sword glinting viciously in the reflected light of the piece of the *bosca fadbh*.

ELEVEN

The doors slammed shut, Bella stared at the closed entrance to the throne room for a moment in complete shock and then rushed toward the doors, only to be blocked by an implacable row of shining rose and gold.

She whirled and ran down the corridor, pushing past anyone who got in her way, until she reached the front doors of the tower and burst through them. In the square outside the Seelie Court, she went down hard on her knees in the snow. It immediately soaked through the fabric of her jeans and numbed her skin, but that only made that part of her body match the rest of her.

All around her, revelers stopped their singing and laughing and stared at her. To Bella it truly was the longest, darkest night of the year.

Before her, on the other side of the square, loomed the Black Tower of the Unseelie Court. All the dark art she'd tried so hard to suppress fluttered deep within her and rose on grief-encrusted wings. All the curses she'd never given voice to beat against the box within her mind where she'd locked them, those for the queen most especially strong. Long-repressed magick bubbled inside her, ready to explode.

She closed her eyes. *No*. She might have Unseelie blood flowing through her veins, but she wouldn't give in to the impulse to hurt others because she was feeling hurt herself. That was not Bella and never would be.

Maybe she could manifest something good. Perhaps instead of weaving curses, she could weave a wish instead. Maybe if it came from her heart . . . She closed her eyes and concentrated as hard as she could on the outcome she wanted. Magick bubbled out of her like water quenching dry earth.

Please, Danu, please.

It wasn't possible that she could have come this far, lost Ronan for so many years, only to find him and lose him again this way. His soul was a perfect match for hers, singing and twining in a beautiful song within her heart. Even his magick complemented hers—more than she could have ever known.

This ending simply wasn't possible.

Would she be able to feel it when they killed him? Would a cold, dark place open up inside her? Maybe they'd already done it. Maybe he was already dead.

She looked up at the Unseelie Court rising across the square. Around her, revelers gave her a wide berth as they sang Yuletide carols. They downed mugs of warm cider and toasted one another with Wassail bowls, yelling in the traditional Old Norse, *"Ves heill!"* Be well and be in good health.

Bella dry-heaved in the snow.

She would never again step foot in the Rose Tower. She could never look upon the queen's face again and not want to give in to the dark impulse within to curse her. Maybe she would give in to the dark pull of the Unseelie Court. It was time to put her fear aside and start a new life.

Someone touched her shoulder and Bella looked up to see Aislinn. The entire square had fallen completely silent. All the fae stared at someone standing behind Bella.

Taking Aislinn's offered hand, Bella stood and turned.

The queen stood in the square, backlit by the light spilling through the open doors of the Seelie Court and dressed in a thick white fur coat, the hem trailing in the snow. No red spray of blood marred its perfection. Hurray for small favors.

"It's Yuletide Eve," she said. It was quiet enough to hear the snow fall. Not even a murmur could be heard from the Unseelie side. "Therefore I've given you a gift."

That was when she noticed Ronan standing to the left of the queen, hidden in the shadow of her glow. Bella's heart stuttered and then started again, beating twice as fast. She took a step toward him, but something in the way the queen stood made her halt. The queen seemed like a raptor ready to strike—one false move and she'd sink her fangs in deep.

"Happy Yuletide to you both, but it's not all sunshine." The queen drew a breath. When she spoke next, it was loud enough for everyone around them to hear, including the *Faemous* film crew. "Bella Rhiannon Caliste Mac Lyr and Ronan Achaius Quinn are hereby banished from the Seelie Court, effective immediately." She turned and walked back into the tower, a brace of guards following her.

The doors shut behind her with a final-sounding thump.

Bella ran to Ronan and threw her arms around him, concerned only with one thing—he was alive, warm and real in her embrace.

Ronan pulled her up against his chest and slanted his lips over hers. His tongue slipped within her mouth and heated her blood, making her forget the snow and cold, making her forget all the other celebrating fae in the square who looked on in curiosity.

When they broke the kiss, she drew a trembling breath. A look of sorrow had enveloped his face. "Because of me you're banished from Seelie. You've lost everything. It's exactly the thing I was trying to prevent all those years ago."

"Oh, Ronan." She reached up and cupped his cheek. "No. Don't you see? I have *everything* because I have you."

"Even if we have nowhere to sleep tonight?"

"We'll figure it out. We're together now and we can overcome any obstacle in our path. Why did she let you live?"

"I've had contact with the Phaendir. I know who might be able to be swayed for a certain price. The queen held a blade to my throat and demanded that information from me after you left, but I refused to give it up. Instead I told that when she had need of me, I was hers. So long as the rest of the time I could be *yours*—warm and alive."

"So pragmatism won out over her slighted pride."

"The banishment is her way of saving face in front of the court."

"Where do we go now?"

Ronan looked at the Black Tower and squeezed her hand.

"Unseelie," she said.

He nodded. "I don't know how this will turn out, Bella. The Shadow King is not pleased with me for turning my back on the Black Tower, and now I've given the Summer Queen a piece of the *bosca fadbh*, something he would like to possess."

She chewed her lip. "Bodes ill."

He pulled her toward him for a quick kiss. "I have reason to believe he'll take us in despite all of this. Leverage, Bell. I have it on both the royals."

"It's a dangerous game we're playing."

"Life in the courts is always dangerous."

They turned and walked toward the center of the square. Bella supposed she ought to be nervous about the fact she was now banished from the only home she'd ever known, yet all she felt was gratitude and happiness, leavened with a dash of excitement for the adventures to come and the things they'd see.

Aislinn stood near the maligned statue of Jules Piefferburg that marked entry into Unseelie territory. "I'll miss you," her best friend said, staring up at the Black Tower.

"I'll miss you too." Bella gave Aislinn a hug, feeling a cloud of loss rising up into her chest and throat. When people were banished from the Seelie Court, that meant no contact with its members. She and Ronan had given up a lot to be together. Bella wiped away a tear. "Can you make arrangements for Lolly?"

"Of course I will."

She parted from Aislinn and took one last look at the Rose Tower. There were many people she would miss— Lolly, her other friends, her family. Ronan caught her hand and followed her gaze. He'd be missing people too.

Then they looked at each other and smiled. They didn't have to say a word, because they each knew what the other was thinking: The sacrifice was worth it.

Hand in hand, they walked farther into the square. Above their heads fireworks sparked and exploded, and all around them Yuletide bonfires glowed. The celebrations had resumed and lighter days were on the horizon.

Before them lay their future, a brand-new path they'd create and walk together.

A
Christmas Kiss

Lora Leigh

ACKNOWLEDGMENTS

A special thank-you to all the dear and special friends who have stood behind me, beside me and in front of me through a very difficult year.

Lue Anne, Natalie, Jennifer and Janine. Jessica, Crissy, Donna and Sheila. For my son, Bret, who always has my back; and my dearest friend, Sharon, who has supported me more times than I can count.

For my daughter, Holly, for running the roads; and Ryan, for putting up the fence. For Renae, for helping when I needed it the most; and for Ann Marie, for the shoes and wonderful e-mails.

All of you have made my life brighter, enriched it and understood when things got crazy.

Thank you.

ONE

Wolf Mountain, Colorado
Wolf Breed Compound, Haven

There was something about a winter snowfall that Jessica Raines had always loved. A sense of warmth, despite the cold. A sense of wonder, a remnant of her childhood that she had never lost.

Now, as she moved through the soft, heavy winter white that fell around her, she had never felt less like a child. At twenty-four, she felt old, worn and tired.

Christmas was coming. Lights were strung around the Wolf Breed Compound of Haven and windows were lit up with the festive colors of the season as lavishly decorated trees twinkled merrily into the winter night.

Christmas was coming and Jessica had never felt less festive.

The snow was beautiful though. She had missed it last year during her imprisonment in the underground cells to which the Wolf Breeds had kept her confined. Because she had been a traitor. No matter how reluctantly, still, she had betrayed the very people she had believed in so deeply.

Even as she had done it, helpless against the compulsions rising inside her, Jessica had raged, fought, screamed silently. But still, she had hidden information, relayed defense maneuvers and revealed the residences of the Wolf Breed alpha and his mate, as well as their second-in-command to her father.

The pure blood society he had worked with had nearly killed them. If she hadn't found the strength to pull two of the mates from their homes before the attack, then they would have been killed.

She pushed her fingers through her hair, tugging at the tender roots as she fought to make sense of the betrayal her father had dealt her. He had been sending her to certain death. He had to have known it. The drug he had slipped into her food and drinks when she visited, the orders he had given her—he had known beyond a shadow of a doubt that she would be caught, and that she would die. And still, he had done it.

She couldn't even ask him *why* he had done it. He was dead now. The society he had been a part of was disbanded. Advert, the small town outside the Breed compound, was under Wolf Breed control, but still, Jessica suffered.

She had lost everything because of his hatred for a species that hadn't asked to be created. One that was determined to survive now that it existed. He had sacrificed his daughter, and then his own life, for nothing.

She lifted her face to the falling snow and imagined the dampness on her skin was the moisture of the melting ice. It wasn't. It was tears, and she knew it. Her father wasn't the only one who had lost in his bid to destroy the Breeds; Jessica had lost as well, much more than anyone could imagine.

Pausing, she leaned against the large trunk of a towering oak and gazed up at the close canopy of thick, dark clouds. The snow was flying thicker, harder. It suddenly had a heavy, ominous feel to it, as though nature were moving in to exact vengeance for crimes untold.

Or perhaps against her.

Grimacing at the flight of fancy, she shook her head before moving quickly to turn back to the cabin she had left. That sudden movement was followed by a loud retort and a chunk of bark striking her in the face.

There was a second of disbelief, a pause as the realization that someone was shooting at her filtered through her system, before Jessica jumped behind the tree, heart racing, fear pounding within her.

Someone had just fired on her.

She was in the middle of the forest with no coat, no weapon, no guards. She was undefended in a place where she shouldn't have needed defending.

Now what?

She stared around the bleak winter landscape, fighting to catch her breath through the pounding of her heart as she tried to think quickly. Logically.

She couldn't see anyone, couldn't sense anyone. Right now she would give her eyeteeth for those nifty supersenses the Breeds possessed. Advanced hearing, seeing and sense of smell would come in handy right now.

She couldn't stand there much longer, she told herself. She was going to have to move soon or the shooter could work his way around until he had a line of sight on her that she couldn't escape.

There was only one course of action. She gripped the rough trunk of the tree, hard, before throwing herself past it and racing for the large rocks and boulders a short distance away.

Shots fired behind her. Clumps of dirt flew up, striking against her as she ran. She slid into the snug embrace of the boulders, flinching on a hard shudder as another bullet exploded against the side of a huge rock.

"Cowards," she bit out furiously, pushing herself as close against the rock as she could. "Bastards."

Surely to God one of the Breeds would have heard the gunshots by now. Haven, the Wolf Breed Compound, was patrolled by one of the best Breed security forces in the world. So where were they now? Maybe it hadn't really been such a good idea to slip away from her bodyguard.

On hands and knees she crawled through the mess of boulders lying around like a child's toys tossed about haphazardly.

The sharp retort sounded again, this time sending chips of stone flying over her head as she wedged herself between upright columns and fought to make herself as small as possible.

She was dead. The Breeds should have just killed her a year ago when they were debating the action, because she was definitely going to die now.

Where the hell were the Breed patrols? Or was that who was shooting at her?

Fear rushed through her system in a surge of adrenaline as the next shot sent a bullet tearing into the stone above her head. They were getting closer. She wasn't going to survive. She would die here, in the cold and the snow, and it would probably take a while for someone to find her body. Evidently no one was too concerned with her now that she had been released, though she was confined to Haven. It was probably a Breed trying to kill her.

"Jess." A hand clamped over her mouth and strong arms jerked her behind the rocks as another shot struck beside her shoulder.

Heated, hard and male, the large body she was suddenly cushioned against was a welcome relief, a place of security as she recognized the voice at her ear.

Hawke Esteban.

Relief poured through her system with enough force to leave her dizzy. One arm curled around her waist, dragging her backward to the security of another outcropping of the large rocks she had been using for protection.

"What the hell are you doing out here?" he hissed in her ear, his dark, brooding voice sizzling with anger.

She tried to shake her head. How the hell was she supposed to talk with his calloused palm clapped over her lips?

"Stay still," he ordered as she struggled against him. "Mordecai and Rule are moving in on the shooter."

Mordecai, the cold, steel-hard Coyote assigned to Haven from the Coyote pack in the cliffs above, and Rule, the Lion Breed who normally worked as personal security for the Director of Breed Affairs, Jonas Wyatt.

Both men were killers, true stone-cold Breeds bred to shed blood.

"Let's get you out of here." His hand slid away from her mouth. "Stay behind me. We'll work our way back to the cabin and let them take care of business here."

*H*awke could feel fear crawling through his system as he gripped Jessica's hand, and following Rule's directions, began to lead her along the most secure path back to the cabin she had been assigned.

Fear was an unknown emotion to him, until now. Until he had faced the realization that someone was shooting at his mate. That he could lose her. That everything he had fought for over the past year could end in her death.

He couldn't face it, he realized in the moments that he, Mordecai and Rule had raced to her rescue. He couldn't face Jess's death. In the past year she had already faced more than any woman should have had to endure; to lose her this way was more than he could contemplate.

Lifting his head, he pulled the scents of the forests into his nostrils, drawing farther away from the sharp tang of evil and gunfire. He could literally smell the intent of the man stalking Jess. The murderous anger; the determination to kill her.

"He's drawing away, Hawke." Mordecai's voice came over the communication link. "We don't have an ID yet, just scent. Rule is moving in place to capture."

"Capture, don't kill," Hawke warned the Coyote Breed, his voice hard. "I want enough left to question."

"If I have to," Mordecai drawled.

"You're dragging me, Hawke," Jess protested behind him.

He *was* dragging her. He was pulling her through the

forests at a quick pace, forcing her to keep up with him as he rushed her back to safety.

There had been no report that she had left her cabin, though there were strict orders that he was to know each time she so much as stepped out on the porch.

"We have to get back to the cabin." He slowed his steps marginally though, knowing she didn't have the endurance that he himself had. "Did you let anyone know you were leaving the cabin?"

"No," she stated mutinously behind him. "I didn't want company."

"Well, you had company anyway," he growled. "The wrong sort."

"Story of my life," she muttered.

He glared back at her before jerking his head forward again and concentrating on getting her to safety.

He should have known better than to look back at her. Each time he looked at her he was struck by a rush of arousal that bordered on painful, just as he had been the first time he saw her two years ago.

With her red-gold hair falling behind her shoulders in heavy, ribbon-straight curtains, her wide blue eyes and porcelain perfect skin, she was like a vision of angelic innocence. Cupid's bow lips, finely arched brows, high cheekbones. Her slender body was sleek and compact; at five feet and six inches, a little on the short side compared to Breeds, but with generous breasts and tempting hips.

She made a man think of all the nasty things he could do to that perfect body even as he felt like a perverted monster whenever he looked into her innocent face.

The innocence was real. Jessica Raines was still a virgin, as medical reports attested. And she was his mate.

"What the hell were you doing out here by yourself?" He snarled at her, angry at himself for the overriding lust tormenting him; angry at her for being the innocent, delicate creature she was.

"I'm always by myself," she snapped back. "Why should a walk in the woods be any different?"

He almost winced at the statement, because it was the truth. She'd been imprisoned for a year, seeing only the doctor, a few of the higher ranking Breed female mates and her interrogators until they managed to figure out why Jessica had betrayed them. When she had been released, it had been into Haven only. She wasn't allowed off the compound. She was given her own cabin, and most Breeds steered well clear of her because she was his mate.

"You have bodyguards," he reminded her coldly. "Sharone and Emma were assigned to you when you were released. They're not exactly unfriendly, so why weren't they with you?"

Sharone and Emma, two of the rare Coyote Breed females, loved trouble. He'd expected any day to have to deal with a situation they had orchestrated where Jess was concerned.

"They have two days off." She shrugged. "I imagine today was one of those days."

"Ashley?" He barked out the name of the other coyote female. "She's on backup."

She shrugged again. He felt the movement through her arm as they cleared the woods and headed for the cabin. The compound was on red alert. Breeds were rushing through the woods now, the main gates were closed and the entire compound on lockdown.

Hawke's lips thinned. Jess was to be protected at all costs. She was to have a guard twenty-four/seven and he would be damned if he wouldn't know, and know fast, exactly why one of those guards hadn't been present.

God help Ashley if she had deserted his mate. Coyote females were rare, and they would be one less if he found out the flighty, girlish little Coyote had literally thrown his mate to the enemy.

TWO

*J*essica had a feeling she was getting ready to see Hawke
explode when they entered the roomy cabin and heard
the muffled thump against the basement door.

Her lips set mutinously as Hawke turned, stared back at
her narrowly, then strode to the door that led to the basement below.

He jerked it open, his expression freezing as Ashley
True sprawled to the wood floor of the living room. Her
delicately streaked long blonde hair fell over her face for
a brief moment before she swiped it out of her way and
jumped gracefully to her feet to glare at Jessica.

Hawke was staring at her too, with that frozen, immobile
expression she so hated. It would almost be worth sharing a
kiss with the son of a bitch just to see some emotion cross
his face.

"She locked me in," Ashley gritted out as she pointed
an accusing finger at Jessica. "I broke a nail." She turned
to Hawke, her voice raising. "Do you even have a clue how
hard it is to get my alpha to approve a trip to the salon? Let
alone pay for it? I have to actually be hurt. If I have to take

another bullet to get my nails done, we're going to fight, Hawke."

Jessica crossed her arms over her breasts. "Do like the rest of us mortals. Clip them down and file them yourself," she told her, her voice laden with sarcasm.

It had been over a year since Jessica had been to a salon. She had no sympathy whatsoever for the girl.

"And I tore my jeans." Ashley glared down at her jeans as though Jessica hadn't spoken.

"Give it another year and the ripped jeans will be in style again." Jessica shrugged, refusing to show even a hint of nervousness at the silent, dark look Hawke was shooting across the room at her.

"She is a menace." Ashley stabbed her finger in Jessica's direction again. "She refuses to stay put. She tries to sneak off. She never takes orders and she will not, under any circumstances, share her soda with me."

Jessica smirked. She liked her soda, and getting it wasn't easy. Most Breeds refused to pick anything up for her in town, and when she did manage to get it, she tended to hoard it. Especially considering the fact that the few times she had shared her soda with Ashley, the other girl had never returned with more.

She had been highly inconsiderate, Jessica deduced. Therefore, she refused to share any longer.

"You're relieved for the day, Ash," Hawke growled, though he continued to stare back at Jessica as though he were doom and gloom coming to set up permanent residence.

Ashley's nostrils flared in annoyance as her gaze slid to Hawke before returning to Jessica.

"Someone should just shoot her and put us out of our misery," she stated with another glare in Jessica's direction.

"Someone nearly did," Hawke informed her.

The statement made Ashley pause, her gaze narrowing on Jessica as the pouting, spoiled features transformed to cool, dangerous intent.

"Orders?" she asked Hawke. "Orders other than simply leaving?"

"Stand by," he ordered without taking his gaze from Jessica. "I'm sure you'll have the privilege of spending more time here soon."

There were no smart-assed comebacks. Ashley gave a quick, somber nod before striding to the front door, opening it and leaving the cabin as quickly as Hawke had dragged Jessica back into it.

"Ashley's not easily duped," he stated with an air of lazy interest as his gaze flicked over her. "How did you get her in the basement?"

Cocking her hip, Jessica stared back at him mockingly. "Soda. I told her I had the extras stored downstairs and I wasn't going after them."

"Soda." He gave a quick, hard shake of his head. "That girl is going to end up rotting her stomach with that crap. Or shooting you to get one. How did you get them this time?"

She kept her lips shut tight. There wasn't a chance in hell she was betraying her source this time. The last time she had so unwisely told anyone who was sneaking her soda, that Breed had been transferred to parts unknown.

"You have no right to restrict them." Dropping her arms from her breasts, she stalked into the kitchen where she moved to the coffeepot and the decaffeinated coffee sitting on the counter.

Another no-no. Coffee with caffeine.

"You have no right to risk your health with them." He followed her, of course. "Dr. Armani warned you that the drinks could have an adverse affect on you and yet you still drink them."

"And still, no adverse affects." She turned back to him with a tight smile as she gripped the counter behind her. "You limit my sodas, my coffee and my chocolate. I can't leave Haven and I can't contact friends on the outside. I thought I was free, Hawke?"

That had been the ruling of the Breed Tribunal three

months ago. She had been drugged, forced to follow the orders she had been given, and still she had managed to save the women that the pure blood society had tried to strike against. They had given her freedom, but it was so limited that sometimes she wondered if it was any different from the imprisonment she had suffered before.

"You are free." But even in his voice she could hear the truth that she was anything but.

Shaking her head, she tossed him a mocking smile before pushing away from the counter and heading back to the living room.

"You can leave now," she told him. "I'm safe and sound, as you can see. I don't need you anymore."

"Did you ever?"

There was a dangerous, warning quality to his voice that brought her to a stop in the doorway. She stared across the room at the fireplace, forcing herself not to turn back to him. Jess reminded herself that the pain she felt in her chest was a side effect of the fear and not any other emotion.

"I did, once," she finally answered. "Did it do me any good?"

She didn't give him a chance to answer. Moving from the doorway, she walked through the living room and into her bedroom beyond, where she closed the door quietly behind her.

Once, she had cried for him. She had lain on a metal cot, sobbed into her pillow and prayed that he would help her, that he'd at least visit her, that he would give her a chance to explain. That he would just talk to her.

It hadn't happened. For twelve months she had lived in near isolation. Month by month the hope that she had clung to at first slowly receded until there had been nothing left.

As she moved across the room the door behind her squeaked open, causing her to turn on her heel and stare back at Hawke in surprise.

Thick black hair fell over his brow despite his attempts to push it back with his fingers. Golden brown eyes—not quite amber, not quite yellow gold—stared back at her with brooding intensity while the savage planes and angles of his face were more defined by the day's growth of beard that darkened his expression.

Snug jeans conformed to powerful legs and thighs, spanned lean hips and tight lower abs. A denim shirt was buttoned over his chest, but did nothing to hide the muscular breadth of it.

He was so handsome he stole her breath. But that was normal for a Breed, she told herself. They were all incredibly good-looking in a rough and alluring way. They had been created for strength, endurance and killing. But they had also been created to please the senses of those who had created them.

As well as those who would see them. Hawke was the epitome of the rough and tough male. His gaze was brooding, his expression hardened, his body muscular and well formed. He was every woman's waking fantasy.

He was the man she had dreamed about, ached for, and had finally given up on.

"I stayed away for a reason."

She'd been out of the underground cell for nearly three months, and this was the first time he had broached the subject. She hadn't dared mention it. She didn't want to discuss it, didn't want to deal with the emotions she knew would rush through her.

"You made the right decision." Jessica stared back at him, refusing to back down, refusing to let him know how much his defection had hurt her.

Of all the Breeds she had known, he alone should have understood that she would have never betrayed them willingly.

"It was the right decision." His nod was short, perfunctory. It was an agreement that sliced at her soul.

"So why bring it up?" And why hadn't she just let the subject drop? Why bring it up when it really didn't matter anymore?

"We've been playing this game since you were released,"

he stated, his voice quiet though dark with some hidden emotion that she wasn't certain she wanted to name.

"And what game would that be? The one where I don't want to be here? Or the one where you insist I stay? Go, do whatever you do, Hawke, and leave me in peace. And while you're at it, keep the babysitters at home, if you don't mind."

"If you'd had a babysitter today you wouldn't have nearly been killed." There was an edge to his voice, an underlying anger that she knew burned inside her as well.

"I survived it." She shrugged, though the fear at the thought of what had nearly happened couldn't be shut off as effectively as she would have preferred.

"You survived it?" Male outrage dominated his features now. His eyes glittered with it; his expression was filled with it. "Son of a bitch, Jess, you were nearly killed."

"Nearly doesn't count. Would you leave now? I'd like to shower."

She turned away from him, trying to appear nonchalant, uncaring. She very much wanted to live, but she had learned in the past year that the rules to her life had changed. Now if someone would just tell her what the new rules were, then she might have a chance at living.

The amazement slowly left his expression, but what replaced it sent a surge of feminine weakness racing through her system. A look alone shouldn't have the power to weaken a woman's knees and send arousal flooding through her system. It shouldn't be bold enough, hot enough, that she could feel her sex flushing, swelling, instantly growing damp.

And a man shouldn't have the senses to detect it. She watched as his nostrils flared, his gaze darkening as he recognized the scent of her arousal. It wasn't fair, because she couldn't sense his emotions, his arousal.

Her gaze flicked uncontrollably to the crotch of his jeans and she found herself swallowing tightly at the sight of a bulge that hadn't been there before.

The front of his jeans were full, the proof of his arousal pressing against the material and filling her head with erotic imagery.

She had to force her gaze back to his face, only to see the heavy-lidded, hungry look in eyes that assured her that he knew exactly where she had been looking.

"We're fighting a losing battle," he told her, his voice darker, deeper. "It's going to happen, Jess, and when it does, there will be no turning back. You know that."

Yes, she knew that. She knew well what mating heat was, and what it would do to her, as well as to him. She knew that once it happened, she was tied to him forever.

But wasn't she already tied to him forever? a little voice questioned her. It wasn't as though she could get him out of her mind, out of her fantasies. He'd been there before her confinement, and thoughts of him had filled her dreams and her thoughts during the entire time she had been there.

The days and nights that she had longed to see him, ached to lay her head against his chest and feel his arms around her. She'd cried for him. They hadn't kissed, hadn't touched, but the time they had spent together had cemented him in her heart.

She didn't understand why. She didn't question it. She knew he was there. It was that love-at-first-sight crap, she thought with self-directed fury. That instant attraction, that instant need, which went far beyond the chemical and biological mating heat that the Breeds experienced.

"I want you to leave," she whispered, though in her heart she knew that wasn't what she really wanted. She wanted him to hold her, to touch her, to ease the burning ache that filled her soul.

He stared back at her for long, bleak moments before nodding sharply.

"This time," he stated with a hint of anger. "This time I will, Jess. Don't expect it next time."

He turned on his heel and left the room. Seconds later she heard the front door close.

She collapsed on the pretty quilted bedspread covering her bed and breathed out with a long, weary sigh. He wouldn't promise he would leave the next time. She was living on borrowed time where the mating heat was concerned, and she knew it. The problem was, she had a feeling that after today's attack, she was living on borrowed time, period.

THREE

"It's escalating." Hawke stepped into Alpha Gunnar's office and faced off with not just his own alpha, Wolfe, but his second-in-command, Jacob Arlington, and Haven's head of security, Aiden Chance.

The three powerful Wolf Breeds were a force to be reckoned with. They were perhaps the most powerful men Hawke knew, Breed or human. They had gathered together the Wolf Breeds, fought for a home, secured it, ensured it before ever revealing who they were or what they intended within their own community.

They had brought peace and safety to the people who followed him.

"We knew it would eventually." Wolfe leaned back in his chair as he breathed out a hard sigh. "I'm surprised it's taken them this long."

"She locked her bodyguard in the basement before going out this afternoon," Hawke revealed. "We can't depend on her to watch her own back."

"Telling her the truth might work." Jacob Arlington, one of the few Breeds with the coloring of the red wolf rather than the gray or black, spoke up then. "She might care more about her own life if she was aware that it was actually in danger."

Hawke threw him a hard glare. "I believe I was ordered to keep that information to myself for the time being." He turned back to Wolfe. "That time is up, Wolfe. It's now time for a measure of honesty with her. I'll lose her otherwise."

Wolfe stared back at him silently for long moments before he began to shake his head.

"Don't make me ignore a direct order, Wolfe," Hawke suggested, feeling the animal he was inside rising to the surface. "We'll all regret it."

He'd followed medical as well as security advice for a year now. He'd stayed away from his mate while she was confined, did nothing to risk the mating heat that would have demanded her release. He gave the pack a chance to secure itself, to determine the extent of damage that had been caused by her treason. When it was discovered that she had been drugged, he had heeded medical advice and kept his distance even after her release to ensure that all the drug was out of her system before the mating heat began.

He had taken all measures to protect his mate. He himself had stood at her door countless days and nights to make certain that her security wasn't compromised. To make sure that she was safe. He had listened to her cry, listened to her whisper his name; he had listened to her pray to God for answers when she couldn't figure out why she had betrayed the people she had sworn to protect.

He had ached with her. His eyes had grown damp with her tears; rage had eaten him alive through those months. And now, to think his alpha would suggest he stay away from her longer, when a threat to her life was clear, caused the wolf he was created from to snarl in fury.

"I would never suggest you refrain from giving her the truth that will protect her now, Hawke." Wolfe surprised him with the statement. "I was merely going to say that perhaps a mistake has been made in keeping the information from her this long. She's clearly in danger, just as we've suspected. Arm her with the truth and perhaps we can regain the loyalty we lost in her when we had her confined."

Hawke's lips thinned at the continuance. It was the Tribunal's belief that they had lost Jessica's loyalty because of their need to confine her, to lock her away from the Breeds as well as from her own people. Hawke didn't believe that. Not once had Jessica tried to escape in the months that she had been free. She had sought solitude. She had sought moments when eyes weren't watching her. But she had never indicated a need to escape, or indicated anger with the Breeds in general. It was more an anger directed toward Hawke.

"I'm pulling in a team from the Coyote base," Aiden informed him. "It will be done quietly, and they'll be placed on protective covert detail around her. We know Haven is being watched. This way, whoever is watching will believe we've become lax about her safety." Aiden leaned forward intently. "We need to capture her would-be assassin, Hawke. There were men we didn't catch earlier this year with the pure blood society we disbanded. We need the information they have, as well as the resources they're using. She's our only link to them."

"Her safety will not be compromised in this quest of yours, Aiden," Hawke growled, the animalistic rumble of his voice burring his words. "I've held back the mating heat, but nothing will change the fact that she is my mate."

Aiden nodded at the statement as he turned back to Wolfe.

"I'm claiming my mate." Hawke stared his alpha down then. "I've given you the time you needed, Wolfe. Jessica Raines is my mate. I'll go without her no longer."

Wolfe shared a look with his second-in-command before turning back to Hawke with a short nod. "I appreciate your trust in me, Hawke. You've denied yourself when others wouldn't have, and given us the time we needed to find answers rather than giving her her freedom based on law. It tells me more than words can say about the loyalty you give to the Breeds."

"My loyalty was to her," Hawke snapped. "My mate was no traitor. There was only one way to prove it. It's been proven. Now, I'll have what's mine."

FOUR

She should have known Hawke wouldn't stay away long.
The bodyguard he had left outside the house was male.
She had noticed both during and after her release that it
was a very rare occurrence for a male of either Breed or
human persuasion to come around her.

She had female bodyguards. Her doctor was female. Her
visitors, namely the alpha's mate, Hope, or his second-in-
command's wife, Faith. Occasionally, Charity Chance visited, but since the birth of her and Aiden's son, she hadn't
been by.

She watched the Range Rover pull into the small grav-
eled driveway in front of the cabin she had been given, and
Hawke stepped out. As arrogant as any man could be, as
handsome as sin, he stood beneath the falling snow like a
force of nature daring the elements to come after him.

Daring anyone to come after him or to oppose him.

He was an integral part of Haven's security team. He
had been an advisor and security leader in the security and
communications station where she had worked a little more
than a year ago. He had been firm and honest, but he hadn't
always been easy to work with. He didn't suffer fools eas-

ily, and he didn't think twice about physically throwing out anyone not performing up to standards.

Did he still oversee security there? she wondered. She realized she had no idea what he did now. She saw him driving through the compound often, stopping, talking to the security teams, directing them to different areas or joking with them. Though she realized she hadn't seen a smile on his face since she had been released.

He had often smiled at her when she worked security for the Breeds. Cautious little half smiles, as though he hadn't known how to express his amusement with her shy jokes or at her attempts to flirt with him.

God, she had so fallen in love with him, she realized. Those months she had spent working with him, sharing the quiet lunches in the small garden behind the security center, she had fallen irrevocably in love.

He hadn't kissed her. He hadn't touched her. He had been courteous, chivalrous. Something she had never known with anyone else. He was larger than life, and the wound she had inflicted on the fragile relationship they had been building had gone deep. In both of them.

She had known, even then, about mating heat. It was hard not to know when working so closely with the Breeds. And she had known the signs of it. It had been building between them. It would have taken no more than a kiss, perhaps a touch, and it would have flamed to life like a wildfire out of control, as Faith had described it.

Faith, Hope and Charity had been brutally honest with her about the mating heat. Despite the fact that she had been called a traitor, they hadn't held back when she had questioned them about it.

As Hawke walked to her front door, she folded her arms over the thick sweater that covered her breasts and wondered about that. Why had they been so honest with her when she was suspected to be a traitor?

Of course, if she had been convicted of her crimes, it wasn't as though the world would have had a chance to hear her side of the story. There would have been no lawyers, and no defense. Breed Law was brutally clear. The papers she had signed in agreeing to it had laid it out in succinct layman's terms. She had agreed to an execution if she ever betrayed the Breeds. And she had signed it, knowing she would never willingly betray them.

She had learned that there was that one little factor though. Unwillingness. The drug her father had slipped into her system had given her little choice.

The front door opened with an air of arrogance and purpose that personified the man that stepped inside.

He carried a bag under one arm. Shifting it in his grip, he turned to close and lock the door.

Jessica cocked her head to the side. More gifts? He had sent her clothes, shoes, boots and coats since her release. During her captivity he had sent her food from her favorite fast-food restaurant, and soft outfits that had kept her warm in the sterile cell in which she had been confined.

He was always sending gifts. This was the first time he had brought any with him.

"We need to talk."

Her brows lifted as he turned and walked into the kitchen after making the brusque statement.

She followed him anyway, despite the arrogance that had her hackles rising.

Stepping into the kitchen, she watched as he sat the bag on the kitchen table and pulled the contents free. A bag of regular coffee, a six-pack of soda, her favorite chocolate cookies and a small clear bottle of what appeared to be capsules, a drug of some sort.

"What exactly do we need to talk about?" She was almost salivating for that coffee. It was her favorite brand.

"These." He sat the bottle of pills prominently in front of the enticing caffeine and chocolate-laced goodies.

Her brows lifted again. "And they are?"

"Hormonal treatments for mating heat," he stated, his expression hard, almost forbidding, as he stared back at her with those odd, yellowish brown eyes. "They're for the more uncomfortable symptoms. You also need to decide if you want to take the additional treatment to prevent pregnancy." He pulled another bottle from his shirt pocket and sat it beside the first.

Jessica felt her heart rate increase. Suddenly, it was pounding against her chest, blood racing through her system and need beginning to burn in areas that she normally tried to ignore.

Between her thighs her clit became swollen and her juices began to dampen the folds of her sex. She could feel lust pouring into her system and emotions she didn't want to face tearing through her mind.

"Have it all figured out, don't you?" she whispered as she stared back at him. "Whether I want this or not, it's going to happen?"

He breathed in slowly, deeply. "You're my mate, Jessica. We both know what that means. I've tried to stay away from you. I've tried to wait until the time was right to court you, to give you a chance to accept what it means."

"Time?" She gave a hard, bitter laugh. "I was jailed, Hawke. You didn't even visit. I've rarely seen you since my release. Perhaps you need to figure out exactly what it means to court a woman before you decide to do it."

His jaw tightened, the muscle bunching almost violently as she watched him clench his teeth.

"I would have given us more time." He seemed to push the words past his throat. "Before I began to court you, I wanted to ensure your protection, your safety. And your freedom." He bit the last word out almost angrily. "I wanted you to *choose* me. I didn't want to force the heat."

"And that's changed. Why?" She almost softened at the words, at the need she could see in his eyes and the fact that, unlike the circumstances of other mates, hers had tried to give her a choice, a chance to turn her back on it if it wasn't what she wanted.

"Because I can't find the man that's been shadowing you since your release," he revealed.

Jessica froze at the statement.

"What do you mean, shadowing me? How can anyone but a Breed shadow me, Hawke? Especially here in Haven?"

He glanced away for a long second, his lips tightening, before turning his gaze back to her. "Certain factions of the pure blood societies have found a drug that can disguise individual scent for a short period of time. Since your release, we've seen signs of a stalker. We can scent his weapons, the fact that he's male, and his intent to kill. He's managing to slip inside Haven and get past our security using this drug. And he's after you."

Fear knotted in her stomach. Turning away from him, she pushed her fingers through her unbound hair before pacing to the window and staring out into the snow that seemed to fall harder now, faster.

"To kill me," she stated softly. "Because I was able to save the mates that they would have killed during that attack."

The attack for which she had given vital information that aided in it's coordination.

"That's what we've learned," he said softly. "Your father had given the orders before his death that once you were released, you were to be killed."

"I betrayed him." She smiled bitterly as she turned back to him. "Father never looked kindly on someone who turned his back on what he wanted."

"There are still several key members who weren't identified before your release. Most of the members of that group were at the party where the Breeds were attacked, but certain players weren't there. We've been trying to learn their identities, but so far we haven't managed to do so."

Jessica nodded slowly. The Breeds had brought pictures to her just before her release, asking her to identify men that she knew her father associated with. She had been asked to name anyone who hadn't been in those pictures. The Breeds had been thorough. She recognized all of her father's friends in those pictures, as well as a few that she hadn't known.

"What does all this have to do with mating heat?" She glanced at the bottles of pills again.

"You're my mate." His voice was suddenly guttural, a primal growl that had every nerve ending in her body suddenly violently sensitive and aware of the man standing in front of her. "I've waited fifteen months, Jessica. I wanted to court you. I wanted this to be your choice, to be what you needed, not just what I ached for. But the danger is escalating now, and I refuse to take chances with your life." His fists clenched at his sides as his eyes seemed to glow with hunger. "I won't let you die. I won't let you be harmed." He moved to her, a slow, steady, stalking movement that made her mouth dry and her lips part in anticipation.

Hard male hands clasped her upper arms as she stared up at him, mesmerized by the man and the intensity of his gaze.

"I protect what's mine." His eyes moved over her face, paused at her lips, before moving up and locking with her gaze. "You're mine, Jessica. You've been mine since the day I saw you. I can't help the animal inside me that claims you. I can't stop the need to protect you. And I would give my life to ensure that you had the time and the freedom to make this choice on your own. But I'll be with you now, day in and day out. I will protect you. And holding back the hunger that will draw us closer will be impossible."

Which was why he had brought her the hormones as well as the goodies. The new hormonal treatments had given the female mates the freedom to enjoy their treats without the adverse affects that came with them. Caffeine and chocolate were known to make the symptoms of mating heat worse. The arousal, the need to mate, to touch, kiss and stroke, were nearly impossible to deny as it was. It could become painful. Jessica knew that the need for sex could become agonizing if a female was parted from her mate, unable to feel his touch, take his sex, or know his body.

She inhaled, almost shuddering, as she fought to breathe through those realizations.

"And if I don't want this mating?" she asked him.

His hands rubbed down her arms, then back up again.

"Then you'd be lying to both of us," he said softly. "There's anger in you, and I don't blame you for that anger. But there's need, Jess, and there's emotion. If you hadn't been confined for a year, you would have come to my arms. We both know that."

"But I *was* confined, Hawke." She moved away, rubbing at her upper arms as she glanced back at him before turning and facing him directly. "You stayed away from me. You never came to me."

"I would have mated you." The words were ripped from him. "I would have taken you, Jess. We needed time to prove your innocence. I knew you would never willingly betray us. I had to prove it."

Surprise filtered through the arousal, surprise that she couldn't ignore.

"You were trying to prove my innocence?" She frowned. "But, Hawke, I wasn't innocent. We both know that."

She had betrayed the Breeds. She had nearly gotten Hope, Faith and Charity killed. She had been responsible for an attack on Haven that could have killed so many of them.

"You were innocent," he stated, his voice filled with determination. "Jessica, whatever happened, you were not a willing party. We have proof of it now. I knew it then."

"Yet you never bothered to tell me that?" she asked with a small hint of mockery. "Wow, Hawke. What would it have taken? A note? A phone call? You could have said that and still given me a choice." The arousal fueled the anger. Need versus pain, the knowledge she had been alone, that he hadn't come to her, pouring through her. "You could have done something, damn you!" Her voice rose as the hurt overshadowed every other emotion.

"In doing it, I would have risked the very investigation I instigated to prove your innocence," he fired back. And though his voice stayed low, calm, there was a power throbbing in it that gave her pause. "If I had done anything, it would have risked your life as well as the confidence our enemies had that you were going to die and take their secrets with them."

"And because you think you had a good reason for what you were doing, then I should just lay down and accept this mating heat as though I have no other choice?" she parried angrily. "Excuse me, Hawke, but doesn't that sound just a little arrogant, even for you?"

One heavy black brow arched over golden eyes in mocking disbelief as he stared back at her.

"Oh, yeah, how stupid of me to have forgotten Breed arrogance," she snorted. "You guys just don't understand limits at all, do you?"

His expression stilled at the comment. "The animal is too close to the surface sometimes, Jess." He finally sighed. "My need to protect you, to hold you close to me, goes beyond anything you might understand at the moment." He grimaced, the heavy canines at the sides of his mouth flashing, reminding her that he was indeed very close to his animal cousins. "You're my mate. Everything inside me demands that I ensure our bond. I'm trying to be reasonable. I'm trying to be human about this, but it's damned hard."

He was trying to be human about it?

Jessica tipped her head and gazed up at him, suddenly curious at this compulsion that urged him to ensure that she belonged to him, no one else.

It was at once frightening and arousing. This man, so big and bold, so unique, wanted her. Just her. Once mating heat was started he could never have another woman. That mating instinct would keep him from even desiring another woman. He would belong to her and to her alone.

Had anyone or anything ever been just hers?

"Jessica." His voice had a soft, mesmerizing quality as he moved closer to her, his big body shielding hers, sheltering it as he lifted his hand to run the backs of his fingers over her cheek.

The gesture was so gentle, so overwhelmingly tender, that she nearly lost her breath.

"I can't leave your protection to others now," he warned her, the brooding, tormented sound of his voice striking at her heart. "You're too important to me. You mean too much to me. And the part of my soul that has claimed you trembles in fear at the thought of losing you."

"Hawke." She wanted to shake her head, to protest his claim.

She didn't know if she was ready for this. Didn't know if she could handle the mating heat as well as the sudden threat against her life.

"I'll be with you, day in and day out," he told her as she stared back at him, silent, confused. "I'll guard you with my life, Jessica, but you know as well as I do that the arousal burning between us won't ease. It's not a product simply of the mating heat; it's a product of what we both wanted before we ever knew that was a factor. We belong to each other."

We belong to each other. Her lips parted as she fought to find a way to deny it and couldn't. Before she had betrayed the Breeds, before she had been confined, she had dreamed of the mating heat. She had dreamed of belonging to him.

Before the betrayal. Before she had lost herself in her father's relentless quest to destroy Haven and everyone who lived there.

"This won't work," she whispered, though she couldn't keep from leaning into his touch for just a moment. "It won't work, Hawke."

She had to force herself away from him. It was the hardest thing she had ever done in her life. When several feet separated them she turned back to him, miserable with the awareness of exactly what she was turning her back on.

"If something happens to me, you'll be alone." She swallowed tightly at the thought. "You won't find another mate. You won't have the comfort of another woman."

"Don't, Jessica . . ."

"You'll be alone," she cried out furiously. "I know what alone is like, Hawke. I know how empty and bleak it can be and I don't want that for you."

Endless nights curled on the cot she had slept in.

Months of agony, dreaming, wishing, crying for someone she couldn't have.

"That won't happen," he gritted out, determination marking his face now.

"You can't be sure of that." She stepped back as he paced closer. "I won't risk it. Not now. Not until we have a chance to clear things between us. Until we know if there's even a future."

"Oh, there's definitely a future."

Before she could evade him she was pressed against the side of the refrigerator, his body so warm, so inviting, touching hers. Heat seemed to surround her, to sink into her.

Pressing her hands against his chest, a breath lodged in her throat as she stared up into his dominant, hungry features.

"There's a future, Jess." One hand slid into her hair, the other gripped her hip. "And it starts now."

FIVE

*J*essica expected a kiss. She'd waited on his kiss for what seemed like forever. Her lips parted as his head lowered; her breath stopped in her chest in anticipation of the pleasure to come.

Once his lips covered hers, once his tongue slid against hers, she knew exactly what was going to happen. The mating hormone that filled the small glands beneath his tongue would release into her system. That hormone would spark a fire to her arousal that couldn't be quenched. It would be an adventure in her own sexuality, as well as his. She knew what to expect. She had dreamed about it, fantasized about it. But it wasn't what happened.

At the last second his lips pressed to the corner of hers rather than covering them. Breathing harshly, his heart beat heavy against her palms as they pressed against his chest. He stood stiff against her, obviously fighting for control.

She was having to fight for her own, and she was failing miserably.

Her hands moved from his chest to his shoulders. As he stood there with her in his grip, she let her hands slide into his hair, let them grip the thick, heavy strands and relish the feel of it. Finally.

How often had she dreamed of simply touching him? Just feeling him against her?

"I don't want to take from you," he growled as he turned his head, his cheek pressing against hers. "I don't want to force this, Jess."

"Then don't," she whispered.

There was no force needed. She let her fingers clench in his hair, rubbing it against her fingertips as she felt the heavy proof of his erection against her lower stomach.

She wanted. Oh, Lord, she wanted him. She shouldn't. He had left her alone for over a year. He had turned his back on her. *But he's here now,* another voice protested. The voice of hunger, of a need, that had whipped through her the first day she met him.

She'd scoffed at the idea of love at first sight until she met Hawke.

"Jess." His voice was rough, rich with wanting. It was primal and brooding and sent a shiver down her back as it caressed her senses. The moment she set eyes on him she had known she would never want another man as she wanted him.

"Touch me, Hawke."

Oh God, who had dared to voice that plea? Surely not her. Didn't she know better? Hadn't she promised herself that she would never make that request awake as she asked for it in her sleep?

She stared up at him as his head moved back. Fierce golden eyes narrowed on her as she fought to breathe.

"You don't have to kiss me," she whispered. "Just touch me."

Let her touch him. There were surely ways to do this without starting something that they couldn't turn the tide back on. It wasn't as though a simple touch was going to turn into a full-fledged wildfire, was it?

"You'll kill me," he growled, but his hand moved from

her hair, his fingertips touching her cheek as she pulled hers from his hair and slid them down his chest.

She could touch as well, couldn't she?

"Jess?" He groaned her name as she pulled the hem of his denim shirt from his jeans.

"Maybe we won't even like each other's touch," she suggested, feeling almost playful in his arms now. "We could be totally disgusted by each other. I think we should be sure before you kiss me."

And maybe it would give her time, just a little time, to figure out what she wanted, or how she was going to handle this big, hardened male.

"Jess, I kind of doubt that your touch is going to disgust me." He groaned, but she sensed an edge of lightness in him as well now. Almost playfulness.

Did he even know how to play? she wondered. Or was his playfulness as cautious as his half smiles used to be?

"You never know," she whispered.

Pushing her hands beneath his shirt, she was rewarded by his sharply drawn breath. A second later he found retaliation by edging the hem of her shirt higher, his fingertips, just his fingertips, touching her sensitive stomach.

"And I can touch you," she whispered. "I've so wanted to touch you, Hawke."

She could feel her juices flooding her pussy now. She was wet and heated, her clit throbbing erratically as she tried to find her breath.

She had waited so long for his touch. Maybe she had waited too long, she thought hazily. Too much anticipation. It was making her dizzy.

"We should be lying down for this," he suggested as he drew back, caught her hand and stared down at her. "We could touch where we wanted to then, Jess. I'd be right there, laid out for you."

"To do with as I wish?" Her heart skipped a beat at the thought.

"Whatever you wish," he promised, his voice low and

rough as he drew her from the kitchen toward the bedroom. "However you wish."

However she wished? She had a lot of wishes where touching him was concerned. She could do a lot of things and never kiss him. Things that could burn through her soul and tie her tighter to him, she thought hazily. Then she disregarded the idea.

Could she really be tied tighter to him? she wondered. She didn't think it was possible. She had thought of no other man, dreamed of no other man, wanted no other man but this one since the day she had seen him.

And she could have him, she assured herself. However she wanted him.

She let him lead her to the bedroom, staring back at him as he guided her easily through the living room and past the opened bedroom door.

As she stopped at the side of the bed she stood, uncertain, watching as he drew his boots off, then slowly unbuttoned his shirt. Long, graceful male fingers released the buttons with confidence as he watched her. He drew the shirt from his body, and she was rewarded with the sight of broad, heavily tanned shoulders. Muscle shifted and rippled beneath the tight, firm flesh. The strong breadth of his chest was bare of hair, but there was nothing immature about it.

Her gaze was drawn to flat, hard male nipples before being dragged lower to tight, rippling abs. His belted jeans hung low on his hips, the heavy wedge of his cock pressing tight against the zipper.

She felt weak, light-headed, as he let the shirt fall to the floor before moving to the bed and dropping on it, lying on his back, his arms splayed at his sides.

His grin was wicked. A true, playful grin despite the hunger that filled his gaze.

"Here I am," he invited her. "Take me as you will, Jess."

Take him as she willed? Sweet Lord have mercy on her, she might not survive this one.

She kicked off the sneakers she wore, and watched as his eyes widened when she gripped the hem of her sweater. She tossed back a grin before pulling it up her body and over her head to reveal the light undershirt she wore beneath it.

She didn't wear a bra. She hated them. The sleeveless undershirt was stretchy and snug and clearly revealed the hardened state of her nipples as she crawled up on the mattress beside him.

Damn, he was like this vision of male perfection. Whichever scientists had decided his genetics had known exactly what they were doing, Jessica thought in satisfaction as she sat on her knees and just stared at him.

She looked her fill, because looking at him could be as erotic as touching him. She could watch his muscles flex as though she were actually touching him. His face creased with a grimace, his jaw was clenched. He was so aroused. Ready for her.

It was a turn-on, she realized. Every move this man made, every word that passed his lips, was a definite turn-on.

"Are you going to stare all day?" he snapped. Not angrily. There was an edge of anticipation and impatience in his tone rather than anger.

"Maybe," she drawled, though her hand lifted, almost of its own accord, her fingers trailing down the center of his chest to his hard stomach.

If she went much further, she'd be in his pants. It wouldn't take no more than a breath to touch the hard crest of his cock. She could undo his jeans . . .

Jessica shook the thought off. That would be cruel. She didn't want to be cruel.

"Lie down beside me, baby." He turned, moving to his side as he drew her to the bed. "Let me touch you as well."

Without kisses.

She would die for that kiss, she thought a second later as he rubbed his hard, bearded jaw against skin and moved over her as she lay back.

Her hands had a will of their own, touching his back, his shoulders, sliding over the tough, hard flesh and relishing the feel of strength beneath it.

She ached for the kiss she was denying herself, almost as though the mating heat had begun without it.

But that wasn't possible.

Her eyes closed as he dragged the rough rasp of his beard over her neck, his heated breath a caress against her bare skin as she arched beneath him, her body demanding more.

This might not have been such a good idea, she thought. Maybe she should have given it more consideration. She was becoming lost in touching him, her hands moving down his back to the edge of his jeans, the temptation to delve beneath the snug band almost more than she could bear.

"I can't kiss you. I can't lick you," he whispered against her shoulder, his lips barely feathering the sensitive skin there. "If I touch you with my tongue, the hormone will touch your skin. I could suck your nipples, and the need for more would burn inside you. I could lick down your soft belly, and your flesh would grow hot, your arousal would build."

The whispered enticement as he brushed his beard against the exposed flesh above her breasts was almost more than she could bear.

"Can I kiss you?" Her nails scraped over his belt before she gripped his hip with one hand, forcing herself not to go lower.

Hawke paused. The thought of her lips against his flesh was both Heaven and Hell. The thought of her caressing him, licking him, had his dick throbbing like an open wound.

Sweet merciful Heaven, give him strength, he thought.

"Yes." He almost hissed the word, because her lips were already at his shoulder, her teeth scraping over the flesh as he bit back a groan. Maybe it was a mistake to give her leave to caress him with her lips, because the pleasure was tearing through him, ripping through his senses and leaving him weak.

She bit him. The rounded curve of his shoulder throbbed as she nipped at it. Then she licked it. His hips jerked, grinding his cock against her thigh as he fought just to breathe.

How insane had he been to agree to this?

She panted against his shoulder. "It takes the hormone to start the heat, right?"

"Yes." His damned tongue was filled with it, the glands so swollen they were painful, filling his own mouth with the erotic heat, making him crazy with the hunger that flooded his system for her.

"The hormone is in your kiss and your semen." Her nails were raking his back.

Hawke stretched into the burning caress. God, he didn't know how much more he could bear.

"I can kiss you." She kissed his shoulder before her lips moved lower.

"God, yes." He cupped the back of her head, holding her closer as her lips moved down his chest, her hot little tongue raking over a distended nipple as he felt his senses catch fire.

"We could play around for a while." Her voice sounded desperate, almost as desperate as he himself was. "Help me, Hawke," she panted. "Please."

She arched to him, her thighs gripping one of his as she rubbed herself against him. The heat of her pussy through her jeans was destructive. He could sense the warmth, the slick dampness. She was so damned ready for him that the scent of her filled the air and left him feeling drunk on it.

"You'll kill me like this," he groaned, but he couldn't stop himself.

Easing the undershirt up over her breasts, he revealed the delicate curves and the candy pink, spike-hard tips of her nipples. He wanted to lick them, suck them. He wanted to draw them into his mouth and fill his senses with the taste of her.

He used his fingers instead. Gripping the hardened little points between his index fingers and thumbs, he rolled them, stroked them, plumped them.

He watched, amazed, as she flushed from her breasts to her forehead. Red-gold hair spilled around her delicate features as her lashes closed over her eyes and her lips parted to draw in more air.

She was lost in the pleasure he was giving her. This was exactly where he wanted her, how he wanted her. He wanted her senses consumed by him, filled with his touch.

And Hawke realized he loved watching her reaction to him. If he had given in to the mating heat and taken her kiss, then he would have been denied the sight of her relishing his touch.

The mating hormone was pumping into his system, spilling from beneath his tongue as he fought to hold back his own lust for her. She wanted to touch. She wanted to love, he thought. But Jessica didn't just want to be touched. She wanted to feel him, sense him. She wanted an assurance that what she would have with him would be enough to sustain a future together.

She had no idea. Mother Nature hadn't made an imperfect mating yet. In all the years that the Breeds had been in existence, she hadn't once created a pairing that hadn't sustained, that hadn't loved.

It was killing him, simply touching her like this, but he knew this was for their future. He couldn't take from her. He couldn't force the mating on her. Everything inside his soul rejected the thought. But he could tease her. He could entice her.

He stroked her nipples with his fingers, plumped them with his fingers. He cupped them, raked his palms over the tips, watched her face and the pleasure that suffused it.

It was almost innocent. Hell, it was innocent. She was a virgin. She came to him untouched by another man's caresses, and he knew it. He knew her background, her history. She hadn't played with boys. His serious, sober Jess had worked hard for a career, worked to escape the legacy her father would have drawn her into.

"So beautiful." He sighed as his fingers trailed from her nipples to her rounded little tummy. "You make me crazy for you, Jess."

She pressed her head deeper into the pillow as he played with the clasp of her jeans, a whimpering little moan leaving her lips.

"I can pleasure you without kissing you," he promised her as he flicked the metal tab of her jeans open. "With just my fingers, I could make you come for me, Jess. Let me make you come."

Hawke watched as she dragged her eyes open, her gaze going to his fingers as he pulled the zipper down.

"Let's get these off, baby." He lowered the material, dragging it from her hips, down her thighs.

He almost came himself when he saw the delicate violet silk of the low-rise panties she wore. They barely covered the fiery triangle of curls beneath, and did nothing to hide the fact that they were wet from her juices.

The scent of her filled his nostrils. Sweet, feminine, fresh. Like a mountain brook, he thought. That was what the scent reminded him of. Pure and clean; untouched.

"Jess." He pulled the jeans from her legs and tossed them to the side of the bed as he fought for control.

She needed to see, needed to know. She needed this moment in time, he realized.

Moving to her side, he laid beside her, his hand covering the small mound between her thighs as he propped himself on his elbow to watch.

His fingers edged beneath her panties and her hips arched closer to him. A gasp, then a hard breath of need parted her lips as he let one finger slide into the narrow slit, feeling the slick wetness, the clench of her folds around his fingers.

His dick was in agony. His balls were drawn tight to the base of the agonized shaft as the crest throbbed in despair.

A dark, spicy heat filled his mouth as the powerful hormone spilled into his system from the tight glands beneath his tongue.

Never had he imagined such agony, such need that he couldn't relieve. Relief was the sweet, fiery heat his fingers were caressing; the delicate, plump folds; the taut, throbbing pearl of her clit.

He wanted his lips there, his tongue. He wanted to taste her as he was touching her, to spear his tongue inside her and feel her coming for him.

He had to end this soon, he realized. His control was shaky now, his hands trembling with the hunger racing through him.

Jessica was breathing hard and fast beside him, little moans breaking past her lips as he circled the entrance to her vagina, dipped his finger inside, then massaged her clit with his thumb.

Her hips arched, a cry throttled from her throat as he felt her clench around his finger.

She was close. So close.

*J*essica felt as though the world were burning around her. Pleasure surrounded her, filled her. His finger caressed the opening to her sex, thrusting inside just enough to stroke nerve endings she hadn't known she possessed, while his thumb raked across her clit before finding a spot that sent her flying.

He stroked it, rubbed it. His finger thrust lightly inside her, his thumb ground against her clit and she felt her mind explode. Her senses disintegrated. Her orgasm was an explosion of sensation and light that tore through her, tightened her muscles and had her arching, crying, fighting to breathe.

She was gasping for breath, short, startled cries leaving her lips as he jerked her to him, holding her close, tight, as shudders tore through her body.

This was pleasure. It was flying in another's arms. It was racing to the sun and exploding in the center of it even as she knew it could have been better, brighter, hotter.

It could have been pure, unfettered sensation with his kiss.

A kiss she now knew she wouldn't be able to live without.

SIX

*H*awke was in agony.

The next morning he slid slowly from the bed, grimacing at the violent sensitivity of his dick as he eased away from Jessica's warm, naked body.

She was sleeping deeply, one arm thrown over her head, the silken, tangled mass of red-gold hair spilling around her face to her shoulders.

Fiery lashes feathered her cheeks. A light flush suffused her face and her soft pink lips were parted as she breathed in and out slowly.

Perfectly curved ripe breasts lifted and fell with each breath and, God knew, they tempted him almost past bearing. It would take so very little to begin the mating heat right now. He could lower his head, take one of her soft nipples into his mouth and suckle her slow and sweet, never waking her.

The mating hormone would lave the sensitive flesh, sink into it and slowly enter her system. Twelve to twenty-four hours and she would need his touch like she needed the air she was now breathing.

As much as he wanted her, as much as he needed her, he couldn't do that to her.

Shaking his head, he turned and moved to the bathroom. A cold shower wouldn't help his hard dick, and he knew it. The spray of the water would only torment already sensitive flesh, but he needed to get ready for the day ahead.

He stepped under the spray and almost moaned at the feel of the water over the flesh. Hell, he was going to have to make this the quickest shower on record.

Grabbing the bottle of liquid soap, he quickly lathered his hair and rinsed it before soaping a rag and going to work on his body.

The quick, hard strokes of the rag were torture to his aroused body. The silky slid of suds over his cock and down his thighs were hell.

He rinsed quickly and gave a sigh of relief as he turned off the shower, grabbed a dry towel and grimaced at the thought of drying. Damn, no man should have to go through this, he thought. But neither should a female. He knew what Jessica would suffer once the mating heat started. A sensitivity of flesh that wouldn't allow for the lightest touch of anything but his hands, his body, his possession.

It was harder for their women, and so far, Breed males were very aware of this. They were selective in their choice of lovers, ensuring that when they went out in public they paid attention to even the smallest signs that mating heat could occur. Enough had been forced on them; they had no desire to force the sometimes painful arousals on a female, whether she was Breed or not.

Wrapping the towel around his waist, he pulled the shower doors back and came face-to-face with Jessica from where she sat on the bathroom counter, watching him.

Her somber blue eyes regarded him quizzically as her gaze flicked to the obvious arousal beneath the cotton.

"You were hard all night," she said softly.

Glancing away from her, Hawke paced to the sink, where he'd placed a clean change of clothes.

"No answer?" she asked.

"What does it matter, Jess?" He let himself watch her in the mirror, saw the suspicion in her face and almost groaned at the next question.

"The mating heat affects you anyway, doesn't it?" There was a knowing tone to her voice, an edge of regret.

"It's not as bad for me as it would be for you." He shrugged as though it didn't matter, when he knew damned good and well that the need was eating him alive. Like acid in his gut, it was tearing at the very fiber of his control.

"Because you were trained to endure pain." That wasn't a question. It was an observation, and more or less the truth.

"Pretty much." He cast her a look of self-mockery. Hell, he might as well try to laugh about it, since raging over it would only make it worse. "We were trained to endure a lot of things. Maybe it's just second nature now."

She ducked her head for a moment before looking to the shower as though desperately seeking a way to change the subject.

"Will it hurt me?" When she lifted her head there was a hint of nervousness in her gaze. "Hope, Faith and Charity didn't say anything about pain."

He'd cut off his own dick before he'd hurt her.

"It's the lack of sex that hurts, Jess," he promised her. "Once mating heat starts with you, I'll ensure you never have to worry about hurting." He shot her a teasing wink as he tried to lighten the information for her.

It didn't work.

Her head lowered as she stared at the pretty ceramic floor of the bathroom.

"Hey." He nudged at her arm with his. "It's Christmas Eve, you know."

She looked up, nibbling at her lower lip as she watched him.

"Wolfe and Hope are throwing a Christmas party for Haven in the community center this evening. Lots of good food, some dancing, a little bit of drinking." He waggled his brows at her. "Want to go with me?"

"I'd like that." A slow, blooming smile lit her face. "I'd really like that, Hawke."

He bent, kissed the crown of her head and then pulled back quickly. "Good. Then we'll leave here about six. Until then, get some warm clothes on. I have some things I need to do today and I thought you might enjoy going with me."

"What kind of things?" She tilted her head, staring back at him with a natural curiosity he'd always been drawn to.

"Oh. Things." He shrugged as he spanned her waist with his hands and lifted her from the counter. "Now get out of here and let me get dressed. When I'm done you can get in here and shower while I fix breakfast."

He guided her to the bathroom door, pushed her through the opening and then closed it firmly. He almost locked it. Son of a bitch. If he wasn't careful, then there would be no way in hell for him to be able to give her the time she needed to decide if this mating was what she truly wanted.

It was all he could do to keep from kissing her now. To keep from taking her. The glands beneath his tongue were so swollen with the mating hormone that it was painful. His dick was as hard as stone and his flesh felt scorched each time he touched her.

Some days it simply sucked to be a Breed.

Jessica showered while Hawke fixed breakfast. Standing beneath the warmth of the spray, she let her hands travel over her body, remembering Hawke's touch from the night before.

He'd been gentle. There had been an air of desperate hunger that surrounded him, but never once had he done anything to start the mating heat that she knew he was craving.

Not once had his lips touched hers, or touched bare skin, period. He hadn't kissed her, hadn't licked her. And she'd been dying for it.

Dressed in jeans, an undershirt and a sweater, Jessica

moved back to her bedroom where she sat on the bed and pulled on thick, heavy socks.

Colorado winters had been particularly hard in the past few years. There was already a foot of snow on the ground from the night before and another foot predicted before the end of the night. And it was Christmas Eve. She had missed Christmas since leaving home at eighteen. Even before that, Christmas had lacked something. A sincerity, a sense of pure affection when the family had come together. During her years in the Army she had stayed in the barracks over the holidays, preferring the solitude to the fake laughter and endless parties her family had forced her to endure.

She wondered if spending Christmas with the Breeds would be any better. She'd heard of the joyous celebrations of Christmases past. The presents the alpha and his mate, Hope, gave out, and the exchange of gifts that the other Breeds participated in.

The Breeds had never had Christmas in the labs, so celebrating it now, as Hope had once told her, was an affirmation that they were indeed free to celebrate, to laugh, to love and to live.

Slipping her feet into hiking boots, she tied them snugly before standing and moving to the closed door.

Breakfast with Hawke wasn't stilted, nor did she feel the old anger rising inside her that she had experienced over the past year.

They ate a simple meal. Eggs, lots of bacon for Hawke, toast and her beloved caffeine-rich coffee. After the dishes were cleared away, he helped her into her coat and they left the house.

There were Breeds with shovels clearing driveways around the compound. Others were stringing more lights. There was always something going on at Haven and there were always willing hands to help.

There was never trash on the grounds, there was never disorderliness. The Breeds were oftentimes much neater than their human cousins, and had a much greater sense of cleanliness.

The frigid winter morning was held at bay by the thermal lining of her coat, and if that hadn't kept her warm there was always Hawke's arm around her waist as he escorted her to the waiting Range Rover, which had been started with the remote ignition from the house.

Helping her into the all-terrain vehicle, Hawke closed the door before loping to the driver's side and sliding behind the wheel.

She noticed he wasn't wearing a coat. Thin leather gloves covered his hands, but other than that he wore only jeans, boots and a dark blue flannel shirt with a T-shirt beneath it.

Breeds didn't get as cold as easily as their human cousins either, she thought with a twinge of envy.

"Where are we going?" she asked as he shifted the vehicle into reverse to turn around and head out of the driveway onto the main thoroughfare that led through the Wolf Breed Compound.

"I'll show you." He flashed her a wicked grin before moving one hand from the steering wheel to grip her hand where it lay on her thigh.

Jessica stared at his leather-gloved fingers as they covered hers and wondered at the warmth that she could feel through the gloves.

It shouldn't be like this, she thought. After a year without him, a year confined to a cool, boring little cell where she hadn't seen him, hadn't heard from him, it shouldn't be like this. She shouldn't feel these emotions shifting through her, racing in her bloodstream and heating her pussy like an internal fire she couldn't put out.

"You could just tell me." Her heart was beating hard in her chest and she had no doubt he could scent the arousal burning inside her.

"If I told you, then it wouldn't be a surprise." There was that smile again. A crooked upturn of his lips, his golden eyes filled with promise.

She was reminded of those days before the attack on Haven over a year ago, when he would tease her with surprise lunches in the small park behind the communications shed, or with sweets to tease her taste buds.

She hadn't realized at the time that he had been courting her, and now she wondered how she could have missed it.

"Close your eyes for me."

She turned to stare at him in surprise as he made the sudden request.

"Close my eyes?" She was actually starting to have fun. "Why?"

"So I can have my way with you?" He waggled his brows suggestively before chuckling, the sound a dark, erotic stroke against her senses. "Just close your eyes, Jess. I promise, you'll like this."

She closed her eyes. She resisted the urge to peek, because she loved surprises. She always had.

"What are you up to, Hawke?" she asked again as she felt the Range Rover make several turns. While she had once been pretty certain that she knew where they were, now she wasn't so sure.

"Just a few more minutes," he urged her.

With her eyes closed it seemed she could hear a more subtle nuance in his voice. Almost a sense of nervousness. She had to be hearing wrong, she decided. Hawke was never nervous. He was always confident and in charge, never anything less.

"I've been working on something over the past year." He finally cleared his throat as the Rover began to slow down. "While you were confined, when I had spare time, there was something I wanted, something I needed, to do."

The Rover came to a stop.

"Hawke?" She whispered his name breathlessly.

"Not yet." His fingers touched her eyes with the utmost gentleness. "I knew you were my mate, Jess. I know it's hard to forgive me for staying away. I know you've been angry, and I don't blame you."

She parted her lips to speak, but his fingertips landed on them.

"Just a minute, baby," he urged her. "It was the only

way to prove you were no traitor. I knew you weren't. I
believed in you, Jess, but I knew you'd never be accepted
by the packs that are a part of Haven if you weren't proven
innocent."

That made sense. A part of her had even known that,
struggled with the idea of it over the months that she had
been in the cell.

"I made certain you were comfortable."

She had been. She'd had warm blankets, home-cooked
meals, warm clothes.

"I made certain you weren't too bored."

Magazines, books and a television had been brought to
her. But even more, sketch pads, pencils and watercolors.
Jess loved to sketch and draw, and the tools for that hobby
had been brought to her.

"I made certain everyone understood that I'd stand between you and any punishment of death."

She hadn't known that.

"I wanted to give you more though." His voice softened
further. "You can open your eyes now, Jess."

She opened her eyes. Her lips parted in shock. There,
by the edge of a mountain lake that she had always loved
to sketch beside, sat the vision of a house she had sketched
so many times.

The house wasn't large. It wasn't ostentatious like the
one her parents had once possessed. The cabin-style home
blended well with the other cabins in the compound, but
with a few noticeable differences.

There was a red tin roof rather than plain aluminum.
It was a little larger, three bedrooms rather than one. For
the children she had dreamed of having with Hawke. She'd
dreamed of two. A boy and a girl. It was exactly as she had
described it to him, as she had drawn it to him so many times.

There was a porch swing on the front porch and areas
for flowers along the edge of the porch, and it had been
built between the gorgeous oak and pine trees that bordered
the lake.

It was breathtaking. Just as she had always envisioned it.

"Hawke." She turned to him, her lips trembling with emotion.

"I didn't just know you were my mate, Jessica." His leather covered hand framed her face. "I knew I loved you. Just as I still love you."

And he had. Everything he had done, every sacrifice he had made, proved he loved her.

"I never stopped loving you," she whispered as a tear fell from her eye.

She leaned forward, an irrevocable decision made, one she knew she couldn't regret, would never regret. This was Hawke. She belonged to him. He belonged to her.

Her lips touched his as his hands gripped her arms in surprise. Her tongue touched his lips as a flare of fear tore through her. What if this wasn't what he wanted? What he meant?

But it had to be. She couldn't accept losing him now. She couldn't accept never having taken this chance.

She licked over his lips with her tongue. As they parted she turned her head, controlling the kiss with experimental passion, her tongue stroking tentatively against his, the spicy-sweet taste of wild lust and desperate hunger exploding against her tongue.

As though the taste of him against her tongue exploded inside him as well, she felt his hand at the back of her head, his tongue pushing against hers as he groaned against her lips and pure erotic need began flashing between them.

Within seconds he had pushed his seat back, pulled her across his lap and taken control of the kiss. His tongue pressed between her lips as she closed them around it, sucking it into her mouth. Her tongue stroked against his, the narcotic taste of him whipping through her system, sizzling through her senses.

The taste of the kiss was as erotic as hell. It was the feel of the kiss, his hand pushing beneath her clothes, the feel of his erection beneath her rear, his tongue stroking against hers. Sensual, sexual. The feel of his body heating against hers, the feel of his heart racing in his chest, his heavy breathing, the deep, dark groan of male need.

It all combined and mesmerized her even before the mating hormone sizzled into her system. She was captivated, arching to him, aching for him even before the sizzle and the heated flames of mating heat began to overtake her.

And then things really got interesting.

SEVEN

Jessica wasn't certain how they made it into the house. She remembered him carrying her, his lips on hers, deep, desperate kisses filled with the spicy taste of the mating hormone and the even hotter hunger that had been flaring between them since the day they met.

Love at first sight. And second. And third. And on and on. As though a part of her had known that they were meant to be together, that they were meant for this moment.

She didn't see much of the house. There were stairs. Most of the cabins were single story; this one was two. The upper story was a loft, she thought. In the center of it was a huge bed covered with a dark, quilted spread. A thick, heavy blanket that cushioned her back as he laid her against it.

She could look at the house later, she told herself. Hopefully much later.

Lying back, she watched as he rose from the bed, his expression dark and drawn with lust as he got to his feet.

His boots were the first to go. He reach down, pulled them off, one after the other, and never took his eyes from her.

Golden eyes locked with hers, eyes filled with promise and passion.

His shirt came next. The buttons were undone quickly, efficiently, revealing his impressive chest as Jessica felt her heart rate increase.

Her entire body was burning now. That was the mating hormone, that burn just under her flesh that only his touch, his kiss, would ease. It was a touch and a kiss that would soon be hers. All hers.

Her heart raced harder at the thought. Blood pounded, rushed through her veins, surging through her system with tidal force as it spread the mating hormone through her system.

When his fingers went to the heavy leather belt around his pants, loosening it before pulling at the metal buttons of his jeans, she swore she lost the ability to breathe for long, precious seconds.

He pushed the denim past his hips, working it over the thick, heavy erection jutting out from his body. The wide crest of the dark shaft glistened damply as pre-come pearled at the tip. The flared head throbbed, spilled more of the dampness and had her lifting her hand as she rose from the bed.

The urge to touch him, to taste him, was nearly overwhelming. She was going to blame it on the mating heat, though she knew the fantasies that had sizzled through her veins for more than a year.

This was one of the fantasies.

There was no need to be shy. No need to draw back or to hold back. He belonged to her now, just as she belonged to him. She could touch him, could taste him as she pleased.

And this would so please her.

"Jesus! Jess." His hands speared into her hair as her tongue swiped over the head.

The same spicy heat that filled his kiss was a subtle flavor on his cock. It exploded over her tongue as a little moan passed her lips, causing his hips to jerk at the feel of the sound against his cock.

His fingers tightened in her hair as his thighs bunched and tightened while her tongue licked and laved over the heavy crest.

She felt intoxicated, a feeling she knew couldn't yet be attributed to the mating heat. Later, perhaps, but not right now. Not yet.

Right now, it was her. Her need, her hunger, her fantasies, and she wanted every last second of them to last forever.

Parting her lips, she enveloped the engorged head, her tongue stroking over the heated flesh as she felt the spill of his pre-come against her tongue.

Lubricating and heated, the fall of liquid had a purpose, and it wasn't just the taste of the hormone or its arousing qualities.

Breed males were very well endowed, especially in the width department. The pre-come that spilled from them had a special hormone, one that relaxed and eased delicate feminine tissue during mating heat to ensure that there was no pain.

"God, Jess. Enough." He pulled her away just when she was beginning to really enjoy the taste, the feel of him.

Eyes narrowed, she rose more fully to her knees, gripped the hem of her sweater and undershirt and pulled them free before tossing them to the floor.

She would have teased him further, but before she had time he pushed her back to the bed, gripped one leg and quickly unlaced a boot before drawing it from her. The second followed just as efficiently.

She hadn't drawn a breath before his hands were at the snap and zip of her jeans. Those were peeled down her legs within seconds, leaving her naked before him.

She felt the flush that suffused her body as his gaze roved over her. From her face to the tips of her toes, he stared at her as though he could consume her.

Hawke had never seen anything, anyone, as lovely as Jessica. Slender and compact, her breasts full and swollen, dark pink nipples tight and hard.

Like candy he thought. Her nipples looked like the sweetest candy.

Letting his gaze move lower, he tracked the pale perfection of her rounded belly, the smooth, pale thighs sprinkled with freckles and then the sweet, lush mound between them.

Her clit peaked out from the swollen, glistening folds. Throbbing and damp, it tempted his lips, his tongue. He'd dreamed of tasting her, of burying his lips between her legs and taking her with his tongue.

The realization that she was finally his, finally here for him to pleasure, had his cock throbbing, the rich essence of his pre-come dampening the shaft as he lowered his body alongside hers.

God, he wanted to touch her all at once. Taste her all at once. His tongue licked over her nipples before he drew one into his mouth and sucked at it hungrily. The tight little bud grew harder, tighter, hotter between his lips before he moved to the other. Its reaction was the same.

He loved them. He suckled at them with delicate sips of his lips, then with the rougher draws of his mouth. One at a time, pleasuring them as she writhed beneath him, her hands spearing into his hair, tightening in the strands as though to hold him to her.

As he drew back, gazing down at the tightened nipples, the sweet, exotic scent of her pussy drew his attention down her body. The lightest layer of syrup glistened against the soft curls that covered her mound, gleaming like dew and tempting his taste buds.

A hard groan left his lips as his head lowered. His lips whispered down her body and his tongue licked over her stomach as he urged her higher onto the bed and moved between her thighs.

She was abandoned, losing herself to him with a trust and innate passion that at once humbled him and left him shaking with lust.

Pressing her legs farther apart, he watched her face as he let his tongue lick through the narrow slit of her pussy. The taste of her ambrosia. It was sweet and wild, causing him to groan with a rumbled growl at the intoxicating essence.

She was like nothing he had ever tasted before. A narcotic he couldn't deny himself. A sweet, powerful drug. Drawing his tongue through the rich juices, he let it circle the hard little nub of her clit. He licked over it, flicking his tongue against it as she jerked and shuddered in pleasure beneath him.

Shattered little moans tore from her lips as she watched him. Her gaze was heavy lidded, her blue eyes almost neon as she panted for air beneath the lash of his tongue.

How long he had waited for her, he thought. And it was worth every agonizing month. It was worth the endless nights to have her now, wet and wild beneath him as he tasted her.

Drawing the tight little bud of her clit into his mouth, he sucked it gently, firmly. She bucked beneath the caress, her hips arching as her hands buried in his hair again.

With his hands beneath her knees he urged her legs higher, groaning in pleasure when her small feet rested against his shoulders. It left her open to him, defenseless. His tongue moved lower, circled the fluttering, snug entrance to her pussy before he tunneled inside it with a hard, hungry thrust.

Her juices spilled against his tongue as the tender muscles of her pussy clenched around the invader. A high, desperate cry spilled from her lips and he forced himself to remain still, just for a second, just until the impending orgasm eased inside her.

Then he licked her. With his tongue working slow and easy inside the gripping opening, he licked at the sweetness, drew ragged cries from her lips and tasted paradise.

The more he had of her, the more he wanted. As she began to tighten, to burn for orgasm, he pushed her higher, harder. His tongue thrust inside her as his fingers gripped her rear, parting the curves as his fingers slid inside the narrow crevice and found the tiny, sensitive entrance there.

He didn't breach it. He massaged it, rubbed it. His

tongue fucked inside her pussy with lightning strokes as he stimulated the nerve-laden area beyond.

Within seconds he felt her orgasm blooming. Her body tightened. High, tight little cries tore from her lips and then she jerked, shuddered, and he felt her explode.

$\mathcal{J}$essica swore she was dying. Pleasure exploded inside her in a wave of light and heat that rushed through her mind and over her nerve endings to detonate in her womb. Like fingers of electric energy it sped through her system, throwing her into the burning center of a sun that she couldn't escape, that exploded on and on until she felt as though she were no more than fragments drifting on a wild wind.

And still, Hawke wasn't finished. As she fought to catch her breath his lips lifted from her sex and he was dragging his body along hers as her legs fell to his hips.

The head of his cock tucked against the tender opening of her pussy as a whimper of impending ecstasy passed her lips.

"Sweet Jess," he groaned as he bent above her, his lips feathering over hers as the head of his cock pressed inside her. "Sweet love. Sweet mate." The last words seemed torn from him as the head of his erection forged inside her, drawing a hard, surprised cry from her lips.

It was pleasure and pain. A mix of sensations so violent, so lightning swift, that her nails dug into his shoulders as she fought to make sense of them.

"Hawke." There was a hint of fear. She heard it in her voice, felt it edge at her mind. She had never experienced anything like this. She had never known that pleasure could be so intense, so white hot.

"Hold on to me, baby." His lips lifted from hers after a sweet, gentle kiss. "Just hold on. It's going to be okay."

It would be okay.

She felt his lips move to her neck. There, he kissed,

licked, rasped his teeth against the sensitive flesh and drove her insane with the sensations racing through her.

As he pleasured her there, his cock began to work inside her. Back and forth, slow and easy, burying inside her until he came to the shield of virginity that she had never quite been able to rid herself of.

She heard the growl at her neck a second before he drew back, the tip of his cock pausing at the tight entrance of her sex before he surged inside.

Jessica screamed. Pleasure and pain erupted inside her and he broke that last veil of innocence. Still, he wasn't fully inside her. He stroked back, drove forward. The wide crest of his cock caressed nerve endings so sensitive, so responsive, that she couldn't help but arch her hips, driving him deeper even as a lance of fire streaked up her spine.

It was so good. Oh God, nothing had ever been as good as this. So hot. So much pleasure.

She was screaming out his name, trying to scream, the word was shattered, throttled as she fought to breathe, to accept the heavy, stiff flesh he was penetrating her with.

Writhing beneath him, she cried out, clenched her thighs on his hips and then threw her head back with a hard, silent cry as he finally thrust fully inside her.

"Sweet Jess." His groan was a harsh growl. "My sweet Jess. My mate."

He was moving then. Hard, heavy thrusts tunneled inside her, parting her, stretching her until she burned, ached and yet begged for more. Nothing seemed enough. She wanted him harder, faster. She wanted his teeth raking her neck more, she wanted air to breathe and she wanted to die in his arms, just like this, immersed forever in pleasure.

The deep, driving strokes were making her insane. Her orgasm was so close she could feel it, ached to dive into it. Her legs tightened around his thrusting hips as he fucked inside her with heavy shafting strokes.

Each desperate thrust pushed her higher, pushed her harder, until Jess swore she met the sun. She exploded with such an intensity of ecstasy that when his teeth pierced her shoulder and she felt him thrust inside her with one last hard, deep stroke, she screamed.

When she felt her pussy stretching more, felt the explosion of his semen inside her and the thick, hard swelling in the middle of his cock, she forgot the meaning of rapture. She didn't just orgasm; she became pleasure.

The rush of sensations that tore through her nerve endings was pure ecstasy. They were white hot, electrical, charged with such feeling, so much pleasure, that Jess felt as though she were flying beyond herself, sinking into an ocean of sensation that had no beginning and no end.

She knew what it was. The swelling in the middle of his cock, locking him inside her, positioning the head of his erection flush against her womb, ensuring the maximum chance of his seed spilling to fertile ground.

Knowing what it was and experiencing it were two different things. Experiencing it was fear, ecstasy, a rush of rapturous pleasure. A bonding. A melding of emotion, sensation and knowledge.

She belonged to him, just as he was hers. She had known that before. But now . . . Now Jess felt it clear to her soul. And now she knew why Hawke had warned her that there was no going back. It wasn't just the mating heat. It was this. A pleasure that would become addictive. A need she would never escape. A man she would love until her dying breath.

EIGHT

*H*ours and one hormone capsule later, Jessica took a deep breath before smoothing her hands over her hips, luxuriating in the feel of the lightweight dark blue velvet dress she had chosen for the Christmas Eve party.

The long, fluid lines of the garment flowed to the tips of the matching high heels she wore and the color brought out the blue in her eyes.

She piled her hair on her head, held it in place with clips that glittered with crystal gems and applied a light application of makeup that Hawke had retrieved from the other cabin, along with her clothes.

She hadn't imagined attending the party, even though she had prepared for it. There was a small bag of gifts that she'd ordered over the Internet and wrapped carefully. On the stove in the kitchen sat the rolls, delicate breads and sweets that Hawke had had flown in earlier.

She felt excited, flushed and filled with anticipation. She had always heard her mother say that Christmas was for kids, and Jessica had wondered as she grew older if that wasn't the truth.

Until tonight. She no longer wondered. The sense of

excitement and anticipation that she could feel emanating from Haven was infectious.

Moving from the bathroom, she walked across the bedroom to the wide windows that looked out over the front lawn and the cabins across the small paved road.

There were two Breed soldiers standing at the side of the road, laughing with two others who had walked out of the cabin directly across from her and Hawke's.

There weren't a lot of cabins in Haven's small community. Perhaps two dozen, some one bedroom, some two. Many of the cabins were inhabited by two or more Breeds though. The pack mentality had survived outside the labs. Males and females often inhabited the same cabin, nonsexually, for the closeness it provided them.

Strength in numbers, Dr. Armani had told her once. The Breeds so believed in strength in numbers that they made certain they were in packs or pairs at all times. Just as they were in the wild.

Touching her hand to the glass, she watched as the soldiers lifted their hands in farewell, each moving away to whatever called them back. Two headed along the street, obviously on patrol, while the other two moved back into the cabin.

Snow was still heaped along the streets, spread out in a pristine cloak around the compound where it seemed the Breeds hesitated to step except where necessary. Yards held no snowmen, the snow was largely untrampled, and she had yet to see a snowball fight. For what it lacked it did nothing to dim a Christmas spirit that Jessica hadn't expected. She could have sworn she had even heard Christmas carols earlier.

Shaking her head at the thought of some of the stern-faced Breeds singing Christmas carols she collected the small velvet purse from the bed, pulled a tiny five-shot .22 derringer from the duffel bag Hawke had brought from her cabin with the other items, and secured it inside the purse.

The Breeds knew she had the derringer. At least, a few

of them did. The tiny gun had been collected along with her other belongings when she was taken into custody.

It was little more than a powerful peashooter, but at close range it could do some serious damage. She wasn't allowed a regular weapon any longer, or at least, her military issue weapon hadn't been returned to her, so she assumed, for the moment, it wasn't allowed.

For the moment. She had all intentions of making certain her weapon was returned, along with her job. Once Dr. Armani was certain there was no chance that the drug she had been given was still in her system, then she would request her post back.

Until then, she had a home to decorate and furnish. Hawke had the basics. A large mattress and box spring, but no true bed. A closet to hang their clothes in, bar stools at the bar. The house was largely empty, and already she was coming up with ideas on how to fill it.

"Damn, you look like an angel."

She turned around, feeling the skirt of the gown as it flared around her feet, to stare back at Hawke in surprise.

His voice had been pitched low, dark with longing, with an element of need that seemed to cascade through her system.

Dressed in dark jeans, black shirt and boots, with his hair still damp from the shower and brushed back, he looked like a dark angel himself. Sensual, sexual and wicked. A being so erotic that he made grown women melt in shameless hunger.

She had seen that melting more than once. Breeds and non-Breeds alike, women took one look at Hawke's roughly handsome face, corded muscular body and deep golden eyes, and they wept in need.

"You look damn fine yourself." She smiled, suddenly nervous, feeling her palms dampen as a surge of sensation seemed to erupt between her thighs.

Wow. The hormonal treatment Dr. Armani had worked up for her evidently didn't do the job the way it should. One look at Hawke and every feminine hormone in her body went nuts. It was a chaotic mixture of arousal, trepidation and pure excitement.

She couldn't blame it all on the mating heat. She'd felt this way before he'd ever touched her, before he'd ever kissed her.

She'd talked to Dr. Armani in depth over the past year about mating heat, and she was beginning to wonder if the heat wasn't just an advanced arousal. An advanced tie. If nature hadn't simply ensured that those who fell in love were pushed together faster, held together more firmly, to guarantee the survival of this species.

"Ready?" He held his hand out to her. A large, capable, strong hand. Calloused and dark, as though his entire body was permanently tanned.

Jessica moved to him slowly, let him envelop her hand in his and draw her to the bedroom door.

"Did you put the presents in the Rover?" she asked, trying to tone down the nervousness. She hadn't been to a party in years. Not since her father had finally stopped forcing her to attend the boring little functions he and his friends had staged several times a year.

"The presents are in the Rover," he promised her. "The breads and desserts are packed snugly in the backseat alongside them."

"Good." She swallowed tightly as they moved down the natural wood stairs to the foyer. "You're certain I should go?"

She wasn't so certain. She was known as a traitor, no matter the reason. How could any of the Breeds trust her now?

"I'm absolutely certain you should go." He drew to a stop at the bottom of the stairs, collected the long dark blue and black cloak that went with her dress and drew it over her shoulders. "You're worrying too much, Jess. Everything is going to be fine."

"Easy for you to say." She licked her lips before raking the lower one with her teeth and staring up at him as worry began to tighten her chest. "I couldn't blame anyone for not wanting me there, Hawke. You didn't force this, did you?"

The faint smile at his lips was chastising, and just a bit amused. "I can't force something like this, mate," he promised her. "If Wolfe didn't trust you to be there, then you wouldn't be."

That was true. She inhaled tightly before straightening her shoulders and forcing in courage for the evening ahead.

She knew Hope, Wolfe's mate. Just as she knew Faith and Charity, the mates of his closest friends. She also knew Amanda Bear, a former president's daughter and mate to a Coyote Breed. She'd met Anya Delgado several times, mate to the Coyote Breed alpha. She knew the mates of those who were influential in this world. She had thought they might even be friends.

"You're worrying too much," he promised her as they left the house and stepped into the cold night air.

Hawke held on to her as he moved her quickly to the Rover, helped her in and then loped around to the driver's side. Jessica kept her fingers laced tightly together and held in her lap.

She knew Hawke could sense her nervousness; it wasn't something she could help. She had always been denied acceptance until she had come here two years ago. During the year she had spent working with the Breeds she had thought she had begun to find that acceptance. Until she had unwillingly, unwittingly, given her father the information he had needed to attack Haven in the worst ways. She had given the location of the alpha's home, as well as the homes of his second-in-command and his head of security. Locations that were kept hidden for a reason: because their lives were in such danger.

The drive to the entrance of the community center was quick. Hawke drew the Rover to a stop at the large double doors where a young Breed stepped outside and moved to the driver's side as Hawke stepped out of the vehicle and walked quickly to Jessica's door.

She took his hand, allowing him to help her to the paved entrance and draw her inside.

The upper, aboveground portion of the community center was filled with large rooms, a kitchen and various work centers. Belowground, reinforced and nearly impenetrable, was the huge open gathering area.

Joining ceremonies, as marriages were called in the Breed society, were often held there. It was there that mates were rushed if Haven was attacked, and this was where various dignitaries were brought for meetings.

Hawke guided her into a large elevator and keyed in his security code. Instantly the doors closed and they were whisked several floors belowground where they were deposited into a wide hallway where both human and Breed guests were loitering. Several journalists were in attendance, though no photographers were allowed. Breeds highly valued their privacy, no matter their Feline or Canine designations.

"You're almost shaking," Hawke accused her softly.

"I don't do well at parties." She lifted her head and squared her shoulders as they passed several Breed soldiers who had escorted her to her cell the day she had been arrested.

"You're going to do wonderfully," he promised her as they stepped inside the wide double doors to the main room and he helped her off with her cloak before handing it over to a helpful attendant. A human attendant.

Coyote and Wolf Breeds mingled amid Christmas music and a display of bright, multicolored lights. At one end of the room was a huge fir tree that had been brought in, decorated lavishly and stacked with presents underneath.

Wolfe Gunnar stood close to the brightly colored traditional tree with Hope, his mate. Hope, with her slightly Asian features and diminutive stature, was dressed in a gay, vivid Christmas green. Her shoulder-length black hair fell to her shoulders like silken ribbon and gave her an almost regal air.

Wolfe, much taller and broader, stood with his arm around her shoulders as he laughed at something another

Breed said. Coarse black hair was pulled back from his face to his nape and secured there. He was dressed in black as well, as were most of the males, with a dark silver silk ribbon stretching from his shoulder across his chest and to his waist that proclaimed his rank of Wolf Breed Alpha.

There were other ribbons present on many of the males. Different colors, all muted blue or gray. His second-in-command wore cloudy gray; his head of security wore a navy blue. Communications wore silver blue.

The women, guests and Breeds alike, were dressed extravagantly in long gowns. For the Breed females, this was their chance to be women rather than soldiers.

"I see you finally got her to join the rest of us mortals." Ashley True stepped up to them, her teasing smile catching Jessica off guard.

"It was a trial," Hawke admitted as he pulled Jessica closer.

"He's the trial," Jessica teased back. She was actually glad to see Ashley now that she wasn't her bodyguard.

"Most male Breeds are." Ashley sighed with exaggerated patience. "We put up with them the best we can."

"Be good brat, or I'll have a talk with your alpha about giving in on those spa treatments," Hawke warned her. "I hear you got the full go-round today."

Ashley's smile brightened as she fluffed a head full of multihued blonde curls and flashed a perfect set of nails. "Del-Rey does so enjoy spoiling me, Hawke. He won't listen to you."

"Brat." Hawke laughed again.

"Always," Ashley agreed. "Now, go find Wolfe. He was asking where you were a little while ago. I'm off to find more punch."

She sped away on heels that should have been impossible to stand on.

"That woman is a menace," Hawke muttered as they continued through the throng of guests.

"She's nice though." Ashley, her sisters Sharone and

Emma, and the Coyote's mate and Coya, the female Coyote alpha, Anya, had always been kind to her. She'd appreciated that, even as she had chafed under their protection.

"She's hell. A prissy little diva by day and when night falls, I swear, one of the sharpest, most lethal Coyote Breeds ever created."

But wasn't that what all Breeds were created to be? They were trained to fit in when they had to, and to kill perfectly, efficiently, when they were ordered to.

Moving to the tree, Hawke sat their large bag of gifts among the others before straightening and drawing Jessica to where Wolfe and Hope Gunnar and Jacob and Faith Arlington stood.

"Wolfe, Hope, Jacob, Faith." He nodded to the four as he drew Jessica closer. "May I present my mate and soon-to-be wife, Jessica Raines."

Jessica almost froze in shock as everyone around them became quiet. Dread began to fill her as Wolfe's black gaze flickered over her. He was imposing, showing little emotion, no acceptance or rejection. His nostril's flared and he drew in her scent.

She knew he could smell the combination of her scent and Hawke's as it merged in the mating heat. He would also smell her fear. But would he know her regret, her pain, and the wish that she had known what her parents were doing, how they had wanted to destroy the Breeds? Did all that come across in a scent? She highly doubted it.

"You've chosen well, Hawke Esteban." Wolfe's arm moved from his mate's shoulder so he could clasp Hawke's hand. "A beautiful and loyal mate, and one I'm pleased to accept into our pack."

Jessica blinked. He couldn't have been speaking of her, could he?

"Jessica, had we not doubted that you could betray us, then you would have died before Hawke had time to declare you as his mate," Wolfe told her softly as she stared back at him. "Questions needed answers, and your loyalty had to be proven rather than simply believed in despite the evidence. We thank you for your patience, and above all, for the grace you showed during your confinement to give us the time to prove your innocence, as well as your bond to your mate."

She shook her head slowly. "What grace, Alpha Gunnar?" she whispered in disbelief.

A smile tugged at his lips. "You didn't throw anything at us, despite months upon months of questioning. You never threatened to call in a representative, though you could have. And not once did you demand rights that were due you. The right of Tribunal rather than confinement during your interrogation. That was grace."

She shook her head again. "It was guilt," she whispered back. "How could I deny what I had done, even though I couldn't explain why I had done it, or stop the actions even as they happened?"

"You saved my mate, as well as Jacob's, despite the drug that enforced your will," he said gently. "That was courage, and it was strength. We need that strength to survive our future. You're part of Hawke's future, and therefore, part of our own. Welcome to our pack."

He nodded with a slow dip of his head, a respectful air of acceptance. He wouldn't hug her, nor shake her hand. No Breed alive would dare to even brush against her during mating heat, especially that first, strongest phase that she was in now.

She had been accepted-though. By his words and his actions, Wolfe had given her mating to Hawke his blessing, and therefore, the pack's blessing.

"Dance with me now." Hawke drew her into his arms even though she was still reeling from Wolfe's proclamation.

She was part of the pack, a family. The pack was like an extended family, drawing together both Wolf and Coyote Breeds, extending an umbrella over each member, an acceptance they could find nowhere else.

The sound of a slow ballad filled the huge room as Hawke led her to the dance floor. Instantly, heat, sizzling energy and a sense of warmth began to invade her. With her head against his chest, his hands settled low at her back, moving her against him, Jessica let the acceptance she had been given sink inside her.

She had found a home; she had found a family. She had people who had believed in her even when it had appeared she had betrayed them.

"I love you, Jessica Raines."

She almost froze in his arms as Hawke whispered the words at her ear.

Jessica lifted her head and stared up at him, her lips parting, tears filling her eyes. "I've always loved you, Hawke Esteban," she answered, her voice soft, trembling. "Since the moment I met you, I loved you."

He was her future, he was her heart.

Lowering his head, he brushed his lips against hers, a sizzling caress that almost caused a moan to break from her throat. She could taste a hint of the spicy essence of his kiss. A taste of lust, need, desire and hunger. A taste that would only fuel her own.

"Soon," he promised, turning his head until he could brush his lips against her ear. "Soon, mate."

Soon. Tonight. When they stepped back into their home, when they stepped back into the heat waiting to flare between them.

Soon. Until then, she had this. His touch, this dance and the incredible realization that she did indeed have a future.

NINE

*I*t was a night made for lovers. Even amid the party, Christmas cheer, exchange of gifts and laughter, there was an air of warmth and intimacy that bound her to Hawke.

Quiet smiles, the touch of his hand, the knowledge that the sexual need was building inside both of them. When her skin was prickling with awareness and sensitivity, he took her hand and drew her back to Wolfe and Hope where they made their farewells.

Anyone watching them would have known why they were leaving, what would be happening that night. Besides the fact that they were Breeds and they could smell the mating heat, Jessica knew that each touch, each look they stole at each other gave them away.

The drive back to their home was made in silence. The short distance was filled with magic though. The twinkling of lights, the heated warmth spearing between them. When they pulled into the driveway, Hawke stepped around the vehicle, opened the door and then lifted her into his arms.

She couldn't speak. Her throat felt closed with emotion

when he pushed the door open and, rather than moving upstairs, moved to the living room instead.

Where once the room had been empty, there was now a Christmas tree and a lush silk-covered mattress awaiting them.

The lights on the tree lit up as they stepped into the room. Blue and gold. The entire tree was lit with blue and gold. There were only lights, no ornaments, but at the base of a tree was a small, gaily wrapped box.

"What is this?" she whispered as he carried her to the mattress and eased her to the thick silk comforter that covered it.

"It's our first Christmas."

*H*awke stared into Jessica's shining eyes. There were tears there. She stared at the tree as though she had never seen one before, much as he had stared at the first Christmas tree Wolfe and Hope had decorated for Haven's first Christmas several years before.

There, amid the colors he had chosen for their family— her blue eyes, his golden ones—he watched as she reached out, her fingers trembling, to touch the point of one tiny light. A golden one. His color.

"Hawke." She whispered his name again, her voice throbbing, as she turned back to him, staring at him as though he had just given her the most precious gift in the world.

He swallowed tightly, his throat nearly closed with emotion. Hell, this was the hardest part to get used to, he thought. So much emotion, when before he had felt so very little. The labs had bred emotion out of the Breeds. The scientists and soldiers beat it out of them, froze it out of them, and in some cases, had killed to be rid of Breeds that couldn't hide emotion.

Hawke had survived. He had hidden all emotion, often even from himself. He had cared for nothing but the survival of the Breeds as a whole, and once he escaped, he had made certain that the survival of their race was all that mattered to him.

Until Jessica.

Now, staring into the velvety depths of her eyes, he knew that he would die, kill, forsake even his race, for this one woman.

"This is my first present to you." He lifted the small box from beneath the tree and handed it to her.

The brush of her fingers against his was like fire. He could feel the tremble just beneath her flesh, smell the arousal and the hint of need that filled her. He could also sense the love that poured from her. He had never smelled love before, not in relation to himself.

He could become addicted to it.

Hawke watched as she took the gift from him and slowly pulled at the bow he had tied around the small decorated box. It came loose easily, allowing her to lift the flap open.

Reaching in, she pulled free the angel that was inside. With red gold hair and blue eyes, the porcelain body was finely made. Dressed in jeans and a sweater, feet bare. Behind her back, delicate crystal wings were attached and a glistening halo circled her head.

At her feet sat a great gray wolf, its golden eyes staring up at her in adoration. Finding an artist to create what he had needed hadn't been easy. The delicate tree ornament had only been finished for a matter of weeks.

"My God," she whispered, her gaze lifting to his as she cradled the figurine in her palm. "Hawke, it's beautiful."

"Not nearly as beautiful as you." He had to clear his throat before he could speak further. "It's our first ornament, Jess. Our first Christmas together."

Cupping her hand, he lifted free the gold tree ring in the back and helped her to her feet before guiding her hand to the tree.

There, in the center, he attached the ring to a branch and watched as the blue and gold lights gleamed around it.

Turning her to him, his hands on her shoulders, he lowered his lips, touched them to hers and whispered a prayer for their future.

A second later, everything went black.

Jessica heard Hawke's muted groan. It wasn't one of pleasure, nor of arousal. The sound was so odd, so animalistic, that her eyes jerked open, even as he pulled her to the mattress.

It was a free fall. It wasn't a man taking a woman down to continue the pleasure that filled both their minds. It was a complete, boneless fall, his arms still wrapped around her as he somehow managed to drag her beneath him even as she felt unconsciousness overtake him.

"Hawke!" She screamed his name as she pushed at his much larger body, trying to get his weight off her, to figure out what was going on.

After struggling from beneath him, she rose to her knees, her hands gripping his shoulders when a sudden, fiery tug at her scalp jerked her back and threw her to the floor.

Bracing her fall with her hands, she lifted her head and tossed her hair from her face as she stared up at the dark, shadowed male form above her.

A tight sneer pulled at his lips as he glared back at her from eyes that were familiar, and had once been warm and filled with friendship. His husky body was tight, tense with anger, and she swore she could feel the need to kill as it emanated from him.

"Todd." She whispered his name, her voice ragged with betrayal and pain.

Todd shook his head, the close cut of his dark blond hair gleaming in the Christmas lights. "I thought better of you, Jess," he snapped. "I never thought you'd become a dog's bitch." She almost flinched at the contempt in his tone, then cried out in despair as he kicked Hawke. A swift, hard jab to the ribs that brought no response from her mate, not so much as a harsh, indrawn breath.

Jessica's gaze moved from his eyes to the gun Todd held. The silenced Trigg Automatic Glacier was built on the old P-90 lines. Fully automatic, it used flesh-searing, armor-shredding ammunition. One bullet could take out an arm, a leg. A shot to the head, chest or back was fatal. It was so illegal that the United States had placed a ban on it more than ten years ago, and all previous sales of the weapon and ammunition were sought out and the owners reimbursed for the confiscation of the weapon.

"What are you doing, Todd?" With her peripheral vision she sought for her handbag. The little derringer she carried was no match for the weapon he was using, but if she could get just one shot off, one to the head or to the chest, then she might have a chance. Hawke might have a chance.

"You stupid bitch." He sneered, his hazel eyes blazing with wrath as he kicked Hawke again before stalking around the edge of the mattress. "What does it look like I'm doing? I'm making certain you pay for betraying God and your country. You stupid whore."

This time he kicked her.

Before Jessica could evade the toe of his steel-lined boot, it connected with her stomach, throwing her back to the edge of the tree as she felt the air whoosh from her body.

Gasping for oxygen, she tried to scramble out of the way of the next kick, crying out as he landed a blow against her hip.

"Are you insane?" she cried out, barely escaping another kick. "The Breeds will kill you for this, Todd."

He had been her friend. They had worked together in the communications center; they had gone through basic training and Breed security together. He had always had a smile, always seemed loyal to the Breeds, always argued for their rights and their right to live with others.

"They'll have to figure out who did it first," he laughed back at her. "How do you think I snuck up on him, bitch? How do you think I managed to hide in the house he spent every waking minute building for you?"

She shook her hair from her eyes as she fought to find a way out of this. How had he managed to sneak up on Hawke? To disable him so easily?

Todd laughed again, the sound ugly, brutal. It echoed with menace and a hunger to inflict pain.

"Can't figure it out, can you, Jessica?" He smirked. "I guess the Breeds didn't tell you all about close proximity and association, did they?"

Actually, she did know about it. Close proximity and association was when a human became so much a part of a particular pack or family that his scent began to blend in with those of surrounding family or pack members. The human began to carry not just his own scent, but also the scent of the areas and the Breeds that he was in close proximity with.

"I made sure I stayed close here." He stared around the living room. "I carried in lumber, I hung around and talked and laughed while it was being built. And afterward . . ." His smile became sly. "Afterward I came inside as much as possible, always certain to wear the same clothes, to make sure when they were cleaned they were washed with Breed uniforms." He shook his head. "How easy it is sometimes to slip up on them. They tightened security on the rest of us after they suspected you betrayed them, but even then, it wasn't enough. Because I knew how to fool them."

He wouldn't fool them for long. Close proximity and close association only made his scent familiar to the Breeds. Hawke might have missed his individual scent mixed with those of his own as well as those of the other Breeds that had been inside the house to set up the tree and lights, but that wouldn't mean he was safe.

His scent now was mixed with that of the weapon, as well as the individual scent he carried that would be stronger because of the length of association with the room.

Her knowledge of the subject was limited, but the Breeds' knowledge wasn't. They knew how to track their enemies, whether or not they had been in close proximity and association.

"You won't get away with it, Todd." She shook her head, knowing she was running out of time. She could see in his expression, in the hardening of the flesh over his cheekbones and forehead, that he was preparing himself to make his next move.

She couldn't get to the derringer.

"How did you manage to knock out Hawke?" She hadn't sensed a blow to his head, and surely she would have.

Todd grinned again. It was a smile of smug satisfaction and triumph. "The champagne I handed him at the party. It was drugged. A special little mix of cocktails that carries no scent, no taste, and takes several hours to react on the Breed senses. I took my chances on it." He shrugged. "Look how well it paid off."

And it had paid off well for him.

"You don't want to do this, Todd," she rasped, rising to her feet, swaying as though she were dizzy, as though the blows and the shock to her system were too much. "You can't destroy the Breeds like this. It won't work."

"I'll get away with it," he assured her. "They will never know it was me."

"You won't listen any more than my father would," she snapped back then, as though angry. "The way to destroy them isn't through this sort of deception. It's through the mating heat."

He paused. "The heat is a rumor." There was an edge of suspicion in his voice though.

Jessica gave a light laugh as she held her hand to her ribs. "I'm going to forgive the bruises for just a moment," she told him. "I'm even going to try to forget that you're a moron acting outside of orders." He frowned at the insult. "Imagine, if you will, that the mating heat *does* exist. How do you destroy the Breeds?"

His eyes narrowed on her. *Oh yes, let that suspicion work through your teeny tiny little brain,* she thought. She was the daughter of the man who had led the pure blood society he was obviously a part of. The daughter who had been imprisoned and betrayed her people. But he couldn't be certain; not really. No one had heard from her in a year before her release.

"You prove mating heat," he ventured softly.

"Father wouldn't listen." She shook her head furiously. "Killing the mates would only enrage them, but they're too heavily backed by too many powerful political figures now. That's not the way to take them down."

Todd nodded slowly. "You have to make people fear them."

She smiled in approval. "I didn't betray my people or my country, Todd. You know I couldn't do that. I loved my father. I love my country."

"You pulled Gunnar and Arlington's mates out of harm's way," he accused her furiously, but the gun leveled off and his attention was no longer on Jessica.

"I did what I had to do," she snarled back at him. "Mating heat, Todd. Prove mating heat. How do you prove it?"

He licked his lips, staring at her like he was beginning to see her point of view.

"Let the heat run it's course," she suggested. "Then escape. Once I do that, and the heat is fully conditioned inside me, then we have what we need to destroy them. Proof."

There wasn't a chance in hell.

"You're fully mated?"

"Close." She pushed her fingers through her hair as though frustrated. "Close, until you decided to play the moron. God, couldn't you have given me just a few more days? That was all I needed."

Was it working? He was suspicious. He was still watching her as though he knew she was lying, knew she was playing him.

"How can I believe you?" He wanted to though, because the thought of finally proving the Breeds were a threat was irresistible.

"Don't you ever pay attention to anything beyond your own inglorious little fantasies?" she scoffed. "Tell me, Todd. Have you ever shaken hands with one of the Breeds' wives? Didn't you ever pay attention to how you are never allowed to touch one of them? How only certain members of any department are allowed around them? They told me about mating heat within my first year there, because the alpha's wife, as well as the second-in-command's, was becoming friends with me. I had to sign waivers to hell and back and swear on everything under the sun that I would never reveal it. To prove it, I had to ensure one of them mated me." She glanced at Hawke as though in disgust and caught the barest flicker of his eyelashes.

Oh God, let him be waking up. Let him be okay. She had no idea how to get out of this other than running her mouth. Todd was too far away for her to jump him, and was too suspicious for her to get him out of the room.

"Hawke still has to die," Todd told her as she turned her gaze back to him.

"Oh sure, kill the goose with the golden egg." She rolled her eyes. "Where do you think the mating heat comes from? Don't you read the papers? It's a hormone, Todd. He has to do all these little 'alive' things, like kissing me, screwing me, trying to make little Breed babies with me. Do you understand yet?"

She was going to throw up. She couldn't believe she was saying these things, that Hawke was listening, that he could hear her. She had fought for so long to make amends for what she had done unwillingly. Now it would only appear as though she *had* willingly betrayed them.

She could see her future draining away before her eyes. She could see her happiness dying, her life becoming forfeit. But, if Hawke lived, if he managed to save himself, then it would be worth it.

Her Hawke was well worth dying for.

TEN

*H*awke could smell the lies coming off Jessica in waves. The desperation to make Todd Bennett believe her went clear to her soul. She sounded convincing, and when he snuck a brief look at her face, she looked convincing. His Jess was playing the role of her life and fighting to give him a chance to get his bearings.

The animal inside him was slowly coming awake. He could feel his senses sharpening, his strength returning. His unique Breed genetics were slowly pushing past the barrier that had clouded his mind.

What the fuck had happened? He felt like he had been hit by a two-by-four, but he knew there wasn't a chance in hell anyone could have slipped up on him that easily.

"I can't believe whoever gave you the order to try anything this insane," Jessica continued with a disgusted sigh. "Really, Todd. Didn't your little attempted assassin inform your group how many times I've been out in that forest trying to escape this place?"

There was a moment of silence.

"The group doesn't know about that," Todd finally admitted. "I was the one shooting at you."

"Father would have had you killed if he were still alive," she spat back at him. "Even he knew not to attempt to kill me. He knew what I was trying to do, he just didn't agree with it. Do you think he would have risked drugging me if I had been truly totally against it? The drug was only there to give me a plausible escape, not because the damned thing actually worked. Use your brain for a change."

Hawke felt her move away from the tree as he opened his eyes just enough to focus, to see if his vision had fully returned yet.

The first thing he saw was the porcelain figure on the floor, one tiny crystal wing lying in fragments against the hardwood.

He had to grit his teeth to keep from growling in fury. That had been his first gift to her, a reflection of what he saw in her. His angel. The beauty that could tame the beast inside him.

Todd Bennett was a dead man walking.

"I wish I could believe you, Jessica." Todd's voice was filled with regret, with hope. "The story is good, I'll give that to you. It's enough to make me want to believe."

"Then kill me," she laughed. "Go ahead, Todd. Make the worst mistake of your life. Because when you do, Uncle Craig will reach out from prison and snap your skinny little neck."

Craig Raines. His arrest had been made so quietly that it hadn't even hit the papers. Only a few people could have known of his arrest. Jess knew, because she had given the Breeds the information that her uncle and her father both had ties to the pure blood groups.

Hawke felt Todd pause then.

"Craig wasn't caught," he said, but Hawke could hear the fear in his voice then.

"Don't be a fool," Jessica snapped, and though the tone of her voice was confident, he could feel her fear increase. "Craig was the mastermind behind the plot to kill the Breeds at the Christmas party in Advert just before my release. He was also my contact."

Hawke was almost ready to move. He could feel his muscles unlocking, adrenaline coursing through his body as he tensed to attack. Just another few seconds. If Jess could just hold on a little longer, distract Todd just a bit more . . .

"I can't take the chance," Todd said softly, his voice now filled with regret. "I'm sorry, Jess. I just can't take a chance on you."

$\mathcal{H}$e was going to kill her.

Jess watched as Todd lifted the weapon, aiming it to her stomach. Damn, that was going to hurt. He was going to make sure that he punished her, whether he believed it or not.

"Uncle Craig will have you skinned alive for this," she snapped.

"Like the Breeds, Craig will have to figure out who did it first," he informed her, his smile tight and hard. "Unlike some who are in the society, Jess, I believe that sometimes we have to take every opportunity we're given to destroy the Breeds. You're his mate. Alive, you still serve a purpose to the Breeds. Dead, you destroy him."

His arm stiffened.

Jess threw herself across the room, diving for the floor, thankful that at least he was shooting at her, not at Hawke. At the same time, a vicious, enraged howl filled the house.

The whine of the silenced weapon could be heard a second before his screams. A second before the sound of chaos tore through the room.

Stumbling to her feet, she rushed for her purse, her head lifting as she stumbled on the mattress, her eyes widening at the sight that met her eyes.

Animalistic, primal. Hawke had Todd's neck in the powerful grip of his hand as he shook him. The weapon had fallen to the floor and Todd stared back in horror at the vision of Breed rage.

Hawke's lips were drawn back from his teeth, his canine's flashing in the low glow of the tree lights. A howl tore from his lips again as Breed enforcers rushed into the room. Leading them was none other than Wolfe, his expression a mask of fury. Hawke shook Todd again before throwing him against the wall and burying his fist in the other man's gut.

The air expelled from Todd's lungs with a gasp. As Hawke stepped back, he crumpled to the floor, gasping, short cries tearing from his throat as he tried to crawl away.

"Hawke." She moved to him, her hand lifting, shaking, as tears began to fall from her eyes.

He turned on her then. Golden eyes flamed with his rage and a sob shook her entire body. He had heard everything. He had heard her speak of betraying him, of betraying him further. He had heard the lies she told to distract Todd, lies that would be her death sentence now.

"My mate," he snarled, suddenly jerking her to him, shocking her with the force of his hold and the snarled demand in his voice.

"Hawke." She whispered his name through her tears as one hand wrapped around the back of her neck, the other gripping her hip as he jerked her closer.

"My mate," he growled again. "Always mine."

Before she could affirm or deny, his head lowered, his lips covered hers and his tongue pushed forcefully between her lips.

Immediately the taste of the mating hormone exploded through her senses. It was richer, spicier than ever before. She could feel the burn almost immediately, the explosion of sensation, hunger and need that lashed through her body and drove her to claw at his chest to get closer.

As though the threat of death had pushed him past reason, he kissed her with a desperation she had never known before, a desperation she returned. Their tongues twined, mated, fought and surrendered in a dance as old as time.

When he managed to jerk back she could only sway against him, dazed and uncertain, as she heard the men behind her, heard Todd's frightened cries, his breathless accusations against her. The details of the plan she had given him, the plan that had never existed.

"Get that bastard out of my mate's home." Hawke turned to Wolfe as Jess struggled to turn in his arms. "I want him dead."

"Quietly," Wolfe stated, his dark eyes going between Hawke and Jessica. "He's bringing some serious charges against Jess already, Hawke," he warned.

"Lies." His arm tightened around Jess. "The bastard thought I was senseless from the drug he slipped me at the party. He didn't give me near enough. I was weak, not unconscious. He lies. He bragged of his part in betraying the Breeds and his connections to the pure blood society that attacked in Advert before Jess's release. I want him taken care of, Wolfe. Permanently. He knows Jess is my mate. He's been deceitful enough that he's put together the information on mating. He's a risk we can't afford."

Wolfe stared back at him for long seconds as Jess watched and fought to catch her breath. She felt as though she were falling, as though the strength had seeped from her limbs the moment she realized Todd was pulling the trigger.

"He'll be taken care of." Wolfe nodded before turning back to the Breeds that had restrained Todd. "Take care of it, Jacob," he ordered his second-in-command. "Quietly."

Todd would never be heard from again.

She watched as he was dragged from the room, kicking, screaming, begging for mercy.

There would be no mercy, she knew. If he hadn't tried to kill Hawke, if he hadn't admitted to being a part of drugging her, of attacking Haven, then he might have had a chance of escaping Breed law.

"I'll need your report in the morning." Wolfe turned back to them.

"How did you know?" Jess finally found her voice, her brain. "How did you know to be here?"

Wolfe turned his gaze back to her, his eyes penetrating, as though he could see clear to her soul.

"It's a tradition," he told her. "We came to hang a wreath on your door, to welcome your union into the pack. That was when we heard your screams and Hawke's howls."

A tradition of acceptance. Her lips parted as emotion swamped her and the events of the day began to clash inside her.

"Hawke, I expect your verbal report tomorrow after you turn in the written report," Wolfe informed him. "Until then, I'll clear your house out and leave you with your mate."

She could still hear Todd screaming outside. It was muted, distant, but the sound struck at her heart and left her shaking on the inside.

He had been a friend. Tonight he had toasted to her union with Hawke; he had smiled and wished her every happiness. Hours later, he had tried to kill her.

The door closed behind Wolfe and his enforcers, leaving them alone as Jess moved, pushed herself from Hawke's embrace and went to the tree.

Kneeling on the floor, she picked up the figurine that had fallen and touched her broken wing carefully.

"She can't be fixed," Jess whispered as another tear slipped down her cheek.

Taking the figure from her, Hawke wrapped his arm around her waist and lifted her against him. She watched, silent, as he hung the ornament again, the broken wing sending fragments of light glittering around it.

"She doesn't need to be fixed." Hawke's voice was soft, his breath feathering along her temple as she stared at the wing. "She'll always remind us of what we survived, Jess."

She bit her lip and tried not to cry.

"I was lying," she finally bit out desperately, another sob tearing from her chest. "What I told Todd . . ."

Hawke swung her around, his finger pressing to her lips as she saw the surprising crooked grin on his lips.

"Breeds can smell a lie, mate. Have you forgotten that?"

Her lips parted. Yes, she had forgotten that. In the fear and the confusion, she had forgotten that Breeds could smell a lie.

"You knew?" Her breathing hitched as happiness seemed to flood her. "You knew I was lying?"

"I knew you were fighting to hold on until I could get my bearings." He touched a tear on her cheek, wiped it away. "I knew you were saving both our lives the only way you could, baby. You didn't hurt me. I never once believed otherwise."

*C*ould he love anyone more than he loved her at that moment, Hawke wondered. Pure joy lit up her gaze; sweet heat and unconditional love filled the air around them. She was indeed a mate he could be proud of. One he knew would always walk at his side.

Turning, he lifted her in his arms and bore her back to the mattress.

"I believe we were in the middle of something when that bastard disturbed us," he stated as he came over her, her arms wrapping around his neck as her lips curved into a tempting, loving smile.

"We weren't exactly in the middle," she shot back saucily. "I believe we were just getting started. Don't go missing steps there, mate."

He had to laugh at her. She'd always been able to make him smile, make him laugh. She had always lightened his heart even as she hardened his dick.

"I love you, Jess," he growled, the man and the animal speaking, the primal need and emotion that erupted inside him impossible to contain.

"I love you, Hawke Esteban. With everything I am, I love you."

His lips covered hers then. Deep, sipping kisses kept them both drugged as they fought with their clothes, pulling them from each other, tossing them to the side, baring their flesh to the stroke and caress of the other.

Her hands roved over his back, her nails rasping over his flesh as she arched against him, urging him with little moans and cries for the possession he couldn't hold back.

He had nearly lost her. So easily, she could have been taken away from him tonight. How the hell was he supposed to live if he ever lost his Jess? Not just his mate, but his woman, his lover. She was a part of his soul that he knew he never wanted to be free of.

Sliding his hand along her side, he reached the ripe curve of her breast. He cupped the mound in his palm and lifted it, rolled his thumb over the distended peak of her nipple before lowering his head to taste it.

Drawing the tight little nub into his mouth, he suckled at her as though he was dying for the taste of her. Actually, he had been dying before he tasted her. Frozen on the inside, locked in a loneliness he couldn't bear. For a year he had fought to prove her innocence, fought for her release. And now she was here, in his arms, touching him, arching to him as he touched her.

He moved down her body and relished each broken cry of pleasure as he fought the heated, slick folds of her pussy. Starving for the taste of her, for the heat of her, he licked through the narrow cleft, moaned at the slick essence of her and devoured her. With lips, tongue and sucking little kisses, he teased and tormented her silken flesh. Tasted her until there was no doubt in his mind that he could ever live without her, then drew in the tight little knot of her clit and sucked it, flicking his tongue over it until she erupted in pleasure.

And it wasn't enough. He could never get enough of her.

He pressed her thighs farther apart, lifted her knees and opened her farther to his gaze.

Soft pink flesh parted, revealing the snug little entrance he sought. Tucking the head of his cock against the fluttering, clenching entrance to her snug pussy, he shifted his hips, moved, penetrated until the crest was pressed firmly inside her.

Tiny eruptions of the pre-seminal fluid jetted from the tip of his cock, filling her, easing the tender, delicate muscles, allowing her to take him without pain, without distress. It increased her pleasure while adding to her natural lubrication and allowing the wide width of his shaft to sink inside her.

Hawke watched as he took her, listened to her excited little cries and knew he wasn't going to last long. His balls had drawn up tight to the base of his cock, a sure indication that his release was only a few strokes away.

Tunneling inside her slowly, working his way in by small degrees, he grimaced at the building rapture surging through his body.

Sweet and so hot. Her pussy wrapped around his cock like the tightest, most silken glove. Each stroke of her intimate flesh against the crest and shaft of his erection was torturous ecstasy. Sizzling fingers of electric current wrapped around his balls, stroked along his cock and had him gritting his teeth to hold back until he was firmly seated inside her.

Lifting his head, Hawke stared into her lovely face. She was flushed, perspiration standing out on her forehead as the tracks of her tears dampened her cheeks.

"My precious Jess," he whispered, leaning closer, pressing himself deeper inside her and moved to steal a kiss. "My beloved Jess."

"My heart." She sobbed against his lip, and he lost it.

The hitched, breathless quality of her voice tore through him. The devotion, the love in her soft whisper, destroyed him.

Groaning her name, he began to thrust inside her. Heavy, probing thrusts that worked inside her, stroking him past pleasure, past ecstasy. He was surging through sensations that he didn't have time to make sense of, sensations he had never known before.

His mate. His woman.

She cried out his name and his thrusts increased and he shafted inside her as he held her hip with one hand and braced himself above her on an elbow. His lips moved over her jaw, her neck.

He could feel the intensity rising inside her as well. Her orgasm was coming closer, the sweet scent of it was wrapping around him, urging him to take her fast, to fuck inside her harder. Nothing mattered but taking her, marking her, blending their scents until they were one, until they were bound so irrevocably that they could never be parted.

Gasping moans fell from her lips as his kiss moved to her neck, her shoulder. So close. She was tightening around him. Her legs lifted, wrapped around his hips, her pussy tightened, the muscles convulsing around his thrusting cock.

One thrust. Two. And she exploded. He felt it. Like an eruption of fire clenching around his dick she clamped on him as she cried out his name.

Hawke felt his own release follow hers. His teeth locked in her shoulder, the mark of their mating, as he thrust inside her again and let sensation tear through him.

A growl tore from his throat as he felt his semen jetting from him, filling her. The fierce swelling in the center of his cock locked him inside her, creating another pleasure, another violent edge of sensation that rocked them both.

Hawke fought to hold on to just enough of his senses to relish this, to memorize it, to know every emotion, every sensation that erupted around him. His and hers. Her pleasure, rising so hard and swift she lost her own senses. Her screams of ecstasy, his growls. The lick of fire across his flesh, the feel of her teeth in his shoulder.

Shock almost tore away that last edge of control. She was biting him as he bit her. Two little canines pierced his flesh and she held on for dear life, just as he held on to her.

Held on until the last pulses of pure rapture tore through their bodies then left them to float back to Earth on a peaceful, comforting cloud.

They were fighting for breath. Holding on to each other like the survivors of a storm. Sweat damped their bodies, their hearts raced and Hawke could feel her, heart and soul, wrapping around him.

Lifting his head from her shoulder, he opened his eyes and stared down at her. She was lax beneath him, her breasts rising and falling with hard breaths as her lashes fluttered open.

"You're my soul, Jess," he stated simply. He knew no other way to say it. "I lose you, I lose all that I am."

Her hand lifted, touched his cheek, before her finger fluttered over his lips.

"You're every breath I take, Hawke," she said, her voice drowsy but echoing with such love that he felt humbled. "Every breath I take, you're a part of it."

They were a part of each other.

Moving to her side, he dragged her coat over them for warmth, pulled her against his chest and let himself believe.

It was Christmas morning, and he held his gift in his arms.

Looking at the angel with the broken wing, he knew that next year there would be another. A perfect one to represent her perfect love. But this one was even more precious for the wing that had been shattered. This one had survived. Just as his own angel had. Survived and still retained its beauty and the essence of what it was meant to be. A reflection of love. Not always perfect, not without trials. But always there, surviving and enduring.

Just as his Jess had survived, endured and loved.

His own Christmas Angel, and he held her in his arms, knew her taste, the feel of her heartbeat, the touch of her body against his.

A true gift from the heavens. His Jess.

His mate.

Always.